THE GREAT LAW OF PEACE

BY ZOE SAADIA

THE GREAT LAW OF PEACE

The Peacemaker, Book 3

ZOE SAADIA

ISBN: 1535200367
ISBN-13: 978-1535200363

AUTHOR'S NOTE

"The Great Law of Peace" is historical fiction and some of the characters and adventures in this book are imaginary, while some are historical and well documented in the accounts concerning this time period and place.

The history of that region is presented as accurately and as reliably as possible, to the best of the author's ability, and although no work of this scope can be free of error, an earnest effort was made to reflect the history and the traditional way of life of the peoples residing in those areas.

I would also like to apologize before the descendants of the mentioned nations for giving various traits and behaviors to the well known historical characters (such as the Great Peacemaker, whose name I changed out of respect even though it was translated into English; Hionhwatha, Tadodaho, and others), sometimes putting them into fictional situations for the sake of the story. The main events of this series are well documented and could be verified by a simple research.

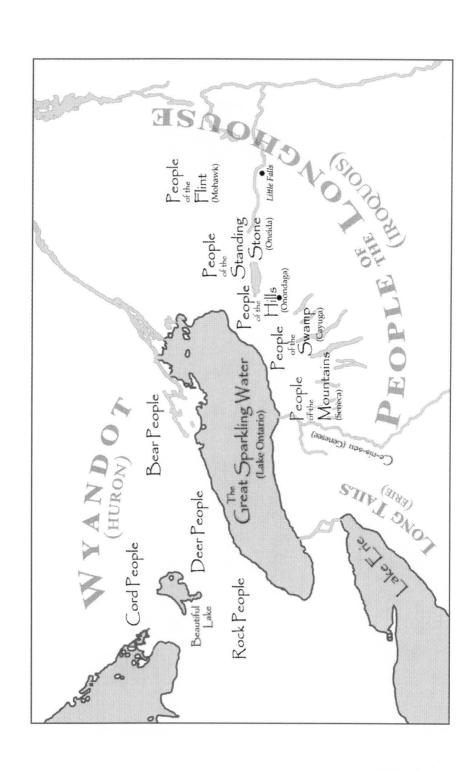

CHAPTER 1

In the lands of the Crooked Tongues,
Thunder Moon (mid-spring), 1142 AD

The breeze ruffled Seketa's hair, bringing relief from the heat and humidity, unusual for such early parts of Awakening Season. Putting the half-finished bead string aside, she pitted her face against the cool flow, shutting her eyes.

Her feet dangled free, not deterred by the height, enjoying the sensation. For the past two moons, this cliff had become her most visited place, the only place she could relax and be herself, without having the eyes of the whole town upon her, reproachful, disapproving, frowning.

So this is how Two Rivers must have felt, sneaking out to sit here and meditate whenever he could, she reflected. No wonder, truly. She had endured it for only two seasons, and it was already wearing upon her nerves, making her wish to scream at people or break something more often than not. Her hometown had no tolerance for a different way of thinking, no room for different ideas or different behavior. You either fit, or you turn into an outcast. *Was she turning into an outcast?*

Shrugging, she made a face. It was their problem, not hers. She was not arguing, not telling anyone what to do. On the contrary. She cared nothing for what people said or did, doing what was expected of her, working the fields of her clan, helping with food preparations, sewing blankets and clothes when required, going to gather firewood and wild berries with other woman. *Doing her duties.* So what did they want from her?

Why weren't they satisfied?

She sighed. There was no point in lying to oneself. She knew what they wanted. The old Seketa. They wanted the old Seketa back, not knowing that the prim, upright girl, the one who cared for her clan, her town, and her people, the girl who was always helping and around, sounding her mind, dancing at the ceremonies, interested in her clan's politics and involved, was gone forever, disappearing into the mists of the lake together with the small, whitish canoe on that frightful evening when everything had gone so terribly wrong.

The pain was back, gripping her insides. It had been so long! The Falling Leaves Season had passed, and the Frozen Season. The Awakening Moons were well on their way, with the crops prepared to be planted. With no raids from the enemy across the Great Sparkling Water, it would be easy to finish the planting in time, to hope for a bountiful harvest at the end of the summer, to make the nearing Maple Ceremony into the merriest affair their town had seen in moons. A little more of this good fortune and the continuous benevolence of the Great Spirits would see her people happy and well-off. Oh, yes, the Sky Deities were smiling upon them, was the conclusion of the entire town.

She didn't care one way or another. Eating was a boring business, anyway, so if they had less food than expected, she wouldn't mind.

Picking up the elaborately woven pattern of beads, she concentrated, contemplating her next move. Would it turn into a necklace or a headband? At this point, it could have gone either way, and she hadn't made up her mind, yet. Like with the rest of her decorations, she never knew what should come out of her work until the pattern materialized into this or that beautiful design. People praised her ornaments, but they frowned when she refused to gift any of it, proving once again how badly disinterested she had become.

She snorted. Why would she give them away for the silly people to show off? These decorations were not for them. They were not for anyone. They gave her the means to pass the time, to cope with the pain and the loss. Nothing more. Like the rest of her activities, they were meaningless, lacking in significance.

"I knew you would be here." The voice made her jump, coming from behind her all of a sudden.

The shadow fell across the cliff and her colorful shells went scattering. Hands trembling, she hurried to catch them before they began rolling down the rocks.

"Are you insane? Why did you have to sneak up on me like that?"

She didn't need to look up to recognize Hainteroh's voice, ringing deeply in the quietness of the afternoon.

"I didn't sneak up on you," he said, coming closer. "You never pay attention to your surroundings anyway, so it's easy to catch you off guard." He shrugged. "You are dreaming most of the time."

"I'm not dreaming. I was just busy with this thing. I come here for some peace and quiet, you know? Not to listen to every troublemaker trying to scare me and feel good about himself." Grinning, she turned around and faced him. "You tried to scare me, you did. To climb this cliff with no sound takes an effort and skill."

He grinned back, pleased with himself. "A good hunter and warrior should move silently, disturbing no leaf and no pebble. And I'm good."

"And so very pleased with yourself, too." She moved to make a space for him. A lot of space. There would be no touching limbs, even if accidentally. "So what is your news? You are not in the habit of wandering the woods, unless you were looking for someone or something."

He shrugged, but there was a tension to his posture now. "No, nothing special. I was just bored, so I went out." He measured her with a glance. "You made this cliff your own, but it's not like other people can't want to enjoy sitting here."

"They can want whatever they like. I found this place first, and I've been here for a few moons by now. It *is* my cliff."

"Yes, I know. This cliff is a part of your change. So you guard it very jealously."

Surprised with his perception, she measured him with a glance in her turn. "I haven't changed. I just grew up."

He snorted. "Is that growing up for you? Turning strange and different, keeping away from people, doing nothing but playing with beads, making ornaments for no one. When was the last time you danced, ceremonial dances or the social ones?"

The open anger in his voice startling her, she said nothing, surprised.

"You do nothing, Seketa, nothing at all. You move like an *uki*, doing your work and nothing else. The only thing that makes you passionate these days are your stupid bead strings, and even those you are making for no one." He peered at her, angered, but troubled too. She could see it clearly, the anxiety lurking in the depths of his eyes. She could read his moods so easily. They had grown up together, their longhouses so very close to each other. "You changed, and not for the better, Seketa. Something happened to you. Tell me what?"

She sighed, then, out of a habit, scanned the lake surface, always empty, bringing no hope.

"It's nothing," she said. "I changed, but it's for the better. I was a silly girl before."

"You? You were never silly. You were always serious, but full of life, of purpose. Now you are empty."

She shrugged. "Why would you care? We are not children to play in the woods anymore. I'm of no use to you, full of life or not."

He said nothing, peering at the lake, as though expecting the bright canoe to appear out of the misty vastness, too. What if it did? she wondered suddenly, the wave of excitement washing her, beginning at her belly, slipping upward, toward her chest, tickling in her feet. Oh, they only *thought* she was empty.

She stifled a nervous giggle. If the canoe appeared, she would have to distract Hainteroh's attention, take him away from the cliff, lure him back into town, then come here running. She squinted against the glow of the lowering sun.

"I talked to my mother," she heard him saying. "Asked her to talk to the Grandmother of our longhouse."

"Oh, why?" Feeling the twinge of well-familiar disappointment, she pursed her lips. The bright bluish vastness was empty, as always, leaving her with the bitter taste in her mouth and her stomach as empty as the neglected lake.

"She'll bring the cakes to the Grandmother of your longhouse."

Her breath caught. "Hainteroh, no!" The lake temporarily forgotten, she peered at him instead, taking in his proud, eagle-like profile. He had grown to be quite a handsome man, she suddenly realized, having not noticed that before. "Please, make her not do that. Go now and tell her not to, before she brings the cakes to our longhouse." She caught his arm. "Please. I can't accept."

He didn't move, didn't take his gaze off the water, but she saw his throat convulsing as though he had swallowed hard.

"Why not?" His voice was also colorless, empty.

She brought her palms up, careful not to scatter the precious shells. "I'm too young for that. I'm not ready."

"You are not too young, Seketa! You've seen seventeen summers. Many girls of your age are taking a man into their lives. Look around you. Are your friends sleeping alone? Tindee and the other girls. Eh?"

She shrugged. "I don't care what they do. I'm not ready."

"Will you ever be?"

"I don't know."

"You liked the foreigner, didn't you?" Now his voice took a growling sound.

She felt it like a blow in her stomach. "It has nothing to do with you."

"So you did like him, that filthy, murderous savage!" Now his eyes were upon her, burning with rage.

She clenched her teeth against the suddenness of her own anger. "He was not filthy and not murderous. Don't you ever say such things about him! He was good and kind and different. He was brave. He killed the giant brown bear with his knife! Think about it. He was decent and he was good." She heard her voice piquing, turning loud and shrill, impossible to control. "Yeentso was the filthy, murderous lowlife. Not the Wolf Clan boy. But no one paid attention, no one cared. Because he was a foreigner, no one was prepared to let him show himself. No one was prepared to listen!" Drawing a convulsive breath, she tried to control her voice. It shrilled in the ugliest of ways, disturbing the sacredness of this place.

He peered at her, his eyes narrow. "No one but you, Seketa. You cared, you listened. You let him deceive you with his filthy lies!" His gaze flickered darkly. "Oh, no, not only you. There was Two Rivers, of course. Another murderer and traitor to his own people. Worse than the savage cub even. Maybe it was him who turned your perfect – *good, decent* – youth into a despicable murderer. Who knows what he had been teaching him during all this time the pair of them spent together, hunting bears and doing all sorts of filthy things."

She gasped, remembering Yeentso's accusation and how angry it made them both.

"Two Rivers had been teaching him decent things. He was a good man, too. People should have listened to him. But, of course, no one did. Our people see nothing, hear nothing. Anything slightly different and they are turning away, in loathing and fear." She clenched her fists tight. "No wonder good people leave, never to return."

But he will return, he will, she thought, swallowing hard, feeling the tears nearing, desperate to hide them, to push them back into her soul. He would return because he promised, and because they belonged to each other, and because they had made their union real.

"They were bad people," she heard Hainteroh saying, his voice calmer now, but trembling, low and strained. "Bad, twisted, murderous spirits. This savage cub, he put some spell on you. He must have been receiving the aid of the Evil Twin himself, that's why he always got away with the bad things he did." The words seeped with difficulty though his pressed lips. "But to earn your affection, he must have done special things for his evil patron spirit, truly bad, outrageous things."

The lake was still there, vast and empty, but now not as bright, not as calming as before.

"Forget it, Hainteroh. Just forget this conversation. We will never agree on that. I knew them better than you did."

He turned sharply. "You knew them better? In what way? Did Two Rivers..." His eyes were now enormous, almost round in the broadness of his face. "Did the loose bastard seduce you?"

"Two Rivers?" She laughed against her will. "No, of course not. He was not of our age, and I don't think he messed with young girls, anyway. Think sensibly, Hainteroh. If he played with girls of my age, he would get in so much trouble with the Clans Mothers and the others, until all his previous troubles would look like a Sky World to him." The very thought made her snort. "And I would never have it, anyway."

He relaxed so visibly, she felt guilty. "I'm sorry. I should not have asked that," he muttered gruffly, turning back toward the lake.

For a while they sat in silence, letting the breeze cool their anger.

"He was a bad man," he said finally. "If not for him, our War Chief might have still been alive. And Iraquas, too. You should have hated this man more than anyone."

The fluttering in her stomach was back. She hadn't thought of her favorite cousin for some time now, too busy waiting for the canoe to appear.

"I don't hate Two Rivers, because it was not his fault. He was speaking against this ill-fated raid, anyway. The War Chief gave him his blessing to go with the Wolf Clan boy, so what happened was not his fault and not his responsibility."

"And the killings that followed?"

She gasped at the open contempt his voice radiated. "The

killings were not their fault. They had been attacked!"

"Oh, please, Seketa! Do you take me for a simpleton? These two had no divine powers. If Yeentso and his friends – all good, seasoned warriors! – had truly attacked them, the notorious pair would have been dead very quickly. Four warriors, against one man and one boy." He turned to watch her, his eyes narrow. "It was the other way around, so you know. The two filthy lowlifes waylaid Yeentso and Yeandawa, shooting arrows and hurling stones, before using their knives. The dirty pair of killers ambushed them, and that's why they managed." His eyes turned into slits. "You understand nothing of war and warriors, so you choose to think like a girl. The savage cub could not kill a warrior of Yeentso's caliber. Once, he caught him off guard, on the day of the game, but he would not have managed to do it more than once. He was a good-for-nothing, stupid troublemaker. I don't think he even killed that bear. I'm sure Two Rivers did it for him, for this or that filthy reason."

Busy fighting for breath, she found it difficult to utter a word of what she wanted to scream into his challenging face.

"It was not like that at all," she managed to squeeze out in the end, too enraged to think straight. "He did kill his bear! He had marks all over him to prove it. And he did kill one of the men that attacked us. I was there, I saw it all! All of it, Hainteroh!" What did it matter, if she told him the truth? What could they do to her? "Yeentso waylaid him, like the cowardly, filthy lowlife that he was, bringing more of his friends along. He was *that* afraid of the Wolf Clan boy! But Two Rivers came in time. And…" She swallowed, her stomach as tight as a stone, the memories still vivid, making her chest hurt. "It was terrible what they did to him… and… I wish none of it happened and they didn't have to leave even if it would mean I'd still have to see Yeentso's ugly face in my longhouse every day."

He turned away sharply, studying the lake once again. "So, if the foreigner had stayed, you would let him come and live in your longhouse?"

"Yes, I would."

He didn't turn to face her. "But he is not here anymore. He left, fled, ran away. Why do you refuse the others now?"

She forced herself into silence, itching to tell him that he would come back for her; of course, he would.

"He is probably dead already."

She swallowed the bitter taste in her mouth. "He is not. I would have known if he was."

"Of course, Seketa!" He snorted derisively, then got to his feet. "You will grow tired of sitting here, playing at being Two Rivers. Oh-so-very-special, different and misunderstood. One day you will be back, and by that time I will prove my worth. You will see that I'm braver than that filthy foreigner of yours."

His paces echoed angrily as he stormed off, down the cliff, kicking stones on his way. She bit her lips, in the corner of her mind sorry to have him leave. It was tiring to always be alone, always waiting. Hainteroh was a good youth, and she had hurt him unnecessarily. But what could she do? She asked him to stop talking about it, but he didn't stop, repeating that hateful gossip the whole town was talking about through the long winter moons and into the spring, speculating, enraged, frustrated in its inability to catch and punish the culprits.

Sighing, she tried to forget the dreadfully long, lonely moons, stuck in her mother's compartment of their longhouse, talked to all the time, admonished, asked questions, longing to be left alone. They worried about her, all of them. They thought she had been sick. If only it were that! If only the medicine she was made to drink and the tobacco smoke accompanied with prayers she was made to inhale could help. But, of course, they could not. Her sickness was of a different nature.

And the next Frozen Season was only some moons away, she realized suddenly, her heart missing a beat. If Tekeni didn't hurry, she would be forced to spend yet another dreadful winter here, with no favorite cliff and no privacy. It had already been two seasons since he left, and it was, once again, close to Planting Moon. Enough time for him and Two Rivers to do whatever they intended to do, establish themselves and make the savages listen. A difficult, dangerous, impossible mission, but if anyone could do that it was this pair. Hainteroh was right in one thing. These two made natural partners. And it must have been an enjoyable work, what they did.

She frowned again. All those places to travel to, people to meet, towns full of good-looking women. Had he found himself a new love? A pretty savage girl of the same origins as his? The pain was back, accompanied with anger. Oh, if he thought of breaking his promise this way, he would be very sorry!

She hit the hard, rocky surface, wincing with pain. Was this why he wasn't coming?

Springing to her feet the way Hainteroh had, she collected her beads hastily, then headed down the trail, in a hurry now. Something had to be done, she thought, the sound of her footsteps bouncing against the towering rocks. Something! She didn't know what it was, but one thing was clear – she was fed up with the waiting.

And another thing was as certain. She would not stay here to endure another winter. Not if she could help it.

CHAPTER 2

The current was strong, rushing forcefully between the high banks, carrying floating objects, from fallen trees to muddied chunks of melted ice, the Great River swelling, as though trying to break free from its confinement.

Tekeni grinned against his will. The winter was over and it was a good thing. Paddling vigorously, he pitted his strength against the current, enjoying himself. The imposed idleness of the long, frozen moons was over. He was sailing again, in the right direction this time, battling against the flow of the Great River, getting closer to his destination.

Admittedly, their small fleet of twenty canoes headed toward the Standing Stone People's largest town, and not toward the Great Sparkling Lake. Still, it was the right direction, and it wouldn't be long before he'd be allowed to sneak off on his own very private side-mission.

Two Rivers had promised, and he had repeated his promise more than once during the cold moons. The moment they were back among the Onondaga People, Tekeni would be free to cross the Great Lake once again, to fetch his girl and be back in no time.

"I need you to return as fast as you can, *and* fully capable," Two Rivers had said more than once through the long winter moons, his eyes sparkling with the well-familiar, easy mischief. "Grab your pretty Seketa, and rush back as though all the creatures of the Evil Twin were after you. Don't stop to take a breath even." The spark was gone, replaced by a frown. "And don't make the mistake of underestimating my people, or trying to trust them and talk to them. It's too early for that. They won't listen. Not before we have made a good progress here. Do you hear me? Don't be tempted to connect with anyone you used to know, or anyone your girl might think you need to talk to." Reaching for the fire that kept dancing despite the opening in the roof being shut tightly against the blizzard, the man reclined more comfortably, putting his palms closer to the flame. "Just grab the girl, hop back into your canoe, and be gone."

"I didn't intend to do anything else," said Tekeni, shifting closer to the fire in his turn. Their small hunting party came back with the worst of the blizzard, carrying a game they managed to hunt, exhausted, frozen, their limbs numb, their woven snow-shoes falling apart. The friendly flames in the middle of their compartment seemed to be a blissful gift.

"I don't like the idea of you traveling those places all alone. If you waited with that until we settled Hionhwatha's people…" Two Rivers stretched, then coughed, waving away the thickest of the smoke. With the vent hole closed tight, it kept spreading along the corridor and around the compartments, making the air blurry, difficult to see through. "Maybe then, I would be able to come with you."

Warmed by those words, Tekeni grinned. "I wouldn't count on that. Between the great gathering of our towns that you are so eager to organize and the couriers that you are about to send to all sorts of places the moment the snow has melted, I'm afraid I'll grow old waiting for you to find the time to escort me back to your people." At peace with the world for a change, he rolled onto his back. Oh, but it was good to be home, it was! He winced, remembering the dreadful winters spent in captivity. "It won't take me long, anyway. A few days forth, a few days back, some time spent trying to find her with no one the wiser, and I'll be back among the Onondagas, in time to see you handling that difficult leader of theirs."

"Tadodaho," muttered Two Rivers. "Curse his eyes into the underworld of the Evil Twin and his minions! Why do I have a feeling he will make it difficult for us?"

"Because he will."

"Yes, I suppose. The filthy lowlife. To kill Hionhwatha's family. What a despicable deed!"

"Do you believe he can do all this alleged sorcery of his?"

"No, of course not. Your suggestion that they died of winter disease made better sense." The man's lips twisted into a contented grin. "How angry it made Onheda back then."

"Onheda? Who is that?"

"The Onondaga girl."

"Oh, is that her name?"

"Yes."

"How do you know?"

"I asked."

Rising on his elbow, Tekeni studied his formidable friend, suddenly curious. "Will you be seeking her company when we are back?"

Two Rivers didn't move, lying on his back, staring at the ceiling. "Of course, why not? She helped us tremendously, and she can still be of a great use."

"Great use, eh?"

The man's grin flashed out, but carefully so. "It's not what you think."

"Then what is it?"

"She is a great woman, very smart, very quick-thinking, as sharp as a polished flint. If she is still at Jikonsahseh's, I would love to have her escort us to High Springs, and then to Onondaga Town."

"Very pretty too, you forgot to mention that," pressed Tekeni, amused by the way the Crooked Tongues man's face closed.

"What do her looks has to do with our mission of Great Peace?"

"That's what I'm trying to understand."

"Well, don't try too hard. Your head may start aching."

Chuckling, Tekeni rolled back onto his mat. "It would be interesting to see you falling for a woman."

"Don't hold your breath. Get busy with bringing back yours."

A creaking of the screen that was pushed aside at the nearest end of their longhouse brought in a draft of a cold air, making the fire dance. Shaking the snow off, Atiron's wife came in, followed by more female figures.

"Greetings."

Both Tekeni and Two Rivers straightened up, returning the polite words, while the women proceeded to shed off layers of thick blankets wrapped around their muffled forms, making them look shapeless.

"It's been a good foray," said the older woman, smiling. "We will feast heartily tonight." From the bag she carried, she pulled out a chunk of a juicy meat. "You were lucky to hunt two mature elks."

"Yes, it was a rare luck," said Two Rivers, his accent heavy, but his words clearly understandable now, after more than two moons of speaking the locals' tongue. "Pleasure hunting with the People of the Flint."

The woman nodded, pleased, as the baby clutched in her younger companion's arms began making mewing noises. The third muffled figure turned out to be Kahontsi, emerging from her wraps, smoothing her hair hastily, her eyes following their guest as the man picked up his mat to clear the space around the fire.

Doing the same, Tekeni watched his friend, amused once again. There was tension in Two Rivers' posture now, in the way he concentrated on removing his mat, in the way he avoided the girl's gaze. What had happened between those two?

"Where is your husband?" he heard the Crooked Tongues man asking, while picking up a heavy pottery container full of snow, bringing it closer to the fire.

"The members of the council were invited to the Bear Clan longhouse, to discuss other hunting expeditions for the rest of the Frozen Moons." Nodding her thanks, the older woman moved on briskly, feeding the fire, making it shine more brightly. "You will be welcomed there. I gather they had been looking for you."

"Then I had better be gone."

With an indecent haste, Two Rivers fled down the corridor, leaving Tekeni to face the women's hubbub alone, now spiced by the crying of a baby that Atiron's elder daughter held in her arms. For another heartbeat, he stared after his friend, puzzled, then noticed Kahontsi doing the same, her lips quivering, eyes flickering with uncertainty.

"Kahontsi, put the pot on the fire," called her mother sharply, eyeing the girl with an open displeasure.

Catching Tekeni's gaze, his cousin tossed her head high.

"Will you go on staring or will you help me with this heavy thing?" she asked, challenging, her uncertainty gone.

"I will do neither. I need to go out, too." But he picked up the heavy jar, placing it above the fire.

"Of course you need to go. You, men, always do. But who will be here first when the food is ready?" Kahontsi's eyes sparkled dangerously. "Sometimes men are nothing but nuisance."

"Oh, please!" Disregarding her glare, Tekeni leaned closer, trying to stay out of hearing range of the other two women. "Don't take your anger out on me. I told you not fall in love with him. I warned you."

She seemed as though about to explode. "Who needs your advice? You understand nothing!"

"Oh yes?" He eyed her contemptuously, but the sight of her narrowed, glittering eyes made his heart twist with compassion, sensing the misery behind her bubbling anger. "Listen, little sister. Don't let it harm your spirit. Forget about it. He is not for this, but there are plenty of young men who would be delighted to have your love." He winked at her. "I know quite a few who would be overjoyed to have you smiling at them. Many are in love with you."

Her lips quivered. "He is in love with me, too. He is!" She took a deep breath and pressed her lips tighter. "He just can't admit it. Because of the town council."

"What? What are you talking about?"

"Don't stare at me like a hit-on-the-head elk! He can't ask our Clan Mothers because he is still a foreigner, even if he is listened to and respected now. He is not one of us, not yet. But he will be, eventually. And then he will admit his love."

Oh, Mighty Spirits! Tekeni felt like taking a step back. "Kahontsi, he is not. Get it out of your head, sister. He is not in love with you."

The girl's eyes flickered like a pair of gleaming coals. "That's how much you know, but I bet he never told you that he almost kissed me once. On that ball game, after the meeting of our town council with the representatives of the other towns. Just before the first snow." She looked at him triumphantly. "He would have kissed me if we had not been interrupted."

This time he did take a step back. "Kahontsi, you are talking nonsense—"

"Would you stop whispering and start working?" Kahontsi's older sister's voice cut into their privacy above the fire. "The water is about to boil, but all she does is exchange whispers with the twin, Mother!"

"We are talking important things, Ehnita! You can put your baby down and start working too, instead of watching how much work I do."

As the two sisters glared at one another, Tekeni deemed it high time to beat a hasty retreat, the way his friend had wisely done before. Women, he thought, heading down the corridor, careful to bypass the fireplaces and the welling activities around each one of them. Sometimes they could be a real nuisance. Especially when they were one's family. Tekeni's real relatives lived in the second Turtle Clan's longhouse, but he preferred Atiron's company, with the man being the closest friend of his father and the first to listen to Two Rivers, even before the test of the falls. Atiron was a great man, and his family was the only family he needed.

Two Rivers had stayed here at first, too, but now he was

enjoying the hospitality of the Town Council's leader and his family. The head of the town insisted, and suddenly Tekeni could understand his friend's inclination to answer the polite invitation better. If Kahontsi was after him, then there was no wonder the Crooked Tongues man preferred to spend his winter confinement elsewhere. After the test of the falls, the whole town went out of its way to accommodate their honorable guest.

The test of the falls!

He shivered, remembering this hideous day, his bottomless worry, his desperation. The hastily concocted plan worked, but it was a near miss, judging by what Anowara and Kahontsi had told him. Two Rivers had nearly drowned in the falls, bashing his head quite open and bruising some of his ribs and limbs. But for the waiting canoe, the man would never have made it. Oh, Mighty Spirits!

However, it all worked out for the best in the end. The people believed the miracle, and they were prepared not only to listen now, but to follow quite blindly, was Tekeni's astounded conclusion. One moment dangerous and rude, the next all smiles, trustful like children. So strange. And yet, not strange at all, according to Atiron.

The wise man had explained it all to him one evening, glancing around, careful not to be overheard. There were too many spans of seasons with bad harvest, combined with too many unsuccessful hunting moons. People were hungry and desperate. The old ways did not work anymore. The appearance of Two Rivers and the miraculous return of Tekeni himself came in right time. A summer or two earlier and they might not have been listened, the jump into the falls or not.

Also, Atiron had said, grinning lightly, nodding as he did; Two Rivers' foreignness presented an unexpected advantage. A local person suggesting such dramatic change was not likely to be trusted, neither by his own people nor by the neighboring enemies. His motives would be suspected, no matter how well he presented his case. While a Crooked Tongues man belonged to no nation and so was expected to be impartial, with his judgment unclouded by loyalties to any of the involved sides. It was easy to believe that he had been, indeed, the Messenger of the Great Spirits, because his passion and the miraculous success of his journey might not be explained otherwise.

Oh, yes, decided Tekeni, taking a deep breath, preparing to dive into the biting cold outside the tightly shut screen. It was a miracle that they had survived so far, making such an unheard of progress. Their entire journey, the encounter with Hionhwatha, their arrival at Little Falls, all this without taking into account smaller incidences and fights; and above all, their departure from the lands of the Crooked Tongues itself. What a miraculous survival it was! Had Yeentso not been so full of hatred, taking pleasure in inflicting unnecessary pain, he, Tekeni, would have been dead by the time Two Rivers had found them.

He caught his breath. No, there must be more to it. The Great Spirits must have wished to keep them alive and successful, to carry out their important mission. Their will worked in mysterious ways, but now it all was beginning to make sense. He should not have survived his last encounter with Yeentso, and Two Rivers should not have survived his dive into the lethal rapids, and yet here they were, not only alive and well, but also full of enthusiastic support of Little Falls and the other towns and villages, because after the test and the miraculous survival, the townsfolk embraced the foreigner's ideas wholeheartedly, as though he had been an appointed leader, inviting him to every meeting of the Town Council and consulting him in everything.

Not wishing to delay the union of the Flint People themselves, the messengers were sent to the neighboring settlements, and a few preliminary meetings were held through the last moon of the clear weather, before the first snow had fallen.

Tekeni grinned, remembering the long, sometimes heated, debates. There was a need to organize a round of a ball game, to distract and pacify some of the hotheaded spirits. And if so, what will the meeting of all the Flint People's towns look like? he wondered, partly amused, partly worried. His people were willing to listen to Two Rivers now, but they were still headstrong, fiercely independent men and women, not prepared to be told what to do. The great gathering of the first spring moon would not be easy to handle, that much he knew. But at least by then, Two Rivers would be able to talk with no need to be translated. The meetings of the last autumn were difficult to handle partly because of that.

Suddenly worried, he narrowed his eyes against the cutting wind. Had Two Rivers kissed Kahontsi? Had he fallen for this girl's sparkling allure? No, it was not possible. She was nothing but a pretty thing, spoiled and willful, confident in her ability to make a man fall for her charm. She spelt danger. As awkward as it might be, he would have to talk to his friend about it, to warn him. There was no need to alienate formidable Atiron. This man's goodwill was important.

"What are you doing wandering outside? Missing the cold of the Crooked Tongues' lands?"

Startled, Tekeni looked up, his eyes taking in another group of muffled figures that carried bags and pots of snow, heading for the second Turtle Clan's longhouse.

"Maybe."

Even though wrapped into too many blankets, he had no difficulty recognizing Anitas' voice and the way the tall girl carried herself, with a cheeky, challenging grace.

"Our winters are too soft for you, aren't they?" Slowing her step, the girl fell behind her group, tilted under her heavy burden. "Help me with this."

He took the pottery jar, his palms going numb with cold.

"It was nice of you to shoot these elk. That foreigner of yours keeps bringing goodwill of the Great Spirits to our people, doesn't he?"

"Yes, he does." He measured her with his gaze, seeking the signs of her teasing him. With Anitas one never knew.

"Was it difficult to convince him to come here? How did you

do this?"

"I didn't. He was the one who wanted to come. I just came along."

"And they let you two leave just like that?" She halted, peering at him, her playfulness gone.

"No, of course not. What do you think? That they gave us their blessing and provisions to make our journey smoother?"

She shrugged. "Who knows? They are savages. Unpredictable. One never knows what such creatures would do."

"They are no savages. Stop talking nonsense." Annoyed, he shifted the heavy vessel, trying to warm his hands. *Would they consider Seketa a savage girl? Would it be difficult for her to live in Little Falls?* "Does Two Rivers look like a savage to you?"

Anitas' eyes sparkled, now with a definite provocation. "Oh yes, he does. He looks alien, outlandish, strange. He talks strangely, and he behaves like he doesn't care for what people think." Her lips, now bluish with cold, twitched. "I think he could make a good lover. I would let him come to live with me in my longhouse."

"Not you too!" he cried out in desperation, before able to hold his tongue.

"Oh?" The girl's eyebrows climbed high, her eyes sparkling. "Who else has been inviting him to warm her mat on the cold winter nights?"

"No one!" Enraged with himself and his stupid slip, he kicked at the snow, watching the tip of his moccasin disappearing in the crispy whiteness. "But women always made fools of themselves over him, and I see that our girls are as silly as the Crooked Tongues foxes were."

"Crooked Tongues foxes, eh?" Her eyes danced as she leaned closer, her breath making white clouds in the air, reaching his face. "I heard that you tasted those wild savage foxes aplenty and that they left a lasting impression on you."

His heart halted, then threw itself wildly against his chest. "What?" The jar began slipping between his palms, and he struggled to get a better grip. "Who told you that?"

"Careful with that pottery. It might break," she said smugly, pleased with herself. Her narrowed eyes studied him, their glitter taunting. "So, do you miss her, that pretty savage of yours? Do you still intend to go back and find her?"

Kahontsi, he thought, his anger splashing, difficult to contain. He should never have confided in her, never. He would go back and break her skinny little neck the moment he had the chance.

"You can tell me." Anitas stepped closer, her enjoyment spilling. "Was she that good of a lover that you would not look on our girls anymore? What things did she do for you? Do savages perform differently?"

He stared into the taunting darkness of her eyes, unable to breathe. Finding it difficult to hold onto the slippery vessel, because his arms shook too badly by now, he thrust it back into her hands.

"Keep away from me," he hissed, his voice trembling too, annoyingly so. "If you ever, ever say something like that again, I swear, I will... I will make you regret this. I swear!"

He didn't remember stalking off, but at some point the slippery path twisted, and he realized that he was practically running, crossing the ground where the tobacco plots were buried under the carpet of white. Numb from cold, he tried to shake off the snow that kept accumulating upon his head and his shoulders, his limbs trembling, difficult to control.

Curse that filthy Anitas into the underworld of the Evil Twin, he thought, clenching his teeth. How dared she talk about Seketa in this way, spreading filthy rumors? What a dirty fox this girl was, always teasing, baiting, provoking, worse than he remembered, because since his coming back she gave him no rest, looking him up, taunting on every occasion, as though enjoying making him angry. But to talk this way about Seketa!

He clenched his fists, out of frustration as much as to return the feeling to his frozen fingers. Oh, but it was his fault. He should never have confided in Kahontsi. Not on his first evening, before the test of the falls, nor on a few other occasions, when the girl had prompted him, asking well-meaning questions. It was tempting to talk about Seketa; it made her real and not just a fuzzy dream of a demented mind.

Some nights, lying on his mat, listening to the groaning blizzards and the quiet conversations floating along the long corridor, coming from other compartments, people speaking his native tongue, laughing or getting angry with each other, he would shut his eyes and feel as though the two spans of seasons in the lands of the Crooked Tongues never happened, that they were just a strange dream, all the good and all the bad, that, in fact, he had never left Little Falls, and that Father was still alive, and so were Mother and his brother.

He would keep his eyes closed, relishing the feeling, but then the sensation of well-being would evaporate, because if it was just a nightmare, then the good in it was not real as well, a fruit of his imagination. Seketa and her wonderful kisses, and the beautiful afternoon of lovemaking on the clearing. And his promise to come back for her.

To talk to Kahontsi helped, so when she would ask, he would tell her more, about his plans and his hopes and about how wonderful Seketa was and how beautifully she danced. Those talks made it all real again. He would cross the Great Sparkling Water, and he would manage to bring her back. As soon as the snow melted and the rivers would be free to flow again.

But how was he to know that the silly girl would tell it all to her gossipy, malicious friend? He kicked at the helpless snow again and again. How was Seketa to come and live in Little Falls now, a savage girl from across the Great Lake, the talk of the town? Would she suffer as he had suffered while living among her people? With Anitas around and ready to sneer, there could be little doubt as to the possibility of her being happy in Little Falls.

And now, rowing against the current, he turned his face into the wind, trying to ward off the troubled thoughts. She would find her new home in Little Falls. They would make it work, somehow. If only there were a way to contact her, to let her know that he would be coming and soon.

CHAPTER 3

Before the boat kissed the shore, Two Rivers was out, careless of the shallow water splashing around his moccasins. It had been a long sail and he was impatient.

The Thunder Moon, the second moon of the Awakening Season, was taking over, making a firm stance upon the waking land. It battled the cold with a firm resolution, melting the snows, releasing the rivers and streams that had been imprisoned by the ice for too long.

It all was coming back to life, the land and the creatures inhabiting it; the plants, animals, and humans, all the creations of the Right-Handed Twin. It was the time to act, time to go back to the People of the Hills, to see how Hionhwatha was faring, to lend him the necessary help and support. With the People of the Flint firmly behind him now, after the second gathering of the nation was held with the first awakening moon, he knew he could turn his attention back to the difficult Onondagas.

Hionhwatha would need help, of that he was certain. The formidable man may have achieved some success in High Springs, but the main Onondaga town would need to be put under more serious pressure than mere persuasion and words full of good sense. The warmonger Tadodaho would not give up easily, would not let his former rival have his way. Hionhwatha would need backing up before his resolve wavered once again. This man was not stable, not yet. And also…

He shook the water off and watched other canoes cutting the gravel of the low shore. He would visit Jikonsahseh on his way westward. It would be good to see the old woman again, to let her know that he was alive and successful. She would be of help, now more than ever. And maybe the Onondaga girl would still be there, waiting as he had told her to do.

His stomach twisted with anticipation. She might have been there, or she might not, an untamed spirit that she was. Maybe she had gone home, forgetting all about him. Or maybe she was waiting restlessly, pacing the clearing in that pliant, forceful stride of hers, with her legs long and fit, and her eyes sparkling angrily, impatient with his delay. He had promised to come back, maybe even before the cold moons, but now it was already way into the spring and here he was, lingering in the lands of the Standing Stone People, heading for yet another gathering of the sort he had just endured back in Little Falls. Why couldn't they see the obvious, joining to his proposed union with no further talks and delays?

"A good polished arrowhead for your thoughts." Tekeni leapt out of his boat, tall and broad shouldered, more impressive than ever, the scars upon his handsome face glittering in the high morning sun, his eyes sparkling, unconcerned.

"Don't spend your arrowheads that lightly." Grabbing the side of the boat in order to help securing it upon the shore, Two Rivers grinned. "You may need them."

"I have enough." Laughing heartily, the young man tossed his head. "I spent most of the time working on those to make the cold moons pass quicker. I have so many. And when all the people around our Great Lake accept your message of peace, what will I do with all this treasure? I'll be stuck."

Eyeing the lines of painted canoes spreading along the shoreline, Two Rivers grinned. "This problem is still far enough for you not to worry about it. Back among the Onondagas your fighting skills may still be of use." He raised his eyebrows. "Also, across the Great Sparkling Water those arrowheads may give you a measure of comfort."

The handsome face closed. "Yes, I know. The moment you reconnect with Hionhwatha I'm free to go, am I not?"

Glancing at his young companion, Two Rivers nodded. "Yes, you are. And if I see that the Onondagas gave our old leader no trouble, I'll go with you." He grinned. "If for no other reason, then to speed the things up, to make sure you are not lingering, making love to your pretty wife days on end upon some abandoned shore. It will be tempting, but I need you here. You are too important for our Tidings of Great Peace to spend your time having pleasure and nothing else."

Tekeni's high cheekbones took a darker shade as the young man scowled, half put out, half amused. "Oh, please!" His lips twisted, fighting an obvious smile. "Also, what do you need me for? You speak our tongue well enough now for my people and the others to understand."

"And this was your only value, eh?" Two Rivers measured his friend with a meaningful glance, reflecting again that the winter spent in his hometown did the youth only good, turning the wolf cub into an impressively large, forceful creature, full of the strength belonging to an adult but combined with youthful energy and vigor. "Our success has nothing to do with your ability to speak this or that local tongue. Well, it has, but there is much more to it, wolf cub. Or mature wolf, should I say? You are not a cub anymore, but a great man, warrior, future leader, the best partner the Right-Handed Twin could have given to me." He grinned again, taunting. "So it'll be only quick lovemaking for you. You have work to do. Seketa will have to live with it."

The momentarily cleared face darkened again. "I was wondering about that."

"What?"

"How will she do in Little Falls?" Shifting his weight from one foot to another, Tekeni eyed the rest of their party climbing out of their canoes. "She will be the foreigner, *the savage*, like I was in your town."

Turning to greet their arriving companions, Two Rivers shrugged. "She'll manage. Women always do."

"I don't know." The young man's face cleared as they began

descending the shore, some distance from their companions again. "Speaking of women, does Kahontsi give you trouble?"

He felt his heart missing a beat. "No. Why?"

"Well, she seems to be determined to get you." Tekeni's voice trembled with mirth. "She told me that much. She was boasting that you kissed her once."

"Oh, please. Will you stop gossiping about me?" Startled by the intensity and the suddenness of his own rage, he tried to control his voice. "I'm not a youth of your age, and I'm busy with a certain work, as you know. Tidings of Peace, remember? You were the one to put it this way! So take it out of your head and tell your cousin to do the same. I don't have time for this silliness." Wrenching his hand out of his friend's grip, he turned away. "Now let us get to work. We have a long day ahead of us."

Desperate to control his temper, he charged down the shore, to keep up with the rest of their party, his anger difficult to contain. The damn girl! As pretty and vital, as attentive and willing to listen, the spoiled little thing turned out to be a real nuisance, chasing him through the long winter moons, trying to talk to him, to corner him into difficult situations, trusting her charm to do the rest. And the damn little fox had too much of that! Beautiful and alluring, her eyes luminous, shining, her figure perfect, curved in all the right places, her mouth folded playfully, inviting to touch it, to taste it, and maybe, to do more. He had almost succumbed to the urge once, before the first snow, when she had managed to catch him alone, all flushed and worked up from the ball game they had just won, his blood boiling, the excitement running through his limbs. She had caught him when he went to the storage room of one of the longhouses, to fetch a pottery jar he was asked to bring. Chatting happily, she came after him, blocking his way of escape, so young and vital and beautiful, so willing and receptive, her gaze telling him that the meaningless talk was nothing, just a pretext, promising the divine pleasure should he put aside any caution for one short afternoon.

Still, he had fought the desire, knowing that she was too young and a daughter of a friend; also, although appearing to offer nothing but pleasure, she had wanted more, more than he was willing to give. He could not forget that he was still just a foreigner, and should he do stupid things, they would stop backing him up, turning against him and his mission, instead.

So he had made the effort to sneak away, but she kept talking, not letting him leave, coming closer, making him feel her warmth, giving him no space to maneuver. He didn't remember quite how, but at some point, his arms were around her and his lips sought hers, but then loud voices interrupted, passing dangerously close to the half-shut screen, making them jump away, frightened, their hearts threatening to burst inside their chests. Oh, but for this blissful interruption! He could still feel the depth of his relief. However, since then, she had chased him like hunters chasing their prey, always there, always watching, seeking his gaze, with her eyes shining and her smile ready, promising, full of smug female superiority, telling him that she knew about his desire and the intensity of it, checked by the strength of his will alone.

After that first semi-successful meeting of the other towns and villages, the head of the Town Council offered his hospitality, insisting that the important guest should reside in his longhouse, but had it not been for Kahontsi, Two Rivers might have declined, not wishing to offend the wise, kind Atiron, the first man of Little Falls to believe in him.

"What a gathering!"

The voice of one of the warriors tore him back from his unhappy thoughts, making him concentrate, his gaze taking in the colorful mess of a small valley spread below their feet, a short walk from the top of their hill. Dozens of tents filled the small space, mats and blankets lining the earthen floor, hiding the brilliant green of the early grass from the eyes.

"What in the name of the forest spirits..."

They looked at each other, unsettled, their gazes taking in groups of warriors that strolled around the tents and the fires, among women busy preparing food.

"We didn't talk about *this* sort of a gathering," muttered Two Rivers, stopping dead in his tracks. "We discussed all the details most clearly!" He shook his head, aware that, again, he had forgotten himself and was talking in his native tongue. "Well, let us see what they are up to."

"Maybe we should go back to our boats," said a tall warrior, the same man who interviewed him back upon the shore of the Great River when they had first arrived at Little Falls. His name was Okwaho, and during the long winter moons, they had come to know each other well, participating in more than a few hunting expeditions, their mutual respect growing. He had asked specifically for this warrior to lead his delegation, although Little Falls' Town Council suggested another man.

"If this was a trap, then they would be alerted, waiting for us to arrive, watching their shore, catching us the moment we stepped on dry land." Two Rivers shrugged, sweeping the valley again with his gaze, seeing a group of respectable men heading in their direction, their headdresses, sporting two feathers each, prominent against the brightness of the sky. "We have little choice other than to go on. And maybe it is, indeed, just a misunderstanding."

"I doubt that," muttered Okwaho, running his hand along the newly shaved sides of his head, rubbing it vigorously. "I don't think that they already decided to kill us, but I don't like the possibility of their deciding to do so later on."

"This gathering seems to be as large as ours back through the last moon, but with twice as many warriors," said Tekeni, coming closer, shielding his eyes to see better. "Filthy creatures!"

Their own dignitaries, three middle-aged men from the three of the most prominent towns, neared in the meanwhile, halting abruptly, standing beside Two Rivers, their frowns well hidden.

He took a deep breath. "Yes, the representatives of their whole nation must be here, which can be a good thing. They have taken our proposal seriously."

"Seriously enough to make sure they can detain us and do whatever they like with us any time they see fit." Okwaho spat, then bettered his grip upon the hilt of his spiked, vicious-looking club. "Maybe we can still beat a hasty retreat."

"Not with such a pompous delegation heading our way," muttered Tekeni. "If they see us fleeing, it will make a bad impression. We came here to talk, after all, and they can plead that they, indeed, had taken our proposals most seriously, gathering the best of their nation to listen to the Messenger."

As the older warrior glared at Tekeni, enraged with the young man offering advice without being asked to do so, Two Rivers made sure his back was as straight as it could be.

"Yes, we'll proceed as planned. And if they entertain silly ideas, we'll deal with it." He shrugged. "This amount of warriors alone shows us that they are not as certain, not as sure of themselves as they would like us to believe they are. So all we have to do is to show them that we better be listened to, and carefully at that."

"Let's hope they won't ask to see a proof of your powers, too," he heard Tekeni muttering under his breath. "What would it be this time? Jumping off the cliff into the sharp rocks of the valley or diving with a stone tied to your limbs?"

Sneaking a glance at his younger companion, Two Rivers grinned, trying to reassure. *We got this far*, he wanted to say, but the flowery greetings in a tongue he found again difficult to understand were already upon them, the eyes of the people measuring them, wary, penetrating, not overly friendly.

We'll deal with them, he thought, concentrating on their leading hosts. They might need some convincing, yes, but they clearly were not seeking to shed blood. Unless provoked. A quick glance at his own delegation's members made him worried.

CHAPTER 4

Onheda watched the squatting men, trying not to be too obvious about it. Sorting the seeds that were spread before her on a folded blanket, she glanced up again and again, her ears pricked. Their guests, all three of them, sat beside the fire that was barely visible in the brilliance of the daylight, gulping a stew Jikonsahseh made out of the meat they had brought along.

"So the gathering of our people wasn't a failure after all?" said the old woman, waddling back with more of the delicious smelling brew.

"Well, no." The younger of the men looked up, smiling politely. "But it was close to getting out of hand."

"The annoying Flint People were unbearably arrogant," said another man, the older of the three. "They came with their usual audacity, as though they can tell us how to manage our affairs."

"But the Crooked Tongues man was the one leading them?" Frowning, Jikonsahseh placed the jar upon the ground, then straightened up, peering at the man, clearly anxious to hear it all. Onheda held her breath.

"Well, yes, the foreigner was the one to do most of the talking. It helped to calm the spirits." The older man shrugged. "He is an interesting man. One moment calm, just a regular person, not too tall, not too imposing; the other – passionate, speaking in a forceful way, making it difficult not to listen to him. Even with this dreadful accent of his." Answering the grins of his companions, the man chuckled. "A strange man. How he made the Flint beasts listen in the first place, escapes me. I would expect them to put such a foreigner on the carpet of the glowing embers with no delays. But what do they do? Let the foreigner lead them, instead! He truly must possess some powers, being the Messenger of the Right-Handed Twin."

Feeling the gaze of her older friend, Onheda hid her smile, scooping the seeds in order to pour them into a basket.

"Was the scar-faced young man with him?" she asked, unable to hold her tongue.

The men turned to watch her, all three of them, and she knew she should not have spoken.

"They were a little more than twenty men, all in all," said the older warrior, measuring her with his gaze, clearly wondering. "With such little force they dared to enter our lands," he added, looking back at Jikonsahseh. "I'm telling you, their arrogance has no limits."

"I remember a scar-faced warrior," said the younger man, his gaze lingering on Onheda with an open appreciation, making her uncomfortable. "He was always around the foreigner, that's why I remember him. A dangerous-looking lowlife that I would love to fight."

This time Jikonsahseh actually laughed, taking their gazes away from Onheda, who felt something close to gratitude. To draw their attention was not a wise thing to do. Although after spending a winter in the old woman's hut, she felt firmly at home here, a part of Jikonsahseh's household and so protected by the unannounced law of this clearing, the awareness of the state of affairs between her people and their neighbors from the east made her uncomfortable. Maybe the Crooked Tongues man made the Flint People listen, and maybe he did manage to start the negotiations between those fierce enemies and the People of the Standing Stone; still, whatever his grand plans were, her people, the Onondagas, were not yet part of this new development. These warriors were still her people's enemy, and her accent was too clear for them to take her for Jikonsahseh's countryfolk.

"They deliberated for days, with the foreigner doing most of the talking," went on the older warrior, scratching the sides of

THE GREAT LAW OF PEACE

his bowl with the spoon in an attempt to fish out the last of the juicy pieces. "And they are still there, waiting for the representatives of the other towns to arrive."

"Can't they conduct their own people's meeting without the Messenger holding their hands?" asked Jikonsahseh, raising her eyebrows high.

The men shrugged in unison.

"They want him there to make sure there is no treachery, I suppose," said the third man, who had kept silent until now. "With the dangerous Flint one never knows."

"They came in good faith, their intentions honorable. Enough people, with quite a few important representatives among them, I suppose." Jikonsahseh's voice rang calmly, her hands busy refilling her guests' plates, yet Onheda could see the signs of the old woman being angry, with her lips pressed and her movements sharper than usual, bumping the spoon against the pot. "What treachery can they plan?"

"All sorts of treachery, Older Sister. Don't forget that those are the People of the Flint, our avowed enemies."

"They won't be our enemies for much longer."

They all stared at her.

"Have you met the Messenger?" asked the leading man, frowning.

"Yes, I have." The old woman looked at her guests sternly. "I have met him, and I have spoken to him, and I had him here as a guest for quite a long time, enough to convince me of the divine nature of his mission. This man should be followed with no questions asked. His motives are pure, and his mission has the blessing of the Great Spirits."

They fell silent, staring at the fire.

"He talked about uniting quite a few peoples along our beautiful forests," muttered the younger man. "It doesn't seem possible to me, even if our people could reach an agreement with the ferocious neighbors from the east. The beasts from around the Lake Onondaga will not hear any of it. They are too bloodthirsty for this, and the man who is leading them now can rival the Evil Twin in his treacherous ways."

"My people will join," said Onheda, unwilling to hold her tongue once again. "They are not bloodthirsty, and they are not treacherous. They are good people, and good leaders are working now to change their minds."

More silence.

"Who is trying to persuade your people? Another foreigner? Another messenger?" There was a frustrated tone to the younger man's voice, his gaze boring at her.

"We do not need foreigners to help us sort out our own affairs. When the Messenger comes back, my people will greet him, eager and ready. They will not argue, and they will not make him stay against his will, to help them get organized."

They stared at her, openly indignant now. She didn't care. Her people were being talked to in those very moments, and he could have been here already if not for the mistrustful skunks of the Standing Stone lands. How dared they detain him in this way?

Her stomach tightened at the mere thought of him. It had been too long. He said he might come back before the Cold Moons, but, of course, it didn't happen. She was right to pin little hope on this. Still, now Planting Moon was imminent, the middle of the Awakening Season. The snows had melted, and the rivers were gushing again with no restraint. How long was she to stay in this hut, waiting for him to return?

She remembered his proud, prominent profile, and the way he moved, resolute and purposeful, but also graceful in some imperceptible way. A perfect hunter and warrior, yet he thought about nothing but his mission. He didn't want to war or to hunt. He fought his attraction to her, as well. Yet, in this he had failed, succumbing to it in the end, taking her to places she had never dreamed to reach. Did he remember?

She had asked herself that again and again, as the Cold Moons dragged on and the blizzards raged, threatening to take Jikonsahseh's huts apart. Was his stomach tightening at the memory of the small clearing by the end of the trail and the way the spirits had taken the possession of their bodies? Or was he too busy making peace between the Flint People and the People of the Standing Stone? Would he come back to have more of the wonderful lovemaking or would he hurry to join Hionhwatha?

She pressed her lips tight. He was alive and well, and it was good news. Through the long, freezing moons they could not be sure of even this, wondering, worried. She trusted the scar-faced youth to ensure that his people didn't kill the foreigner on the spot. Still, even with the brave resourcefulness of these two, the danger was too imminent, too great to feel safe about it. However, here he was, surviving the winter and obviously achieving his goal, now busy making peace between such avowed enemies as the two eastern nations. How did he manage?

"Your people are not doing too well." The voice of the younger man tore her from her reverie, his gaze not thawing, burning holes in her skin. "They were fighting each other last summer, and they are still arguing most violently, so I hear. It's only a matter of time before their two leading towns start fighting for real."

Oh, Mighty Spirits! She felt her heart sliding down her chest, to fall into the emptiness of her stomach. Her High Springs and Onondaga Town. And here she was hoping that Hionhwatha was more successful this time.

"They will sort out their differences in a peaceful way," she said stubbornly, tossing her head high and bestowing on the young warrior a look of cold contempt. "By the time the Messenger comes, they will be ready to listen."

Folding her blanket, careful not to let the seeds scatter, she got to her feet, heading toward the house, keeping her back straight and her head proud, knowing that their gazes would follow her.

She knew the intimidating Tadodaho was proving more difficult than ever, having heard about it already when the warriors' party from High Springs stopped by earlier through this moon. Her hometown was eager to support the old leader who had come back from the dead, enthusiastic to resume his work. But Onondaga Town remained dangerously quiet, ominous and aloof under the firm grip of the deadly War Chief, still larger than High Springs, wielding more influence.

The war would break out, unless the Crooked Tongues man hurried, she realized, clenching her teeth, fighting the familiar wave of despondency. Yet, he was busy elsewhere, pacifying the eastern nations, not caring for her or her people, damn his eyes into the underworld of the Evil Twin.

Pressing her palms to her face, she fought the tears, desperate not to succumb to the moment of weakness. Oh, but she was a fool to delude herself the way she did. He was not in a hurry to come back. He cared for nothing but the Great Peace. She would do better to forget all about him.

They were still squatting when she came out, carrying an empty jar, heading for the spring.

"And so they cut the tree, to fall straight into the worst of the falls," she heard the older man saying, leaning closer to Jikonsahseh who, atypically for her, stared at the speaker, clearly thrown out of balance.

Onheda slowed her step.

"It disappeared into the raging water, with only the broken branches coming out, to fall into the lower rapids." Pausing, the man glanced at his companions, satisfied with their nods. "The warrior who told me that said that one of his adoptive sister's cousins was there, seeing it all with his own eyes. It was a sure death. No man could have survived that fall."

"And then?" Jikonsahseh seemed to be holding her breath.

"And then, the next morning, he came back, just like the Town Council told him to do."

"Wounded?"

"No, not a scratch. As though he had never been in the rapids at all."

Frowning, the old woman leaned back, while Onheda felt her heart accelerating, despite the firm resolution not to think about him ever again. It was always the same. They seemed to be able to talk about nothing but him these days, Jikonsahseh, and now even total strangers.

"Like I told you, this man is the Messenger of the Right-Handed Twin himself. Our people should help him along instead of giving him trouble."

"He could have started with our people. He didn't have to go all the way to Little Falls. You said he talked to you before. Why didn't you tell him that?" The man frowned. "Did you know he was going to that foul town?"

"Yes, of course. I told you that he confided in me. I was dubious at first, too, but when he went to see Hionhwatha of the Onondagas and came back unharmed, having converted the deranged man to carry his word on to the towns of the Hills People, I knew he didn't need my advice. Or anyone else's, for that matter. He thinks differently. Like an eagle, he flies high, higher than any of us can imagine. He sees it all, the general view and the smallest details. We can't understand his plans. We can only follow and help him along."

The man grunted. "Well, if he truly has all those powers, why doesn't he just make it all happen? Why is he running around, getting in trouble?"

"He is not running around. He is traveling and talking to people, making them listen. What good would it do if he changed everything in one wave of his hand? We would all be confused and resentful, wouldn't we?" The old woman leaned closer, peering at her guest. "He is trying to help us *arrive* at the right conclusion. He wants us to change our lives by our own efforts. Otherwise the changes he makes won't last."

They lapsed into another bout of silence, staring ahead, each in their own thoughts, their half finished meals forgotten. Hesitating, Onheda shifted her weight from one foot to another, reluctant to leave, but unwilling to sit down, too, wishing to talk to the old woman, but not in front of these strangers.

As though sensing her need, Jikonsahseh got to her feet,

springing up with the agility of a younger person, surprising considering her age and girth.

"If you are staying for the night, I had better make more bread," she said affably, talking to herself. A light grin flashed, directed at Onheda this time. "How about this last basket of dried berries? Do you think our guests deserve a treat?"

No, they do not, thought Onheda, turning to follow her benefactress into the smaller hut that served as a storage place. They should go away hungry, for making trouble to the Crooked Tongues man, and for talking about him the entire day on end.

"We'll dry up the remnants of the meat," said the old woman briskly, poring through the baskets and jars. "And we better hurry to work that wonderful hide they brought before it begins to rot. It was a good shot, so very clean. Almost no cuts in the entire pelt. But in the meanwhile, fetch more firewood, would you?"

"Yes, of course." Hesitating, Onheda lingered at the doorway. "You will need me to plant the maize, won't you?"

A pair of squinted eyes looked at her, suddenly concentrated. "Well, yes, I would let you do this, but," the woman's smile flickered, small and lacking in mirth. "But I can do it without you, if you have other plans. What are you up to, Onondaga girl?"

Onheda took a deep breath. "I want to go to High Springs."

"Why now?"

She almost shut her eyes, her stomach tightening again, interrupting her ability to think. It would be so easy to lie, to say that she missed home and it was time for her to return to her family.

"I want to find Hionhwatha. I want to help him. I know I can't do much, but I think, at this point, he needs all the help he can get."

The woman straightened up, measuring Onheda with a probing gaze. "The Crooked Tongues man will be here shortly, I believe."

"I don't want to wait for him." She swallowed the knot in her throat. "He is not in a hurry. He doesn't care for my people. Not the way I do. He will come in a good time, when he has finished with the east. But it may be too late by then. Hionhwatha needs help now."

"I see." The old woman nodded thoughtfully. "Well, I will not try to detain you, but I want to warn you most sternly. Be careful. Don't underestimate that War Leader Tadodaho. He sounds like a dangerous man, a bad enemy. Don't endanger yourself more than necessary."

She fought the urge to reach out and touch the woman's arm, maybe to hug her even. Jikonsahseh had never shown feelings, but she loved her, Onheda, all the same. She knew it now, and it warmed her spirit.

"I will be careful, and I will not endanger myself. And I will come back to you when it's all done and ready."

"And when you have shown the Crooked Tongues man that you are not a girl of no significance."

She felt the blood rushing up, making her cheeks burn. "I do not want to show this man anything. It has nothing to do with him."

Her companion's good-natured laughter made her wish to hit the shaky wall, but the merry sound died away quickly.

"Promise that no matter what Hionhwatha asks you to do, you will keep away from Tadodaho and Onondaga Town. Promise!" The old woman came closer, catching Onheda's hands between her large, abrasive palms. "I mean it most sincerely, porcupine girl. I had a dream, a disturbing, unsettling dream. This man spells danger, for you in particular. I couldn't see what happened, but it was all about you." The usually squinted eyes were now wide open, peering at Onheda with such intensity it made her shiver. "I told you nothing because you were here, with me, protected, but of course, I should have expected you to leave. Dreams never lie to me. So now all I can do is to ask you to stay in High Springs until the Messenger comes. Then the danger would be over."

She felt the fear enveloping her, crawling up her spine, making her heart freeze. The woman's voice had a low growling tone to it, as though she had been prophesying. Resisting the urge to wrench her hand from the warm grip, to push her companion out of her way and run into the brilliance of the outside, with no darkness and no frightening visions, Onheda let her breath out.

"I… I will be careful." She licked her lips. "But what did the dream tell you?"

Jikonsahseh sighed and the magic broke. Again she was just an old, shrewd, courageous woman, amused with the world and its restless inhabitants, observing.

"I don't know. I didn't catch the details, but there were roaring falls, and you were in a grave danger, about to die, maybe." An imperceptible nod. "I can't hold you here against your will, but I would have if I could."

Now it was Onheda's turn to press the old woman's palms. "I will not die. I will be careful, and I will come back in time to help you with your field, either to tend it or to harvest the crops. I will not leave you alone to do that." Feeling stronger and calmer, she smiled reassuringly. "I will be back, and when… when the Messenger comes, tell him I went away to help."

CHAPTER 5

The warriors were back, victorious. As the drums rolled and the hubbub of the excited town enveloped her, Seketa pushed her way through the crowd, anxious to see the captives.

The whole town talked about nothing else since the word reached them in the early afternoon, brought by a messenger from the neighboring town. This last expedition was large, comprised of warriors from many settlements – close to hundred men crossed the Great Sparkling Water in an attempt to punish the enemy, to make the fierce savages pay for the raids of the last summer – still, no one expected such overwhelming success. No single warrior from their settlement was killed, while the spoils were passable, and the captives numerous enough to distribute between the participating towns. Oh, the vile enemy was made sorry. Once again, they had learned the lesson. They would fear the Wyandot men, thinking twice before coming here again.

Excited, people poured into the square, assembling around the ceremonial ground, waiting impatiently. But, of course, she had managed to miss it all, enjoying the solitude of her cliff, instead. Like always. As a result, by the time she came running, the warriors were already there, exhausted and sweat and dust covered, some wounded, some caked with a mixture of mud and blood, but all of them happy, victorious. They had invaded the lands of the terrible enemy; they had fought and bested the fierce savages, coming home, bringing spoils and captives, making their countryfolk burst with pride.

The captives! Seketa's heart made strange leaps inside her chest, as she pushed her way through the crowds, trying to see better.

The prisoners, a sorry-looking lot, huddled around the pole that served the War Dance before the raids were commenced. Much dirtier than their captors, their clothes in tatters, the group, indeed, looked pitiful, their eyes fixed upon the ground, trying to hide their desperation. Four women and two wounded men. Seketa's stomach heaved in relief. None of them looked familiar; she had never seen them before.

"Oh, glorious sons, tell us about your victories," cried out the elderly medicine man, coming forward, eyeing the warriors with open admiration. "Tell us how you struck the enemy, how you made them suffer, how you made them pay, how you crushed them in their own heartlands, and made them see the valor, the bravery, the strength of the Wyandot men."

Bowls and pots were brought, spreading the delicious aroma of stew, with the elders being the first to receive the offering. And while the warriors' eyes sparkled, they controlled their hunger with an admirable self-control.

"They are invincible," whispered people, covering their mouths, agog with excitement.

Seketa didn't listen. Holding her breath, she watched the Clans Mothers, as those neared in groups, inspecting the captives. Aloof and unmoved, the women measured the huddled together people through their narrowed eyes, as though offered a dubious gift, suspicious of the giver's motives.

Is this how he was chosen to be adopted into the Wolf Clan three summers ago, a young, frightened boy, wounded and alone?

She tried to remember, but this particular event did not come to her memory. She had been too young back then, too indifferent, and anyway, there were no other prisoners brought along with him, with no execution ceremony following. He had probably just been picked, dumped in his new longhouse, in the compartment of his new family, and forgotten, expected to adapt and do well.

Sighing, she dropped her gaze, her stomach heaving in a familiar way. He did not adapt, carving a path of his own in the history of her people, instead, taking a part in Two Rivers' mysterious destiny. Were these two still alive and well, doing what they intended to do, or was she waiting in vain for him to come?

Oh, but he promised, he did! Even if he was dead, he said, he would come, but she wanted him unharmed and bursting with life forces, with his arms strong and forceful, holding her tight, and his eyes as large and as beautiful as she remembered, peering at her with desire and admiration.

Clenching her teeth against the dull pain in her chest, she tried to take her thoughts off him by studying the captives. Did these people belong to the same people he did? Did they come all the way from the mysterious lands belonging to the People of the Flint? He had told her once that his people called themselves after the sharpest of the knives' blades, the finest of the clubs' spikes, the strongest of the arrowheads; that they were as fierce and as brave as those weapons were, like the most polished flint she had ever seen. She laughed into his face back then, offended on behalf of her own countryfolk, but the words stuck. If his people were like he was, then there was no wonder they were called after the most lethal of the material.

Pushing her way closer, she tried to see the prisoners better, having no difficulty studying the two men, standing in a comfortable proximity, arising no interest in the Clans Mothers. Both were mature warriors, obviously no candidates for adoption, with their faces bloodied and their eyes returning the gaze of the townsfolk angrily, challenging, not afraid. In addition, one of the warriors, the older of the two, seemed to be wounded worse than the other, with a cut under his ribs oozing blood and some other substance. She had seen him leaning against the pole, trying not to be too obvious about it, while the younger man, although bloodied and pale, looked as though he could stand up with no support for as long as need be.

With the curious townsfolk watching the warriors, talking agitatedly, the Clans Mothers inspected the women, coming closer one after another. She saw the Grandmother of her own longhouse tugging at the hair of a young girl, making her lift her face. Heart twisting with compassion, Seketa watched the girl shutting her eyes, her mouth twitching, tears coursing down her mud-smeared cheeks. She seemed to be of the same age, or maybe even younger, a cute round-faced thing, trembling with fear.

"Maybe this one," said the Grandmother thoughtfully, releasing the girl. Turning to the other women, she shook her head with a certain amount of doubt. "She seems of a good disposition, and she is young and healthy."

"Do we need additional members?" asked another woman, Seketa's great aunt. "We passed the Frozen Moons with no difficulty. No member of our family died."

"Yes, but sometimes, when an appropriate person comes along, you don't wait for someone to die, do you, younger sister?"

The aunt quailed and held her tongue, eyeing the girl in her turn.

"So typical of you to come and take everyone you fancy without consulting the others," cried out one of the Porcupine Clan Mothers, coming closer. "We did bury two dear members this winter. We are the ones that should get the replacement, not you."

"Go and take another of the prisoners." Shooting a scornful glance at the Porcupine woman, Seketa's Grandmother turned back to inspect the foreign girl once again. "There are enough to pick, and Porcupine Clan Mothers should be able to make up their own minds, instead of following the choices of the others."

"Oh, please! No one followed your choice," shouted the Porcupine woman, enraged. "This girl is in the best of conditions compared to the others, and this is so typical of the Beaver Clan to rush forward and snatch her."

As the argument peaked, Seketa stopped listening, pitying the girl, who, by that time, sank onto her knees, as though trying to fold into herself. If not for the ties securing her hands, she would be covering her face, thought Seketa, catching the worried expression of the younger warrior as he leaned closer, whispering to the girl, frowning painfully.

She tried to listen. Was he talking in the Flint People's tongue? She didn't know, but the muffled words sounded foreign, bringing back painful memories.

"What are you thinking about, sister?" Tindee's voice tore her out of her reverie, interrupting the unhappy direction her thoughts were talking.

"Nothing. Where were you?"

"All around." The non-committal wave of the young woman's hand indicated the longhouses behind their backs. "After we finished preparing the field, and after you scattered away as you always do, I had to do some cooking." She made a face. "Sometimes it's better to have no man in your life."

Earlier in this season, with the end of the Frozen Moons, the Grandmother of their longhouse received an offering of marriage cookies on Tindee's behalf. Surprisingly, Seketa's wild-tempered friend did not argue. The man was a renowned hunter of enough summers to make a welcome addition to their longhouse, bringing honor to a woman of his choice. Still, she expected Tindee to enjoy the benefits of the free life for more moons to come. It was hard to imagine her free-spirited cousin living with a man. It also put additional pressure on Seketa herself. The Mothers of her Clan were eyeing her with almost an open displeasure now, as she kept refusing the offering of the marriage cookies coming from all sorts of clans and longhouses.

"Poor thing," she said, taking her thoughts off her troubles. "She is so scared."

"She is a forest mouse!" declared Tindee. "I hope they don't actually bring her to our longhouse. To cringe the way she does, and in front of everyone!" The girl's face contorted with distaste. "And when their men behave with such dignity. See? Even they are disgusted."

Glancing at the younger warrior, Seketa saw him turning as

much as his ties allowed him, glaring at the crying girl, as though trying to will her up and onto her feet.

"Yes, he is angry with her. But he is worried too, one can see that."

Narrowing her eyes, she studied him, seeking for clues, some sort of resemblance. There was none. Tekeni was broadly built and handsome, with large, well-defined eyes and mouth, while this man was thin and long-faced, his eyes narrow and dark, lips pressed into a thin line. Still, there was strength in this face, so maybe there was some resemblance. And they both came from the lands of the savages.

"I think the warrior and the girl know each other," she added, frowning. "I think he worries about her."

"Well, he should worry about himself. He will be the one required to run the gauntlet, not her. They started the preparations."

"Where?"

"On the ceremonial ground behind the Turtle Clan longhouses." Tindee measured the warrior with a long gaze. "He is passable looking. Not like your savage boy, but nice enough."

"Stop this," said Seketa sharply. "This man is to die tonight, and you should give him the honor he deserves."

The glittering eyes met Seketa's, unabashed. "Maybe you should talk to him, ask him if he met your savage boy while still in his lands." The taunting grin kept spreading. "Don't tell me you didn't think about that."

"I did not!" She stared into her friend's face, finding it difficult to catch a breath. "Also, there are many peoples on the other side of the Great Lake. He may belong to a different nation."

"Which people did the Wolf Clan boy belong to?"

"The People of the Flint."

"Oh, so you know even this, eh, sister?" Openly delighted, Tindee raised her eyebrows in a showy manner. "Do you think they fled there, Two Rivers and him?"

"I don't know, and I don't care. Stop implying silly things!" She watched the arguing Clans Mothers, hearing not a word of what they said. *Was she that obvious? Could they all see through her that clearly?*

"I'll go back now, to our longhouse. They would want us to warm the food."

"Don't miss the ceremony. If it doesn't rain, it might commence today."

As though she would miss something like that! Pursing her lips, Seketa hurried down the path, listening to the distant thunder that kept rolling above her head. Maybe it would rain after all. And if so, the ceremony would be delayed until tomorrow, and then…

She caught her breath at the suddenness of the thought. And then, she would find a way to talk to the prisoner, to ask him if he had actually seen or heard anything.

The rain was pounding upon the bark walls, leaking through the opening in the roof, which wasn't covered tightly enough. Stealthily, Seketa looked up, watching the sleeping figures, her mother and father sprawling on the lower bunk, with her sister curled on the opposite shelf. She would usually sleep there too, snuggled beside her younger sibling, but this night, she had different plans, so declaring that she was cold and wanted to sleep closer to the fire, she took a blanket and dragged one of the straw mats out of the storage space under the bunk. It put her in the corridor and on everyone's path, but she didn't care. Of all things, she didn't plan to snore through the whole night.

Sitting up carefully, she inspected the sleeping figures anew. They were breathing evenly, wandering the world of the dreams. Good! Slipping her moccasins onto her feet, she listened to the rain, disturbed. How was she to run all around, looking for where the prisoners had been put to weather the night? The rain was a blessing, postponing the ceremony of the execution, but now it was a hindrance, too. She could use a bright moonlit night, come to think of it.

As quiet as a forest cat, she slipped down the corridor, passing other compartments, afraid that someone might still be awake. Light snores shook the dimly lit space. She breathed with relief, then slipped into the darkness of the storage room.

With the screen shut tightly because of the storm, it was pitch black, forcing her to grope her way, slowing her step. Picking her way carefully, she bypassed piles of baskets and scattered tools, the scenery familiar from the deep childhood, no need to light her way even.

The darkness to her right came to life, moved with a sobbing, strangled sound, and her heart missed a beat, then began pounding wildly as she jumped aside, scattering baskets on her way. Struggling to move the screen, breaking her nails against the hard wood, she felt like screaming, her fear primitive, overwhelming. What was there in the darkness? The door screeched and a little moonlight poured in, breaking through the weakening rain.

Safely outside, she fought not to slip upon the muddy ground, the drizzle sprinkling her face, making her come to her senses. No, she could not run away into the night, escaping her own longhouse, with all her family sleeping there. If some animal got into the storage room, she would need to wake people up. Even if it was an *uki*. She shivered, then peeked in carefully, ready to spring back.

The darkness was deep, encompassing, yet now she could make out muffled silhouettes of scattered jars and containers, of neatly folded heaps of hides. No, it was not empty. Someone was breathing in the darkness, suppressing sobs, more scared than her, apparently.

"Who is there?" she whispered.

No answer came, but now the breathing stopped, too. It was as though the creature died of fear. She waited patiently, until another muffled sob erupted, followed by a hiccup.

"Come on," she said more sternly, stepping back in, her fear receding, giving way to a wave of anger. She had reacted in a silly, cowardly way and it shamed her. "If you won't say something now, I'm going to bring the light and see what you are up to."

Still no answer, but she could now make out the dark form, curled up in a helpless, defensive manner, shuddering violently. Another pace and she realized who would be hiding here, scared beyond words.

"Don't be afraid," she whispered, suddenly anxious to attract no attention of the family who slept in the compartment next to the storage room. "Why are you hiding here?"

Kneeling beside the trembling girl, she tried to see through the darkness.

"Can you understand my words?"

It seemed that the girl nodded, but it was difficult to tell.

"Come," whispered Seketa, taking her unexpected companion's arm and pulling her firmly onto her feet, disregarding the feeble attempts to break free. If it scared the poor creature even further, she didn't care. She needed to ask her questions, and fast. The girl was sent to her by benevolent spirits, making it all easy. No need to seek the hostile, tied-up enemy warriors now.

Outside, the rain had almost stopped, although the thunder kept growling, threatening, not friendly in the least. She wasn't afraid. Heno the Thunderer was her favorite deity anyway, but since the wonderful afternoon in her chosen mate's arms she knew the benevolent Sky Spirit would be the one to help her find her love back, no one better. She had told Tekeni so, she remembered, that Heno was always helping lovers in trouble and he would help her, too, somehow.

The girl stood next to her, trembling so badly, Seketa was afraid she might fall. In the meager moonlight, she looked as pitiful as she had back on the ceremonial ground, small and thin and oh-so-very-afraid, her shoulders sagging, eyes boring holes in the wet muddy ground.

"Don't be so scared. I will not hurt you."

The girl shuddered and said nothing.

"Look at me!" She felt like shaking the stubborn creature, exasperated.

Still nothing. She grabbed the girl's shoulder, pulling her closer, making her sway, her grip firm but not hurtful, relating her message.

"If you don't talk to me now, I'll drag you back inside, and I'll wake the Grandmother up and tell her you were trying to run away. Do you understand me?"

The horrified sob told her that some of her words were comprehended. "Look at me!"

This time the puffy face, smeared with dust and tears, peered at her through the darkness, the girl's eyes huge and glittering, full of terror.

Seketa's heart twisted with compassion. "Listen, you don't have to be that afraid. I won't hurt you. I promise." She peered into the wide-open eyes, holding their gaze. "I just want to ask you something. Do you understand me?" She pressed the thin shoulder, frustrated. "Say it. Say if you understand me."

"I understand… little," whimpered the girl, her voice breaking. "Some words… understand. Please, no hurt!"

"Good." Seketa tried to force a reassuring smile. "But you have to talk quietly. We don't want to wake them up, do we?"

Testing the girl's ability to understand, she waited, but a blank gaze was her answer. Not good.

"Well, it doesn't matter," she muttered to herself. "Come, I want to talk to you."

This time the girl followed dully, with no need to pull her on. Encouraged, Seketa headed away from both of her clan's longhouses, toward the more open ground.

"What's your name?" she asked when no bark walls towered around them, allowing a good glimpse of the clearing sky. "Name?" she simplified, when no reaction came, the wide-open eyes just peering at her, afraid and expectant.

"Oh, name," exclaimed the girl, suddenly beaming. "Me

name?" Her accent was terrible, hurting Seketa's ear. Tekeni had also spoken strangely, but it was not an unpleasant sound, with his words rolling in a different, even exciting way.

"Yes, name. Your name." She put a hand on her own chest. "I'm Seketa."

"Oh, Seketa." The girl beamed again, her fears temporarily forgotten. "I... Gayoah. Name Gayoah."

"Oh, good!" Relieved, Seketa glanced at the sky, hoping to see the clouds dispersing. The darkness was oppressive in its thickness, and it frayed her nerves. "Well, now tell me something." She returned her gaze to the girl beside her, trying to see her better, curious. "Where do you come from? What your people are called?" Frowning against another blank gaze, she simplified. "Name, not your name, but your people's name. Tell me how they called. Across the Great Sparkling Water."

The girl's face fell as quickly as it lit up before.

"Onondaga, the People of the Hills," she muttered, staring at her feet once again.

"People of the Hills? Who are they?"

"My people. They... my people."

"Where are they?"

The girl's gaze leaped up, puzzled. "The Great Sparkling Water. Other side."

"Right across?" She fought the urge to shake the girl into talking more sensibly, telling her more. "If you cross the Great Lake where they usually cross it, do you get to your people?"

She tried to explain with signs, exasperated. Finally, the girl nodded.

"Yes, yes. My people, other side."

She took a deep breath. "Do you know the People of the Flint?"

Her companion seemed as though about to take a step back. "Yes, I know. Bad people."

"Bad people?"

"Yes, very bad."

What chances did she have to learn while communicating like

that? She plodded on. "Where are they? To the east, to the west?"

"Oh, east. You sail, sail Great River, down, with current."

So Tekeni and Two Rivers had to pass through those Onondaga People's lands. Her stomach tightened.

"Did you hear of people coming from here, from this side of the Great Lake? Strange people, talking strangely."

The girl stared at Seketa blankly.

"Two people," she insisted, shivering against the gust of cold wind. "In a canoe. They must have come before the snows."

The wide-open eyes didn't blink, staring at her as though she was the one talking strangely.

"Through Harvest Moon. Or maybe Hunting Moon." Reluctant to hear an obviously negative answer, she went on, breathless. "They crossed the Great Lake. Two men. One tall, and... and different. And the other, the other young and... and he was wounded, and..." She swallowed, suddenly unable to go on. What if he... "They crossed the Great Lake, some time during Harvest Moon," she finished, a stony fist gripping her chest, making her struggle for breath.

She felt a warm palm brushing against her arm. "Please, no cry," whispered the girl. "Please. The men, I didn't see men, but they come back, they will, I'm sure." She was so tiny, this captive girl, hardly reaching Seketa's chin, and yet suddenly, she was not so unimportant, standing there, firm and not trembling anymore, radiating warmth, comforting, her accent more pleasing now, reminding of *his*.

"I'm not crying," said Seketa, embarrassed. She wasn't crying, not truly. It was the silly drizzle that gained power again, the distant thundering still rolling, refusing to go to sleep. "I just thought you might have seen them."

"No, no see. Maybe they no cross." The girl's eyes sparkled. "Or maybe stone canoe. Cross stone canoe. Maybe they." Her laughter was light, caressing the darkness.

"What stone canoe?" Absently, Seketa watched the dark alley, spreading between the nearest longhouses. They should go back and get some sleep.

"I don't know, I didn't see," the girl was saying. "Stone canoe. It's hard to believe. But people kept talking, talking about it. Tidings of peace, they said. There was a messenger. He came to bring tidings of peace, sailing a white stone canoe. He said everything will change now."

It was difficult to follow as the girl fell into the blabbering of her strange sounding native tongue. Still, the key words stuck.

"He talked about peace. The man was talking about peace? What did he look like?"

"No, he was no man." The girl shook her head firmly. "He was messenger. Messenger of the Right-Handed Twin. He was no person. How could he sail a canoe made out of stone if he were a man?"

"Oh." She fought the wave of acute disappointment.

"But he looked like a man, they say. He talk strangely. My brother—" The girl's voice broke suddenly, with no warning, cut by a sob.

"What about your brother?"

"He saw, saw the man who saw…" It was hopeless, the poor thing was trembling again, her tears rivaling the intensifying rain.

Seketa eyed the girl helplessly. "What happened to your brother?" A redundant question. He must have died in this or that fight.

"He is die, to die," sobbed the girl. "He is to die tomorrow."

She caught her breath. "He is one of the prisoners?"

More sobs were her answer, but she needed no confirmation. The young warrior who was trying to talk to this girl, growing angry with her when she wouldn't behave with dignity back in the square. The man she had been going to look for before running into this silly, weeping mess!

She grabbed the thin shoulders once again. "Stop it, stop crying. Tell me what he saw. Tell me now!" It was difficult not to shake the whining creature into calmness, so she did just that. "If you tell me, we will go and find your brother now."

More whimpering. "He saw man who talked to the messenger."

"When did it happen? On what season?"

"Hunting Moon, I think it happened on Hunting Moon. There was fighting in our settlement." Again, the stupid mouse was blubbering in her tongue, but Seketa didn't mind as long as the information kept coming. She could put together enough words to understand the general gist. "Two clans were in dispute. Not our clan, but our people got involved, too. And it was turning ugly, people were giving dark looks to each other. They were talking of leaving the town, or fighting it out."

"And then?"

"And then Ganuk and some other hunters came, and they say there was a man, a Messenger of the Great Spirits. He sailed stone canoe, and he said there will be no more fighting." The girl frowned, as though trying to recollect. "And then later, Hionhwatha was reported to come back. He was dead or maybe he just lived in the woods. But he came back, and he said that the Messenger of the Right-Handed Twin sent him to prepare people. He said it was time our people unite for real. I didn't see any of it. It was in High Springs, away from our town. Our village is small, not important. And now…" The rivers of tears burst anew, impossible to shake back into non-existence anymore.

"Oh well," said Seketa, trying to organize her thoughts. "We will now go and find your brother. And we will see what he knows."

Her stomach churned as though she were hungry, but it was not the lack of food. The idea was so wild, so unacceptable, she found it impossible even to put it into words. It made her head reel. Could she truly do this? Would she? But oh Mighty Spirits, if caught helping prisoners to escape…

"I wish I knew in what longhouse they put the captives," she muttered, afraid that her courage would leave her now. Of all reckless deeds, this one was most imprudent. It would make Two Rivers and Tekeni's crimes look like a child's play.

CHAPTER 6

The delegation looked tired. Squatting beside the fire, they maintained calm dignity appropriate for the important people they were, but their faces were ashen and their eyes ringed, their warriors, about twenty of them, resting nearby, looking exhausted.

"We rowed for the most part of our journey, hardly stopping to rest," said the broadly built middle-aged man, clearly a leader of the delegation. "The lands of the Onondagas were never a safe place to travel, but now they are practically boiling, like a pot of stew put on too large of a fire."

Two Rivers' stomach twisted, but he curbed his impatience, saying nothing, giving the courtesy of the opening move to the leading Flint People, as was appropriate. They were back at Little Falls, for yet another gathering, of both united nations this time. Which was a good thing.

The results of his venturing into the Standing Stone People's lands, that looked disastrous in the beginning, were much better than he had anticipated. He was forced to stay there for too long, days upon days, throwing all his energies and so much unnecessary time into the attempt to make them listen, while his anger soared and his patience was wearing off. A short journey to talk to a few representatives turned into a gathering of the whole nation, and yet again, he had been required to organize, to conduct, to calm, and to pacify each time important people grew angry, or tired, or impatient. Much like the gathering of the Flint People only a moon earlier, but this time actually easier, with his fame going ahead of him. The Messenger of the Great Spirits!

He hid his grin. Well, it was as good a way to put it as any. His mission *was* important, more than he even thought it was before crossing the Great Lake. The matters on this side of the huge water basin were worse than he had expected, and who knew? Maybe he, indeed, was sent to make a change. Maybe his strange, far-fetched ideas stemmed from a place more hallowed than his mind alone. After all, there was a prophecy and the dreams, and so far, they had all come true.

So, when the Standing Stone People had insisted on having him conducting their unification, he didn't feel as resentful, as enraged by their audacity as the rest of his followers were. He plunged into the work enthusiastically, instead. But now, back among the people of Little Falls, his impatience welled. He should have gone to the Onondagas more than a moon ago, like he promised. To leave Hionhwatha with the entire work of convincing his stubborn people, alone and unaided, was not a wise thing to do, not with the man's previous history. The old leader would need a strong backing against the vicious Tadodaho. A long winter of lonely work was enough. He, Two Rivers, should have come sooner, backed by the agreement of the Flint People as promised.

On the other hand, now he might be able to offer more. The Standing Stone People's goodwill was secured. How surprised and delighted Jikonsahseh would be to hear that, concealing her smile and proceeding about her chores as though nothing happened, yet the old woman's eyes would glitter, nevertheless, satisfied and pleased for her people. And for him.

The thought of Jikonsahseh brought another, this one less welcome. Onheda, the Onondaga girl. Another good person disappointed and hurt. He seemed to have a tendency to betray Onondaga people, the closest of his associates too, curse all the delays into the realm of the Evil Twin. When telling her to stay at Jikonsahseh's he had promised to come back, if not before the snows then right after them. But now the fields were already planted and he was still here, in the east, busy organizing these people while neglecting hers against all promises.

He clenched his teeth. She must be furious by now, hating him most probably, hurt by him and his actions, when he didn't mean to do any of it. Of all people, the brave, smart, fascinating woman deserved better treatment than a quick lovemaking and a promise to come back. He would have to find time to travel to Jikonsahseh before he sought out Hionhwatha. Oh yes, he would leave after this meeting, hopefully in no more than a few dawns. Unless the new delegation of other foreigners brought nothing but trouble and more work. With an effort, he brought his thoughts back to the present.

"It seems your journey was not an easy one, brothers," one of the Flint People's leaders was saying, sure of his stance in his homeland to behave with a measure of politeness.

"Oh, no, it was not. But the word of Good Tidings of Peace has reached our ears, and it filled our hearts with joy."

The accent of the newcomers was strange, difficult to understand, but Two Rivers felt his own heartbeat accelerating. Whoever those foreigners were, they came to join out of their free will, with no need to travel and talk to them even. The word was getting around, gaining power.

"Those are the People of the Swamp," whispered Tekeni, coming closer and standing behind him. "You can tell by their dreadful accents, of course, but also by the way their feathers are tilted in their headdresses, as though they can't stick it straight enough."

Indeed, a large feather on each magnificent-looking hat of the two leading men was tilted jauntily, surrounded by smaller, simpler-looking decorations. The impressive headdresses made it easier to tell the dignitaries apart, as the Flint People adorned their heads by three upright feathers and their neighbors, the People of the Standing Stone, wore their two feathers upright and one lying to the side. By now he had learned this and many other differences between the two eastern nations. Yet, the west was still a riddle for him. Who were those People of the Swamp? He tried to remember.

"Next to Onondagas, westwards. A small nation." Tekeni's

whisper brushed past his ear, most welcome in its timing.

The young man was getting good at reading his thoughts. Two Rivers stifled another grin. He would never have gotten this far without the helpful presence of his most loyal of companions, but every time he tried to stress Tekeni's importance to their cause, the young man would dismiss it with a shrug, strangely content with his role of a person acting behind the scenes, unwilling to be acknowledged up to the point of being irritated by the attempts to do so. Why?

Of course, the young man was impatient to get back to the Onondagas, for his own reasons, which had nothing to do with the well-deserved glory among his own people. Still, it was strange that, despite the accumulating respect and admiration, Tekeni kept to the shadows, quite stubbornly at that, always there and helpful, as forceful and as enterprising as a great warrior would be, but never confirming to the others, never bothering with their intentions or opinions, acting as though he were alone and not a part of the crowd. Another puzzling change in this ever-changing companion of his.

"What do you think they want?" breathed Two Rivers, barely moving his head, wishing to be able to go away for a while and discuss it all with no interruptions. Both people's leaders were busy exchanging regular platitudes, not getting to the point, but their guests were stealing glances at him, while their escorting warriors were staring quite openly.

"They are impressed with your mission and all that. My guess is they want in, but for a price. They need something from us."

"How surprising." He studied the speakers once again, trying to understand their words. A difficult feat for a person who had mastered the tongues of the eastern nations only recently, too recently to feel comfortable about it.

"May we address the Messenger?" one of the two elders was asking.

He met their gazes. "You do not need to seek anyone's permission to speak your minds," he said smoothly, hiding his impatience. "I am honored by your arrival."

The other people shifted, their glances suspicious. They clearly did not trust the foreigners that readily.

"We came to believe that your mission is blessed by the benevolence of the Great Spirits. We are in awe of the broadness and the depth of your vision. You are like an eagle, floating on the invisible currents, seeing the earth with the clearness of this magnificent spirit."

The flowery phrases went on for some time, while Two Rivers studied the man, deciding that they approached him with unusually humble spirits. Finally, they got to the point.

"Our towns are troubled by bloodthirsty enemies from either side of our beautiful lands. The beasts of the Onondagas are attacking our villages on the east, while the evil warriors of the Mountain People are giving no peace to our western settlements. We need your help and protection. We need the benevolence of the Right-Handed Twin you bring along."

Understanding the general gist, Two Rivers nodded. "I will do what you ask. The message of the Great Peace will be delivered to your lands."

He could feel the disapproval of his peers spreading like a cloud around him. Neither the Flint People nor their recently acquired allies liked him making promises on his own, discussing nothing first. He disregarded their displeasure.

"But you will have to accept the Good Tidings of Peace with your hearts calm and your minds open, with no hesitations or misgivings," he went on, peering at his conversers now. "Your neighbors to the east and the west will be a part of it. They will not be left out of the Great Tidings of Peace. You must understand that before you accept my message."

That reassured his followers, but not their guests.

"Neither the monstrous Onondaga nor the beastly Mountain People will consider accepting your message," said the leading Swamp man, his tilted feather rustling with the gentle breeze, seemingly as unsettled as the owner of the spectacular hat.

"Why do you say so?"

"The bloodthirsty People of the Mountains are united in

nothing but their hatred toward other human beings populating the Turtle Island. In all other things they are divided, finding it impossible to agree with each other, following two, or even three different leaders, each of them a ferocious beast. They will not listen to you and your message."

This was vital information he welcomed eagerly, hoping that Tekeni listened, remembering every word. He would need to hear it all again, retold in a more understandable manner, maybe even in his own native, *crooked* way of speaking. He hid his grin. Living among the people of this side of the Great Lake, he came to actually think about his own people in these terms.

"Do you know the people who are leading your neighbors to the west?" he asked, pushing the amused thoughts away.

"Yes, we know them. They will not listen to you."

"What are their names?"

"The leader on the nearer side of the river is called Skanyadahriyoh," answered the other man after a pause, when his peer pursed his lips and said nothing. "And his rival is leading the settlements near their main Ge-ne-see river. He is called Sadenkarohhyes. They are bitter enemies, although, for the outsiders, they pretend they are not. Not many seasons will pass before they start warring on each other."

"And the Onondagas are in an even a worse situation," added the first man, his frown deep. "They have two leaders now as well, and those are declared enemies, one being a powerful sorcerer and the other – a fierce war leader who came back from the dead not long ago. Unrelenting in their hatred, they will never agree to sit beside the same fire."

He felt his stomach constricting. "The leader who has come back from the dead, does he have many followers?"

"Oh, yes, the Onondagas are thoroughly divided these days." There was a flicker of satisfaction lurking in the depths of the broad man's eyes.

"I must go there at once!" Turning back to face his people, he saw their surprise, their astonishment open, written clearly across their faces. They had forgotten the day before the test of the falls, when he promised that the powerful Onondagas were made to listen already.

"We shall discuss it at length," said the head of the Little Falls' council, in whose longhouse Two Rivers resided during the winter, spending many pleasant evenings by the crackling fire. "Let us now proceed to make a worthwhile welcome to our guests from the foreign lands."

The man's tone, even though affable enough, brooked no argument, and so the people began getting up, openly reluctant, clearly eager to stay and hear more. But it didn't matter, thought Two Rivers, his anxiety splashing, difficult to keep at bay. He would rush to the Onondagas now, with or without the agreement of his current allies. He could go wherever he pleased, and their choices were limited to the decision of whether to follow him or not. He could go all by himself, without the local warriors' escort and protection. He and Tekeni had done it before.

"It's just like the good old times, isn't it?" said the young man, catching up with him as he headed down the trail, deep in thought. He recalled that the people tried to stop and talk to him, but he told them that he would attend to their conversations later. He needed to be alone now.

"What?"

"You, acting with no concern to the others, making people angry, storming off to get morsels of solitude. I wondered how long it would be before you made this cliff over the falls into your favorite spot, to sit and think and fume about the stubbornness of the people in general."

"I will not make anything into anything, because I will be busy sailing your river against the current. They can't tell me what to do!" His fists clenched, Two Rivers kicked a stone and watched it rolling down the trail. "I've been holding their hands for too long, guiding and calming and pacifying them like little children. They can go on managing their own affairs, letting me go about my mission uninterrupted." Angrily, he kicked another stone, making it hurl into the bushes. "We have forgotten our purpose."

"Which is?"

"To make peace between all peoples. Not to play with councils and talk for days on end, feeling oh-so-very-superior. Since reaching the agreement with the People of the Standing Stone, your countryfolk became too pleased with themselves, carrying themselves like powerful chiefs, looking down on today's delegation as though they were their superiors, receiving a humble request of help from some nearby village."

"They were the first to back you up." Tekeni's indifferent shrug made Two Rivers yet angrier. "Of course they feel good with themselves, being courted by the other nations now, with the Great Messenger living in their most prominent town. I don't think there is anything wrong with that." There was a twinkle in the familiar, well-defined eyes.

"Oh, please." Halting by the cliff's edge, Two Rivers restrained himself from kicking more stones. "They made me jump those falls to prove the divine nature of my mission. It's not like they just accepted our message with no questions asked." Well used to the roaring of the vicious cascades by now, he still found the need to shout at the top of his voice annoying. "We are here to do more than just make your countryfolk feel good about themselves. We are here to make it work between all peoples. Or have you forgotten that, too?"

"No, I have not forgotten, and there is no need to take your frustrations out on me." The young man turned abruptly, the scars upon his face glaring. "I wanted to rush up the Great River the moment the ice broke and the current began to flow. You were the one wishing to detour through the Standing Stone People's towns, sailing around with a respectable following like an important War Chief, *enjoying yourself*."

"Oh yes, you wanted to rush up the river, but for your private reasons. I doubt you were that greatly concerned over Hionhwatha and his mission."

"Oh no, I was not. And I didn't care for pretty, high-spirited women hiding at Jikonsahseh's, either. Don't forget to mention that."

For a heartbeat, they glowered at each other, too enraged for words. *You are an annoyingly cheeky piece of rotten meat,* Two Rivers wanted to scream into the handsome broadness of his young friend's face. *Go and cross the Great Lake and never come back if all you can think of is your stupid girl.*

But he said not a word, knowing that, of all people, Tekeni deserved this accusation less than anyone. He was the most loyal of friends, but there was more to it. He was a part of it all, a part of the prophecy, a part of the dreams. Without this young man none of it would have happened. By now, he knew it beyond any doubt. Without his enterprising, cheerful, often challenging presence, the Great Peace would not have been achieved. The youth was a true friend and a rare asset, even if by now the damn cub had learned to see through him, Two Rivers, too easily to feel comfortable about it.

"You can come with me, if you like. Or you can stay here. I will not tell you what to do this time." He shrugged. "I will give your people the courtesy of a few days of deliberating, but if they won't join me, I will go all by myself, and they had better not entertain stupid ideas like trying to detain me, like the annoying People of the Standing Stone did to us. I don't have any more patience." He turned to watch the swirling mist, where the water cascaded strongly, in an unstoppable, surging mass. The dreadful jump was still fresh in his memory, too fresh to think it was long in the past. "You can come along and leave the moment we reach the Great Lake. I will not insist on you coming to High Springs with me."

But you better insist upon coming with me yourself, he thought tiredly, wishing to go back and put as much distance between him and the accursed falls. This place had nothing in common with his favorite cliff back home.

"As though I can truly do that," muttered Tekeni, not taking his gaze off the angrily flying drops. "But after we are done with the Onondagas, I'm off. We'll reach another Frozen Season this way, and I can't make her wait for so long."

"I wish we could just send someone to fetch her and bring her back to you. A large well-armed party, eh?" Two Rivers chuckled, then turned to go. "It would solve all our dilemmas, would it not?"

The broad face crinkled with laughter. "Not all of them, but some." Picking up a stone, the young man hurled it into the swirling mist, then turned to go, too. "It's good that the Swamp People came on their own. Saved us spending time running between their towns."

"But their neighbors to the west will not be as comfortable to deal with." Sniffing the air, Two Rivers became aware of his growing hunger. Another feast, this time welcoming their unexpected guests, seemed to be well on its way somewhere down the valley. Counting the newcomers, three nations would be sharing their food this afternoon. Quite an achievement. "Tell me more about these People of the Swamp."

"Oh, well, they live on the shores of the Great Sparkling Water, to the west of the Onondagas." Tekeni shrugged, still deep in thought. "Their towns are small, and not as powerful as ours. They are scattered all over their lakes and springs, it is said, and so these people are growing waterfowl aplenty. It's said they never go hungry." Another shrug. "But, of course, they have it bad from both sides. The Onondagas and the People of the Mountain are not the sort of neighbors one would feel comfortable with."

"And they want in. Badly enough to send their dignitaries all the way here," muttered Two Rivers, trying to imagine the lands with small towns upon small lakes, with fowl waddling all around, making silly sounds. Such a pastoral living. "Well, they will be of help, come to think of it. It will put additional pressure on the Onondagas. To be surrounded by our union of three, or even four, nations might not seem like a comfortable position, even to that warmonger Tadodaho."

"So you expect to be able to convince the Mountain People?" There was wonder in Tekeni's voice, an expectation diluted by a considerable amount of doubt. "It doesn't sound as though they will be as forthcoming as their eastern neighbors. But what do we need them for? They are far, stuck in their hills, growling like mountain lions but not truly that dangerous. They can rot in their mountains, as far as I am concerned."

Warmed by the friendly sun and the sensation of being back in time, walking with Tekeni, airing his thoughts aloud, Two Rivers grinned, feeling almost content. They'd had no opportunity for an idle talk since the cold moons.

"They are far away from here, wolf cub, yes. But when we make peace with the other nations, we will be obliged to participate in their wars, to help defend their settlements. Those Swamp People came here for a reason. They want to join so we will help them defend themselves, against both of their fierce neighbors. But while Onondagas have been taken care of and hopefully will be under control soon, the People of the Mountains are still unheeded, still in the dark. And they can't be left out, not a strong, warlike nation like them. They will give us too much trouble if not a part of our union."

Tekeni slowed his step. "We can crush them, make them fear us, make them keep to their stinking mountains, can't we? Now that we are three nations united, we are quite strong, aren't we? And if the Onondagas join us…" The young man brought his palms up, his uncertainty obvious. "Won't they fear us and leave their neighbors alone?"

Grinning, Two Rivers slowed his step in his turn. "Well, yes and no, my most prized companion and adviser. Yes, we will be strong and intimidating. Like a bunch of arrows tied together, we will be impossible to break." Picking up a stick, he broke it in two, throwing the splintered parts away. "See? It breaks easily." He searched the ground for more of the dry, creaking twigs. "But I want to see you break a whole bunch of those."

Tekeni was laughing loudly now. "Oh yes, I see your point. And I like what I see. Together we will be truly strong. Not to say invincible." He took the offered pack of sticks and actually put an effort until the bunch snapped with a loud crack. "Yes, difficult to break, but not invincible, not yet."

"Well, my example referred to arrows, not to the wobbly twigs." Two Rivers laughed in his turn, his gloom receding. "I won't be wasting good arrows on you. I will save this demonstration for the meeting of the councils, maybe for the first gathering of the Five Nations, eh?"

Tekeni brushed the splinters off his palms. "So five nations?"

"Yes."

"And why can't we crush the fifth one, or force them into joining?"

"Because, old friend, we are uniting for peace, not for war. They are following us because of our message. They believe us when we say that the Right-Handed Twin wants the war to be stopped. But what would happen if we forced one of the nations into our alliance, or used our accumulated power to war on someone?" He sniffed the air, his senses welcoming the aroma coming from the town. "We would be contradicting our own message, and the perceptive people would see it. They would be hurt and disappointed, and they would stop believing us."

Eyeing the cheerful melee of the adjacent valley, where the Standing Stone People's delegations were joined by the tents of the newly arrived guests, he again thought how fortunate it was all turning out. The People of the Swamp might have been a small nation, tucked between two warlike giants, but they were still the first to come of their free will, not being approached yet at all. And if they saw the truth in his mission, then why not the others?

"To make our union strong, impossible to break, we would need every nation to join us out of conviction, out of belief, and not because they were forced to do that," he went on, sorry for their privacy to end. People were rushing up to them, anxious to talk, as always these days. If he was not listened to before, now he was listened to too much. "And we would need to make sure that our laws are just and efficient, to stay forever and make people happy and content, and our alliance strong, functioning, alive." He glanced at Tekeni, seeing the young man's smile. "A lot of work is still ahead of us, wolf cub. To make them listen was only the first step. So many laws yet to be formulated, so many agreements reached. We will not rest much through those summer moons, I can promise you that." Grinning, he shook the vision off. "And now we need to grab some food to keep us going."

The boiling pots were already stormed, attacked from every direction. Answering the greetings and keeping his conversations to the polite minimum, he searched the crowds for the Swamp People delegation. The newcomers might be an interesting company to spend one's afternoon with, a wonderful opportunity to learn about the difficult Mountain People. And maybe they could tell him more about the goings on at the Onondagas.

His stomach twisted with anticipation. What if they stopped at Jikonsahseh's on their way here.

"Here, this came straight from the fire!" A voice broke into his thoughts, startling him.

Kahontsi's braids jumped prettily as she rushed toward him, a steaming plate balanced in her hands, her eyes dancing. Her festive dress was a celebration of colors, revealing the prefect smoothness of her neck, with the wide, beautifully embroidered girdle tying it in a playful fashion, hiding none of the trimness of her figure.

"Oh, well, thank you." Shifting his weight from one foot to another, he wished he had reached the town's elders and their guests earlier, not lingering here all alone. "It is very considerate of you." It came out coldly. He forced a smile. "I was just gathering my courage to try and dive into this mess."

"No need for that. I brought you the best of the meat." She beamed at him, her excitement spilling. Such a pretty sight! He frowned.

"I'm grateful." Taking the offered plate, he tried not to wince as the heated wood scorched his palms. "It's very nice of you."

"It's no trouble." Her eyes clung to him, expectant.

He hesitated, aware of the people around them.

"You were busy preparing the food since the sun came up, I suppose." It was too cruel to be that cold to her. She didn't deserve this sort of treatment.

"Well, yes. All the women were busy doing that. We didn't go to the fields today, but the planting will start soon enough."

More of an awkward silence. She watched him like a child expecting a treat.

"Oh, well, this is good. I hope the *Three Sisters* will flourish this span of seasons."

"Oh, yes, many offerings were made already." Her fingers kept crushing the fringes of her sleeves. "The Maple Ceremony will be held soon. Will you stay in Little Falls to participate?"

"No, I'm afraid I won't be here. There is much to do back in the west. I will have to travel most of the spring and summer."

He saw her eyes losing their spark, turning frightened. It made him feel bad. She was a good girl, pretty and vital, and she had saved his life back in the falls.

"But the ceremony… There will be dances…" Her eyes glittered with gathering tears. "You have to stay for, at least, this ceremony."

The urge to gather her into his arms, to comfort her, grew. "I wish I could. But maybe some other ceremony. The Strawberry Festival, maybe. Or the Green Corn Celebration. I would love to see how your people celebrate that event. In my lands, it was the second most important ceremony."

"Yes, it is the most important ceremony, yes." She pressed her lips, obviously trying to push the tears back. A courageous little thing. He remembered the head of the trail near Jikonsahseh's hut and the Onondaga girl, screaming at him, struggling not to let her tears show. Oh, Mighty Spirits! Was he going to hurt every good woman he met?

"I will try to reach Little Falls for the Green Corn Ceremony." Seeing her eyes brightening, he swallowed, angry with himself. What a coward he was. "It is very nice of you to want to show me all the wonderful things Little Falls has and the things your people do. I'm grateful! But listen," he licked his lips, suddenly not hungry anymore, the cooling food just an annoying thing to keep his hands busy. "You are a wonderful girl. I'm grateful for everything you have done for me, from saving my life to bringing me food right now. You are a truly beautiful spirit."

She leaned forward, drinking in his every word, peering at him with so much expectation he found it difficult to find words, although the Flint People's tongue was not such a challenge for him anymore. He felt the people's gazes. Atiron must be there among them, and his wife, and all the people of their longhouse, her family, and the others.

"Listen, you have to stop thinking about me in the way you may be thinking now."

It came out awkwardly, in an annoyingly halting manner. Her deepening gaze told him that, the same unsettling feminine superiority filling it, making him feel stupid.

"In what way do you think I think about you?" she asked, her face closing, losing some of its trustful freshness that touched him so.

He sighed. "I don't know, but you must understand that it is not possible."

"Why?" Her eyes narrowed defiantly, but her lips began quivering again.

He fought the urge to touch her, to caress her, to reassure. She didn't deserve this. "There are too many reasons to tell them all now—"

"Then meet me this evening, behind the ceremonial ground, close to the southern entrance." It came out in a breathless rush, the shine of her eyes returning. Some of it. "Tell it all to me then."

"No!" He felt like taking a step back, finding it hard to keep his instincts in check. The public nature of this meeting kept him safe, but it would not be the case when in the darkness and alone. He wouldn't make the mistake of overestimating his ability to control himself. He had failed with the Onondaga girl, but Onheda was not a child. She knew what she was getting into, and she had already proven her worth back then. Strong, smart, courageous, she made a good partner. He might have considered moving into her longhouse had she belonged to one, and had he been free to settle in these lands. But with the wild, spoiled little thing like Kahontsi, however pretty and tempting and willing, it was out of the question.

"Listen, I need to go and talk to people. I thank you for the food."

Not daring to look at her, he stalked off, trying not to be too obvious about it. Damn it! Why had he had to run into this sort of complication, time after time? Women were such nuisance sometimes, from opinionated, headstrong matrons, the Mothers of the Clans, always eager to tell their minds and to force their opinions in the matters that had nothing to do with them, all the way to the silly girls who could think about nothing but dancing and flirting and complicating a man's life.

All but the Onondaga girl.

He felt his heartbeat accelerating. It would be good to meet her again. She might be surprised to see him alive and well, unless the rumors reached Jikonsahseh's hut already, and in this case, she would wait only more impatiently. Oh yes, she would greet him most eagerly, and after spending a day and a night at Jikonsahseh's, they would go to High Springs together.

CHAPTER 7

"Did he send you? Why didn't he come himself?" The question hung in the air, making it denser, more difficult to breathe.

It wasn't easy to recognize the man, so much had Hionhwatha changed. As though the gloomy, wild-looking recluse had never existed. Stout, imposing, his back straight and his bearing dignified, the man looked at the world now out of the shrewd, dark, unreadable eyes, the creases on his face adding to his newfound calm dignity, making him look like a respectable member of society, like the leader he was.

Surprised by the change, Onheda watched him, unable to forget the grim, violent man from the other side of Onondaga Lake. Oh no, she thought, unsettled. Even though followed and accepted now, having a purpose in life and a clear direction, the man was still torn, still suspicious, still uncertain of his ability to turn the tides; he still needed help.

Answering the heavy gaze, reading the frustration behind the narrowing eyes, she shook her head with a matching impassiveness. "He did not send me. I came on my own." She didn't drop her gaze, but it was an effort not to do so. "He is still busy with the eastern people."

"What eastern people?"

"People of the Flint and People of the Standing Stone. He has organized a council of the two nations, right after the snow melted. They had reached an agreement."

There was no harm in embellishing the truth, she thought, welcoming the breeze coming from the river, cooling her sweaty face. The interview was as unsettling as she expected it to be, but she came here for that purpose and she regretted nothing.

She hadn't lied to Jikonsahseh. Her people might end up being left out of his Great Tidings of Peace, but she would not let it happen, not if she could help it.

Oh, but it was frustrating, the manner in which the annoying People of the Flint had clearly begun getting an upper hand, hosting him now for so many moons, acting as though he were one of them. Even the Standing Stone People were annoyed. She could see it in the faces and the words of the hunters back at Jikonsahseh's hut. They felt that the pushy Flint were taking the lead, presenting his ideas as their own, maybe, proud at being first to receive his message. But it was not so! She and Jikonsahseh were the first to hear him out, and maybe another Onondaga hunter. And then Hionhwatha. They were the first to listen to him, and to start helping, not the arrogant Flint, who now claimed him as being one of them, while, in fact, he belonged to no nation, coming from the cold lands of the Crooked Tongues, from across the Great Sparkling Water. He belonged to no one, no nation, no man, and no woman.

Suppressing the familiar twinge of pain in her chest, she concentrated on the man beside her.

"I wonder how he made the violent beasts listen," Hionhwatha was saying, shaking his massive head. "His young companion must have still had a great influence in his annoying Little Falls, although it doesn't make much sense. He was too young to be of any importance, and he is still too young to be of real help."

"He left his people when he had seen close to fifteen summers," said Onheda, mostly because she felt it was impolite not to respond. "Yes, he must have been too young to be remembered, let alone expected back or listened to."

"Then it must have been something else." The formidable man nodded, answering a greeting of two passersby, whose eyes lingered, wondering at his company. Onheda forced a smile to answer theirs. It was good to be home, greeted warmly and eagerly by the people who remembered her, her family and friends, her longhouse and her clan's people, all those who cherished her memory although thinking her to be lost forever. Oh, it was certainly a homecoming.

Still, something was different, changed. The town was as large, as bubbling with life as she remembered, but not cheerful, not cozy. There was tension, and fear. The people spoke quietly, less openly, avoiding matters concerning management and councils, as though afraid to sound their minds. They talked silly nonsense, discussing the weather and the fields, careful even when ceremonies were mentioned, and their eyes would dart everywhere, as though reluctant to be overheard. Oh, how it annoyed her, those empty conversations. It was such a waste of time! Since when had her people turned into a bunch of forest mice?

"Why are you so restless, Onheda?" Her mother would ask her, time after time, almost through every evening. "So nervous, so agitated, so lacking in patience? What happened to you, my child? Did the beasts of the Flint People harm you that much? They are such brutes, every one of them!"

"No," she would say, staring at the fire, unable to meet the well-meaning gaze of the older woman. "They did not harm me, and they did not break my spirit. But the world is changing, and I wish our people were more open, more receptive to changes. Why can't they just listen?"

"They do listen, young one." At this point her mother would move closer, dropping her voice to a whisper, shooting careful glances all around. It made Onheda twice as furious. *Who were they afraid of?* "High Springs has been hosting Hionhwatha since he came here before the snows. Our people are warm and generous, and we ask no questions. We listen to what he says. Even though we risk the wrath of Onondaga Town and its mighty leader, we listen. Why do you accuse us of not being attentive?"

"Because you are listening half-heartedly, Mother. And because you are afraid. Our people should back this brave man up, should go after him and work together, help him change the minds of those who follow that evil Tadodaho." For her

mother's sake, she would drop her voice, but it only served to
make her angrier. "Hionhwatha paid a terrible price, but he did
not give up, Mother. Think about it. Instead, he met a
wonderful man, a man who helped him back onto his feet, a
man who showed him the right path. So he came back, afraid of
nothing. Why can't our people be like him? Why do they make
difficulties? The People of the Flint are now busy changing, and
the People of the Standing Stone. All the peoples, Mother, but
us, the strongest, the fiercest, the most advanced nation in the
Turtle Island, the creation of the Sky Woman." She shrugged.
"Well, we will be the strongest for not much longer, if we will
not change our minds and start listening."

But her mother would only caress her shoulders, her eyes
glittering with unshed tears. "Oh, my little girl, you are the one
who changed. Oh, how much you have changed. Why won't
you tell me what happened to you in the foreign lands? What
made you so eager, so anxious to change our way of life?"

But she would not, *could not*, share any of it, not even with her
mother. Her inner thoughts and fears were to be faced alone.
Until he came. And then Hionhwatha himself had sent for her.

Back in the present, she concentrated again, meeting the
contemplating gaze of the formidable leader.

"So he did not come or send word?"

"No, he did not. Or maybe he did send word. I was not privy
to every conversation Jikonsahseh had with her visitors. But we
heard many accounts of what is happening in the eastern lands,
and it seems that the Crooked Tongues man was successful in
uniting both peoples. He faced many challenges, of course, but
now they are united."

"So where is he now? Why isn't he coming?" Nodding to
another group of people, Hionhwatha turned to head toward
the opening in the fence. "Did he find his life among the
eastern savages so pleasant that he is not in a hurry to help his
friends achieve what he himself commissioned them to do?"

"I'm sure he is working day and night, with no time to rest,"
called out Onheda, ridiculously offended. "He has achieved the

impossible. He came to them, just a foreigner, and instead of being executed as a war captive, he made them follow him and make peace with their immediate neighbors. I'm sure such an undertaking takes time."

Passing the opening in the fence, they headed up the trail, both knowing where their destination lay, in the wonderful privacy of the shores that the gushing spring provided.

"You don't have to scream at me, girl," said Hionhwatha, surprisingly calm and well-meaning. "You seem to be as incensed with him taking so long. Although something is telling me your reasons are somewhat different, grounded in more than just an anxiety to see our people stop fighting each other, uniting to either squash or join the enemy who is growing stronger thanks to our mutual friend. Of all things!" The man shook his head, picking his step lightly, his breathing even, not disturbed in the least by the steep climb. "Well, I can reassure you that I want to see our people leading this union and not the filthy Flint People. So stop taking your frustrations out on me. I will not take your screaming well for much longer, woman."

Pressing her lips together, Onheda concentrated on the trail ahead, picking her step, trying to breathe as lightly as her companion. Such a rude beast! But the formidable man was always like that, back in his neglected hut, on the shores of Onondaga Lake, worse than now. The winter spent among his own people, accepted and not alone anymore, listened to, even if reservedly, had obviously agreed with him.

"Well, now tell me, why did you come here, High Springs' girl?" They reached the top of the hill, watching the nearby valley and the small brook spreading ahead, glittering in the high morning sun.

"I came home. I missed my people."

The grin of the man was wide, atypically amused. "And the real reason?"

"That is the real reason," she began hotly, but the hearty laughter stopped her words in midair, made the wave of the rising rage abate.

"Stop wasting my time, girl. You are after something, and it all has to do with the Crooked Tongues man and his dubious enterprises. Tell me exactly what you heard about his escapades in the east, word for word."

She made an effort to put her temper into as rigid control, desperate to impress the formidable man.

"Like I said before, people who visited Jikonsahseh reported the large gatherings and the small ones. Both People of the Flint and the Standing Stone People now seem to be well-organized into a sort of councils that are supposed to deal with the matters of the whole nation. I don't know how he did it, how he managed to make them reach an agreement, but they are organized now." She took a deep breath. "Moreover, the gathering of both nations seemed to be already held. The Crooked Tongues man went there, representing the Flint People. They got into some sort of troubles, but in the end, they were successful." Some more embellishment. She couldn't tell for sure if he was successful or not, alive or dead by now, but if he was still alive then he was successful. There could be no doubt about that. He would not agree to go away, taking 'no' for an answer.

"I'm sure our Crooked Tongues friend refused to leave until they agreed to do as he wanted, if only to get rid of him," muttered Hionhwatha, echoing her thoughts, his eyes glittering with a certain amount of satisfaction. He wanted the Crooked Tongues man to succeed, reflected Onheda, surprised. He was proud of him as much as she was, although it did not bode well for their own people, unless they would be as successful as the foreigner was.

"So, by now, he may be heading back toward our lands already," she said, hopeful.

"Unless they keep finding more work for him to do." The amusement left the creased face, the gloom coming back, darkening the sharp features. "The canny Flint may be too devious even for him. They are obviously liking what he has done for them so far, putting them in the lead without noticing.

I bet they were running this mutual council as though it were their own, giving the Standing Stone People not much of a chance at saying anything. It would be so much like them to do so."

She remembered the resentment in the visiting hunters' faces, the open displeasure in their words. Oh yes, this was exactly what happened, she was sure of that.

"He will see through their ploys," she said, sounding more convinced than she felt. "He will not let it happen."

"What's to stop them from holding him there against his will?" The man kicked a stone, sending it flying down the cliff, bouncing off the sharp edges. "He is just one man, after all."

"There is his companion, the scar-faced youth. He will not betray him, I know he will not."

"Which makes them two men. Quite an intimidating warriors' force."

For a while they said nothing, listening to the wind rustling at the treetops far below their feet.

"So what can we do to help?" asked Onheda finally, feeling surprisingly comfortable talking to the impressive man as though he were her equal now.

"We need to unite our people." Hionhwatha's voice gave out no resentment, no sign of displeasure at her initiating the question. "Before the snows came, I made the High Springs people listen. Unlike my native Onondaga Town, this settlement keeps its ears open, not clouded by prejudice. Your Great Messenger should have come here first."

"You both decided he should go and secure the goodwill of the Flint People first."

"Yes, we did that." The man grinned, his glance making her uncomfortable. "I remember you arguing, making me angry with you. I thought you were just a silly girl back then, but you obviously are anything but that, aren't you?"

"I don't know what I am," muttered Onheda, dropping her gaze. "But I know that we should help our people get rid of their fear at the face of the Onondaga Town's leader. We should be united and ready to join our eastern neighbors."

"Oh, yes, that we should." The man's face closed once again as he turned away to face the whispering valley. "The trouble with Tadodaho is that he is very strong, and his powers are great, far beyond the abilities of a regular person. Not only Onondaga Town, but all the surrounding villages are subdued, afraid, groaning in his heavy grip. People are afraid to go against his wishes, and with a good reason. He stops at nothing, and if enraged, he can be more cruel and vicious than the Evil Twin himself."

"Your family," she whispered, a shiver going down her spine.

"My family, yes." The man's voice rang hollowly, hardly audible in the strengthening breeze. "And many other people. Your warrior, too."

"What?" She felt the air escaping her chest, the ring around it tightening, not letting a new gust of fresh current in.

"All people who listened to me and followed died. He promised it would happen, and it did." Her companion's shoulders were as rigid as a wooden beam, and as lifeless against the brightness of the clear sky. "He said so when we argued for the last time, just before the first meeting of our people was to be commenced. His eyes glowed, and his twisted right arm twitched. And his voice was as deep as the groaning of the earth when it breaks sometimes, wishing to swallow people and animals, all living creatures, as low and as ominous." The man's own voice shook. "Even his hair seemed alive, moving as though with a breeze, but there was no breeze at all. It seemed to be composed of living snakes."

She fought the urge to look behind her, to take a step back or maybe to rush down the trail, toward the safety of the town. The strengthening wind was alarming, setting her nerves on edge, making her hair rise with the sensation of being watched by some evil powerful presence.

"But my man, he died on the raid, like many warriors. His death had nothing to do with Tadodaho or you and your... disagreement."

"It has everything to do with it!"

Not wishing to annoy the grief-stricken man by arguing, Onheda stared at the valley below their feet, pushing away her fears. Tadodaho was a mean, powerful, revengeful person, but only a person. Her man had died a warrior's death, and Hionhwatha's family died of a winter disease, with his youngest daughter's fall being a mere accident. There was a good explanation to it all. Or was there?

"Why didn't you just kill him, if he is so evil and powerful? It would have solved it all, wouldn't it?"

The man whirled at her, enraged. "Why don't you say sensible things instead of being impudent and outright stupid?"

She gasped. "I think I had better go back, back to my family's longhouse, or maybe back to Jikonsahseh, where I can actually help instead of listening to tales of sorcery and evil."

Turning around, she hesitated at the head of the trail, eyeing the forest ahead, her heart beating fast. It was darker now, with the sun hiding behind the vast mass of clouds. Another natural occurrence, but it made her think of all sorts of strange, dangerous things, of eyes watching them both.

"You can't run away from this. It won't help you." His voice was quiet, but somehow ominous too, the gloom in it menacing, impossible to miss.

"I'm not running away from anything," she muttered. "I'm just tired of waiting, of doing nothing of consequence."

The silence was heavy, and she took a step down the trail, clenching her fists to stop her hands from trembling.

"If you are tired of doing nothing, go to Onondaga Town. If you want to be of help, this step might, indeed, prove helpful."

"Onondaga Town?" She stopped again, her heart beating fast. "What will I do there?"

He said nothing, and she hesitated, wishing to flee, but needing to hear it, too.

"You will see what can be done there. You will talk to people, see how many are dissatisfied with Tadodaho's rule, how many of them are willing to join us should we prove our worth."

"If he is a powerful sorcerer, he will see through my intentions." Unable to fight the temptation, she turned back, wishing to see what his face held, but it was closed, impossible to read, the eyes studying her blank and as dark as a moonless night.

"He will not bother to look at the mere woman. He won't think you are important enough."

"But what if he does?"

"Then you will be in a grave danger." His eyes came to life, flickering with cold challenge. "Especially if he learns of the affection our Messenger may cherish toward you."

She felt her heart coming to a halt. "Then why would I do this?"

"You want to help, you are tired of waiting." Squatting, he picked up a stick and began drawing upon the crumbling, dusted earth, his fingers nimble, not trembling. "You want to impress the Crooked Tongues man, this much is obvious. Well, he will be impressed, when he bothers to see what is happening in our lands, I can promise you that. Especially if you are successful in bringing more people to our side, in sending us useful information." The drawing upon the earth was that of a wolf with its fangs bared and its ears pointed, a wonderfully detailed likeness. "I'm still remembered in Onondaga Town, so you will be welcomed cordially, offered a place to stay. I will tell you what people to approach, what story to tell."

"You have thought about it for some time," she said, making it a statement.

He nodded his admittance. "That I have."

"That was why you sent for me?"

"Well..." Looking up, he measured her with a penetrating gaze. "I expected you to come and seek my company on your own. It's been a few dawns since you appeared."

"You are a very prominent man. Always have been. How could I seek your company on my own?"

"Oh, well." He was improving his drawing, adding a line

here, a stroke there. "We have some history to share. You should never hesitate in seeking me out."

Coming back toward the edge, she sat upon the crumbling earth and let her feet dangle free, undeterred by the height.

"What exactly should I do in Onondaga Town? What shall I tell them about me?"

"Tell them the truth. Or some of it. Tell them you spent the last few seasons in captivity. Tell them you fled but that you are afraid to go back to your town, as to not make your family angry with the unspeakable deed of yours, being adopted but leaving anyway. Tell them you need a place to stay and think it all over." He studied his drawing once again, seemingly immersed. "I'll tell you what clan, what longhouse, to approach. These will be the people who know me, and they will be prepared to offer you a home without asking too many questions."

She watched the spot where the distant sky merged with the brilliant green of the forest.

"How will I contact you if I need to send you word?"

"The people who will house you will take care of this."

It was all sounding too smooth, too well-thought-out.

"And what am I to do exactly?"

"Listen to people, all sorts of people. Talk to them. Ask probing questions, make them talk to you and share their thoughts. Can you do this?" He got to his feet and was now standing beside her, his arms crossed upon his chest, eyes measuring her openly, unashamed. "Most women can do this, but you are anything but an ordinary female, aren't you?" An amused smile flashed, to be replaced by a frown. "But you will have to act like such when you are in Onondaga Town. You will have to control your temper, behave nicely, demurely, and be ready to chat and gossip. Do you think you can do this for the sake of *his* mission?"

The way he stressed his last words, made her angry.

"Yes, I can try to do this for the sake of *our* mission, so our people will not have to face the united enemy instead of leading the proposed union." She hesitated. "And what about Tadodaho? Should I try to approach him?"

His face darkened. "No! Stay away from him. Live as a part of this town until the Crooked Tongues man comes, then return here. Gather information, see what the situation is, talk to people who are willing to listen, but don't tell anyone of your acquaintance with the Messenger. This piece of information is better not to be circling around Onondaga Town." Shrugging, he squatted beside her, but at a respectable distance. "Your information can help us to decide on the better course of action when the time comes."

She sighed. "I want to think about it."

"Of course. Let me know before our Father Sun goes to sleep tonight."

"That early? Am I not allowed to take my time?" Turning her head, she saw his grin, a good-natured, well-meaning grin. "You think it's all amusing, don't you?"

He ran his palm through his thinning hair. "Yes, I do. The Crooked Tongues man introduced me to an interesting group of people, I have to give him that. He might have been a strange person himself, with this dreadful accent of his and the unacceptability of his ideas, and most of all, the way he keeps making people listen. Yet, the followers he gathered in the beginning of his journey seemed to be an even stranger lot, from the fierce, scar-faced young man to you, the woman who refuses to know her place." He shook his head, lifted from his gloom permanently now, as it seemed. "I'm telling you, this man made life interesting around our side of the Great Lake, and I want to see where all this is leading."

But you are one of those early followers, too, she thought, strangely calm now, once the decision was made. *And you are the strangest of us all, a complex man with a mind as devious as that of Tadodaho, if one believes half of the stories concerning this man. Well, I'm glad you are on our side, but I will keep away from you if I can help it. No wonder the scar-faced youth didn't not wish to leave Two Rivers traveling alone with you.* She pitted her face against the breeze, not bothered by its strength anymore.

"You don't have to wait until sunset. I will go to Onondaga Town. Just tell me what clan to approach, and who are the people that I need to find and can trust."

CHAPTER 8

The arrows swished, one, then another, then some more. Crouching at the bottom of the canoe, her limbs jutted against the hard wood, the sobbing of the other girl fraying her nerves, Seketa tried to control her panic. They were being shot at, actually *shot at*, by warriors, people, maybe her own people. She was going to die by her own people's hand! Oh, Mighty Spirits!

The monotonous splashing interrupted as their canoe flinched, jerked to the side, pushing her into the bags she remembered packing hurriedly only four dawns ago, afraid but full of excitement and memories. Oh, but it was her second time to pack in this way, in the darkness and by stealth, however this time it was more dangerous, but more exciting. She was the one to sail, and not only to say her farewells and pray and hope for the best.

Clutching to the side of the boat, she looked up, first at the rowing man, to make sure he was not hurt, then to the shoreline as it was drawing away. The warriors were still there, shouting and waving their clubs and spears. *Were those her people?* She pushed the terrible thought away and winced as another arrow came from the sky, diving into the water in front of their boat like a hunting bird.

"Get down," muttered the man, and this time she had no difficulty understanding his words. What he said made sense. And yet…

She glanced at his sweaty, haggard face, taking in the exhaustion, and the blood seeping from his shoulder, where one of the arrows brushed against it, leaving a gaping cut. Combined with his previous wounds, the man didn't seem capable of rowing efficiently. She grabbed the other paddle.

"What are you doing?" he groaned, exasperated, but his face lit for a heartbeat.

She crawled the length of the canoe, flinching as another arrow descended from above. Their attackers were obviously furious, almost out of range by now but reluctant to give up.

Another missile scratched the bottom of their boat, next to the girl who was curled into a ball, not looking up, shuddering and letting out a helpless moan, instead. Seketa forced her thoughts off the razor-sharp flint that, in a strange fashion, descended upon them like scattered rain, in oblique sprays. How did they manage to make the arrows come this way? Weren't the warriors shooting forward, after taking a good aim?

The water splashed under her paddle, and it took her time to fall into their rower's tempo, but once she did, the canoe shot ahead, in a satisfactory manner. Soon no more arrows came, and the shouts of the people upon the shore melted into a dim hum. Still, they didn't dare to rest, paddling on and on, saying nothing. And what was there to say, anyway? she thought, her heartbeat slowing down, the calmness coming back, spreading through her body. The immediate danger seemed to be over, and somehow it reassured her, made her think that she would survive the reckless adventure she had plunged into without thinking.

Only four dawns, four dawns of fear and misgivings, traveling with this pair, *the enemies of her people*, a wounded warrior and a scared girl, both unable to protect her or make her journey smoother. Why, the opposite was true! It seemed that their safety and well-being rested with her, actually, although the man did his best while rowing at nights and finding small hideaways with the coming of each dawn, too exhausted to help her pitch their camp or prepare their food, usually just the mix of sweetened powder she'd made sure to tuck into their bags before leaving. They could not even converse properly, had they had any energy left to talk, with both fleeing captives speaking their tongue and her being in the minority all of a sudden, an uncomfortable feeling.

What made her do that? she wondered, as the nights had dragged on and the streams merged into each other, hurrying to drain into the huge water basin, the Great Sparkling Water. What made her do something as reckless, as wild, as unspeakable, interfering with the oldest of customs concerning the prisoners and the manner of their execution, going against every tradition?

She remembered that night, only four dawns ago, when the rain poured and that girl, Gayoah, wiping her own tears and turning so nice all of a sudden, telling her that the men she wanted to know about might not have crossed the Great Lake at all, trying to comfort, doing the opposite. And then the strange story of the stone canoe and the messenger of the Great Spirits, told haltingly, in a barely understandable manner. Oh, but their way of speaking was so unpleasantly twisted.

She sighed. The story didn't make much sense, and yet she kept clinging to it, thinking that maybe, somehow, it might have been Two Rivers, or Tekeni, or hopefully both of them, making those people believe they were divine messengers. Somehow.

Had she had time to think it all over, she would not have done this, she knew. But as it was, with the rain strengthening and the night deepening, and the tempting way this warrior was not guarded but placed in a storage room of one of the longhouses, with his companion dying but him still alive and relative well, she just knew that it was the only way, her only opportunity to cross the Great Lake and come and look for *him* all by herself. He was not dead, even if it was not him posing as some messenger. He had made it to his own lands, and for some reason, he still didn't come back, but he would if he could. He would still come, maybe, but she was fed up with the waiting. Six long moons were more than enough.

So she did the unspeakable, and now, the water of the Great Lake spread ahead, offering not only hope but a shelter too, because the people who had shot at them might go back and fetch their canoes and try to chase them, but in such a grayish-blue, limitless mass what were their attackers' chances in finding them?

"We need to go there." The man pointed to their left, then wiped his forehead, smearing a mixture of sweat and blood upon it, not doing a great job of cleaning his face. "East."

"Why east?" she asked, appreciating his effort to talk slowly, for her sake. When speaking to his sister, his words would gush like a current, impossible to follow. His name was Sgenedu, she had learned by now.

"Crossing, difficult here. Too much sail. East better." He shrugged, then pressed his lips and resumed the paddling, checking that their boat's prow turned the way he wanted, his face breaking out with a new coat of sweat, losing the last of its coloring. "If not for those people, we would not sail here. We would set off later, in a dawn or so."

Although he switched back to his normal way of talking, she understood too well. Fleeing their attackers had made them dive into the mists of the huge mass of water too early, before finding a good crossing spot, and before making solemn offerings to the spirits inhabiting these waters. The other side may not see them at all.

"Maybe we can sail back to the shore later on," she said, falling again into his step of the paddling. "Then move to the east?"

He shook his head vigorously, his face twisting with pain. The old gush upon his leg was not bleeding anymore, but it glared angrily red, the crust upon it wet, alarmingly so.

"They will be waiting. Our only chance is to start crossing now and pray for the mercy of the Great Spirits."

Their voices rang clearly in the breaking dawn, and it seemed to bring the girl at the bottom of the canoe back to her senses.

"Did they leave us alone?" she asked in a small voice, raising her head, her face grayish, lacking in color.

Seketa wanted to laugh hysterically. "We left them alone, more likely," she muttered, understanding the girl's words with almost no effort. For some reason, since that rainy night of their first meeting, it was easier to understand the timid little thing. The girl was smiling so readily, so friendly, and she had always spoken slowly, for Seketa's sake, even when addressing her brother. Her gratitude knew no bounds as it seemed, and for all her timidity and her tendency to cry upon the slightest of provocations, Seketa tended to like this girl more than the grim warrior, their protector.

The smile flashed as expected. "Good. Glad. I'm glad we left them alone. It was nice of us to do that." One glance at her brother and the smile disappeared all at once. "You are bleeding!"

The boat swayed as she jumped to her feet, rushing forward, making them lose the rhythm of their paddling. The man cursed.

"Shut up and stop being useless," he muttered through his clenched teeth. "Get busy. Take care of our food or something."

"But you are wounded again," insisted the girl, not deterred by the way she had been addressed. "We need to clean your wound, and you need to rest. You rowed for the entire night."

Which was true enough, reflected Seketa, already tired, hungry, and sweaty under the strengthening morning sun. If they had reached the crossing point, they would still have a whole day of incessant rowing ahead of them, and if they didn't... She shuddered at the thought of being lost, of drifting for days on end in the intimidating vastness, of dying slowly, of hunger probably, or exhaustion, or both.

"You'll take my place in a short while," she heard the man saying, as his brief glance measured the sun. "We'll keep up on this course for some time. When we turn south, I'll rest."

Sensible thinking, decided Seketa, hating the way her dress clung to her back and under her armpits, sticky with sweat, her head pounding, eyelids heavy with lack of sleep. Some of the men's work was not pleasant at all.

"Would you like to drink, sister?" Gayoah's smile was back, as she leaned over the side, filling a bowl she fished out of their bags.

Seketa smiled. "Yes. How do I say 'thank you' in your tongue?"

"My tongue? Yes? Oh!" Her grin playful, the girl made her way carefully along the side of the boat. "You say *nyaweñha*. Like that. *Nyaweñha*." She crouched back beside their bags. "I can teach you more words, if you want me to."

"*Nyaweñha*, yes. Why not? But," Seketa paused to wipe her brow, then glanced at the warrior, uncomfortable with his gloomy disapproving presence. "Do you and the Flint People understand each other?"

"Oh!" The smile disappeared once again. "Well, yes, we do. But we don't want to. They are bad people." A frown. "Nothing to talk about. Bad people. Don't go to their towns. They kill you. Or do other bad things."

Seketa pursed her lips. "You said the messenger, that strange man in the stone canoe, he said make peace, peace with Flint People too, no?"

The frown was back, distorting the girl's pleasant features with an attempt to understand. "Oh, the Messenger, yes, he came in stone canoe, yes."

"Didn't he say to make peace, peace with Flint People?"

The girl reared back, almost in horror. "No, of course not! Why would he say something like that?"

Her disappointment was so vast she felt her limbs going numb for a moment, unable to move. Which made her stop rowing, and their canoe jerked, began to turn about. Cursing, the warrior rushed to stabilize the boat, paddling more vigorously, from both sides now, his forehead breaking with sweat.

"You either row or you don't," he muttered through his clenched teeth.

Seketa didn't care, her thoughts in a jumble, stomach heavy with desperation. If he came alone and didn't talk about Flint People, then it was someone else, maybe truly not a person but a divine messenger. How else would someone sail a canoe made out of stone? Enough of a miracle, but it had nothing to do with her predicament. Had she left her people, crossing into enemy lands, in chase of a silly dream, an impossible promise?

"Please, no sad again," said the girl quietly. "I'll row instead of you."

"No!" Clasping her lips, Seketa made an effort to fall into the tempo their wounded protector provided again, paying no attention to the skeptical glance he gave her. He looked worse by the moment, with his old wound glaring and the new one oozing blood with every move of his paddle. "Row instead of him." She nodded toward the man. "Let him rest."

He didn't argue, letting his sister take his place, sliding down the side of the boat, too tired to make his way toward the more vacant space in the middle of their vessel.

"You need to wash your wound." The girl leaned forward, not doing too good of a job with her paddle. It struck the water lightly, diving not deeply enough to keep them progressing in the previous pattern.

"I know. In a little while." He shut his eyes with a sigh of relief.

"If Seketa can keep us going until I'm done with your wound—"

"Just keep moving toward the south." He groaned, pulling himself up, obviously seeing the sensibility of his sister's advice. "Put your paddle deep into the water, don't just caress it, for the divine spirits' sake! You may as well not row at all the way you do this." Reaching over the board as carefully as he could without making it harder for them to go on, he began splashing the water over his cut, rubbing the crusted blood off, pressing his lips so hard they lost color. "I never thought the Crooked Tongues could teach us anything, but when it comes to you, sister, I'm not so sure anymore."

What was he talking about? The wary glance the girl shot at Seketa made her wonder.

"Oh, please, Sgenedu," said the girl scornfully. "You are truly bad-tempered at times, you know that?"

But her gaze rested on him, worried, and her rowing improved not a little bit. In this pace they may never reach the other side, not this evening and not the next, thought Seketa, still wondering about this crooked tongues remark. Who were those people? More of the other side's savage dwellers? She could imagine their tongues sticking out, gnarled or just tangling, drooling saliva. A disgusting sight, but with the savages one never knew.

"So what is your thing with the Flint People, mysterious girl?" he asked, lying back on the bottom of the canoe, his eyes half closed, but his face actually looking better, some color creeping back into it.

She stiffened. "Nothing."

He shielded his face with his good arm. "Nothing, eh? But this is the second time you bring them up. Second time talk about Flint People," he added, simplifying. "What seek there? Revenge?"

"No, no revenge," she said, unwilling to talk to him about any of it. His sister was a different matter.

"Then what?"

She kept rowing, keeping silent. She didn't have to tell him a thing. He owed her his life, and she owed him nothing in return. She wasn't obliged to answer his questions.

"The Messenger came to our lands before the Cold Moons, before the snows." His voice rang eerily, lacking in emotion, his eyes closed again. "The man of our village, a prominent hunter, was the first to listen to him. He came to his companions all excited, telling them about this strange encounter. But when they came back, the stone canoe had vanished, along with the man. Disappeared with no trace." He paused, opening his eyes, his frown light. "So this is how our village received the message first. Not haughty Onondaga Town, and not influential High Springs, but us, a meaningless village, four longhouses all in all, with our fields small and our fence just one row of palisade."

She tried to understand, finding it difficult to follow his gushing words. The Messenger talked to someone and then he… disappeared? Why?

"And then what happened? The Messenger, he came back?"

"Well, no, not to our town." All of a sudden, his face lost some of its previous challenging smugness. "But he was reported to visit the woman who is feeding the warriors, and, of course, he went to see Hionhwatha!" It came out triumphantly, in a complacent manner again. "So before the snows fell, that formidable leader, Hionhwatha, was back, in High Springs this time."

"And the Messenger?"

"Oh, no, the Messenger didn't come. Some say he went to talk to the Flint lowlifes. Such a reckless decision. Even for the divine person like him, it was not an advisable journey to undertake. He must have thought too much of his powers."

She caught her breath, fearing to ask, knowing she had been due for another disappointment. "Was he traveling alone, the Messenger?"

The warrior didn't move, and she thought he might have fallen asleep, which might have been a mercy, actually. She didn't need to hear yet another confirmation as to the recklessness and the futility of what she had done.

"Some say he was alone, just traveling from place to place and talking to people, telling them what should have been done, making them listen, somehow." The man shifted to make himself more comfortable, his words flowing slowly, too quiet to understand half of them. It seemed that he was talking to himself. "I wonder what he said to the fierce leader from Onondaga Town, because at that time, the man was crazed with grief and disappointment. He lived in the woods, alone, dangerous, and insane. No one knew what he did, and no one dared to come and ask. He was certainly not above killing people for his meals. Everyone feared him and left him alone, even the enemy warriors. But the Messenger went to see him, and then Hionhwatha was back among our people, as bright and as formidable as before, ready to confront Tadodaho again."

"Who is Tadodaho?" asked Seketa, not overly curious but wishing to make him talk. He fell silent again, not asleep, but deep in his thoughts.

"Oh, Tadodaho, he is the War Chief of Onondaga Town. That's what the title says, but don't make a mistake, Crooked Tongues girl. He is the leader of the whole place, if not the whole nation. You don't want to cross his path, you truly don't. You will be made sorry for such a try. I'm not sure Hionhwatha will weather this repeated confrontation. I wonder what help the Messenger promised to make him face this battle once again."

"And where is the Messenger now?" The canoe almost stopped, not drifting with the current, but not progressing much either, with Seketa's halfhearted rowing matching Gayoah's attempts on the other side of the boat.

"How should I know?" His voice suddenly shook, taking an angry tone. "I've obviously spent some time away from home, have I not?"

She pressed her lips, angered too. "Maybe he disappeared again. Maybe he won't help your people anymore. Maybe there is no Messenger at all! Maybe this man from your village lied to you all, or just imagined that, eh? Do you people believe so easily in what you are told?"

He straightened up abruptly, turning his head to face her, squinting against the glow of the high-noon sun. "What nonsense, woman! Many people had met him, people respected and held high by the community. There are so many changes in our lands and even the lands of the despicable enemy. Who are you to question any of it?"

The last sentence was too clear not to understand, his indignant expression reinforcing the challenge in his voice.

"I am the woman who saved your life," she retorted. "I am the woman who made your return to your lands possible. So you can start by treating me with respect!"

Oh, he evidently understood her well enough. His eyes narrowed to mere slits. "So what is your purpose? What are you seeking on our side of the Great Lake? The Messenger?"

She glared at him. "Yes, maybe I'm seeking the Messenger. Maybe I have something to tell him."

The lifted eyebrows were her answer, then he flopped again onto his back, closing his eyes.

"You, Crooked Tongues people, are strange," he mumbled to himself. "Some say the Messenger is Crooked Tongues too, you know. So maybe you do know him."

Who are those crooked tongues, she asked herself again, but didn't utter the question aloud, reluctant to receive yet another rude answer. This man was unbearably annoying.

"Ganuk, the man who saw the Messenger first, did not lie to us. He is not that sort of a man. He is a very respectable hunter, a member of our council. We are just a village, not a large, haughty settlement like Onondaga Town or High Springs, but our people are as respectable and as trustworthy." His eyes were shut once again, but his voice rang loudly, cutting the misty air. "He met the Messenger and he talked to him. And to his companion, too. He was the first to receive the promise. I talked to him, I heard it all more than once through the long winter moons. He did not lie to us." For a few heartbeats he fell silent, and Seketa could see the worried gaze of Gayoah relaxing. He needed his rest, obviously. "The messenger talked strangely, so Ganuk had to listen to his companion instead, while the man just stood there, in his stone canoe, with the sun glowing all around him although it was not the right angle for Father Sun to shine at this time of the day. It was truly a divine message. His companion explained it all to him."

His companion! She felt the paddle slipping out of her grasp, and fought not to let it go, her numb mind not noticing the canoe jerking to a stop once again.

"Seketa!" Gayoah's cry tore the crisp air, the worry in it obvious. "What happened? Are you all right?"

"Yes, yes." She clutched the paddle in her sweaty palms, trying to concentrate. "I'm all right." Leaning forward, she peered at the wounded man, who straightened up, staring at her, puzzled. "His companion. Who was it? What did he look like?"

His frown deepened. "How would I know? I didn't meet any of them."

"But what did this Ganuk say? Please! I need to know."

He brought his good arm up, rubbing the side of his head, which was covered with thick stubble, not shaved for some time, for obvious reasons.

"He was a strange man too, of course. A fierce warrior. Full of scars. His face and his body. He must have seen hundreds of battles. Although Ganuk said he seemed young." A shrug. "Who knows? The Great Spirits are mighty and never erring."

She tried to bring her thoughts into order, her head aching with the effort to understand. He said the other man was a warrior full of scars, but he also said he was young. No, it could not be him, no more than Two Rivers could be considered the messenger of the Great Spirits. Wise and wonderfully eloquent, the formidable man was too much of a human to fool anyone, from his tendency to laugh and see the ridiculous side of many situations to the difficulty he had controlling his desires when it came to women. Oh, Two Rivers was human, very much so.

As for Tekeni. The stony fist was back, squeezing her insides. He would grow into an outstanding warrior, a fearless leader, but he was not any of these, not yet. No, he could not be the fierce, intimidating warrior with hundreds of scars. They would never try to make him pose as such, even if they would have thought of this sort of a trick. Yet, if the Messenger and his follower were not them, then where were they? Where were Two Rivers and Tekeni? Wandering the enemy countryside? Dead or alive?

She clenched her teeth tight, determined. Oh, but she was going to find them, and they had better be alive and well.

Bettering her grip on the slippery paddle, she looked at Gayoah resolutely. "We better put forth an effort now, before Father Sun begins his journey toward his resting place."

CHAPTER 9

"I can sneak into High Springs and try to talk to both of them." Stifling a yawn, Tekeni stretched beside the fire, watching the stormy face of his friend as Two Rivers sat there, rigid and stiff, refusing to make himself more comfortable. "You don't truly need me at the Swamp People's, do you? Not with that impressive escort you've got yourself now. Fancy going around with six dozen warriors, like the most important War Leader in the land."

But even this light needling did nothing to lighten Two Rivers' mood. They had been on the way for some dawns, sailing against the current but in a grand state. No more careful sneaking around, traveling by night and resting by day, making sure to leave no marks. No more concerns at being discovered and killed before the hasty explanations were concocted. This time their party was large, impressive, the dignitaries of both eastern nations accompanied by many warriors, heading for the gathering the Messenger was to organize among the Swamp People, coming there invited, expected eagerly, or so the delegation of the western foreigners had assured them.

Traveling in such a state, with so many important people, was a novelty, but not always a welcome thing. There was no fear, but also no freedom of their previous progress through these lands. Even the detour to visit Jikonsahseh required some explanation, a measure of convincing of other people, instead of just going there, doing what Two Rivers decided to do on the spur of the moment. Not their style of doing things, decided Tekeni, seeing the same impatience in the depths of his friend's eyes. He missed the freedom of their lonely traveling.

"I can detour through Onondagas, reassure our mutual friend and the girl, and be back with no one the wiser," he repeated, serious now. "I think I can do that."

"You? You will stick out among the Onondagas like a lit torch in the middle of the night." Two Rivers' grin was fleeting, lacking its usual baiting quality. "Jikonsahseh will send a word. She has enough contacts to do that, I suppose." A shrug. "And her reasons for being difficult."

But it wouldn't be as good as a personal reassurance, reflected Tekeni, watching his friend, his heart filling with compassion. He knew how Two Rivers felt, no one better. Hionhwatha's state of affairs had worried him for some time, but the old leader could handle the difficulties, if aware that help was on its way. A word sent through Jikonsahseh might be enough to strengthen the formidable man's spirit. No, this is not what made Two Rivers sink into gloom this morning, while reaching the familiar clearing, leaving their party camping upon the shore, taking a well-deserved rest.

Tekeni grinned, remembering how good it felt to find both strange-looking huts unchanged, the part of the scenery, with the smoke coming out of the smaller dwelling, inviting and friendly. It was a sort of a homecoming, he felt, smiling, answering the greetings of the old woman, whose eyes sparkled with excitement and pride, lifted out of her usually reserved, practical self. Oh, she was glad to see them back, genuinely glad.

However, the clearing was empty, safe for them and the old woman, abandoned. Her living here alone again was evident, too clear to miss. He watched Two Rivers talking, answering the questions, charming as always, enjoying his improved ability to speak their tongues, but the impressive man's gaze kept drifting, scanning the huts or the edge of the clearing where the trail would lead toward the spring and the cluster of smaller fields. The Onondaga girl was not around, but maybe she just went to fetch firewood or to work the fields.

"She is not here," said Jikonsahseh finally, when another uncomfortable pause ensued.

"Oh!" Two Rivers' eyes were back upon their hostess, their concentration exaggerated. "As I was saying, the council…" his words trailed off under the meaningful gaze of the old woman.

Jikonsahseh sighed. "She went back to High Springs less than a moon ago. You left her waiting for too long."

Two Rivers said nothing, but his jaw tightened, and suddenly, Tekeni wished they had not insisted on leaving their people on the banks of the Great River and coming here. It was good to see the old woman, satisfying to show her how successful they were, how his people were not the beasts she assumed them to be. She was a good person, very wise and very kind, a loyal supporter, and yet, her straightforwardness was embarrassing. Two Rivers did not owe her explanations or reasoning on the ways he might have behaved with the girl. Whatever happened, his mission was more important, and he had made efforts to come back as soon as he could. The Onondaga girl could have waited patiently. Seketa was forced to wait for much longer!

The old pain was back, clutching his stomach in its painful grip. It had already been near Planting Moon, and he had not been even close to the shores of the Great Sparkling Water, let alone able to cross it. For how long would he have to wait?

"I see." Two Rivers' voice rang calmly, in perfect control once again. "I suppose it was the best thing for her to do."

"Unless she runs into trouble." The old woman's eyes drifted toward the swaying trees on the edge of the clearing, dark, thoughtful, worried.

"What do you mean? What trouble?"

"She didn't go home to live with her family. She went to help Hionhwatha. She asked me to tell you that."

This time Tekeni thought his companion's jaw would crack, so tightly did his teeth seem to be pressing against each other.

"What else did she say?"

Reaching for the pile of dry branches, Jikonsahseh stirred the fire, refusing to look up. "Nothing. She said nothing. Typically to her, she went away on the same day, the moment she decided to go. It was after we received the news about you getting in trouble with my people and their gathering."

"What did you hear?" The words came out muffled, seeping with difficulty through Two Rivers' clenched teeth.

"Oh," Jikonsahseh smiled, her face clearing of shadows. "We hear many things – strange, fascinating stories, from men jumping into falls and coming out unharmed to them strolling in the head of the Flint People's delegation, presuming to organize my people's affairs. Quite arrogantly at that, or so my people said."

Tekeni stifled a chuckle. So the word was getting around.

"The Onondaga lands are swelling with stories, too. Stone canoes, divine messengers." Her frown deepened again. "Hionhwatha seems to be gaining trust among High Springs' dwellers and the surrounding villages, but Onondaga Town is still firmly in the grip of that ominous Tadodaho. There will be trouble there, unless you find the way to get rid of the evil man." The old, generously padded shoulders lifted in a shrug. "Or to sway him onto your side. You seem to have a talent for making the most stubborn people listen."

Two Rivers was staring at the fire, as though he didn't hear any of it.

"I need to go to the Onondagas now," he muttered, finally. "We can't afford any more delays."

"Weren't you two on your way there?" Their hostess looked up, surprised.

Embarrassed by his companion's continuous silence, Tekeni shifted uneasily. "We are heading for the Swamp People's main town," he said. "They invited us formally, by sending an important delegation. They asked for Two Rivers' guidance and advice. They were wise enough to wish to join the peoples uniting in a Great Peace."

The old woman looked genuinely surprised. "And your Flint People agreed?"

"Yes, of course." It was annoying, the way she kept taking his people for mindless brutes. "My people were the first to receive the message, the first to embrace it and back the

Messenger up. They listened to him. They were the ones to follow him to the lands of your people, offering peace. Even though your people chose to make trouble, testing his patience, my people remained patient alongside with him. Why do you keep questioning their motives?"

Jikonsahseh's eyebrows climbed so high, they almost reached the receding line of her thinning hair.

"I may live all alone in the woods, young man," she said, ominously quiet, bestowing on Tekeni one of those squashing gazes the elders save for impudent youths. "But I can see through some pretty words. I'm not your regular audience, boy, to preach to me about the Great Peace and the will of the Right-Handed Twin. I know exactly what happened, and I know what your people are getting out of it. So spare me your pretty speeches. Save them for the People of the Swamp's meeting."

It was difficult to hang onto his temper now, but by this time, Two Rivers was back from his wandering the realms of the daydreams.

"The People of the Swamp should not prove difficult," he said with a grin, his confidently affable self again. "But their neighbors to the west may give us trouble. I hear that there is no peace among the People of the Mountains now; no peace and no concord."

"The People of the Mountains? So now you want to go there!" Jikonsahseh shook her head, slightly put out, or maybe just grimly amused. "You cannot rest, can you? Those people would make the Onondagas, and even his Flint People," a rough nod indicated Tekeni, "look tamed. Why would you go there, into their unfriendly hills? It would certainly be looking for trouble."

"Are they that intimidating?" Two Rivers smiled, actually looking pleased with himself, as though having hidden advantages he didn't bother to reveal yet.

Her brow creased. "You don't seem bothered at all. Did they send an important delegation, too?"

"No, they did not receive our message of peace, not yet. But they will. In due time. After we have dealt with the stubborn Onondagas."

"I see you are in great spirits this spring." Jikonsahseh's laughter shook the air, but it was not a light-hearted sound. "At the Onondagas you may have a chance, although it doesn't look like it as of now. You have a powerful ally who did not give up on your mission yet, waiting for you to come and help. Not to mention your other loyal friend and follower." Her gaze deepened, lost some of its affability. "I fear for her. She may be in danger."

Two Rivers' face closed abruptly. "Why? What did she intend to do?"

"She didn't tell me, but her determination and impatience were obvious, impossible to miss. She was tired of waiting, tired of hearing about you spending your time organizing the eastern nations while neglecting her people. She went away determined to do something. And also…" The old woman hesitated, her face losing most of its forbidding expression, turning softer, uncertain, openly worried. "She should keep away from Onondaga Town and Tadodaho. This man spells mortal danger, particularly for her."

The air hissed loudly as Two Rivers drew a breath, his eyes wide open, clinging to her. "Did you warn her? Did you tell her not to go to Onondaga Town?"

"Yes, I did, and she promised to stay with her family in High Springs. But…" The old woman's hands came up, her palms brushing against her face. "She won't listen. She will do whatever she thinks is necessary. I can tell that. She was determined to help, and…" A dark glance bestowed on Two Rivers. "And to show you that she is not a girl of no significance. To leave her here with no word was not a decent thing to do, not to the sort of a woman she is."

Tekeni held his breath, not enraged at the open reprimand, not this time. He remembered the Onondaga girl, the first time he had met her, here in the woods, spying on him, thin and haunted, but still beautiful, still fierce, yelling at him, angry and unafraid. And the other time, when they fought on the shores of Onondaga Lake and she didn't panic but helped and did what he asked, helpful and matter-of-fact, not her usual argumentative self all of sudden, saving his life in the end. And how she told him not to make Seketa wait, but to go and fetch her with no delays.

He remembered her eyes, how they gleamed with a pure feminine know-it-all spark, promising to shelter his Crooked Tongues love until he was done and ready, still defying and not easy to handle, but now kind and well-meaning, a true friend. What if she did something to make that evil Tadodaho angry? What if he killed her the way he had killed Hionhwatha's family?

He watched Two Rivers' taut face, seeing the jutting jaw, the sharp cheekbones, the dark, stormy eyes. No, the girl better be safe and unharmed, he thought, shivering. Friendly teasing aside, the Crooked Tongues man clearly cared for her, more than he was prepared to admit. If something happened to her, and because of him and his mission, of all things, the great man would not take it kindly. Divine messenger or not, if Tadodaho harmed her, mighty sorcerer he might reputed to be, most likely just a very formidable person, the despicable murderer would be in a grave danger, but so would be their mission. It would look bad if the Messenger of Peace did violent things, killing leading men of the nation that weren't even persuaded to join yet. No, the Onondaga girl had better not get into trouble. There must be a way of ensuring her safety.

"Do you have a way of sending word to High Springs?" Two Rivers' voice broke into his reverie, echoing his thoughts. "Somehow?"

Jikonsahseh shrugged. "They are not my people."

The tall man leaned forward, his gaze penetrating, imploring. "I want her to stay in her town, to do nothing wild, that's all. I want her receive this word from me." He nodded, pressing his lips under the accusing gaze. "I should have done it earlier, yes. But I want her to know it now, so she won't do anything rash before I come."

"Go and tell her that yourself. With so many followers, you will be in no danger, even if strolling among the Onondagas." Another shrug. "I don't know many of their people. They are not my people."

"You know many men, no matter what peoples they belong to. For many moons you were opening your dwelling to every passerby, no matter where they came from and where they were heading. You treated them with kindness, and your visitors appreciated that, honoring your rules as long as they were your guests."

Fascinated, Tekeni listened, forgetting his unhappy thoughts that again flowed into the usual channel of fuming with yet another delay. If Two Rivers went to the Onondagas now, he, Tekeni, could not leave him alone, facing that dangerous beast Tadodaho. Six dozens of followers or not, he trusted no one against the alleged sorcerer, curse him for all the trouble he caused into wandering the afterlife for endless spans of seasons, not finding his Sky Path at all.

"You belong to no nation, and in the new state of affairs, when we are one and not different peoples, you will have a prominent place. You ensured it already, while acting like a true mother of our united people, moons before it started to happen. They are all your people, Jikonsahseh, all of them!"

Now it was her turn to stare at him, mesmerized. Tekeni suppressed a grin. Oh, the great man knew how to talk, knew what to say to his listeners. The old woman was now his to command, and she would find a way to send the word, to warn the Onondaga girl, of that he was certain now.

CHAPTER 10

The thunder rolled again, bringing along the distinct smell of rain. Two Rivers pulled his blanket tighter, shivering with cold. The nights were still chilly, with the wind doubling its efforts, as though angry with him personally. And why wouldn't it?

He glanced at the fading moon, willing the dawn to come faster. It was annoying to just sit there, but he dared not wander about as he would have done back home or even at Little Falls. Here, camping among the people who were supposed to become their allies, with the negotiations still in progress and suspicion and bad memories still ruling both sides, wandering about in the pre-dawn mist was certainly not a wise thing to do.

He rubbed his eyes, then glanced at the sleeping silhouettes spread all around, comfortable under their blankets, beside the barely glowing embers of last night's fires. After five days of negotiating, the people were tired. And restless. Which was not a good thing. His experience at the Standing Stone meeting taught him what limits should not be pushed. It nearly got out of hand back then, and he saw the signs of impatience coming from both sides now, with his eastern followers already offended by a certain lack of cooperation, coming from the stance of power and superiority, united and strong.

However, this was not the right attitude, he knew, not the approach he wanted to take. He needed both sides respectful and content, reaching the agreements in a good faith, with no pressure and no coercing. The People of the Swamp may have been a smaller nation, but they were proud and fierce, no less than their powerful neighbors. Intimidated those people wouldn't be, and their willingness to cooperate was as vital as that of the others.

The exhaustion was creeping up on him, so he got up, wrapping the blanket around him, to keep the chill out. Anything but to return to the world of the dreams, although the lack of sleep was taking its toll, making his head dizzy, his thoughts slow to organize. Tomorrow he would need his concentration, his ability to talk sensibly, to look into the people's eyes and make them listen. The lack of sleep would undermine that, taking more of his strength away.

Yet, if he went to sleep, the dream would return. He knew it would; he had grown too familiar with the signs. The remnants were still there, lurking too close to the surface, the terrible images clinging to his mind's eye, although it had been some time since he jerked awake, sweaty and trembling, to stare at the star-sprinkled sky and try to get grip of his senses.

Shuddering, he searched his bag for his pipe and the ground leaves of tobacco he always made sure to bring along. His hands still trembled, and he cursed softly, trying to make as little noise as he could.

Why? he asked himself. Why yet another of *these* dreams? And why now? And what did it mean? And where?

The dream was different, strange. He had been somewhere upon the top of a hill, with a clear view of a small valley and the bare hilltops towering on the other side of the lake, far below his feet. A place he had never seen before, a place strange and not especially friendly. There was a danger in the air, but he was not afraid. Not like in the dream of the falls, where he had felt shamefully terrified. This time, it was a place of danger, but he was not alone, not challenged. There were people around, people who came with him, and people they had come to visit, their hosts not happy with their arrival but behaving cordially, not grabbing their weapons, not yet. Maybe later. Oh, yes, it might have come to a confrontation, but he was still calm, still confident in his ability to make them listen. *And then it happened.*

He shuddered again, and the tobacco bag slipped from his sweaty hand, the fragments of the dry leaves scattering, rustling in the darkness. Cursing softly, he hurried to scoop the bulk of them up, at the same time glad to put his thoughts on the effort to salvage as much of his treasure as he could. To think about what happened in the dream was frightening. It made his heart flutter, leaving his stomach empty, as though he had just vomited all of its contents.

If only the vision were not so vivid. If only the brilliance of the sun that was shining down that strange valley was not beginning to dim. If only the sounds of the midday forest would not disappear all of a sudden, along with the fading light. If only the darkness would not come and swallow them all, as though the Evil Twin and his minions had risen to claim the Turtle Island and all its inhabitants for themselves.

He took his time searching through glowing embers, lighting the pipe, deep in thought. It was the same sort of a dream that had plagued him back home, before he came to these lands. *It was going to happen.* But where, and when, and most importantly – why? Back home, it had taken him long moons to understand. He didn't know the dream was about Little Falls until the Great Spirits made him meet Tekeni. And even then, it had taken him time to put the pieces together.

Yet, this time the dream was even vaguer. The place was bleary, the people around him faded, not important to any of it, neither his followers nor the leaders he was trying to convince. He himself was nothing but a part of the landscape, not significant, not prominent, just a disposable form of life, like anyone else. The morning was important, the trees, the towering hills, and the lake down below, but those were dying away, fading along with the rapidly disappearing sun. A terrifying sign!

He shook his head, inhaling deeply, feeling some of his calm returning along with the friendly sensation of the strong, aromatic smoke sliding down his throat, reaching his chest, spreading its tranquility. With the coming of the dawn, he would make another effort to lighten the mood, to reach anything tangible, to make them listen to each other. And then he'd be off, rushing to High Springs as fast the rapids of the rivers would allow him. The prominent people from Little Falls and the Standing Stone representatives should be able to stay and take care of the rest. Hionhwatha could not be left waiting any longer. The old leader's resolve might prove not enough, not in the face of his former rival, that evil Tadodaho and his desire to lead. And if Onheda got involved in any of that...

He clenched his teeth, fastening them around his pipe, suddenly wishing to crack it in two. She would go straight into the heart of the action, he knew. The warning of Jikonsahseh would not manage to deter her, would not make her stop and think. She was not that kind of a woman.

The image of her rushing out to bring him a spear, pale and disheveled and smeared with blood, *her blood*, but oh-so-determined, so vital, her jaw clenched and her eyes sparkling, invaded his mind, uninvited. She had saved his life back then, probably, and she thought nothing of it, just an ordinary deed that one person does to another. But it was no ordinary deed at all. Maybe between the warriors, yes, but with a woman? The fair sex had its strengths, there was no doubt about it. Woman were courageous and smart, many of them, but their way of doing things was different, never straight, never outright, even the Clans Mothers, wise and opinionated women as they were. But the Onondaga girl behaved like a man would, concealing no feelings, no inner thoughts, telling her mind, doing what was necessary and not feeling embarrassed about it. Like Tekeni, she was a perfect partner, and like Tekeni, she had been made to wait for too long.

He thought about his young friend. Maybe after they dealt with the Onondagas he might manage to accompany the wolf cub back across the Great Sparkling Water. Just a few days, five, six at the most. They could do it if they hurried. One day for the crossing, another two to get to his former town, snatch the girl, and rush off with no delays. If that pretty Seketa was still waiting, still willing to go, then it could be done very quickly, with no one the wiser. And if not...

He shrugged. Then they still would rush back, of course,

heartbroken as his young companion might be. They had nothing to do among his former people, not yet.

His grin spread, to disappear as promptly. If they sailed tomorrow, even through the second part of the day, they might reach High Springs in just a matter of a few dawns. And she had better be there too, not venturing to do anything wild, heedful of Jikonsahseh's warning. Still beautiful, still alluring, still full of desire, even if angry. She had been made to wait for too long, but he would explain it all to her, he decided, heading up the trail, heedless of his direction. He would explain, and she would understand, and then, and then…

The memory of the small spring made his heard race, spreading the warmth through his limbs all the way to his stomach. It made him shiver, but smile too. Oh, he would make love to her, and he would not leave her for so long again. He would take her along to Onondaga Town despite what the people might think or say. Her family or not, if she wanted to come, she'd do just that, and he would not be the one trying to stop her. She was a worthwhile partner, as useful and important as Hionhwatha himself, maybe, even if in a different way.

Yes, tomorrow he'd go to the Onondagas, whether his current allies agreed with him or not. Would it be wise to travel there with an ample escort like this time or would he and Tekeni do better sailing alone, like in the good old times? The Onondagas were still the enemy, and until they reached Hionhwatha, they would be vulnerable, subject to attack. Yet, if he came to High Springs in the head of the delegation composed of three surrounding nations, escorted by several dozen warriors… An alluring prospect. Very tempting, indeed. Oh, this would make the stubborn Onondagas listen more readily, already prepared by Hionhwatha and softened. A few speeches, a few meetings with the local leaders, and they would be ready to head for Onondaga Town, to confront its ominous leader.

He tucked his blanket tighter as the wind grew upon reaching the end of the trail and the cliff facing a small lake. Eyeing the grayish darkness of the nearing dawn, he briefly wondered how he'd gotten here. With the fresh, smokeless air and the freedom of being alone for a while, he felt the remnants of the dream receding. Why would the sun disappear from the sky in the middle of the day, and why in such dreadful fashion? No, it was not possible. The dream was wrong, or maybe, like other dreams, it was just a fragment, not a vision. He had had no visions since he left his people's lands. He had thought he was done with them.

The darkness rustled, and he leapt aside, his instincts alerting him to the foreign presence before the figures materialized, coming into his view, two or three men beside the bushes, and another one blocking the trail behind his back, their clubs ready, clearly visible in the thinning darkness.

His heart racing, he tore his knife from his sash and waited, hardly daring to breathe, the unfamiliar cliff offering no possibilities of retreat. The silence that prevailed was interrupted by the wailing of the wind alone. The figures didn't move, watching him warily, of that he was sure. If they wanted to kill him, they were in no hurry.

He bettered his grip on the knife, deciding to slash at the nearest man the moment he moved, then to try to deceive his companions into coming closer and, maybe, earning him a chance to push one of them down the cliff.

"You are the Messenger," said one of the men, his words difficult to understand, ringing hoarsely in the swishing of the wind.

It was no question. He stared at them in silence.

"You need to come with us." They were still frozen, surrounding him like stony ghosts, not daring to come closer but not about to leave him in peace.

"Where?" He heard his voice ringing clearly, steady and firm. It pleased him, as his heart raced, thumping in his ears.

They hesitated. "Not far. Our canoes are hidden in the inlet, by their main shore. It's a short walk."

"Why would I do this?" His laughter was loud enough to

shake the air, surprising him as much as it surprised them. He saw them shifting uneasily, even the man at the head of the trail. "Do you take me for a stupid forest rat? If you have anything to say, come with me to our camp and we shall talk."

They hesitated once again, not moving, not clearing the way. But, of course, he did not expect them to do that. People do not track a person in the darkest of the night to talk in a regular fashion.

"We need you to come with us. Our prominent men want to see you." Their accent was terrible, worse than that of the Swamp People.

"Who are you?" He tried to play for time, watching them carefully, wishing the dawn would come faster. His people would be waking up soon, and Tekeni would notice him missing, turning suspicious and rushing to search for him right away.

"Please come," repeated the man, as though reading his thoughts. "We need to hurry."

He felt his anger beginning to rise. "And what if I refuse? Will you take me there by force? It will cost you a few lives, and the noise it'll create would do no good to the rest of you, those who will manage to survive."

The leading man sighed. "Yes, it may create a trouble and cause us to fail, but we have no choice." He shrugged. "We were asked to bring you down there, to talk to our leaders. I promise that no harm will come to you."

"Who are your leaders? What people do you belong to?"

"The People of the Mountains."

Two Rivers felt his heart missing a beat. Now it was more apparent why he was approached in this way. He took a deep breath.

"How many canoes are waiting there by the shore?"

"Three. We cannot travel those lands in a larger state unless ready to fight, and our message is important."

"Why can't you relate it to me here?"

"This is not my message to relate. I'm just a simple hunter."

The man seemed to be more at ease now, his posture not as tense. "I promise that no harm will come to you. The word of your mission reached our lands, and although not all our leaders are in agreement, some of the people thought it wise to contact you. The gathering in the valley on the lake will be held in a matter of a few dawns, with both leaders from the valleys and this side of our mighty Ge-ne-see River promising to honor it with their presence." The man hesitated. "The leader of our delegation will be able to explain better."

The valley on the lake! He remembered the dream: *the top of the hill, the view of the lake, other hilltops towering on the opposite side.* The urge to run away welled. To charge through the men who blocked his way – let them fight him if they wanted to – anything but to take one step toward the accursed place from the dream. Was that the valley from the Mountain People's lands? He didn't want to know.

Their gazes were upon him, piercing the darkness, tense but expectant, trusting him, after a fashion, their faces barely visible in the darkness, yet now he was certain of their sincerity.

"I will come to talk to your people upon the shore," he said tiredly. "But I promise nothing. The People of the Mountain may have to call another meeting when the time comes. It's possible that neither I, nor my allies may be there in time."

CHAPTER 11

"So tell me, sister." The girl smiled, revealing a row of large, even teeth. "How long were you forced to live among the savages of the Flint?"

"Two moons." Frowning, Onheda took the flat stick off the gash in the maple tree, making sure that not a drop of the precious sap was still seeping. Satisfied, she cleaned her tool and measured the amount of the collected liquid in her jar.

"Two moons is a long time to survive without being adopted," commented the girl, shooting a gaze full of curiosity at Onheda. She bent to pick a greenish strawberry that hid among the bushes and eyed it dubiously before giving it a hesitant bite. "How did you manage to get away?"

"I slipped out in the middle of the night." Absently, Onheda caressed the cut bark, muttering a silent prayer, thanking the old tree for being so generous. Pine, hemlock, elm and basswood were honored, highly esteemed, but the maple trees were the special gift of the Right-Handed Twin himself. Its returning and raising sap let people know that the new span of seasons had truly begun, with the Great Spirits' blessing, benevolence, and goodwill.

The eyes of her companion did not stir, sparkling with expectation. The girl's name was Hanowa, and she was a funny, restless, sweet little thing. "Weren't you afraid to make the matters bad for you by running away?"

Onheda raised her eyebrows. "They didn't seem to take it badly. It's not like their entire warriors' force was chasing me all the way to our lands."

The girl giggled. "That would be a sight I could do without.

And surely you, too." Her eyes sparkled again. "But how did you manage to live there for so long without being adopted?"

"Oh, well..." She fought the urge to tell the stupid fox to mind her own business, proceeding toward the next maple tree, instead. "It was their fault, actually. They took their time. I thought I was adopted, and then, all of a sudden, that annoying woman from that longhouse I lived at told me I was not actually adopted, demanding that I do things to make it happen." Onheda snorted. "Such an annoying ground snake she was!"

"What did she want you to do?"

"Well, all sorts of things. She said I was not adapting well. She wanted me to be nice to people. But I was nice, I was! Not to all of them, but to some." She shrugged. "They were not so bad, all things considered. But not all of them."

"There are quite a few Flint people's women in Onondaga Town," said the girl thoughtfully, fishing a long knife from the basket she carried. "But our clan has none, so you are lucky, I say. There was this youth — a very good-looking boy! — but he fell in love with a girl from the nearby village, and when the Grandmother of her longhouse agreed, he went to live there." The girl laughed. "To the deep disappointment of more than a few cute-looking foxes from all over the town, I say. He was truly good-looking and nice. I would have fallen for him myself had he not been from our longhouse." Another bout of laughter. "I bet you would be running back to your High Springs if he were still there. You must hate them all truly badly, to take such a terrible risk like running away."

Taking the knife from her chatty companion, Onheda hesitated, studying the tree.

"I don't hate them all. I met good Flint People, too. In fact, I have a truly good friend among them." She scanned the bark closely, looking for signs. "He was captured too, and he lived among the Crooked Tongues, imagine that. He ran away too, and now he is back in his Little Falls."

But maybe not anymore, she thought hopefully, her stomach twisting. Maybe he is on his way here, he and the Crooked

Tongues man, rowing against the current, hurrying to visit her people, to bring them the message of the Great Peace, hurrying to find her like he promised. What would he do when he heard that she was not at Jikonsahseh's? Would he be disappointed? Hurt? She hoped he would.

"Among the Crooked Tongues?" cried out the girl, aghast. "Oh, Mighty Spirits! I would take my own life if captured by those savages."

"They are no savages," said Onheda, returning her attention to the tree she was scanning. "Didn't you hear about the Messenger?"

"Yes, of course." The girl caressed the wet bark, tapping it lightly, searching for the best place to cut. "Who hasn't heard about the Messenger of the Great Spirits in the stone canoe?"

"He will come here shortly, you know?"

The gaze her companion shot sideways made Onheda uncomfortable. They were in the middle of the grove, not inside the town's fence even.

"Well, he may not be welcomed here too eagerly," muttered the girl finally. "He may do better going elsewhere."

"Elsewhere? I happen to know about his mission, and I can tell you that if he goes elsewhere, our people will be made sorry. Deeply sorry. We will pay a terrible price."

The girl refused to look up, but her palm tapping the tree froze. "What do you mean, sister?"

"Just what I said. If he goes elsewhere, we will be left alone, facing our enemies united and powerful."

Taking a deep breath, she reminded herself to be careful and patient, not to get carried away explaining the obvious over and over again. She had had such talks with quite a few women by now, mainly the dwellers of the longhouse she had resided at, but also some of their guests. The family who had sheltered her seemed to be making it their business to invite as many people as they could, and then to prompt her to talk, about the Messenger and her time spent among the strangers.

It was Hionhwatha's doing, she knew, not resenting her

newfound duty, but actually enjoying it. She was helping, helping for real. She was reaching people, and if not changing their minds, she was, at least, making them think, preparing the most difficult of places for *him*, when he would deign to appear.

"Think about it," she said, bettering her grip on the knife, reading to make a cut. It needed to be two or three fingers deep and, at least, a palm long. Otherwise, the sap would be difficult to collect. "The eastern nations, the Flint People and the Standing Stone People, already accepted the message, so I hear. They are united now. After the snows melted, they welcomed the Messenger and listened to his words. They stopped fighting and followed him, and now they are together, not enemies but brothers. Think about it. What do you think will happen if we refuse to listen to the news of the Great Peace? Will we manage to face our enemies united?"

"No one can best our warriors," the girl cried out, forgetting to lower her voice for a change. "No one!"

Onheda smiled gently. "Don't be not so sure about that." Disregarding the resentful look shot at her, she bent to apply her stick to the cut up bark, prompting the sweet juice to start seeping. "The Messenger carries the words of the Right-Handed Twin himself. He wants us to stop fighting. He wants us to make peace with our neighbors to the east, and maybe to the west, as well. He wants us to live together and to prosper, working our fields without fear, without the need to keep our watch and run back into our towns upon every alert. He wants us to live our lives the way the Right-Handed Twin intended for us in the first place. The Great Spirits are displeased, watching us ruining the world of their creation."

The girl said nothing, bringing her jar when Onheda's became full.

"Did you truly meet the Messenger?" she asked finally, careful to speak in a low voice again.

"Yes, I have."

"And how is he? I mean, what does he look like? How does he speak? What did he tell you?"

Onheda hid her smile. Since coming here to Onondaga Town – was it only ten dawns ago? – she had encountered this question often enough, of course, while talking about him and his mission. Always careful, she would disclose very little, telling only general things; yes, he was an impressive person, probably not a mortal man at all; yes, he had been talking to her, about the peace among the people, about the displeasure of the Great Spirits; yes, he was to come to their lands soon, but she wouldn't know when, the Messenger of the Right-Handed Twin was to come when the time was right.

Hionhwatha had been insistent and clear. She was not to let people know about her real connection with Two Rivers. Not that she had any inclination to gossip about her state of affairs with that man, anyway.

"He said what I told you just now. He said it's time we stop warring."

The girl's eyes were as round as a pair of wooden plates. "But what is it like to speak to him? Did he let you talk back to him?"

"Well, yes, of course. He is kind, not forbidding or rude. Of course he let me talk to him."

"What did you tell him?"

The familiar twisting in her stomach was back, squeezing her insides, making her chest heavy with longing.

"I asked him questions." She hesitated, looking around in her turn, seeing nothing but the clearness of the crisp morning and the trees swaying with the light breeze. "I didn't want to accept his message in the beginning, either."

"You didn't?" Hanowa gasped, bringing her palms up to cover her mouth. "And what did he do? Did he grow angry? Did he bring lightning down on you?"

Against her will, Onheda laughed. "He did grow impatient at some point, yes. But as the time passed, I came to know him, and well, then I understood. He is incredibly wise, wiser than anyone you've ever met. There are no people like him."

"Oh, I wish he would come already. I would like to get a glimpse of him." The spark was back, lighting the glittering eyes. "Tell me what he looks like? Is he old? He must be old, no?" The know-it-all look was creeping in, impossible to miss. Onheda fought the urge to cover her cheeks, which felt suspiciously hot. "Oh, sister, don't tell me! He is not old, is he? Does he look good?"

"Stop being silly, Hanowa!" Now it was her turn to cry out, frustrated. "He is the Messenger of the Right-Handed Twin. His looks have nothing to do with it."

"So he *is* good-looking!" exclaimed the girl, triumphant. "Tell me more!"

"No, I won't tell you. You are too silly!" Furious, Onheda pulled the stick off, seeing a few precious drops of the sap dripping out of their full jars.

"And you think you are so important because you talked to this man?" This time her companion's eyes sparkled angrily. "Well, you are not. Maybe he'll dare to come here, maybe he won't. Or maybe our leaders will prove more powerful than he is. But in any case, he will probably not remember you at all. So stop thinking you are better than anyone else!"

Enraged, Onheda was about to flare at the stupid rat with more cutting, poison-dripping words, but the sense of being on a mission prevailed. She didn't come to Onondaga Town to pick fights and alienate people. She could have stayed at home to do that.

"I'm not thinking that I'm better than you, or anyone else," she said, taking a deep breath, despising the silly fox, but suppressing the feeling. "I just think that we should take the message of the Great Spirits and their messenger seriously. Whether women or men." Narrowing her eyes, she studied the jar. "We should think about the future of our towns and people. Not about his looks or whether he suggests something that is slightly different from our customs and traditions, you see?"

The girl smiled reluctantly. "Yes, I see. I'm sorry. I didn't mean to say that you are not important. I just grew angry when you said I was silly."

And you are, you are silly, reflected Onheda, but kept this thought well hidden, picking another jar from her basket. "I can't wait for the ceremony to begin. I haven't danced for moons!"

"Do you dance well?" Hanowa's glance was dubious, her hands busy arranging the content of her basket. "They don't let just anyone in, not until the Strawberry Festival. This Thanksgiving Ceremony of Maple Tree is for the sprits alone. Only girls who know the proper way to dance and who can wear, at least, a few pairs of turtle shells can participate."

"I know that. I'm not a foreigner, remember? I come from High Springs. Important... town... Onondaga...people," she added, imitating heavily accented speech of Crooked Tongues. It made her feel better.

They laughed and proceeded toward another maple tree, making sure the cuts they made were deep enough to give them wonderful sap aplenty, but not too vicious to wound the revered trees. All forest giants deserved respect, but maples were revered and thanked profusely, with silent prayers offered each time it gave people of its wonderful juices, to be enjoyed for the whole span of seasons, as sweetener, energizer, medicine, and what-not.

"I've never even been to High Springs, let alone to the foreign lands," said Hanowa dreamily, as the sun climbed higher and higher. "You must tell me how it is."

"Where? In High Springs?"

"No!" The girl laughed again, then threw a branch at Onheda, who avoided being hit out of an instinct. "You behave like a warrior, you know that? You ducked as though I threw a spear at you."

"If you are throwing spears this way..." Onheda faked a laugh, not wishing to get into a tale of her battle experience, remembering the fighting upon Onondaga Lake and what she did to save the scar-faced youth. The mere memory of it still made her shudder. And later that day, *him* and the two warriors on Hionhwatha's clearing, when she brought the spear and watched him fencing, faking moves, making the man with the club make mistakes. She still needed to lean against something when she remembered what happened next.

"You saw battles, didn't you?" The girl's voice broke into her thoughts. "I mean when you were captured, obviously. But later on too, no?"

"When I was captured there was not much of a battle. We were nothing but a bunch of silly women sailing our lake with only two men as an escort."

The pair of wide-open eyes was upon her again. "How was it? I mean, what did it feel like to be captured? It must have been horrible."

"It was."

"Did they kill many?"

"Well, yes." Onheda studied the patterns upon the jar that she had picked up, readying to start filling it. Once upon a time those memories would make her shudder, turning her insides into stone. Now, they were nothing but recollection. So much had happened since! "Our men fought well, so they got killed and not captured. And some of the women, too." She shrugged again, willing the rising dread away. "Still, they managed to tie the three of us."

"Did they… did they force you?" Now the girl was studying the ground.

"No, of course not! They wanted us for adoption, and what's the point in forcing a woman who is supposed to live in your own town? She will be an enemy for life."

"Yes, I see." Hanowa's relief was evident, but so was her disappointment. "I just thought how terrible it might be."

"But they wanted to force me into a marriage later on. This was one of the reasons I left. I told them I would not take a man until I was ready to take a man. But that filthy rat, Kwayenda, told me I would not get adopted until I did this. What a dirty, sickness-stricken forest rat this woman was!" Enraged at the mere memory, Onheda kicked a stone and watched it rolling against the muddy ground.

"But you had a man in your life, hadn't you?" The girl's

curiosity knew no bounds. "You are not young."

"Yes, I had, but it was a long time ago."

"What happened to him?"

"He died in a raid. He was a great warrior."

"And you knew no man since then?"

Startled, Onheda stared at the round, well-meaning face, feeling her cheeks beginning to burn anew. "What?"

"When did your man die?" Hanowa's eyes were all innocence.

"It was two spans of seasons ago, and it's none of your business what I did since then!"

"You get mighty upset, sister." There was again that glitter in the girl's eyes, her smile suggestive, full of mischief. "I'm sure your story would not shame the best of the storytellers, but you are as touchy as a mother bear with newborn cubs. Not a natural storyteller."

"And I don't presume to be that, anyway. Let us finish collecting the sap before the women of your longhouse get angry with us for lingering. They need some of it for the ceremony today."

With the tones from the flute peaking, the drums began fading away, now just the background, throbbing, rolling softly, intermingling with the rustling of the rattles. The flute dominated, as though maintaining the sacred fire all alone, to shimmer under the maple tree on the edge of the ceremonial ground, along with the murmuring of the turtle shells upon the legs of the dancers.

Onheda did not try to suppress her happiness, lost in the music, floating, her spirit soaring with no connection to her body, giving her and her people's thanks to the benevolent spirits of the Sky World. The maple sap was the first gift the creators sent to the people after the long, stern winter moons; a wonderful gift that needed thanks offered for it. Hence the ceremony with the sacred fire, the sacred dances, and plenty of tobacco offerings.

Oh, it was so wonderful to dance again, the weight of four pairs of turtle shells tied to her upper legs not hindering her movement, the rhythm of their beat giving her feet more strength. She was able to handle twice the amount of shells, but since she had not participated in the ceremonial dancing for almost two spans of seasons, the Porcupine Clan woman responsible for the society of dancers decided it would be best to start with four pairs, like a new girl.

There was strength to this claim too, so Onheda didn't argue. Aside from maybe losing some of her skill due to the lack of practice, the skin of her thighs was softer now, not used to the rattles and the leather straps that tied it to the leg. It would be covered with sores if she tried to go for the acceptable amount right away. But oh, Mighty Spirits, it was good to dance again. Through the times of her grief when her man died, and the moons of her captivity, followed by her self-imposed exile at Jikonsahseh's, she'd forgotten how wonderfully healing, fulfilling, and gratifying the ceremonial dancing was.

Her troubles forgotten, she just floated, connected with the music and the smoke and the magical chanting, letting her spirit go straight up to the Sky World and the Great Spirits themselves, carrying her prayers, her private prayers too, asking for help and guidance, and for, maybe, a little bit of private happiness as well.

Sensing the dancers slowing down with the fading beat of the drums, she shook her head, feeling as though awakening from a dream. The Faith-Keeper of one of the clans was talking, thanking the Great Spirits for the gift of life. Beside him, other important people of the town stood rigid, the members of the council, the War Chief and his aides, other prominent leaders, followed by the Clans Mothers, watching the sacred fire, their offerings ready.

Still under the spell, Onheda studied them until her gaze met a pair of dark, deeply set eyes that measured her openly, full of cold, slightly surprised interest. Shuddering, she fought the urge to step back, taking in the long, unkempt hair set on a large head, the exaggeratedly wide shoulders, the withered right arm pressed tightly against the man's broad chest. Tadodaho, the War Chief and the unofficial leader of Onondaga Town, the man responsible for as many deaths of her own country-folk as those of the enemy warriors.

Her heart skipped a beat, then threw itself against her ribs. He was studying her. Why?

The Faith-Keeper was still speaking, his voice monotonous, tranquil, pleasing the ear. She could feel the people listening and the dancers drawing away, melting into the crowds. The War Chief's eyes left her, but her back was covered with cold sweat as he was still close, standing along with the other dignitaries, his presence repressing, making the breathing more difficult, her instincts screaming danger.

Since coming to Onondaga Town, she had seen Tadodaho once or twice, from far away, strolling between the longhouses and along the alleys, always in a hurry, not answering people's greetings. Safe in doing so, she used to study him, trying to understand him, to learn the enemy, to find his weakness, maybe. It wasn't dangerous to do this. She was nothing but an insignificant girl, a stranger in this town, just a part of the scenery. But now, all of a sudden, that man was very near, and aware of her, curiously interested. His eyes told her that, as they brushed past her again, before she dived into the safety of the crowds, her festive dancer's attire uncomfortably colorful, drawing attention, not allowing her to blend into the crowd, the shells still tied to her legs rustling with every step.

Her heart thumping, she tried to go away, but the people surrounded her, standing still, listening. To push them out of her way would be rude, truly bad manners. And it would draw more attention. She willed her hands to stop trembling.

When the thanksgiving speech ended and the crowds began moving toward the food, she was calm again, except the pounding of her heart. What was there to be afraid of? She'd done nothing untoward by dancing at the ceremony. The War Chief had noticed her, but only because of the dance. He must have forgotten all about her by now.

"Let us help you out of the rattles, girls," said the woman from the dancers' society. "Come, hurry up, before they eat all the food."

The other girls giggled, talking excitedly, but Onheda just nodded when addressed, anxious to get away from the ceremonial ground. Just in case.

"You danced so well." This time it was her hostess, a pleasant looking woman in her thirties, with her face as round as a full moon and as friendly. Her name was Gwayeah and Onheda had grown to like her a great deal, pleased to share her compartment in the longhouse, despite the presence of a silent, not especially friendly husband and two noisy, mischievous boys. "I didn't know you were a professional dancer."

"It was a long time ago," said Onheda, following the woman toward the delicious smell coming out of the boiling pots, relieved to move around without rustling with every step.

"But you danced on the ceremonies?"

"Yes, I love dancing. I was trained since I was very young."

"Oh, I wanted to be a dancer, too." Her companion smiled, revealing a row of large, beautiful teeth. "But the Grandmother of our longhouse thought I was hopeless." She laughed, navigating their way in the crowds. "So I have to make do with social dances when even the small kids are allowed to join."

"The Grandmother of our longhouse insisted, so I had to practice when the other girls were out playing. It was not such a joy, either."

Smiling in her turn, Onheda looked around, seeing that most of the men were already served, standing in groups or seated comfortably on clusters of mats. Meeting some of their gazes, she looked away. It was silly of her to draw so much attention by participating in the dance. She needed to change her clothes, and soon.

"I would switch with you, nevertheless. I still want to dance like you, dressed in pretty colors, with rattles tied to my legs, making beautiful sounds."

"It's heavy and not always comfortable."

"You looked comfortable enough up there beside the sacred fire." Pushing her way more forcefully now, Gwayeah shook her head. "They are going to leave us with nothing but leftovers, stew with no meat."

"I don't mind."

With their plates finally full, they made their way toward one of the groups, surrounded by laughter and lively chatter, the mood of the townsfolk bubbling with well-being. The amount of the collected sap promised a good stock for a whole span of seasons, enough to make plenty of sweeteners for food and medicine for aching stomachs. The Great Spirits were generous, smiling upon Onondaga people.

"We'll be out cleaning the fields in a dawn or so," one of the leading women of their longhouse was saying. "With the weather holding on, it might be the time."

Onheda could see Hanowa making a face, winking at the other girls, but she didn't mind the work. Being in the fields would give her more opportunities to talk to people, women of this clan, and maybe some others, too. So far, she was satisfied with the results. Even if carefully, guiltily, they were listening to her, most surely talking to their men in their turn, making them wait for the Messenger, too.

"But not before we collect more maple," said Gwayeah. "The Great Spirits are generous to us this span of seasons, so we should not let their gift go unwanted."

"We can split." The first woman shrugged. "Some will start preparing the fields, some will go on collecting the sap."

"Oh, yes, I know in what group I want to be," whispered Hanowa, leaning close to Onheda. "Not clearing fields!"

Turning to watch the argument peaking among the men, Onheda remembered licking the sweet juice of the trees, cleaning their sticks, allegedly. Yes, the fields offered no treats this time of the planting season. It was a work with no small rewards.

"High Springs may think they are so important as to try and tell us what to do," one of the men on the nearest cluster of mats exclaimed, waving his hands. "But they are nothing but a large village. How dare they presume to question the decisions of our wise leaders?"

"A village they are not, brother," said someone, shrugging. "Even if they have the temerity to make you angry."

"Well, we are not a village, either! And yet they want to take the lead, don't they?" The angered man waved his hands again, refusing to notice the attempt to lighten the mood. "This is an outrage. In the light of what is going on in the lands of our despicable enemies, we need to unite, but instead, we are quarreling, refusing to settle under a good, renowned leadership. It will be us fighting against each other instead of the enemy in the end."

"When some leaders are more concerned with old grievances and grudges, what can you expect from smaller settlements and clans?"

"It's High Springs' fault," exclaimed the first man again. "By letting Hionhwatha in, they showed us that they are rivals and no brothers to us. They declared war!"

"You are taking it too far, brother." Putting a comforting hand on the angry man's back, an older warrior sighed. "Such words are dangerous to utter, such thoughts dangerous to let in. Trust our leaders to settle their differences. They will not let us down, and they will not let the foreigners come here and poison our minds."

There was a fleeting pause, the silence heavy, disturbing. Onheda's heart made wild leaps inside her chest.

"Did you mean the mysterious stranger in the stone canoe?" whispered someone, shooting a wary gaze at the other groups of eating people.

"Any foreigners, anyone!" said the older warrior firmly.

"But did you hear about the man with the stone canoe?" The

man looked around again, lowering his voice, forcing Onheda
to come closer, the silly chattering of the women interfering
with her ability to listen. "They say he was the one to bring
Hionhwatha out of the woods. They say he can do more than
just sail a stone vessel."

"Oh, yes," said another man. "I heard he was killed by the
eastern savages, but that he came back, alive and well, on the
next morning."

Their food forgotten, the men peered at the speaker, their
eyes wide. "How?"

"No one knows. That hunter from the village upon the
Great Sparkling Water told me all about it. He said they had
thrown him into the most vicious waterfalls you have ever seen,
and they saw him drowning with their very eyes, bashing his
head on the rocks."

"And then what happened?"

Onheda found herself holding her breath, like they all did.

"They promised to do his bidding if he came back the next
morning. And what do you think happened?" The man
encircled his audience with a piercing gaze, clearly enjoying
himself.

"He came back the next morning?" breathed a young warrior
in the end.

"Oh, yes, that he did. Dry and well-clothed, displaying not a
scratch, as though he had never dived into those rapids at all."
Another gaze, pregnant with meaning. "Since then, they are
doing whatever he tells them to do."

"The Standing Stone people?"

"I wish it was them!"

"The savages of the Flint?" It came out as a collective gasp.

"Well, let them think they are strong enough to come here
and try something stupid. Our leaders are no children also, and
some of them have powers beyond the obvious. That wonder
from the foreign lands may find it difficult to take our towns,
miracles or not."

"He doesn't want to take our towns."

She heard the words coming from her own mouth, loud and clear, impossible to stop. It surprised her as much as it surprised them.

They all turned to stare as the women around her fell silent, their merry chattering dying away. She fought the urge to step back, or to shoot a quick glance at her surroundings. To apologize and sneak away was still a possibility.

"I met the Messenger when he came here for the first time, before the snows. He came to bring peace, not war. He wants us to unite and live in peace." Her voice rang clearly, not trembling or shrill, and it surprised her. She felt as if she were walking in a fog, with nothing to hold onto and no possibility to see her way. "He will come here, yes, before the hot moons. But he will not come to war. He will ask us to join the peace. The Right-Handed Twin himself sent him."

The din of the other feasting people seemed to fade, as though the whole town were listening to her. It made her skin crawl, this heavy silence and their astounded gazes, boring into her, piercing.

"Who are you?" asked one of the older men in the end.

And then Gwayeah was beside her, her presence warm, reassuring. "Oh, she is a guest of my family. The sweet girl spent horrendous time in captivity and now she is here, resting, gathering her strength."

There was an unspoken message in the hurriedly uttered words, and it angered Onheda. Yes, she was not wise to burst into the men's discussion, but what she said was true, not to be dismissed as the blabbering of the deranged, silly woman who had seen too much hardship in her life.

"What I say is true," she said stubbornly, refusing to drop her gaze and go back as she had clearly been expected to.

"Did you truly meet the Messenger?" asked one of the younger warriors, whose eyes were upon her for some time, fascinated.

"Yes, I've met him, and he has spoken to me. He brings an important message that should be listened to."

"Oh, and what *is* his message?" A new voice tore the silence, and the people shuddered, turning toward the newcomer, as frightened as children caught doing mischief.

Tadodaho did not bother to come closer, standing on the edge of the group, surrounded by a few of his closest aides, minor leaders of the warriors and some people from the Town Council. His voice was calm, slightly amused, and yet there was a threatening tone to it. Or maybe it was the way he stood there, his legs wide apart, arms crossed upon his barrel of a chest, hiding the withered hand, his shoulders as wide as logs, his eyes squinted, peering at her as though she were a bothersome insect to be squished out of the way. It made her legs tremble.

The wide lips twisted into a hint of a grimly amused smile. "Don't be afraid, girl. Tell us about the message of your wondrous foreigner. I'm sure he must have been a good orator, to make you and your like, even the savages from the east, listen. Even my previous colleague, our glorious Hionhwatha, has fallen under the foreigner's spell, so I hear. Although, I suppose it's not such a difficult feat to sway the mind of a deranged man." Another heavy glance. "Do tell us about this man."

She felt as if she were in a dream, like a rabbit staring at the huge snake, mesmerized, her danger signals up, screaming, running through her skin, making it tickle. It was a frightening sensation, but also strangely pleasant, making her blood come alive. She was no rabbit.

"This man is not a foreigner, but the Messenger of the Great Spirits, the Right-Handed Twin himself. Everyone whom he met listened to him. Everyone! People and nations, towns and villages. The east is united now, and when he comes here, we will join him too, because we can displease the Great Spirits no longer."

As the amusement fled from the broad, slightly misshapen face, she saw it hardening, turning to stone. The squinted eyes narrowed even more, taking a darker shade.

"You took it upon yourself to interpret the foreigner's words in a way no girl of your status is allowed to do. You are a young woman with no skill and no training to know about the will of the Great Spirits. You can be punished for presuming to preach to your elders and betters, do you realize this, dancer girl?" His eyes bore into her, glowing fiercely, burning her skin like a pair of blistering coals. "Did you come here to Onondaga Town to bring us this irrational message? Who sent you?"

She tried to collect her thoughts, which were rushing about like squirrels, in panicked circles.

"No one. I came here on my own." It was difficult to recognize her own voice now, so low and broken it sounded. She cleared her throat. "I didn't come to preach, but I do think we need to listen to the Messenger."

"What you think is of no consequence to the leading people of our nation." The man turned his head slightly, measuring his audience through the squinted eyes, looking down his aquiline nose as though towering above them, although he was shorter than many. "Do we need the foreigners to tell us how to live? Do we need the eastern enemy, coming here as though owning our forests, directing us, giving us orders, telling us how to manage our affairs because some enterprising foreigner has made them unite between themselves? Are we nothing but clueless children? We, the People of the Hills, the strongest nation on either side of the Great Sparkling Water. Are we that weak, that defenseless, that desperate?"

People murmured, their frowns deep, shifting uneasily under the dark gaze of the fierce leader.

"We are proud and powerful. For many spans of seasons, we've kept our neighbors in fear and our heads held high. We do not need foreigners to tell us how to live our lives, neither enemies nor friends. We do not need the traitors among our own people, neither insignificant women nor deranged former leaders who could not even be trusted in their better days. Don't we know how to please the Great Spirits? Don't we see their goodwill manifested in bountiful harvests and plentiful forest fruit?"

The dark gaze was back upon her, making her legs jelly. "I suggest you go back where you came from, strange girl. You dance well, but this is your only way to connect with the spirits. You talk nonsense, and your understanding of life and war is like that of a forest squirrel. Take this well-meaning advice from your elder and better. Keep your thoughts to yourself, or better yet, change your mind and stop thinking of strange foreigners and the ridiculousness of their words."

His steps ranged heavily as he walked away, resounding against the dry earth, bringing up clouds of dust.

Onheda just stared, her limbs still frozen, but tickling now, coming back to life. It was as though a mountain lion, or a huge mature wolf, had stood there a heartbeat earlier, pondering her worth for his next meal, calm and in control, not crazed with hunger, just contemplating, turning away eventually, not reaching any decision, not yet. The immediate danger was over, but she would be a fool to think herself safe, and a fool she was not.

CHAPTER 12

The lake glittered merrily in the soft morning light, reflecting the rays of the strengthening sun. Seketa hugged her knees, curling in the relative safety of the bushes, fighting the urge to come out in an attempt to catch some of its warmth. She was cold, but not like the night before, frozen and desperate under the beating rain and the cutting wind of the storm that raged on and on, for most of the day and the night.

It was bad enough to be lost in the endless mass of the Great Sparkling Water, drifting for three days, sunburned and hungry, giving up on the hope to make it to the other side alive, between the warrior's grim, ever-scowling presence with his short, cutting remarks and the stench of the blood and other smelly discharges coming out of his wounds, and the constant sobbing of his sister, curled on the bottom of the boat, not helping at all, just a burden, a silly fox.

Shuddering, she peered into the clearness of the water, relishing the sensation of being on the firm ground again. Even if lost, cold, and dizzy with exhaustion and hunger, and in the heart of the enemy's lands, she was still alive, although she had given up on the hope through the second day of the crossing, when the sun had begun diving into the water once again. At that point, she knew she was going to die, to shrivel and weaken, eventually to fall asleep and never wake up again, a lifeless form in the endless mass of water, to drift until their canoe would sink and nothing would be left, not even a memory.

But maybe when he came to the town, to kidnap her as he promised, she had thought, curling on the bottom of their boat, the sobs of the other girl not irritating her anymore, giving up on the rowing long since, maybe he would guess, somehow. He would find out that she had not broken her promise, had not taken another man into her life, even though she didn't wait, and so maybe he would not be too angry, remembering her for the good things she did, the only person to remember.

However then, on the dawn of the third day, the water flow had changed, turned brighter, swirling with currents, and Sgenedu, already a shadow of the warrior she had helped to escape only six or seven dawns ago, his face glistening with sweat and his eyes with fever, came back to life, renewing the rowing, muttering about the proximity of the land somewhere behind the merciless glow.

Paddling again, putting all her strength into it, helped Seketa to come back to life as well, and so, toward the second part of the day, they had found themselves climbing the bank with the last of their strength, exhausted, starving but happy, smiling foolishly at each other.

"We did it, Crooked Tongues girl," he had exclaimed, helping her up, although his wounded leg did nothing to support him anymore. Desperate to steady himself, he clutched onto the trunk of the tree as though his life depended on it, before fishing his sister out of the boat. "And I must say, you are quite a woman."

And although dizzy with exhaustion and not liking the way he kept calling her by this unpleasant sounding epithet, she beamed back at him, elated. She was on the other side of the Great Lake, *on Tekeni's side*. She had made it across the Great Sparkling Water, and she would find him now, no matter what. She would let nothing stand in her way.

However, their troubles were far from being over, she had discovered, when Sgenedu, his exhaustion and sickness that he had forced down with the sheer power of his will prevailing, had left them hiding in the nearby grove and went scanning the countryside. Yes, they had made it to the other side, he had told them grimly upon his return, but they had drifted too far westward, landing upon the shores belonging to the People of the Swamp, curse their eyes into the underworld of the Evil Twin and his minions.

"Who are those people?" whispered Seketa, greatly perturbed.

"More of the filthy enemy," he said, cursing again. "Not as disgustingly bad as your Flint People, but bad enough." He took a deep breath, sliding against the wide trunk of an old tree, drained of the last of his strength. "We'll wait until nightfall, then we go eastward," he muttered, closing his eyes. "And we will hurry."

However, she was not about to take orders from him, venturing into the woods and gathering some early berries, wild onions, and ground nuts. And then, disregarding his protests, she made a small fire and boiled the onions and the fruits into a decent tasting brew, for them to drink and maintain their life forces, if only a little.

The fire had also kept them warm, and as the night fell, all three of them felt reluctant to abandon the grove, craving a good night's sleep beside the warm glow, but the forceful warrior prevailed, and they traveled through the whole night, and another day, until the storm caught them, as though not enough foes had befallen them so far. And now, here she was, trying to warm herself upon the shores of this long, misty lake, too tired to be afraid of being detected by whoever might roam these shores, with both her companions being in a bad shape, the warrior by now too sick, and his sister too worried to think sensibly.

"We need to go on," she said finally, to no one in particular. "Do you know this lake? Did we reach your lands already?"

The girl frowned, dipping a piece of cloth she had torn from her skirt in the water, to place upon her brother's burning forehead. "It might be Onondaga Lake. It's so misty. I think, yes, it might be that."

"It *is* Onondaga Lake," groaned the wounded, blinking against the strengthening sun.

"Then we've reached, reached your lands, no?" After so many days in their company she found it less daunting to try and talk their tongue from time to time.

"Yes," whispered Gayoah, beginning to sob again when her brother's eyes closed, making his face look like a wooden mask with no color applied to it.

"Then let us try and find the nearest settlement!" cried out Seketa, jumping to her feet. "There is no use sitting here until he dies." She looked around, then knelt beside the prone man, touching his good, unwounded shoulder. "What towns are situated on this side of that Onondaga Lake?"

He opened his eyes and stared at her blankly.

"What towns?" she repeated, trying to pronounce their foreign-sounding words. "What towns on Onondaga Lake?"

She saw him concentrating with an effort. "What side are we on?" he whispered finally.

"Oh, well," she glanced at the sun, which was glowing to their right now, at a sharp angle. "We are on the southern side of it, I think. And closer to the east than to the west."

His nod was almost imperceptible. "Onondaga Town... it's not far. We are on the right side."

"How far?"

He shook his head lightly. "Not far. Less than half a day of walk."

Half a day of walk? Oh, Mighty Spirits! How were they to drag the half-conscious man for such a long journey, two starved, exhausted, and frightened women?

She got to her feet briskly. "Well, then, that's the plan. Gayoah, help me to lift him up. We will walk as long as we can, then we'll rest, and walk again. By nightfall, we'll be at Onondaga Town."

The tearful eyes clung to her, irritating in their unconcealed doubt and fear.

"Come! He needs to see a healer or he'll die. So get on with it, and I don't want to hear you crying. One moan and I will leave you two here in the woods to do as you please. I will go on alone, never think I won't!"

The terrified gaze was her answer. She paid it no attention, leaning toward the wounded, shaking his shoulder once again.

"We need to bring you to Onondaga Town, so please try to hold on," she said as he peered at her, his eyes glittering with fever, trying to focus. "Need walk. Until reach Onondaga Town. Please try." His nod reassured her, so she helped him up, staggering under his weight, her memories welling. This was just the way she had helped Tekeni to walk on that terrible evening when they had sailed away and left her behind. Oh, how stupid she was back then. She should have insisted on coming along, Two Rivers or not. The two of them would have prevailed, would have made the formidable man agree. She should have listened to her, and her chosen mate's, hearts; instead, she had yielded to the authority of the man now half of this side of the Great Lake seemed to be listening to. Or was it not him after all?

Shaking her head to get rid of the disturbing thoughts, she struggled to help the wounded find his balance. "Help me, for all the great and small *uki*'s sake!" she hissed at Gayoah. "Stop being so useless!"

Grinding her teeth, she glared at the girl, regretting the decision to take the silly thing along at all, getting angrier when the clumsy fox slipped in, stumbling, making the three of them sway. She would have done better dumping the silly mouse in her people's longhouse and helping her brother escape all alone. He was a bad-tempered piece of rotten meat, but useless he was not. Wounded and sick, he had still managed to bring them across the Great Sparkling Water and to the lands of his people. And maybe, just maybe…

She pushed the tempting thoughts away. Maybe he would feel grateful enough to help her look for their mysterious messenger in a stone canoe and his fierce companion full of scars. Tekeni might have been scarred after that evening. He had been cut badly enough.

Oh Mighty Spirits, oh the Right-Handed Twin, please let me find them, she prayed. *I will offer to you every morning, as long as I live. I will have a small plot of tobacco, no matter where I'll dwell, and I will tend it myself, and I will offer you the best of its fragrant smoke. I will do only good, working the land and living according to your guidance. Please, let me find him and let me be with him.*

CHAPTER 13

The current rushed strongly, gushing between the towering hills, filling Tekeni's heart with fear. Crouching in the back of their canoe, clutching his paddle so tightly his palms went numb, he held his breath every time the boat jerked, bouncing between the protruding rocks, turning sharply, leaping to avoid yet another hazard, offering possibilities of an inevitable crush.

They would end up in the water, fighting for their lives in the angrily hissing sprays, he knew. All of them, the suspicious, unfriendly hosts and the reluctant, distrustful guests in their array of narrow canoes, too narrow and unstable for this turbulent flow. But of course! When, in the beginning of this moon, they had headed out for the gathering of the Swamp People, they didn't plan to invade the intimidating mountains of their neighbors to the west.

He stifled a reluctant grin. Who would have thought that Two Rivers would go back to his old ways, gambling and taking risks in the best of the reckless fashion, as though they were still alone, wandering the shores of the Great Sparkling Water, bluffing more times than not, having nothing to lose but their lives. As though they had no backing of the three powerful nations now, enjoying the prominent, leading position, advancing slowly and carefully, working around the ever-arising problems, bringing the great Crooked Tongues man's vision to life against all the odds.

Shaking his head, he blinked in the drizzle to clear his vision. Less than one span of seasons, and here they were, listened to, respected, revered even, followed and assisted so readily that it all looked like a dream, too good to be true. Some nights he would lie sleepless, staring into the sky, watching the stars, asking for their guidance. It was all working out perfectly, all but one thing, one very important mission. Planting Moon was almost over, the last moon of the Awakening Season. The summer would be upon them soon, and she would not continue waiting for so long. He could not expect her to do that, with not a word from him, not a hint as to even the simplest knowledge of him being dead or alive, intending to come back or not.

Oh, Mighty Spirits! His time was running out, and he was still here, still busy, always so near, but never actually doing it, never taking his canoe to cross the Great Lake on his own, always about to finish one more task, one more mission before embarking upon this most important of his enterprises. Two Rivers needed him, yes, but Seketa needed him too, and he had been sacrificing her for the sake of the Great Man's vision over and over, waiting for the right time. Recently, he began to fear that the right time would never come.

"Keep to the middle." A sharp cry tore him from his unhappy thoughts, bringing him back into the dubious reality of raging water and the grim enemy warriors all around, guiding them into the heart of the enemy land. *Why had Two Rivers insisted on coming here?*

Paddling with all his strength, he didn't even try to look forward, knowing that he would see nothing but the sharp rocks and the angrily spitting water, readying his body to jump out the moment their canoe would be overturned like the empty shell of a ground nut. He only hoped that Two Rivers was as ready to do the same.

Tearing his gaze off the hissing white foam, he caught a glimpse of the Crooked Tongues man, clenching his paddle in the middle of their boat, his eyes narrowed and his jaw clenched, his tension obvious, but why would the Great Man feel at ease? They were in trouble, oh yes, no matter how one chose to look at it, and it was entirely his, Two Rivers', fault. There was no reason to agree to the most strangely put, unacceptable invitation of the fierce foreigners from the hilly west. No reason whatsoever, and yet here they were, riding the wild current, sure to end up in the water, to drown or bash their heads open, breaking their limbs against the gleefully expectant rocks. The foreign river was ready to do the work, sparing the effort for the People of the Mountains, unless they didn't want their guests killed, planning to keep them as hostages instead, the treacherous enemy that they were. After all, there were many important people in this delegation, the Messenger himself, accompanied by enough representatives of the three nations, those who chose to follow against any better judgment. Not to mention the warriors, who were not enough to put up a decent resistance, but enough to keep their prospective captors happy with quite a few execution ceremonies.

"Now we get into this channel!" The man upon the prow turned his head briefly, glancing at his passengers, making sure they understood. "Just row with all your might, and don't let the boat turn back into the main current."

Obediently, Tekeni attacked the water, glad to pit his strength against the powerful flow, enjoying the confrontation. His anger kept gathering, difficult to control, but now he had the means to spill it out, to fight and punish the furious river for its attempt to kill them all.

Their canoe jerked, screeching, its sides grinding against the underwater rocks, titling dangerously. *But oh no*, he thought furiously, pushing yet another sleek surface with his paddle, striking it away. *You are not going to win this. Not this time.* Whatever awaited them at the Mountains People's gathering, they were going to arrive there in one piece and relatively dry. He was going to make sure of that.

Shortly thereafter, a small lake jumped upon them, striking in its tranquility and calm as opposed to the raging current of the river. Grateful, the boats slipped into the safe haven, relieved. Taking a deep breath, Tekeni caught a glimpse of the towering hills on the opposite side, their tops bluish, clouded by puffy fog. It was a breathtaking sight. He shivered, wondering what powerful spirits might be occupying this place.

"We will put our boats in there," said the man on the prow, jumping out and pointing at the small, cozy inlet, separated by a piece of land from the main body of water. "Just signal the other vessels to follow."

They were a small fleet of twenty boats, all those who came here reluctantly, unwilling to let the Messenger go alone. It was a strange thing to watch, how all those people were following the Crooked Tongues man now, almost as loyally as he, Tekeni, did. If the Messenger had found it necessary to visit the Underworld, descending the realm of the Evil Left-Handed Twin, they might have argued but, eventually, they would have come too, because if not, Two Rivers would still go, all alone and unconcerned for his own safety. Typical of the adamant, wild-tempered man!

Leaping into the shallow water, Tekeni lifted the boat along with another man, carrying it to the shore, his heartbeat calming. It was good to reach the safety of the dry land, even if this particular place was not where he wanted to be at the moment. If they had made it out of here alive, he decided, he would insist on bypassing by foot many of the rapids their guides made them sail.

"What a strange place," he muttered, watching the lofty hill that they were clearly expected to ascend, intimidated by the towering mountains on the other side of the lake. There was something strange about this place, about the way the clouds darkened the bright morning sunlight, the way the wind howled in the tops of the trees as though warning them not to proceed, not daring or threatening, but letting them know that something bigger than them was going to happen.

His heart sinking, he took in Two Rivers' wide-open eyes as the man peered at the opposite side of the lake, his face draining of color, twisting with fear. Oh, Mighty Spirits! He had never seen the Crooked Tongues man that openly frightened.

"What's wrong?" he asked quietly, coming closer, unwilling to let the others see what he had glimpsed.

"No, no, everything is well." Two Rivers shook his head, as though trying to get rid of a vision, his face clearing, but the shadows still lurking, refusing to disappear out of the dark, tension-filled eyes.

"Something is wrong. Tell me!"

The man bit his lips. "Everything will be well." Taking a deep breath, he concentrated his gaze, grinning lightly, making Tekeni feel better. "There will be something, something unsettling, if my dreams are to be believed yet again. But we will handle it. Like we handled the test of the falls, eh?"

Tekeni frowned. "We handled the test of the falls because we knew all about it beforehand. We were able to prepare." He peered at the well-familiar face, seeking reassurance. "Is there anything I should know?"

"Well, I had this dream, five nights ago, at the gathering of the Swamp People. And then again. The sun—" He jerked to a stop when their guides and the others neared, their faces presenting a gamut of expressions, from suspicious and doubtful to just sealed, cold, unreadable.

"Let us hurry, honorable visitors," said the man whose skill in navigating had brought them so far, clearly the leader of the local delegation, his multitude of tattoos gleaming eerily. "We have some way to go before we reach the gathering."

"I hope they are expecting us," muttered someone. "Maybe we better send someone to bring them the word of our coming."

"No!" Two Rivers came back to life at once. "We can't wait. We need to hurry."

He measured the sun with his gaze, wincing most visibly once again. It was shining brightly, climbing up its regular path, but there was a tiny shadow on its edge, as though the glaring, sparkling ball had a crack, like a pottery bowl with a broken edge. Tekeni felt his skin crawling for no reason.

"I'm confident they are expecting us," repeated the Crooked Tongues man, standing their puzzled stares, calm and sincere, his impatience well hidden; yet, Tekeni recognized the signs. "I believe we should not leave our prospective allies waiting. Our journey has taken longer than expected, and I would rather we head home no later than the next dawn."

They turned to go, not reassured, neither their allies nor their guides. What was the Great Man's game? Following his friend's sure-footed steps, Tekeni fought his uneasiness. *You always trusted him,* he reminded himself. No matter where they went or for what reason, no matter how wild their spontaneous missions seemed to appear, it turned out to be for the best, always. This man's dreams were powerful, and they never erred.

Perturbed by the eerie silence surrounding the trail they were about to ascend, he glanced at the sun once again. No, there was something wrong with this place.

The silence, it was this silence! It had some ghostly, frightening quality, as though there were no life in those bushes and behind the trees, all those small creatures, always a part of the forest, rustling all around, busy going about their business. Where were they?

He listened intently. Some rustling reached his ears, and the birds were chirping, but hesitantly, as though ready to flee. He remembered crouching behind the small fence, waiting for the bear to appear. Had it happened only one span of seasons ago? It seemed that a lifetime had passed since he curled behind his pitiful cover, terrified and numb, his senses honed, listening to the life gushing all around. There was so much of it, everywhere. Yet, when the bear came, all those small creatures scampered away, diving into the safety of their lairs, leaving him with nothing but the hideous silence interrupted by the buzzing insects alone, too silly or too small to be threatened by the dangerous beast.

Well, the silence around the trail they were climbing now seemed familiar, making him shoot worried glances around. What sort of beast was waylaying them this time? It must have been huge enough to make so many creatures hide in the middle of their usual daily activity. And the sun was still not whole, still lacking its prefect roundness. If anything, its broken edge seemed to grow, eating more of its brightness away. Oh, Mighty Spirits!

The top of the hill was swarming with people, many men, most of them armed, even the elderly among them. Tents spread on the edges of the clearing, with women sweating above the fires, stirring large pots.

"One might think they had been living here since the end of the Cold Moons," muttered Tekeni, his hand caressing the hilt of his club. "Such a homey feeling."

"Lots of warriors in this home, I say," whispered one of their men, a tall, heavyset hunter of the Standing Stone town. "I don't like it. The Messenger should not have agreed to come here."

"He knows what he is doing. He is the Messenger of the Great Spirits. He enjoys their guidance, always." The words helped. He almost believed them himself. Hadn't Two Rivers said something about a dream? But that frightened expression on his face...

Tekeni felt his stomach convulsing. Would his friend be required to do another feat of strength, another demonstration of the divine nature of his mission, like back at Little Falls?

He peered at the tall figure, seeing him standing there, upright and dignified, backed by his followers, not too many, but not too few, either, all those people belonging to the three powerful nations, warriors and elders, representing a considerable force, a true belief in what he had been doing.

The realization that clearly impressed their hosts, too, as they strolled to meet the new arrivals, both leaders in the front, followed by their men, the feathers of their headdresses rustling in the wind, arrogant and aloof but wary as well, not as confident of themselves as they clearly strove to appear. They were on their home ground, all the advantages on their side, thought Tekeni, his stomach churning, his hand going numb from clenching his club with too much force, his senses screaming danger. And yet, they were afraid and uncertain in the face of this man, this foreigner from the lands of the Crooked

Tongues. His allies may have been many, but his personal power was the one to shatter their hostile hosts' confidence. Although to force these people into the alliance would be a difficult feat, their expressions mirroring the unfriendliness of their terrain. And yet, all the same, they were not so certain now, strolling toward the Messenger. No powerful currents and easily defended narrow passages would help them against the divine displeasure. If angered, the Right-Handed Twin might turn his face away, abandoning the People of the Mountains, leaving them with no *Three Sisters* to harvest and no game to hunt. Even now, before the first word was uttered, there was a general sensation of a disaster looming, with the wind getting stronger and colder, and the sunlight dimming as though it were late afternoon and not high morning.

Against his will, Tekeni glanced at the sky, hoping to see Father Sun bright and clear of shadows, knowing that his hope was as slim as their chances to come out of this enterprise alive. Indeed, what he saw made his chest tighten, as the same damaged edge of the blazing circle kept being eaten away by the ominous darkness.

"Greetings, visitors from the east." The deep voice broke the silence in time, bringing Tekeni back from the brink of panic. He blinked, trying to see through the flickering dots dancing before his eyes, as it always happened after staring at the sun directly. Even if eaten away, it was still bright enough to hurt his vision, reassuring in a strange way. "You came a long way, and we are honored by your eagerness to see us."

"Indeed, we came a long way, carrying the message of the Great Spirits." Two Rivers' voice rang somewhat eerily in the strengthening wind. "The Tidings of the Great Peace are upon us. The Creators wish to see our people working together in peace and accord."

"Our people?" The owner of the deep voice turned out to be an imposing, broadly built man of enough summers to make his braided, partially shaved hair look more silver than black. "Our people, or your people, or their people? Whom are you speaking of?"

Tekeni held his breath, trying to understand what was behind Two Rivers' neglect of the opening politeness. Why did he have to anger their not-very-affable hosts any further by dispensing with the greetings and speeches which was customary with every nation, no matter where one went?

"I'm speaking of all peoples, of all creations of the Right-Handed Twin." The dimming air seemed to thicken, difficult to breathe, heavy with enmity and suspicion, but Two Rivers didn't move, standing there, on the very edge of the trail, an immaculate figure outlined against the darkening sky, his hands folded upon his chest, his carelessly tied hair the only thing to stir in the strengthening wind. "The destruction and war we've been conducting displease our creators. The way we've been killing our brothers makes the Great Spirits sad. We've been disappointing them for too long. The war between our brothers will stop and the Great Tree of Peace planted."

Fascinated, Tekeni watched the silver-haired leader's frown deepening, a hesitation peeking out of the squinted eyes, changing their challenging expression, even if for a heartbeat. The other people murmured, staring at Two Rivers, clearly impressed.

He strained his eyes to see better, watching the well-familiar face, seeing it closed as though chiseled out of stone, unwavering and compelling, the large eyes not even blinking, gazing at their hosts, mighty and forceful, as bright as the diminishing sun.

"You presume to come here, to our lands, our forests, our towns!" Another voice tore the silence. This one belonged to the second leader, a younger man, tall and full of scars, the amount of which could rival those of Tekeni's. "You came here uninvited, and you presume to tell us what to do? We are aware that the arrogance and the audacity of the enemy know no bounds, still, this time it has surely surpassed itself." The younger man turned to the crowds that, in the meanwhile, gathered behind the leaders and their warriors, the oiled patch of hair upon the top of his head swaying fiercely. "Didn't our enemy outrival itself by coming here in this fashion, presuming to order us about?"

"We did not come here uninvited," said Two Rivers calmly, unperturbed. "We've been interrupted by the delegation of the Mountain People while conducting our own meeting in the lands of the Swamp People, the meeting of the three powerful nations who decided to put the end to the war between the brothers. We listened to your messengers, following your guides, coming here with no delay. We've not been presuming to act with arrogance, but the message of the Great Spirits cannot wait any longer. The war must stop."

Was he pushing this man on purpose this way?

Tekeni felt his fellow warriors drawing closer, their tension obvious, ready to fight. The impending clash seemed inevitable, with their rivals glaring at them from all around, wary and undecided, but furious too, ready to spill their indecision in the bout of violence and bloodshed.

There was no way out of this, but why? wondered Tekeni, his mind numb, eyes drawing to the sun every now and then, seeing it diminishing slowly but surely, still fiery and bright but eaten away bite by bite. Had the great man seen the end of the world in that dream he did not have time to share? Was he wishing to finish it all in a spectacular manner of a fierce fight to the death? He tried to make his mind work.

"How do we know those are not lies?" cried out the younger leader, bringing his hands up in a showy way. "From the supposed agreement of the three nations to the allegedly divine nature of this man's mission, how do we know those are not arrogant, presumptuous, audacious lies?"

The wind tore at them, bringing along the scent of a nearing storm.

"I tell no lies. The other nations have listened to the message of the Great Spirits. Some asked for proof, some have accepted with no evidence of the divine intervention." Two Rivers' gaze drew to the sky now too, if only momentarily. Tekeni held his breath, seeing the familiar lips pressing tightly, the large eyes clouding, turning unreadable as he took a deep breath. "I tell no lies, and my mission carries the blessing of the Right-Handed Twin himself. He wants to see his children living in peace with each other. The people of this side of the Great Lake are like a longhouse, spreading from the east to the west, with five nations like five families, living together with each having its own fireplace and independence in managing all but their mutual affairs." He looked at them gravely, encircling them with that penetrating gaze of his. "He will be displeased to see that one of the families refuses to live alongside the others."

More people were glancing at the sky now, unsettled, their frowns deep. Tekeni forced his eyes off the diminishing circle, feeling the cold spreading. Was it his fear or was it truly getting colder? Further down the clearing, around the tents, the women were pointing at the sky, talking rapidly.

"Listen to me," cried out Two Rivers, and Tekeni clung to the familiar voice, watching the Great Man as he stood there, paying no attention to the disquiet that kept growing around them. "We can make it work."

"How?" The silver-haired leader stepped forward, also refusing to look at the sky.

"Like I said, in the way of our traditional longhouse." As though no deepening shadows were gathering upon the ground, Two Rivers knelt, picking up a small stick. Like in a dream, Tekeni watched the long fingers drawing a square, then another, five in all, connected by a thin line. "These are our people, five nations, five families residing side by side. The People of the Flint," the stick pointed toward the first square, "they have already held the gathering, choosing the leaders who will represent each town at their national council. They are organized now, not a loosely coordinated group of settlements anymore, but a nation." The stick kept moving, sliding above the next rectangle. "The People of the Standing Stone have chosen their council too, already." A slight hesitation above the middle square. "The Onondagas are yet to organize the meeting of the whole nation, but their neighbors to the west, the People of the Swamp, are holding the main gathering at these very moments. I was present at their meeting when your messengers came to invite me here." He looked up, not needing to squint anymore, with the glow of the sun dimming rapidly.

Unable to stop himself from doing so, Tekeni looked up, a stony fist squeezing his stomach. What started as the dark crack on the edge of the blazing sun was now a blot of ominous blackness, swallowing the shining deity like a snake devouring its prey, unhurried, sure of itself. For a heartbeat he shut his eyes, his senses clinging to the familiar voice, so calm and well measured. Didn't Two Rivers notice that something was amiss?

"You are the fifth family, the keepers of the western door. Without you, our longhouse will not be whole."

Most people were staring at the sky now, some gaping, some pointing, murmuring, looking around, their fear unconcealed.

"It all sounds very well," the younger leader's voice boomed, overcoming the growing hum. "But what happens if we refuse to join? Will the Great Spirits direct you to gather the warriors of the four nations in order to force us into your union? What will you do if we refuse to guard the western door of your metaphorical longhouse?"

Two Rivers got to his feet, looking suddenly tired, almost exhausted.

"I think the Great Spirits are not trying to conceal their displeasure," he said quietly, his jaw stubbornly tight, but his eyes clouded, thoughtful and oh-so-very sad. "Listen to this." Gesturing widely, he pointed toward the forest behind their backs. Not a chirp of a bird came from between the swaying trees. Even the insects kept quieter now, as though afraid of the darkness.

"What does it mean?" the people were shouting. "What is happening?"

"The Great Spirits are displeased." Two Rivers' voice rang calmly, but there was an obvious tension to it now.

Unable to fight the urge, Tekeni came closer, but whether to protect his friend in case someone decided to attack him, or to seek the safety beside the man who seemed to be doing all this, he didn't know.

The cold was growing, definite now. And so were the shadows. He noticed the flowers down the clearing were closing up, as though the night were nearing. People were rushing about, openly afraid, peering at the sky, murmuring prayers. Two Rivers stood there alone, watching the sharpening shadows, his jaw tight.

"Your dream?" whispered Tekeni, stepping into the void surrounding his friend. Even their people kept away from the Crooked Tongues man now, stealing terrified glances.

The warm palm rested on his shoulder, heavy, reassuring. "Yes. But it is going to be well in the end."

The distant shadows loomed over the western side of the lake, like a gathering storm.

"What is happening?" He swallowed, hearing his own voice husky and high, full of panic. The urge to run away welled. It was obvious that the Left-Handed Twin was coming to claim their world for himself and his underworld minions and followers, the bad, poisonous *uki* and the giants that were still reported to roam the earth. The cry of an owl confirmed this assumption. *An owl in the middle of the day?*

"I don't know," Two Rivers' voice shook now too, his self-assurance gone. "I wish I knew!"

The sun was a pitifully thin crescent, like a moon on certain nights. Oh, Mighty Spirits! Tekeni watched the strips of light darting across the ground, alternating with patches of black, both moving fast, like attacking predators. It was as though the light and the darkness were fighting each other. The epic battle of the Celestial Twins?

He felt his heart fluttering, the stony fist gripping his stomach, squeezing with all its might. But for the presence of Two Rivers, he would turn around and run into the woods, to crawl somewhere quiet and maybe vomit in fear. The world was ending in front of his eyes, and he was not ready for this. It was one thing to risk one's life, facing death, fighting or sailing, or hunting a bear, but another to watch the world dying, collapsing on its own, with Father Sun being devoured by a feral beast.

He heard Two Rivers' murmuring, and he knew it was a prayer, repeated over and over in the Crooked Tongues words. He had almost forgotten how they sounded.

Many people prayed all around, but he listened to the foreign speech, thinking about Seketa and how he didn't keep his promise, after all. She would disappear with the crashing world, and he would disappear too, and nothing would be left of them, nothing, not even the memories.

The darkness fell, but the ring where the sun had previously shone was still there, a dark plate surrounded by the glowing aura of light. Fascinated against his will, Tekeni watched it, forgetting his desperation. It was a beautiful sight, reinforced by the orange glow spreading above the lake. It would be over soon, they would all die, however at least the world was ending more beautifully than he expected. But for the cries of people, and the urgent murmuring of their prayers, he might have tried to prepare himself to leave in peace, in dignified tranquility maybe, not drowning in his own fear. If only there were a way to let her know…

The glow on the western side of the ring began to dim. He didn't dare to believe it yet, but the hope was creeping in, impossible not to pay attention to. It made his stomach flutter, but this time with hope, his excitement difficult to contain. He heard Two Rivers releasing a held breath.

"Is it over?" he whispered, not sure if he had said it aloud or not.

No answer came, but he needed none, anyway. The sliver of the light returned, the other side of the dark circle clearing now, creating yet another crescent. The light was getting the upper hand. The Right-Handed Twin was winning once again.

He heard the people's murmur growing, their prayers still rustling but losing the desperate tone. No one moved, but their eyes were glued to the sky, their hopes filling the light with more force, sure to win now.

Someone rushed back toward the tents, and soon a fire was made, and the prayers went up, accompanied by the fragrant tobacco smoke, and the beautiful chanting, the beating of the drums and the trilling of the lone flute. Everyone joined the prayer, and the people were moving, some dancing in a pure gesture of thanksgiving, some just talking, the locals and the newcomers alike, united in their gratefulness at being alive and well, with their world surviving a difficult trial.

However, the void around Two Rivers remained. Tekeni could feel it most clearly, catching the peoples' wary glances, their eyes wondering, full of suspicion, even fear. Oh, but he felt it too, this small, nagging voice in the back of his head, asking, wondering. Had the Crooked Tongues man done this? Did he make the sun disappear in order to frighten the stubborn People of the Mountains into obedience?

He felt the hair on his nape rising. What if it was truly him, his friend of more than one span of seasons, his best friend, the man he had trusted most, the man he owed his life to, what if he was capable of doing this? The man was afraid, yes, but he was in a hurry too this morning, when they arrived; he was anxious to proceed, as though he had known all along that the terrible thing would happen, trying to be on time to use it to the maximum effect. And there was this dream he mentioned. It was something about the sun, now Tekeni remembered it most clearly. *He had known all along!*

Fighting the urge to move away, almost afraid to stand next to his only friend, he glanced at the tall figure, seeing the set face, cold and unreadable, the generous lips just a thin line, the eyes blank, dark, giving nothing away. Oh, benevolent Spirits!

"Is it over for good?" he asked, the challenge in his voice impossible to conceal. Had they been alone he would have turned around and left. Yet, with all the hostile glances, he could not do even this. They were afraid of the Crooked Tongues man, yes, but furious, too. No one had ever scared them so thoroughly, of that Tekeni was sure.

"I hope so." The eyes of the man filled with life all of a sudden, turning to Tekeni, sparkling with familiar warmth. "I certainly hope it is over and will never happen again."

"But you knew, didn't you?" Almost limp with relief, Tekeni smiled. The Two Rivers he knew was back, and if he managed to forget this incident, all would reverse back to normal. A big 'if.'

"I'll tell you all about it when we are alone. I should have told you before, I wanted to, but it all happened too fast."

"They are convinced now, aren't they?" Glancing at the fire and the people gathering around it, dancing and chanting, Tekeni hid his grin. "Your fifth family will not make any more trouble."

Two Rivers nodded, but his face darkened all of a sudden. "Only one stubborn family remains."

"The Onondagas will not make much trouble, either. They are surrounded. They have no choice but to accept our offering of peace. With Hionhwatha working on them since before the Cold Moons, I'm sure they are waiting for us to arrive as we speak."

"I hope so." Two Rivers' shrug was mirthless, lacking his usual vitality.

Tekeni looked at the fire. "You are worrying about the girl."

"Yes." His friend's voice rang faintly, hardly heard in the rising clamor. "I should have sent her word, somehow. I should not have left her waiting like that."

"I can say the same."

The warm palm resting upon his shoulder made him feel a little better. "Yes, I know, old friend. We've been lousy with our women, haven't we?"

"I will cross the Great Lake the moment we are done with the Onondagas. I hope they make no trouble, because if they do, I will leave before the end of this moon, whether they have joined your metaphorical longhouse or not."

"Then I hope they make no trouble, because I will not let you go alone. You never abandoned me, and I could not do this to you. We'll cross together, and we'll make it a truly fast campaign. A few dawns in each direction, back before anyone would notice."

"Your girl will not be happy to let you go again."

Two Rivers' laughter rolled down the hill, attracting the attention of the nearby people. *As though it was not enough that they had been watched openly or covertly all this time.*

"Onheda? Oh yes, she will not be happy, but we will bring her along. She will make our small warriors' force stronger."

Tekeni could not hold his own laughter. "Oh yes, that she will. She is a real warrior, this Onondaga woman. I'm glad you did not forget her. She deserves better than to be one of many."

Two Rivers raised his eyebrows, his eyes turning challenging. "Have you been counting?"

"No, but one could not help noticing things. Atiron could have been a valuable ally, but he chose not to come, neither to the lands of the Swamp People, nor here. He is barely civil with both of us now."

"Oh, please. I haven't been fooling with that pretty cousin of yours!" Angrily, Two Rivers kicked a stone, then turned to go toward the celebrating people. "It's time we extracted a few promises from this stubborn lot. I would love to see us starting back no later than the next morning." The dark gaze brushed past Tekeni. "And I will appreciate if you don't bring up my love life anymore, either."

CHAPTER 14

"If I don't reach the lake shore right away, I will scream and die of exhaustion. And of the stench, too!" Hanowa's round face twisted with mischief, as she wrinkled her nose and rolled her eyes, waving her empty basket in a showy manner. "I can't bear being so stinky for much longer."

"Oh, please!" Another girl laughed, passing them by. "You are such a spoiled baby. What would you say if forced to go out there since the beginning of the Awakening Moons, like some of us?"

Hanowa stopped abruptly, her playfulness gone. "It's not like I've been loitering in my longhouse since the end of the Cold Moons. I've been working, too, just to let you know." The frown didn't sit well with the girl's cheerful features. "Where do you think the maple sap you are going to sweeten your food with came from? We've been collecting it, Onheda and I."

The other girl's provocative grin lost some of its baiting quality, as her eyes brushed past Onheda, acknowledging her presence with a reserved nod. Since the Maple Ceremony and her argument with the powerful War Chief five dawns ago, it had been the regular thing, those wary, cautious glances, and the hurried farewells. Aside from her hosts, who were irritated and displeased with Onheda's careless escapade, but who still didn't see fit to just throw their troublesome guest out – they must have owed Hionhwatha a truly huge favor – Hanowa was the only person still cheerful in her presence.

"Well, see you by the river," said the girl, rushing off, her skirt swirling.

They watched her for a heartbeat.

"What cheek," exclaimed Hanowa, bringing her palms up. "To imply I was being lazy. Me!" She glanced at Onheda. "And you, too. You have been working like two women, with the sap and today at the field."

Onheda just shrugged. The last three days in the fields were actually quite enjoyable, the work keeping her busy, too busy to think. Since the Maple Ceremony and the argument with the powerful man, she had been all nerves. Collecting sap with her talkative partner didn't help, while the difficult work of cleaning the fields, readying the earth for planting, molding it into conical mounds, helped to take her thoughts off what happened at the ceremony. *And of what happened last night.*

She shivered, taking a deep breath to stop her heart from beginning to pound again. Last night, she had been scared senseless. Sent to fetch fresh drinking water, she had taken a pot and went out to the elevated part of the town, where the small spring ran all the way to the poles of the fence and beyond it.

It had been a clear evening, and she lingered, enjoying the light breeze, relishing the sensation of being alone with her thoughts for a little while. What was he doing now? she asked herself, pitting her face against the new gust of wind, remembering them being together in just the same kind of weather, before the cold came. He was holding her so tight on that only evening, stroking her hair and her shoulders, careful not to touch her wound. Back then, she had known that he was hers and hers alone, no matter what his plans were. She knew she was special to him, like no other women in his life, although, according to the scar-faced youth, there were females lining his history aplenty. Still, she knew she was special. What he felt for her was new, even to him. It scared him so much that he had fought his need for her, trying not to be involved. Trying but failing. He had fallen for her, and they made marvelous love, drowning in their feelings, perfectly tuned to each other. Back then, she knew that whatever was his mission, whatever it took him to do all that he intended to do, he was her man, and he would find the way to be with her for more than a quick lovemaking every now and then.

She shivered, remembering her confidence, confidence that had been weakened by long winter moons, gone by the springtime, when he had stayed in the east, pacifying its fierce residents while neglecting her people, relying on Hionhwatha to do all the work among the Onondagas. She didn't think he had found a new woman to love, but the realization that his mission was so much more important than her and her people was difficult to face. He would never come to live with her, not until all the people on this side of the Great Lake were brought together, to live in peace. And maybe not even then, as his Crooked Tongues countryfolk may need to be pacified, too.

Clenching the heavy pot with both palms, she had put it aside and knelt beside the glimmering stream, washing her face, listening to its calm trickling. Would she ever see him again? Did he know what she had been doing by now?

"Tell me about him."

The deep, slightly amused voice tore her out of her reverie, making her jump. The water splattered all around, as she flapped her hands in the air, desperate to catch her balance. He was almost invisible in the darkness, just an obscure, threatening shadow, his eyes gleaming at the same level as hers, so short was he, his voice warm, the only thing that made him alive, not letting her mistake him for a vision.

"Don't be so scared." He came closer, materializing out of the darkness, looking even shorter with no imposing headdress of his high status adorning his head. "I will not harm you because I need your knowledge, little woman. You say you met this mysterious foreigner who claims to carry the message of the Great Spirits. Tell me about him."

"I…" She tried to collect her senses, her heart pounding in her ears, interrupting her ability to think. "I didn't… I don't… I don't know…"

His laughter parted the darkness, ringing softly, openly amused.

"You are afraid, aren't you, young one? But you needn't be.

He might be in danger. Hionhwatha certainly is. But you? Oh no, you are a good girl who will help me to organize our people, help me make them immune to the blasphemy of the foreigners, and the traitors among our people."

She didn't see him move, but suddenly, he was so close she could feel his breath on her face. It made her hair rise.

"He is the Messenger of the Great Spirits. He can't be stopped or obstructed," she said, mustering the last of her strength, resisting the desperate need to step back, to turn and run away.

"The foreigner can do nothing here, and his success among the savages of the east is temporary. Both of their nations will be at each other's throat at the first opportunity. Do you trust the bloodthirsty Flint People to keep to their peace for longer than a mere span of seasons? Or even less than this? These savages will be fighting their sworn enemies, the People of the Standing Stone, before the summer moons run their course." He paused, and she knew he would feel her shuddering, sensing her welling dread that was threatening to get out of control. "And for your admired hero's sake, I hope he won't be alive to watch it happening. I could not be so cruel as to wish to see him break, watching his creation crumbling all around him."

She tried to contain her trembling. "He will make them live in peace. He will not let them fight again. He knows what he is doing. He is strong in his beliefs. He will succeed."

He laughed once again. "He left quite an impression on you, little woman. And yet, I don't think you believe your own words now."

The night enveloped them, sheltering in its thickness and tranquility, but also a trap. It was like standing next to a forest beast. He was quiet and calm, but for how long? Her instincts told her to run, but she wasn't sure her frozen limbs would obey. And she was not a silly little woman.

"Tell me about him," he repeated, his voice quiet and sincere. "Where did you meet him?"

"It was on the other side of our lake." She picked her words carefully, trying to play for time. Why wasn't she wise enough to prepare her story? But who would have thought that the powerful man would stop to ask her all those questions, and in a conversational way, too.

"Well?"

"He was there, and well, he talked to me. He told me all about the Good Tidings of Peace. He convinced me."

"Just like that?" His voice trembled with mirth. "You are a terrible liar, dancer girl. You should either practice or stick to the truth."

"I did not…" She heard her voice trailing off, shamed by his open contempt. "I don't have to tell you anything! You have no right to ask me or to laugh at me. He is the Messenger of the Right-Handed Twin, I can tell you this much."

Again, she didn't see him moving, but his good hand was suddenly upon her shoulder, pressing it painfully. "Don't be insolent with me, woman. I will ask you whatever I want to, and I will get my answers, too."

She fought to break free, the crushing grip making her gasp with pain. His palm seemed to be made out of stone, his fingers rigid, pitiless, having no life in them despite their warmth. In desperation, she kicked wildly, feeling her foot connecting with his shin, making him wince. He growled, and his grip loosened, but apparently, only to slip down her arm. Struggling to break free again, she felt herself whirling, with her arm twisted behind her back now, in a merciless grip.

He pushed it up, making her double over with pain. Unable to keep her balance, she would have fallen to her knees, but for his firm grip. He stopped pushing, maintaining the achieved balance, and she found no strength to fight on, trying to catch her breath, instead.

"Stop fighting me," he hissed, still careful to keep quiet. They were behind the ceremonial grounds, with no real privacy the woods might have provided.

Her teeth seemed as though about to crack from the force with which she clenched them, now busy struggling not to cry out. The option to break free no longer existed, but he would get no satisfaction of her whimpering and maybe begging to be left unharmed.

"Stop fighting," he repeated, now more calmly, his breath normal, as though he had spent no energy on this struggle. "When I release you, you just turn around and listen to me quietly and calmly. Is that clear to you?"

She said nothing, but when his fingers tightened around her wrist, not pushing her twisted arm up again but suggesting that it might be done, she nodded and felt him hesitating for a heartbeat, before the pressure was gone.

"Now listen to me carefully, wild girl." He paused, waiting for her to finish checking her arm. It went numb, and she wondered if it had been broken, or maybe taken out of its place at the shoulder, the way it happened to the Crooked Tongues man back at Jikonsahseh's, when she had met him for the first time. It felt safer to get busy with her injuries. To turn around and face the War Leader was a challenge she was not yet prepared to handle.

"Stop messing with your arm and look at me!"

Now she truly had no choice.

"It's not broken, so you can let it go. If I wanted it to be out of place, it would have been by now. So leave it at peace and pay attention."

She watched his broad face, barely visible in the darkness.

"I know who sent you, dancer girl, and I think I can guess for what reason. Hionhwatha must be desperate to resort to such means, to use women in his struggle. Fancy sending pretty girls to spy on me, or to stir trouble, or to do both. Which one, eh?" His mirthless grin flickered in the darkness, evidently not put out with her lack of response. "And you must owe him a huge favor to agree to do that. I wonder what made you cooperate." A soft chuckle, then his fleeting grin was gone. "Well, let us continue with our game as though nothing happened. For a few more dawns, at least. You stay with the Porcupine Clan and pretend to be just a lost, harmless girl. And

I will attend my usual duties, keeping this nation safe from the enemies and the intruding foreigners." He nodded thoughtfully, as though agreeing with himself. "We'll keep it on until either your wondrous messenger, or Hionhwatha, or both of them, come. Then we shall see. He will come, won't he?" He paused, his frown sudden and visible. "Does he know you are here, spying on me? Or was Hionhwatha acting on his own? I wonder to what extent the old snake will use the foreigner to gain his own means. Because this is all he wants, pretty girl. To reach his old status, to gain back his influence among our people, to be the War Leader again. Nothing more. Your Great Peace and its tidings worries him no more than an empty shell of an old nut. You realize that, don't you? I hope you do."

She tried to contain her trembling, ashamed of this reaction of her body, her anger rising, impossible to control. But *oh no*, she thought. *You will not trick me into telling you anything, not this time. One time of opening my silly mouth was one too many.*

"Go back, girl. Bring your water before they think you got lost wandering around the town. And remember, no more silly escapades, no more talking to people about your wondrous messenger. And don't think of running away, either. If you do, you will regret it. You will never make it to High Springs alive, and you will miss interesting developments when the two men, who are oh-so-very brave as to hide behind the back of a pretty girl, will gather enough courage to come at long last. Stay here and wait for them together with me."

He was gone, disappearing back into the darkness in the same way he had appeared, soundless like a forest spirit. One moment here, the other gone. Leaving her to stand there, limp with relief, finally able to breathe the crisp night air, which previously was heavy, difficult to take in.

Even now, a day later and in the clearness of the afternoon light, she could feel that same relief returning, welling in her chest. It was good not to have this man anywhere around, and in a few days, she would be gone. He would be watching her now, but not for too long. A War Chief had more important things to do. He would not notice her disappearance, and by the time he did, she would be back in the safety of High Springs. She could make this journey in less than two days of a fast walk. She had spent little more time while coming here, but now she would run all the way, of that she was sure. Hionhwatha needed to be warned, while she needed to get away from Onondaga Town. It was a terrible place to be, and it would get worse when the Crooked Tongues man finally came, but by then, she would be beside him, protected and not alone anymore.

"What is going on out there?" Hanowa's words tore Onheda from her reverie, as the girl slowed her step at the head of the path leading toward the lake shore.

"What?" Incensed with the small wave of fear that went down her spine, Onheda halted, listening to the voices coming up the trail. "Are they partying down there?"

"I can't hear any drums, sister, but there are definitely too many voices to my liking. Do we not deserve some privacy to wash after a difficult day?" The girl hastened her step, sliding down the trail with the familiarity of a person who could find her way here with her eyes shut.

The small shore seemed to be packed with people, women mainly, those who came to wash up, but dotted with men. They crowded around something, talking all at once.

"What in the name of the Great Spirits?"

A group of newcomers brushed past them, with the elderly healer of the Wolf Clan in the lead, carrying his bag of medicine and pipes.

"Move away, girls."

They moved obediently, but their curiosity was too great, and they needed to wash up, anyway.

"Come."

She felt Hanowa's palm clutching her arm, pulling her on with the determination worthy of a war leader. Looking around carefully, she found no trace of the important people of the town, aside from the old healer; just a bunch of sweaty, mud-smeared women of all ages, and a few curious men.

"What happened?"'

"Those people, they were found here." One girl moved a little, allowing them a view of a young warrior spread upon the sand, looking dead.

"Move away!" cried out the healer, kneeling beside the unconscious man, irritated. "Stop crowding around like that. He needs air to breathe, and I need light to see."

"They just found him like that?" whispered Hanowa, her eyes so wide they looked rounded.

"No, no!" The women backed away reluctantly, making the circle around the wounded larger. "He was not alone. There was a woman carrying him. Or trying to."

"Two women!" exclaimed someone. "You weren't there from the beginning, but I was. There were two young women carrying him here. See? There!"

Following the woman's impatient gesture, Onheda saw that, indeed, two girls crouched beside the sprawled man, not looking much better than the wounded. Pale, mud-covered, and disheveled, their clothes torn and their faces stark, both seemed to be about to join their unconscious companion in his wandering state of mind.

The memory of her own flight from Little Falls made Onheda's stomach twist with compassion. She must have been looking no better when Jikonsahseh had found her. Where were those people fleeing from?

She studied the girls who might have been sisters, so alike they looked in their miserable state, but when one was peering at the wounded, all puffy with tears, mumbling incomprehensibly, the other glanced around, concentrated and wary, clearly on guard despite her state of exhaustion.

"We need to carry him back to the town," said the healer, shaking his head. "I will need better light and assistance. His wounds are not looking good." He got to his feet, then hesitated, as the first girl burst into a new bout of noisy tears. "How long has it been since he was wounded?" he asked, studying her through his narrowing eyes. "Did his mind begin wandering shortly thereafter?"

"Oh, oh, oh, I truly don't... don't remember. It's been a long, long time. I think..." The girl was wailing, rocking back and forth, useless.

"Three dawns," said the second girl firmly, shooting a furious glance at her hysterical companion. "His mind wander three dawns. But he wound, got wound, before. One wound five dawns. The other, I don't know."

The silence prevailed, as they all stared at the girl, speechless. Onheda felt her heart stopping, missing a heartbeat, then another, the longing so sudden and overwhelming it gripped her chest. Oh, it had been so long since she had heard that way of talking, this halting manner in which the Crooked Tongues were uttering their words, twisting them as though their mouths were full of hot porridge.

"I thank you, young one," said the healer gravely, eyeing the girl with a measure of compassion. She blushed and looked away. "Help me to carry him into the town," he added, addressing the others briskly, but when the people began rushing about, Onheda saw several elderly women staring at the girl, their eyes narrow.

"Who are you?" asked one of them, a heavyset but good-looking woman, a member of the Bear Clan council.

The girl dropped her gaze, but as her companion seemed to be utterly useless, lying on the ground, crying so lustily the air shook, she looked up again, her frown deep. "Onondaga Town. We look, Onondaga Town."

The woman smiled in a motherly fashion. "You found it." A brief pause. "Come with me, young one."

"Why would she come with you?" cried out another woman, one of the Turtle Clan Mothers. "You can't just pick any girl you fancy. This matter has to be settled officially."

"Who said I was taking her into our clan already?" The Bear woman reared in indignation. "I just want to feed her. They both look no better than the wounded man. They may die."

"Oh, yes, of course. As though we don't know what you are

up to!"

The hubbub that broke could rival the storm raging two nights before. Amused, Onheda watched the men picking up the wounded, anxious to get away from the women's problems. Adoption business had nothing to do with them, in this case more than ever, with even the captive girls coming here on their own, with no warfare involved.

The other girl was on her feet now, crying and trying to follow the men. "Where are you taking him?" she screamed, fighting the hands that held her, supporting more than detaining as she was anything but steady, trembling badly and swaying.

"Stop it, girl, stop it," admonished the women. "He is taken to the town. He will be taken care of. Stop crying. Tell us who are you? Where are you from?"

The name of the village was difficult to understand through the hysterical sobs, but the women nodded, satisfied. The crying mess seemed to be of local origins, as was, probably, the wounded man.

Onheda glanced at the Crooked Tongues' girl, seeing the set face and the pressed lips, as starved and exhausted as the other, but in control, not sobbing and not terrified. She might have been pretty even, if washed and fed properly, she thought. And she was certainly set on going away as soon as possible. Onheda knew the signs, no one better. No matter what this girl was doing, running around this countryside with those other two Onondagas, she was not a frightened captive, and she wasn't about to give up. She would be crying and screaming and resisting now if she was. The way she walked on, following her captors, her paces steady, refusing offered help, conveyed her determination. This girl was after something.

CHAPTER 15

"We will hold the gathering of all people after the end of Planting Moon." The silver-haired leader of the Mountain People shifted, making himself more comfortable beside the flickering fire.

Two Rivers frowned, bottling his impatience. He had pushed these people too far already, and it was not wise to keep doing so. When he first came here, following the dream, he had counted on the help of the terrible event promised by the vision, so he pressed hard, with no consideration to the acceptable way of negotiations. But now it was back with the waiting game, letting the people he had just forced into the alliance proceed in their own unhurried pace.

"Of course." He nodded gravely, taking the offered pipe – a beautiful affair of exquisite patterns, carved in decisive lines. "Having attended the meeting of the other three nations, I will be honored to be present if my presence would be required."

Both leaders acknowledged his offering with grave nods, while the others, the locals, various minor leaders, and the people who had come here with him, representatives of the three nations, said nothing, staring ahead.

There was no cozy atmosphere around this particular fire, and it had ceased to puzzle him long since. The terrible darkness that scared so many people this morning made them wary of him, his allies and adversaries alike. They were not about to forgive, and he wasn't sure he would have felt differently in their place. To cause Father Sun to disappear from the sky was not an admirable thing to do, and he did nothing to allay their suspicion. On the contrary, he had used it in front of everyone, whether he was the one to cause it or not. It did the trick, made the fierce, warlike people agree to enter his proposed alliance with no further argument, and that's what counted. After so many moons, he had little patience for all the mounting delays.

He suppressed a snort, determined to be honest, at least with himself. Was he impatient because he wanted to go to High Springs since the end of the Cold Moons, or even before that? He had promised to return with the end of the winter, at the latest. He had promised, telling her to wait at Jikonsahseh's, and she did as he told her, she, who had never followed orders before. She had waited and waited, and when she lost patience, she didn't go home, forgetting all about him, but went to do his work, to try to help his only ally among her people. She had stayed loyal, when he had failed her.

The guilt was back, gripping his stomach, making it as tight as a stuffed ball. She deserved better. She deserved to be loved, cherished, and respected. She deserved to live with the man of her choosing, but he was not that sort of a man. Or was he? Maybe after all this was over, after the Great Council was established and functioning and the Great Tree of Peace planted, with the national councils and all the laws worked out and determined, maybe after all this, he would be free to do whatever he liked, maybe yes, settle with a woman and make a family. With her it seemed like a possibility.

He shook his head, banishing the silly thoughts. He had known this woman for a few brief days when his life was nothing but living on edge, battling the odds, having not much hope of achieving anything. She had probably forgotten all about him, anyway, but he would see her in High Springs, because this time, he would let nothing stand in his way. Swamp People, Standing Stone People, Mountains People, they had all managed to push themselves ahead of his plans, but now he would go to the Onondagas, even if no one would follow him there.

His eyes sought out Tekeni's dark silhouette, curled not far away, fast asleep. The young man had a long day behind him, rowing most of the way up here, for a few days in a row, since they set out on this last of his spontaneous journeys, working cheerfully as always, asking no questions. Oh, the Great Spirits were truly generous giving him a partner like that. No matter what others chose to do after what happened here today, he would never be alone as long as that wolf cub, now a splendid young warrior, lived. One could never ask for a more loyal friend and follower. Oh, but for that he was truly grateful!

Inhaling deeply, he passed the pipe to the leader of the Swamp People, who squatted next to him. The silence was more comfortable now, so he drifted back into his thoughts. Tekeni was content but only up to a certain point. The youth needed to go and fetch his girl, and he, Two Rivers, needed to do something about it. There was no other choice but to accompany the young man to the lands of his former people. His friend deserved that and much more.

If only he could be certain that the girl was still waiting. He tried to recall that Beaver Clan beauty, the cousin of his best friend, long since dead; the demure, upright, pretty thing, one of the future leading women of her clan and her longhouse, surely. He had never thought much of this type, but the girl surprised him, falling in love with the wild boy, fighting alongside him, saving him and then helping them flee as though there was no more natural deed to do than to pillage the storage place of their longhouses to equip them with as many supplies as possible, the fleeing criminals. Oh, this girl was full of surprises, so maybe she was still waiting. She had better be, he decided. The wolf cub deserved no nasty surprises.

"What is the nature of this gathering?" asked Okwaho, the man of Little Falls, one of the few who came with them that far. Little Falls kept being the most heavily represented town in every gathering he'd organized until now, his most loyal followers, and, Two Rivers suspected, anxious to keep its dominance in all the proceedings. "Can't you decide this matter now? It seems to me there are enough representatives of the

Mountains People swarming this hill?"

The silver-haired leader gave the pushy guest one of the most freezing glances Two Rivers could remember seeing.

"There are enough of our people around here, yes," he said, stressing his words, reminding his insolent guests of their inferior position if it came to the worst. "Yet, the way the Messenger wishes to organize our nations needs to be ratified by the Clans Mothers of every important settlement, together with their nomination of the worthy people to represent them in the Great Council of the Five Nations." Another freezing glance. "I assume that the proceedings are simpler, not as sophisticated, in the lands of the Flint People."

"You assume wrong." The man of Little Falls held to his temper, but barely, and Two Rivers concentrated, abandoning idle thoughts concerning the fidelity of his friend's girl.

"We have no need to hurry," he said, making a special effort to sound as calm and as sincere as he could. "Our first meeting of the Five Nations will be held in a general manner, dealing with the mutual agreements and understandings between each other. The Clans Mothers of each nation will have ample time to choose the best of your people after it happens."

They nodded, thoughtful.

"Where will the first gathering be held?" asked the man of the Swamp People, narrowing his eyes.

Two Rivers took a deep breath. "In the lands of the Onondagas."

Their glares could have burned his skin had they had the ability to do so. Many pairs of indignant eyes stared at him, flashing. He said nothing, letting them sound their protests, not about to justify his decisions.

"Why?"

"Their location is most convenient, easily reached by any of the participants of our 'longhouse.' No nation will have to travel too far."

"They have not even joined our union yet!" cried out the man of the Standing Stone. "They are still our enemies as far as my people are concerned. And you already give them this honor?"

"Our location is not that inconvenient, either." The Swamp People's representative's voice shook with an equal rage, matching the indignation of his neighbors to the east.

"The People of the Flint will have to travel farther than the others." He kept his voice calm, not especially worried. So close to the terrible event yet, he knew they would not challenge his authority more than necessary.

"Oh, yes," called out Okwaho. "Why not hold the meeting at our eastern neighbor's, the Standing Stone People's, lands. They have quite a few pretty locations I'm sure our current hosts wouldn't want to miss visiting, even if they would be required to travel farther than the others."

Two Rivers suppressed a grin, letting them argue, watching the two fiercest adversaries, Flint and Mountain People, united for a change. Their lands were not under consideration for the grand meeting place, so they could handle this matter with a certain amount of objectivity, pointing in favor of the absent Onondagas. Which was a good development. He needed something to bargain with before meeting that formidable Tadodaho. An honor of having a permanent meeting place among this leader's people would be a good concession to offer, if made at the right time.

He sighed. He would need more, much more. Something truly significant that would make the arrogant leader feel as though he and his people were favored over the others, while the others would not feel cheated out of their rights. But what? What could that be? Could he count on another miracle, like the disappearance of the sun, while meeting the dangerous man? He didn't hold his hopes high.

CHAPTER 16

The evening was pleasantly warm, with only a slight breeze disturbing the dark tranquility. Hurrying along the nearly deserted alleys, Onheda smiled, pitting her face against the warm flow. She hadn't felt comfortable or safe when leaving her longhouse after dark, but now, wandering around for some time, she began feeling better.

Gwayeah insisted she should not be going out tonight, or on any other night. She had actually hinted, more than once, that Onheda might be better off returning back to her High Springs, the sooner the better. The kind, pleasant woman seemed to be genuinely worried about her guest since the argument with the War Chief on the day of the Maple Ceremony. Or maybe she was worried for herself and her family.

Onheda had little doubts. To shelter a nice harmless girl was one thing. Organizing all those clandestine meetings with people interested in listening about the Messenger, pushing their goal discreetly and carefully, held little danger and much thrill. But to confront the intimidating leader of Onondaga Town, openly and in front of everyone, was not something a careful woman with a family to risk would do. Onheda didn't blame her merry, outspoken hostess for changing her mind. She had decided to leave anyway, and had Gwayeah known about that violent nighttime encounter three nights earlier, she would faint, at the very least.

Suppressing a shudder, she tried to take her thoughts off the troublesome evening. Her first reaction was to keep very low and then run away at the next opportunity, but now she changed her mind. Intimidated she would not be, she had

decided last night, turning around on her bunk, the sleep
eluding her, for the second night in a row, the memory of this
man's nearness and his stony palm tightening around her arm,
twisting it until it felt like breaking, making her cover in cold
sweat.

Gwayeah may have insisted for her to keep at home, very
quiet, or to leave, but she went out this evening all the same, to
walk with Hanowa and the other girls, as they laughed and
gossiped, huddling behind tobacco plots, close to the gates. And
then, later, looking around like real conspirators, they began
asking her about the Messenger, some questions silly, wanting
to know if he was handsome, some serious, wishing to hear
what the man actually wanted, what his mission was.

It made her afraid and elated at the same time. If the War
Chief heard her, he would be furious beyond measure. He
would kill her this time, most probably, just to make an example
out of her. And yet, here she was, asked about *him* again,
prompted to tell more, to talk about his mission. People were
curious; oh, yes, they were ready for him to come. Even here, in
the heart of Onondaga Town, the people were waiting, wanting
the change. She hadn't come here in vain, and he would
appreciate her help when he arrived.

The Bear Clan's longhouse towered ahead, a dark,
threatening shape, so she hastened her step, anxious to reach
home now. If Tadodaho had known about her meeting with
those girls, he would be waylaying her, she realized, sweat
covering her back, wishing to catch her alone and with no
witnesses.

A branch cracked, and her heart missed a beat, then tossed
itself wildly against her ribs, making her head spin. Frozen, she
watched a shadow slipping out of the gaping entrance, moving
carefully, by stealth. She wanted to run, but her legs were too
heavy, glued to the ground, useless and trembling, barely
supporting her.

The silhouette came closer and then halted, very abruptly at
that, gasping, clearly afraid. Taking in the slender form, Onheda

felt her relief welling, making the trembling subdue. It was just a silly girl, tall and delicate, not the broad-shouldered, dangerous leader out to kill her.

"You scared me!" she hissed angrily, unable to control her fury, or maybe wishing to conceal her embarrassment. "Why are you running around in this fashion?"

The girl just stared, evidently as petrified as she herself had been just a few heartbeats earlier. Narrowing her eyes, Onheda took in the outline of the pretty face, the narrow shoulders, the thin arms clutching a bag. The Crooked Tongues foreigner, found on the shores of Lake Onondaga only two dawns ago along with the dying warrior and a local girl! She'd forgotten all about this strange trio, but the warrior must have still been alive as no mourning platforms had been laid out during these last days.

Biting her lower lip, she held her breath, understanding without the need to ask. The girl was alone, sneaking around, carrying a bag. Oh, what memories!

"You are running away," she whispered. "Aren't you?"

The girl didn't move, clutching the bag protectively against her chest. She remembered the feeling too well, the fear, the hope, the excitement. It didn't happen too long ago. But where was this girl going? Was she planning to cross the Great Sparkling Water, somehow? Onheda's journey was a possible thing, and she had succeeded with almost no help, anyway.

"I won't tell on you," she said, leaning closer. "If you want to go, go now."

The girl let out a breath, which she had probably held all this time.

"You not tell?" she whispered, her voice hardly audible, like the rustling of the wind, her accent bringing back painful memories.

"Come," said Onheda resolutely. "I'll take you to the tobacco plots. From there, you can sneak out with no trouble."

The girl fell into her step easily, her walk light, barely heard in the darkness. Like walking next to a forest spirit, thought

Onheda, her mind blank, refusing to function properly. She should have been in the safety of her hosts' longhouse now. Not running around, helping strange prisoners to escape. And yet, she had been in the same situation, and it was her duty to help. The Great Spirits had sent Jikonsahseh to save her, and they were requiring of her to help this girl now.

Faint voices floated not far away, and the girl winced, ready to dart into the shadow of yet another longhouse. Onheda reached out, hoping that the touch would reassure her companion instead of scaring the poor thing even more.

"If we run into people, they will think you are strolling with me."

"Why do this?" asked the girl quietly when the voices died behind them, melting in the darkness. "Why help?"

Onheda grinned. "It happened to me, too. I know how it is."

"You capture?" The girl halted, staring with brief astonishment. "You here, you not live here, you not..." Evidently finding no appropriate words, she resumed her walk, catching up with Onheda, who didn't stop.

"I *am* from here," said Onheda, amused. "Well, not exactly from here, but I am an Onondaga woman." She shrugged. "It's all complicated. I was captured before, and I ran away."

"Oh." The girl nodded, staring ahead.

"We'll cross the ceremonial grounds, and then it will be a short walk toward the tobacco plots. You'll be out of this town in no time." Hesitating, she eyed her companion, so thin and underfed, but so determined. "Where will you go?"

The girl's shrug could be felt most clearly.

"You can't cross the Great Sparkling Water."

"I crossed it already," muttered the girl, talking her tongue again, bringing along more memories. He was always trying to speak in their tongue, slipping into his people's way of speaking every time it was something important he wanted to say. How difficult it was to understand him! She pushed the memories away.

"You didn't cross by yourself. You've been captured."

"No, I no captured," said the girl angrily, slowing her step again. "I keep tell, no one listen. I no captured. I can't, can't adopted. I tell, and they don't listen."

"How did you come here if not through being captured?" What the girl said made no sense, but Onheda couldn't help but believe her. This little thing was so young and fragile, yet so determined.

"It long... long story. But I no captured. I come because I want. I need... need find person."

Onheda felt like laughing. "You make no sense, but do whatever you want. Go look for your person, or swim across. It has nothing to do with me, anyway."

The mass of the fence greeted them, dark and unfriendly.

"Just cross the tobacco plots and you are out of here," she said, suddenly anxious to go back, not wishing to be outside anymore. The War Chief was out there, she was certain of it, all of a sudden. She could almost feel his presence. It made her skin crawl.

"I thank, very thank. Grateful," began the girl, and then she shuddered and fell silent, hardly breathing, and Onheda stopped breathing too, because the voices carried too clearly, just whispers but nearing, coming their way.

Not looking at each other, they dived behind the bushes, scratching their limbs, getting in one another's way. The girl's stupid bag was heavy, hitting Onheda's leg.

"Are you sure you saw her?" The familiar voice made Onheda's heart skip a beat, then another.

"Yes, she was out here. It was a usual gathering, silly girls, chatting away." The other voice belonged to no one she knew.

"But she was there?"

They were passing next to their bushes, not slowing their step. It made Onheda feel better, but disappointed too. She needed to hear more.

"Yes, she was, and she was speaking about the Messenger again."

His curses shook the air, too loud not to be heard, although

both men were now reaching the fence. Clenching her teeth so
they wouldn't clatter, giving her presence away, Onheda slipped
alongside the bushes, hearing the man halting beside the poles
of the entrance.

"They held the meeting at the Swamp People's lands, beside
the Long Lake." Tadodaho's voice was calmer now, but it still
dripped with anger, like a poisonous plant.

"With the Messenger?"

"Yes, the filthy lowlife was there, doing most of the talking.
With that ugly accent of his, but they still listened like a bunch
of tame children." The man paused. "He is running circles
around us, and I bet you the best of my bird traps, he is doing it
on purpose. He doesn't dare to come here, not yet. He needs
the backing of many peoples, but it eludes me why they
continue listening to him." Another long pause, full of so much
rage Onheda found it difficult to breathe. "They were all there,
the Flint lowlifes, and the Standing Stone beasts, coming
together, patting each other's backs." More of a colorful
cursing. "He is trying to organize them all, and I wish I knew by
what means. It must be something good, some very good
promises he won't be able to keep. Or maybe sorcery. He must
have mastered the secrets of the Left-Handed Twin himself,
enlisting the support of the powerful spirit."

"But what can we do?" asked the other man when the silence
lasted too long to be just another pause.

It was so quiet, Onheda could hear the buzzing of the night
insects and the cries of the nocturnal birds out there in the
woods. The breathing of the other girl tickled her ear, her thin
body pressed too close, her sharp angles jutting against
Onheda's limbs.

"Get the girl and bring her to the falls. She is a pretty little
thing and quite passionate about the foreigner. Maybe he has
the same interest in her."

The man hesitated. "What if she fights?"

"Don't harm her more than necessary. We need her alive and
well." A mirthless chuckle. "I hope the divine messenger comes

soon. I don't want to house her for too long. The wild thing will give me trouble for certain. Such a pretty, high-spirited fox. I was almost tempted to pursue her for myself. I bet our mysterious messenger was tempted as well." Another pause. "Also, I wouldn't want Hionhwatha to get suspicious and start looking for his delectable spy. Pity she didn't heed my advice. It would be easier to keep an eye on her here."

The sound of their steps began melting into the night, but it was impossible to understand their direction, whether they headed out into the woods or returned back to the town. Her heart pounded too strongly, allowing her to hear nothing else. The darkness was oppressing, not sheltering anymore, but a threat. She was supposed to do something, maybe go back to Gwayeah's longhouse, or burst into a wild dash all the way to High Springs, to run for a whole night and a whole day without stopping to catch her breath.

"They go, go away," whispered the girl, getting to her feet carefully, as soundless as before, truly nothing but a forest spirit.

Onheda just stared, unable to slam her mind into working.

"Who men, who these men?"

"I..." She got up clumsily, stumbling on the girl's bag. What *was* wrong with her? "It doesn't matter. I... I better go back." She studied the delicate face, the narrowed, attentive eyes. "You should go. Before they start looking for you. If you want to run away, you should hurry now."

Turning to go, she winced as the gentle hand caught her arm. "No, please. Wait. I need... need know... know what they say."

"Why?" It was still difficult to make her mind work. She didn't care for what this girl wanted, and she didn't have time for the awkward conversation of many broken words. She needed to think what to do, and she needed to do it fast.

"He say the Messenger. He say something, the Messenger. I need know."

Now her mind snapped into attention. "What do you need to know about the Messenger?"

"I need find, find the Messenger." The girl's eyes narrowed, sparkling resolutely, not about to unclench her grip or to stop her questioning.

"You what?" Startled by the ring of her voice, Onheda covered her mouth hurriedly. "What do you mean? Why do you need to see the Messenger?" she whispered, her words muffled, coming from under her palm.

The girl pressed her lips, her gaze not wavering. "Need talk, need ask, ask something."

It all felt like a bad dream, wandering the darkness, finding no stable ground, nothing to cling to. First getting out, talking to Hanowa and her friends, playing brave and not caring; then overhearing the terrible War Chief whose spies seemed to be all around, knowing her every move; and now this Crooked Tongues girl, bringing so many memories with her accented way of talking, making no sense. What did she want from the Crooked Tongues man? Why was she looking for him?

Crooked Tongues!

The thought hit her like a blow in her stomach. Oh, but the pretty fox came from his homelands. She said she was not captured. She crossed the Great Sparkling Water on her own in order to find *him*.

"You know him!" She stared at the girl, aghast. "You came looking for him."

It came out as an accusation. She could see the girl's lips pressing tightly, the defiant look creeping into the narrowing eyes. For a heartbeat, they just stared at each other, wary and hostile, measuring, gauging one another's strength.

And then they were not alone anymore. She could feel the evil presence before the man materialized out of the darkness, a dark shadow in the corner of her eye. A wave of alarm cascading down her spine, she darted aside nevertheless, her stomach hollow, her legs weak, finding it difficult to support her, with the annoying girl still there, blocking her way. *Did they conspire together, to get rid of her, each for their own reason?*

He grabbed her easily, like the previous time, his palm as rigid as a stone, and as cold.

"So, wild High Springs' girl," he said calmly, his voice quiet, ringing lightly, as though in a regular conversation; as though they had just bumped into each other, and he was not holding her from behind, twisting her arm in a way that didn't let her move without hurting herself. "I think it's time we had a more serious talk."

"Let me go," she hissed, trying to break free in spite of the pain.

He didn't even move, holding her with no effort. "It saddens me that you chose to disregard my well-meaning advice," he went on as though she had not spoken at all. "I had a better opinion of your thinking abilities."

Two more men came out, jumping over the low bushes, not bothering to circumvent the obstacle.

"I'm not going anywhere with you," hissed Onheda, trying to kick backwards, missing her target when he twisted her arm higher, causing her to cry out with pain.

"Oh, yes, you are coming, warrior-girl. And you are coming along quietly and with no trouble, because I do need you alive, but with broken limbs or not, that will be your choice."

She bit her lips hard, finding it difficult to keep her balance, held so awkwardly, all her power turned to the attempt not to make even the slightest move, the pain near unbearable, yet she knew it could be made worse. The tears were rolling, tears of anger and frustration, but she was afraid they might interpret them wrongly.

"Let her go!" She felt the other girl by her side, struggling against the stony grip, her hands small and warm, not strong enough to make a difference.

"What about the other one?" asked the nearest man, catching the girl easily, although she squirmed and kicked, twisting like a snake, yet held expertly, at arm's length.

"Bring her along." The War Chief shrugged. "She has seen too much, and maybe she can be of use, too. These two were clearly planning something smelly, hiding here in the bushes like that. Maybe she is involved in some way."

"She is not," groaned Onheda, giving up on her struggle and wishing the foreign girl would stop squirming so wildly. The man who held her was clearly growing impatient, about to strike her to make her behave. "She is a foreigner. She won't tell. She can't speak our tongue."

"Let us go."

The push in the direction of the entrance made her sway, but it caused the arm holding her to loosen its grip. Momentarily free and not giving her actions too much thought, she whirled around, pushing the man away with all her might, while leaping aside, charging straight through the bushes. They scratched her limbs, but she didn't care, anxious to get to the other side, to put as much distance between herself and her captor, trusting her ability to run faster than him.

A futile hope. He was again beside her, having barely moved at all. Oh, but of course. Hionhwatha was right about this man being a powerful sorcerer.

She fought desperately, kicking and squirming, biting the hand that clasped her mouth, making it difficult to breathe, or to scream. His curses rang in her ears, but then the pain in her head exploded, and the darkness came, merciful in its thickness, offering shelter.

CHAPTER 17

"Where is she?"

He knew she was not there, he knew it from the moment they had arrived in a magnificent array of canoes, when the sun was still high, washing the river, sparkling off the transparent water and the brilliant green of the wet grass adorning the banks.

It had taken them only a few days to reach High Springs, with the large town situated in the comfortable proximity to the fast-flowing river, its current being in their favor. A few days of strenuous rowing, pausing only to forge yet another outburst of rapids, or to consult the guides they had been given.

His followers were puzzled, but he paid them no attention, not bothering to explain. He was going to the second largest town of the Onondagas, and that was that. He was fed up with the delays, arguments, and explanations. He'd had enough, and they did have their choice, to follow him or not to follow. He never forced anyone to go anywhere he went.

Well, as expected, they had chosen to follow, and to High Springs they arrived in a grand state, a fleet of large canoes containing many representatives of four nations. An impressive achievement he might have enjoyed but for the nagging worry. All was not well at the Onondagas. His gut feeling was insistent. Something was wrong, terribly wrong. But what was it? Had Tadodaho gained a total control? Would he find Hionhwatha frustrated and powerless, isolated in the only town he hoped might have listened? And then, there was Onheda. Was she in High Springs, waiting patiently? Was she angry? Would she understand?

Putting all his energy into forcing their canoe to move faster, rowing most of the time with no pause to rest, he had managed to push those thoughts away. Why should he care? She was only a woman, beautiful and courageous, clever and wonderfully responsive, but only a woman. He had had his share, never feeling too bad about disappointing any of them. They tended to demand more than he was willing to give, most of them, expecting unreasonable things, but it was just a part of life. He was too busy to give them more than a fleeting pleasure, and they had no choice but to accept. The Tidings of the Great Peace were more important.

And yet, why had he been so anxious now? Why did he hope she was living in her town, helping Hionhwatha but waiting for him, Two Rivers, to come and join their struggle? Not angry, not disappointed, offering her vital, sparkling presence and maybe more of that inspiring lovemaking, the memory of which still made his stomach twist with anticipation.

However now, the moment he reached High Springs, he knew she was not there. Another gut feeling, as she was not likely to push herself in the midst of the leading people who came to greet them upon the shore of the nearby creek, having clearly been informed about their impending arrival.

Busy talking to people, answering their flowery greetings, trying to convey a calmness he didn't feel, he searched the faces that crowded the shores and then the wide alleys twisting between the longhouses, the smells of the impending feast tickling his nostrils, inviting but bringing no joy. These people were expecting him and his delegation, they were openly glad, greeting him with a genuine pleasure, but the worry was nagging, getting stronger with every heartbeat. She was not here, not a part of this town. Hionhwatha's flickering know-it-all grin had told him so. *But if not here, where was she?*

He had pushed the troublesome thoughts aside, concentrating on the elated mood of this town, talking to them and letting them talk. Hionhwatha had done a splendid work, he decided. He had clearly spent no time in idleness and gloom.

These people wanted to join, with no special concessions even, but the real challenge was still ahead of him.

"Tadodaho is holding his town and the settlements surrounding Onondaga Lake in his firm grip. He is fiercer than ever, and by now, quite eager to meet you, to pit his strength against yours. He doesn't fear me more than he should, so my life is in no danger. But yours is."

"Then we shall grant him his meeting."

Refusing the food, Two Rivers sought out his pipe, always within an easy reach. He was relying on its calming effect too readily these days, he reflected, crushing the dry tobacco leaves, not paying attention to the familiar process. Of an old he had not been smoking his pipe at every opportunity.

"Join us, and we will sail to Onondaga Town in a real strength, with our intentions peaceful but our spirits strong, unwavering, ready to face any challenge."

He forced a grin, missing Tekeni's presence. For a change, the young man had lingered back on the shore, supervising the warriors who remained behind in order to guard their canoes. As though there was a need to guard their vessels, camping in such a friendly place.

"Maybe," said the old leader thoughtfully. "Maybe we'll do just that." His grin spread, along with an unfamiliar slightly mischievous sparkle. "And to think that when we separated on the shores of Onondaga Lake you were no more than a strangely spoken foreigner with a few outcasts for followers. But look at you now! Two seasons later, you come to me, followed by four united nations, speaking our tongue, more sure of yourself than ever. And more impatient." The glimmer in the dark eyes deepened. "You will need every grain of your patience now. While dealing with Tadodaho, you will have to be firm and confident, as unwavering as always, but this sparkle of arrogance I see in you now will have to go. You cannot force my people into your union, four nations or not. You can only persuade them."

"Can Tadodaho be persuaded?" Momentarily alone, as, out

of respect, people moved away, letting the two leaders converse in private, Two Rivers eyed the older man, pleased with the changes. The haunted, violent look was gone, replaced by the dignified bearing, the slightly amused twinkle new to the wrinkled face. The old fox knew what Two Rivers wanted to know, and he was not about to volunteer the information without making the visitor ask.

"Maybe he can be persuaded. Who knows?" The wide shoulders lifted in a shrug. "He has been waiting for you to come. Not much had been done around Onondaga Lake to make it ready *against* your arrival. The old beast is clearly playing for time, curious, confident in his ability to deal with you, to put you in your place or to get rid of you. Curious and expectant. Maybe he has more wisdom than we credit him with." Another shrug. "He could have gotten rid of me, could have swayed High Springs to his side, but he did not. Why? Only his devious mind knows. I think he is eager to meet you."

"Then we shall grant him his wish." Uneasily, Two Rivers shifted, leaning against the warm tiles of the bark lining the wall of the longhouse. "Maybe when he sees the size of our delegation, it will make him pause."

"It won't. He knows his strengths and our weaknesses. He knows that we need to make it as peaceful as we can, resorting to no violence, as tempting as the option may be. But, of course, we shall sail in a day or two. We have not much choice, do we? And we do have the power now."

"Yes, we do, more than he may think we have." Picking up a small stone, Two Rivers hurled it into the fire, watching it bouncing about, rolling out unharmed. "He may think he has power, but he has none. He has nothing to bargain with, nothing to blackmail us with. Judging by our reception here in High Springs, I bet many people of Onondaga Lake are ready to receive us as eagerly. They may be afraid, but when we arrive, they will be heartened."

"Oh, yes, they will. We haven't been idle, as you can see. Onondaga Town is ready for your arrival. I have my spies there, and the information I've been receiving is more than encouraging. Much work has been done there. None of your loyal followers remained idle."

And then he saw it, in the dark, suddenly guarded eyes and the pursed lips, in the sadness that invaded the tired features. And the waiting game was over, the silly play of who will ask first.

"Where is she?"

Wisely, the older man didn't succumb to the temptation of prolonging the confrontation by asking whom.

"She is in Onondaga Town. She went there at the beginning of Maple Moon."

"Why?" It came out angrily, an open accusation.

The bushy eyebrows climbed high. "She wanted to be of help."

He heard the creaking where his fingers pressed against the old wood of the pipe with such force that he could not feel them anymore.

"You sent her into the nest of the snake. You sent her there knowingly, aware of the danger." His voice had a growling sound to it, but he didn't care. She was there, at Tadodaho's mercy, possibly risking her life, swaying people's minds, powerless against the rage of the filthy old sorcerer should her activity be discovered. He squeezed his pipe tighter, wishing to feel it break. "You should not have let a woman do our work. It is our mission, for us to do. Why make a woman fight your battle?"

"Oh, is that so?" Hionhwatha's eyebrows shot higher, the challenge in his eyes unmistakable. "And where have you been? Doing your battles elsewhere, while my people – *and hers!* – were left alone, facing the breach, ready to turn against each other." The narrowed eyes sparkled. "You were the one to abandon us to our struggle, leaving us to make do with our own means to face your war." The gaze of the older man was now blazing ferociously. "Yes, I sent her to Onondaga Town, but she was the one to come to me. Torn, lost, wishing to be of use, eager to do something. To leave her in the old woman's hut, in the middle of nowhere, was not a decent thing to do, oh Revered Messenger of the Great Spirits. Whether she was just another friend and follower, like the scar-faced Flint youth, or whether there was more to it, this young woman deserved a better treatment. I gave her something useful to do. You gave her nothing, unsettling her and her world, then leaving her to her own devices." Pursing his lips, Hionhwatha turned away, staring into the fire. "She is a brave woman, and she did the right thing."

Unable to utter a word, Two Rivers stared into the fire too, his heart beating fast, pumping in his chest. The urge to launch into the older man and strangle him with his own hands welled, but he clenched his palms tight, willing their trembling to subside.

Hionhwatha was right. Of course, he was right. It was his fault. His fault and no one else's. He had neglected these allies of his, Hionhwatha himself, and her, the only woman he had cared for, the only woman that meant more than just a passing fancy to him. He had let them all down. He had no right to complain about their way of doing things. When he had been busy elsewhere, they were struggling to keep his dream alive, in these lands and among these people, loyal to him and his ideas no matter what he did.

He got to his feel slowly, exhausted. His muscles ached from more than two days of rowing, his chest heavy, hollow with desperation.

"I will sail for Onondaga Town," he said, refusing to meet the older man's questioning gaze. "You can organize your people and those who came with me and follow when you are ready."

"Will you be sailing alone?" Hionhwatha's voice held an open surprise.

"I will bring a few of the warriors, those who would volunteer to come. There is no need to make Tadodaho wait any longer."

"Your scar-faced companion will be with you, surely." The older leader was on his feet now, too. "Where is he, anyway?"

"He is down there by the boats."

He thought about Tekeni, always there, always helping, doing all the right things without being asked to, putting his private happiness and his promise aside for his, Two Rivers', sake. What sort of a person was he, to make people closest to him unhappy, forgetting their own goals?

His shoulders felt heavy, made out of stone. The tiredness was annoying, refusing to go away. He felt like lying down and resting for at least one afternoon, with no need to think or act or answer people's questions, with no nagging worry at the awareness that there was more than a day and a half of walking between here and Onondaga Town, and that he might be too late already.

"Why didn't he come into the town? Is he afraid?"

"He is afraid of nothing. There is no braver warrior and no more loyal companion, and you know it as well as I do." Shrugging, he fought the urge to rub his face in an attempt to bring his numb skin back to life again. It was tiring, to pretend to be strong and unwavering all the time. "He has his own private matters to settle. He will not come with me this time."

"Too bad." Hionhwatha narrowed his eyes. "Your people need rest, and they need to mingle among my people, to talk and to share a pipe. You can't rush them more than necessary."

"I'm not rushing them. I will send the word when the matter with Tadodaho is settled. When it happens, I will invite them to leave High Springs and come to Onondaga Town."

The old leader gave him a long, measuring glance. "Let me show you something."

"I need to go to our boats."

"It will not take long."

The man was gone, leaving Two Rivers in a blissful solitude, which didn't last. People were coming and going, surrounding him, talking, requiring answers, or just polite greetings. He answered them without thinking, his mind in a fog, craving the

privilege to be left alone. Back in his lands, he had had too
much time to himself, rarely listened to, never for real. Now he
had been listened to too much, making his vision come true in
the manner he had never imagined was possible, far beyond his
wildest dreams. And yet, something was still wrong, still
missing. Somehow, he kept making the people close to his heart
unhappy, too busy to think about their private needs. The needs
of the nations and their united purpose were more important,
and yet...

He glimpsed Tekeni's broad shoulders blocking the sunlight
as the young man neared with the long, forceful stride of his, a
mature wolf on a trail. Shielding his eyes, Two Rivers watched
him, reflecting how this youth had grown in stature, turning
into a real man, imposing and prominent, the scars not marring
his handsomeness but adding to it.

"They claim no one would dare to put their filthy paws on
our boats." The youth's grin was wide, flickering with mischief.
"And the smells of the feast reached us even down there on the
shore."

"Get a quick bite because we are leaving in a short while."

"What?" A pair of widening eyes peered at him, startled.
"What's wrong?"

"Nothing is wrong." He shook his head, trying to make his
mind work. "I'll ask Hionhwatha to organize a good bag of
provisions for you. Enough for half a moon, or so. All that
dried meat and cakes, and a lot of maize powder with maple
syrup."

The eyes peering at him narrowed into slits. "Where am I
going?"

"Where you've wanted to go since we left my people. Get the
girl, and make it as fast as you can. I want you back here in time
for the first gathering of the five nations. If all goes according to
our plan, it will happen here, on the Onondaga soil, probably
around Onondaga Lake, somewhere near their main town. You
have half a moon to be back, with your pretty Seketa by your
side, all happy and smiles." He forced a grin. "I want at least

one of my countryfolk around and watching, witnessing that I had not been talking nonsense all these long summers back in my lands."

The smile of the youth beamed at him, making him feel a little better, so happy and unreserved it almost shone. "Yes, I'll do that. I'll bring her back in time for the first gathering. I would not miss it anyway, even if I have to travel with no sleep at all." A shadow crossed the handsome face, making the smile dim. "But what about Onondaga Town and Tadodaho?"

"We'll take care of the old fox, Hionhwatha and I. As you know, we have enough power behind us now, the promise of the four nations and the backing of many Onondagas. Tadodaho will make no trouble."

"What if he does?" The smile was gone, replaced by a frown. "Judging by the rumors, the old beast might be quite upset by now, throwing everything he has against you, and you in particular. With you gone, the promises of the nations will disintegrate. The bonds are not strong enough, yet. I know it, you know it, and I bet he knows it, too. Your bunch of arrows needs to be tied by a few more rounds before you loosen your grip."

Oh, the youth had grown to be too wise, too perceptive!

"Yes, I know it, and I will be careful. But I want you to go now all the same. You've been putting your private happiness away for too long. There will be something, always something. After Tadodaho's matter is resolved, something else will come up, preventing you from leaving." He put his arm on the wide shoulder, feeling odd. "Get yourself some food, and we'll set you off right away, before Father Sun starts hurrying toward its resting place."

"Why not tomorrow with dawn?"

"Why do you ask so many questions? Do you want to go or not?" He moderated his tone, knowing that his frustration had nothing to do with his friend. "If you want to stay, stay."

"*Tsi:ron*! But you are touchier than a mother bear about to give birth." The young man frowned. "Are you sure everything is well?" The large eyes narrowed with suspicion. "The Onondaga girl, is she here?"

He saw Hionhwatha coming back, carrying a large strip of what looked like another of his shell works. Which was a good timing, as a little more questioning would see him yelling at Tekeni.

"Oh, the scar-faced warrior finally graced my humble town with his presence," said the old leader, grinning widely. "My people are honored."

Tekeni's smile was surprisingly shy. "We needed to guard our canoes."

"And here I was thinking you were praising the Messenger higher than your boats. Of an old, you used to guard him and not his vessels." The older man's grin faded, lost some of its mirth. "I used to admire your loyalty to him, but now I'm not so sure anymore. It's not a good timing to go away on your private missions."

"I did not…" The young man's face was a mask of bewilderment. "What are you talking about?"

"Let us leave it at that." His hand still on the young man's shoulder, Two Rivers stirred him away, toward the pots that were bursting with hungry people. "Go get some food."

He turned back to Hionhwatha, wishing to get the ensuing conversation over with, but Tekeni was still there, refusing to leave.

"I want to know what *is* going on!" he demanded, the easy-going young warrior of the last few seasons spent on this side of the Great Sparkling Water gone, replaced by the angry cub of his hometown, growling and refusing to be put back in his place.

"Will you be making a scene right here in the middle of the feast thrown in the honor of our guests?" Hionhwatha was clearly more amused than put out, but his voice sounded stern.

"Not if I'm told what is going on," retorted Tekeni, not about to give up, standing the glare of the High Springs' leader bravely.

Two Rivers sighed. "Do what I told you. Cross the Great Lake, and be back in no more than half a moon. In the meanwhile, we'll make it all ready for the First Gathering." Was he required to act as a peacemaker between these two, in addition to doing that for their nations? He felt like cursing and chuckling at the same time.

"I would say you put it a little too simply, but if your so-called friend is eager to leave, then I suppose it's a good enough way of saying it."

"I'm not eager to leave. This is the first time I've heard about it."

Now the questioning glare of the Onondaga man was directed at Two Rivers, scorching his skin. "I see."

He sighed. "Listen, you two. I know what I'm doing, so please, just let me do it. It's going to turn out well, like the rest of our last autumn's adventures."

"And if it's not?"

"It will."

"You told me you two are going to talk to Tadodaho."

Hionhwatha's mirthless chuckle shook the air. "He told you wrong. He is going to confront the malicious sorcerer all by himself, because that's what the evil man is expecting him to do. And he has his private reasons, as well." The dark eyes were now mere slits in the paleness of the wrinkled face. "He expects me to handle this lot from all over the lands of the five nations in the meanwhile, make sure they don't start fighting in his absence. Which, of course, will occur, especially if something happens to him, preventing him from returning at all."

Another pair of indignant eyes were boring at him. "You said nothing of the sort!"

"I don't have to tell any of you anything."

Oh, Mighty Spirits! He could not control his temper anymore, and the people were looking at them, puzzled, openly wondering; the guests and the locals, people who had followed him here, ready to support him and his idea of the union, ready to try and live in his Good Tidings of Peace.

He took a deep breath. "Please, let us leave it at that. I know what I'm doing."

"And so do I." Tekeni's eyes glowed stonily, reminding him of the eventful evening in Little Falls. "I'll go with you to meet Tadodaho, then I'll sail." He shrugged. "It's on the way to the Great Sparkling Water, anyway."

"What can I do to make you both leave me in peace, to do as I decide?"

They raised their eyebrows in unison, as though following a signal.

"You start thinking like a man with an important mission, like a man responsible for the welfare of five powerful nations and their future well-being. Not like an angry youth eager to chase a pretty face." Hionhwatha kept his voice low, and Two Rivers was grateful for the small mercy. "I hope you have brought along some good people whom you can trust to handle this lot in your absence, because we both are coming with you. And anyone else who would choose to join us. As if no one comes, than it will be the three of us, in the best spirit of the last autumn's adventure you are remembering so well." The long, purple-white belt rustled pleasantly as it was thrust into Two Rivers' hands. "See this? It's the symbol of your Great Peace. We will take it along, and we will use it in the First Gathering, to make everyone remember their commitment. I liked that idea of yours, and I had enough time during the long winter moons to do something about it."

Dazed, Two Rivers stared at the pattern of white rectangles upon the purple of the background, a neat line of five connected forms. "How did you know?" he whispered, awed.

He could feel Tekeni holding his breath, himself remembering the dimming light of the swallowed-away sun and him kneeling, drawing on the ground, talking about the metaphorical longhouse composed of five nations, trying to dominate his fear in order to keep their attention, to gain the most out of the terrible event. *Drawing exactly the same rectangles in the sand – two from each side, and the diamond in the middle.* The diamond was different, but the rest were exactly the same.

"How did you know?"

"Know what?" The older man seemed to be surprised with the effect.

Paying him no attention, Two Rivers peered at the wide string, studying it more closely. There were differences, of course. Unlike his drawing, the rectangles were of various sizes, spread unevenly, and the middle section was decisively larger, too prominent, but in a fitting way.

"Those are your five nations, tied together in the way of a mutual management, just like you suggested to do when we first met."

"Like a longhouse," muttered Tekeni, peering at the white-and-purple belt with the same intent. "Five families."

"Well, yes, in some way." Hionhwatha nodded appreciatively. "Good thinking, young man."

"I didn't think it. He said it when he drew your belt in the People of the Mountains' gathering, when he made Father Sun disappear from the sky in order to make them listen."

"He did what?" The Onondaga leader's eyebrows were very high once again, reflecting his doubts.

"It doesn't matter now." Suddenly lightheaded, Two Rivers shook his head. "This is a wonderful symbol that represents exactly what will happen after we are through with Tadodaho. Five Nations, living together in peace." He ran his palm along the tightly woven shells, enjoying the rough smoothness of its surface. "Oh, it represents our future longhouse perfectly. Perfectly!" His fingers lingered around the middle, overturned form. "Those are Onondagas, yes? Why is its form different?"

"Oh, well," Hionhwatha shrugged, but his eyes were guarded now. "We are in the middle of your union, so it made sense to stress it, somehow."

"What else would have to be different because you are in the middle of our longhouse, an indispensable part of it?"

The older man's smile was free of guilt. "You know very well what it would be."

"The meetings would be held in your lands." Two Rivers made it a statement, his smile matching.

"Yes. The Keepers of the Central Fire, I love that title."

"It will give your people no power over the others."

A shrug was his answer, but he held the man's gaze, wishing to make himself clear.

The smug expression faded, disappeared, leaving the broad features cold, as though chiseled out of stone. "We'll see about that." It was quite a growl.

"There will be not even the slightest inequality. The Great Council will work in the way that will give no nation power over the others. There will be no leading peoples." He stared at the dark, stormy eyes, remembering the hut on the shores of Onondaga Lake and the violent man throwing knives, one after another, each throw a perfect hit. "The nations will benefit from joining the league, but never at the expense of the others. I made sure of that already."

"Did you?" The thin lips quivered, twisting into a defiant smile.

"Yes, I did. The laws that will govern our union are already made. They will not be discussed among any of us. They will be presented to the people on our First Gathering, to be ratified, yes, but not to be adjusted. They will be either accepted or rejected. There will be no changes."

He liked the sound of it, although he had thought it all out only now, standing before his oldest of allies, knowing that it was a crucial moment. The laws, indeed, were all in his head since before the Cold Moons, or even earlier, maybe before he had left the lands of his people.

He remembered discussing it for the first time with Atiron, before the test of the falls, meeting an apprehensive suspicion at first, and then the conviction. Every discussed issue, every new law would have to be passed through the positive vote of every council member. With one single representative's objections, nothing could be passed, no law made, no solution reached. A difficult procedure, but a necessary one. This way no represented town would feel overruled, and no nation would gain control over the other. There were different amounts of towns in every land, and so would be the amount of representatives, but with an unanimous voting it would not matter at all. Too bad Atiron had chosen not to come. He could use the man's calm, wise, witty support. Damn that silly daughter of his into the world of the Evil Twin and his minions.

Hionhwatha's glare was not easy to stand, but before they could start arguing for real, Tekeni was between them, distracting with his swift, silent way of moving, and the air of determination he radiated.

"Let us worry about it later. If we want to set out for Onondaga Lake before the sun has left our world, we had better hurry."

And that was that, thought Two Rivers, pleased with his younger friend's timely intervention. They had a difficult task ahead, and by the time they were able to discuss the lawmaking again, the old Onondaga leader would have come around.

He smiled at Tekeni fleetingly. "Yes, let us get organized."

CHAPTER 18

Seketa watched the shadows dispersing, the dim light creeping in through the cracks in the wall. The darkness turned grayish, cold and unfriendly but encouraging too, giving hope. The morning was near, and she always felt better in the mornings. She was not a night person like many of her friends.

Her friends!

The thought of her hometown, her people, made her stomach turn, bringing a bitter taste to her mouth. She should never have left, never. It was a mistake, a rushed decision made out of a stupid impulse. She was always thoughtful, always clever. How could she have acted so stupidly this time, not only leaving on a wild adventure with her chances to find him, the Wolf Clan boy, her chosen mate, so slim they were almost nonexistent, but also the way she had left, helping the war captives to escape, doing the unthinkable.

So now here she was, with her way back blocked by the Great Sparkling Water and the unreasonableness of her deed, with nowhere to go but to wander about, to be captured or kidnapped, or worse. It all had happened already, and she could not even try to imagine what the future held in store for her. The Great Spirits were clearly displeased with her actions, rightfully so. She deserved all the trouble that had befallen her, from losing her way in the Great Lake, barely surviving the crossing, to falling into enemy hands right away, almost forced into adoption and then kidnapped again while attempting to escape. Oh, she must have made the Great Spirits truly angry!

The rope tying her hands behind her back loosened a little, and it brought her back from her desperate thoughts. She had been rubbing it against the sharp edge in the wall since they had been brought here, into this small hut in the woods, with the waterfalls roaring not far away. The moment their captors left, she had crawled toward the corner and began working on her ties, with the other girl still unconscious, or just disoriented, very quiet in the darkness, moaning lightly every now and then.

She thought about that girl and the way she had argued with the man who kidnapped them, so brave and in perfect control, almost calm, challenging, but then losing her mind and fighting like a wild creature, in panic. They had to hit her hard to make her stop fighting, but it forced them to carry her all the way here, which clearly displeased the two men that were ordered to do so. They were enraged and very rude, ready to knock her unconscious too, so Seketa deemed it wise not to anger them any further, but to do as she was told. To walk mainly, and to keep quiet. And now, here she was, in this strange-looking hut, barely hearing her own thoughts with the roaring of the damn falls, but blissfully alone and with her ties coming off. At long last!

In the strengthening light, she looked around, seeing scattered tools and utensils, with the bag she had stolen from the Bear Clan's longhouse earlier in the night thrown carelessly beside the door. It made her chuckle. Why had they bothered bringing her bag along? It was silly of them, but helpful.

Hurriedly, she went through its contents, remembering herself snatching two flint stones on a spur of inspiration, thinking of the possibilities like needing to make fire. Both pieces were small and round, but one had a broken edge, sharp enough to cut the tough leather.

The other girl groaned and moved, trying to sit up.

"Wait!"

Armed with the flint, Seketa came closer, kneeling awkwardly, afraid to cut the girl instead. Her palms were numb from being tied for half a night, but a few strokes of her flint helped, making the rope fall off, so easily she felt like laughing. Eyeing her newly acquired weapon with satisfaction, she allowed herself a grin.

"Where are we?" whispered the girl, sitting up, grimacing with pain.

"I not, not know." It was annoying, this necessity to speak their foul-sounding tongue. "Men bring, bring here. Men kidnap."

"Oh!" Hesitantly, the girl touched the back of her head, feeling it out, while Seketa made her way toward the wooden cistern, pleased to see it half full of water. A stack of dried meat and berries made her feel like a winner.

"We good. Have water, have food," she informed her companion, dunking her whole face into the cistern, drinking thirstily.

"We need to go. We need to run away from here, and fast." The girl's face had a pasty color, and the way she clutched onto the pole of the entrance, made her look unfit to cover even the distance to the wooden bin, let alone to run away and fast.

Picking up a small, round bowl, Seketa filled it with water. "Here. Drink. You look no good."

Her companion drank thirstily, almost choking on the clear liquid. "Thank you. You are brave. I'm sorry they kidnapped you too. They are after me, not you."

"What want? What they want?" Without thinking, she tucked the dried meat and berries into her bag, fighting her hunger off. This woman was right, they had better get away first.

"It's complicated." Biting her lips, the girl inspected her head once again. "Am I bleeding?"

"Let see." The base of the loosely tied braid was stiff with dried blood, and upon a careful inspection, Seketa could see the sticky mess of her companion's nape. "Yes, blood, yes. There wound, but I can't, can't find. Need wash, need light."

"It doesn't matter," muttered the girl, grimacing again. "I feel better now."

Picking up her bag, Seketa didn't try to hide her concern. "Need see healer."

"Later, yes." The girl went toward the shut screen, her steps steadier.

They listened carefully, then, satisfied, tried to pull the screen away. It moved, but only a little, getting stuck very soon. Stifling a curse, Seketa pulled harder, with all her might.

"Wait." A warm palm rested on her shoulder, cautioning her.

They listened.

"It's tied. Outside," whispered her companion, apparently satisfied with the silence. "Give me that flint you used earlier."

A flint? Cursing her inability to understand faster the stupid way of their talking, Seketa fished in her bag again, grabbing the sharper stone.

"I cut."

Carefully, she pushed past the girl, knowing how easy it would be to knock her dizzy companion off her feet. Twisting her body, she reached for the knot that held the wooden screen in place, trying to find the way to make the first cut. The rope vibrated, making her mumble in fury.

By the time it gave in, her arm was numb, its joint twisted, sending rays of pain down her shoulder. The girl disappeared, then came back, holding a pole that would be used in the fields to prepare the ground for planting as though it were a club. Seketa raised her eyebrows, then moved the screen, frowning at the way it screeched.

The bright morning light poured in, giving a good view of the clearing and the man coming out of the woods, adjusting his loincloth. Her heart stopped, freezing in her chest. One heartbeat, then another. The man stared at them for only half of that time. In one powerful leap, he was beside the doorway, shoving her in with a violent push.

Waving her hands to keep her balance, Seketa grabbed his sleeve when another forceful shove sent her crashing down, onto the earthen floor. Half stunned and panicked, she didn't let the well-tanned material of her attacker's shirt go, and it made him waver and crush beside her, spitting curses.

His palm grabbed her face, shoving her head into the floor, making her cry out with pain. Her vision blurry, she brought her free hand up, then remembered the flint. It was still there, grasped tightly in her palm. Frantic, she thrust her arm out desperately, aiming for the momentarily exposed side of his face, but the sharp edge slipped, brushing against his cheek harmlessly, hurting it maybe, but drawing no blood.

He cursed again, catching her arm easily, slamming it against the floor, making the flint fall.

"You filthy rat!"

She squirmed wildly, in panic now, his limbs pressing her, hurting, making it difficult to breathe. When his face slammed into her, she gasped, stunned by the blow, but still pushing, her instincts screaming danger, not aware of his body suddenly turning heavier, limp in a revolting way. The wriggling out was easier now, and she shut her eyes, gathering the last of her strength, pushing him off with a final effort, staring at the roof, gasping for air.

"Get up, we need to hurry. Are you hurt?"

Focusing, Seketa's eyes took in the bright surroundings, the light pouring in through the gaping entrance, illuminating the other girl as she stood there, legs wide apart, like a warrior, the improvised club firm in her hands, glittering darkly.

"Yes, yes, I no hurt." She felt out her face, pulsating with pain but not wet, not bleeding. "I... Sorry. It fast, too fast."

She got up shakily, then took in the girl's pose again, her stark, lifeless face and the pole held expertly, still glittering. The man was on the floor, a lifeless form with the back of his head a mess of wet hair and seeping liquids.

"You kill, you kill him," she whispered, and it brought the girl back to life all at once.

"Yes, I think he is dead, or maybe dying." Her voice was steady, livelier than before the violent encounter. "We won't stay to see if he recovers. Come."

Peeking carefully this time, they slipped outside, scanning the clearing, searching for signs of danger. Seketa's legs shook so badly she needed all her concentration to just walk straight. It was like a bad dream, and it kept getting worse. They had just killed one of the men who kidnapped them, and the girl by her side was not perturbed in the slightest, doing the killing with the natural efficiency of a warrior and feeling no remorse whatsoever.

"Hush!"

A warning hand clasped her arm, making Seketa's heart leap. It pounded in her ears so loudly she could hear no other sound, but the girl was already pulling her, making her sway. Diving behind the back wall of the hut, she caught a glimpse of another man coming out of the woods, strolling leisurely, not in a hurry.

The girl kept pulling, and before she knew it, they were in the thickest of the grove, following a small trail that kept narrowing, forcing them to climb between the twisted roots and the slippery rocks, with the roaring of the waterfalls getting closer, drowning out other possible sounds. Seketa stopped thinking and just followed, her mind in a jumble, refusing to work. The man did not seem to chase them, but why?

The answer presented itself when the trail ended at the edge of a high cliff, the breathtaking view of a powerful surge cascading into the glittering rocky surface far, far below, a magnificent flow, awe-inspiring in its forcefulness, the brilliant green all around completing the beautiful picture. It was a dead end. They had nowhere to go.

"We will have to go back," muttered Seketa, unable to take her eyes off the rocks that glittered viciously far below her feet. She'd heard of people jumping into falls and coming out alive, but she was sure it never happened in these particular cascades.

"We can't. The other man will either follow or wait." The girl measured the nearest cliffs with her gaze, chewing her lower lip. "Maybe we can get down there, if we are careful. Just follow those rocks. Maybe they'll bring us to the bottom of the falls."

Seketa hoped she did not understand her companion well this time.

"We have nothing to lose," went on the girl, clearly talking to herself now, trying to convince.

"I no go there," said Seketa, determined. "I wait, then go

back."

The pair of dark eyes flew at her, flashing. "He'll wait too. But you can go. I won't hold you here against your will."

"You fall if go. No crossing. Can't jump." She mimicked a movement of a person slipping, flailing her hands in the air. "You fall."

The girl shrugged with an obvious contempt. "I'll go there, you go back, and we'll see who will make it out alive."

Seketa felt like pushing the annoying fox down the cliff. "Do as you please!"

Turning abruptly, she heard a hiss, as though a large, vicious insect just rushed past her ear. There was another sound, a sort of a gasp, and as she turned back to find out what happened, she saw that she was all alone on the cliff now, just her and the sky, and the roaring water, and the chirping of the birds on the trail behind her back.

Stupefied, she looked back, then saw a glimpse of a movement, and another hiss, not as clear or as close as the first one. Aghast, she dropped to the ground, remembering the other side of the Great Lake and the hurried flight, and the frantic rowing under the same murmur of the lethal, razor-sharp arrows.

Crawling toward the edge, her heart fluttering in her chest, making her dizzy, she peeked down, her stomach as tight as the stones it pressed against. The distant rocks glittered undisturbed in the turbulence of the swirling foam. The other girl was nowhere to be seen, an *uki* vanished into thin air. She was alone now, truly alone, between the vicious cascades and the people who wanted to kill her.

The scream was close, near the surface, a scream of rage and frustration, and not of fear. It all had been in vain, all of it, her waiting, her journey, her love. She had been struggling for nothing, like an insect caught in a flask, with the Great Spirits displeased or indifferent, not favoring her desperate efforts.

Her vision blurry, she scanned the distant rapids one more time, then looked at the rocks below her cliff. Should she try to climb down the way the other girl had suggested before the man with the bow came? It didn't seem like a way out, but what choice did she have? No more arrows flew, but she knew the man was coming, maybe in those very moments, climbing the trail, his knife out and ready.

Leaning over the edge, she sought the next tier, lowering herself on her hands carefully, the ice in her stomach piling. If she slipped, it would be such a long fall.

On the solid surface again, she looked around, then gasped. The girl was there, not far below, a crumpled form lying on a relatively wide tier, her eyes wide open, blinking, as round as two plates in the grayish pastiness of her face, her dress askew, one of the long, decorated sleeves torn, glittering darker than the other.

Seketa clutched to the cold, slippery stones, trying to make her mind work.

"Are you all right?" she cried out, fighting for breath. Her voice rang eerily, not belonging in the clearness of the blossoming morning and the forcefulness of the tumbling water, her tongue not good enough for those gods-accursed lands.

The girl blinked again, then moved awkwardly, struggling into an upright position. "Yes, I think I am." Her words drowned in the roaring of the angry water, but Seketa knew what she meant.

"I come. Wait. No move, I come, come down," she shouted, seeing the unsuccessful attempts, one of the sleeves on the girl's dress soaked and glittering. "No get up."

Her fear of the fall forgotten, she worked her way down hurriedly, regretting that her bag was not at hand, abandoned, still in the hut. She might have found something useful there.

Breathing heavily and scratched all over, she jumped the last of the gaps, knowing that under no regular circumstances would she have attempted such leaping between the slippery rocks, with the prospect of a long fall that might have ensued should she miss her footing.

"You wound?" she panted, kneeling beside her companion who, by now, was sitting, leaning on her good arm. The other hung useless, the tanned leather of the dress clinging to it, dark and stiff with the accumulating blood.

"The damn arrow," said the girl hoarsely. "It stuck. I tried to pull it out. Maybe it was not a good thing to do."

Now she could see the broken shaft, thrown carelessly, defeated, the remaining part of which was still there, in the fleshy part of the girl's upper arm, sticking out, short but menacing.

"I... I think... think what to do," she muttered, helpless. "We need help."

The girl made a face, her color returning. "Oh, yes, we do, but we can't have it." She shrugged with her good shoulder, flinching. "So I say we go on, try to get down there," she concluded after a painful pause, as determined and as domineering as always.

"You can't."

"Yes, I can and I am going to. And so are you."

But the attempt to get up proved Seketa right. Wavering and almost falling into the roaring abyss, the girl slipped back into her previous position, her lips colorless, pressed tight, face stark and sweat-covered, lifeless again.

"Maybe in a little while," she mumbled, panting, clinging to the ground as though trying to absorb some of its strength. "You go. Don't stay here."

Seketa squatted more comfortably, holding her companion lightly, afraid to touch the wounded shoulder and the broken shaft that stuck out so awkwardly, not belonging in the delicate flesh of a young, beautiful woman.

"We think, find what to do. You rest now," she muttered, listening to the wind in the bushes above. *Were their pursuers searching the cliff now? Would they manage to see them huddling here?* It was a good hiding place, provided help was on its way.

Pursing her lips, she tried to think hard. Maybe she still could climb back up, reaching the town not later than on the early afternoon. It was not far, and she remembered the way well. But whom would she ask for help, a runaway Crooked Tongues captive that she was?

Suppressing her fury, she thought about that ugly name her people were apparently called here. Crooked Tongues! As though the locals spoke any better. She remembered wondering who those crooked tongues were when Sgenedu first used this term.

Sgenedu!

If he didn't die and maybe got better, he might be willing to help her. He owed her his and his sister's lives, and he was a decent person.

"I bring help. In a little while," she said, helping the girl to recline as comfortably as she could on the damp stones. "Call help."

"No one will dare to help us. They are afraid of the War Chief, all of them, and..." The girl licked her cracked lips, then took a convulsive breath, clearly trying to dominate the pain. "He is a powerful sorcerer, they say. He could be anywhere, listen to anyone. No one will dare to help us."

"The man who kidnap?"

"Yes."

"Why kidnap? Why you and me?"

"He wants to use me against the Messenger. It is my fault. Hionhwatha had warned me not to let him know, but somehow, the War Chief knew. He wants to use me when the Messenger comes." The girl sighed, then her eyes concentrated, peering at Seketa, suddenly wary, even hostile. "You know the Messenger, don't you?"

"The Messenger?" It was again difficult to understand the rapidly flowing foreign words. "Think maybe know, yes. Maybe."

"From the Crooked Tongues lands?"

"Yes."

"Why? Why did you come all the way here, risking your life like that? What do you want from him?"

The gaze peering at her was so intense, Seketa felt like taking a step back. Into the roaring chasm, she reflected, not amused.

"I don't have to tell you!" she said hotly, then switched back to their tongue, just to make sure she was understood. "Can tell, can not tell. Don't owe you, nothing."

A fierce glare and the pressed lips were her answer. "You will have to wander quite a lot looking for him. He is running all over. It will take a while before he comes here." The girl's gaze darkened. "If ever."

"Where is now? Where is he?"

"I don't have to tell you that, either!"

Seketa moved away as much as their small hideaway allowed, fighting the urge to push the filthy fox down the cliff, to put her out of her misery, maybe.

"You are nothing but a stupid piece of rotten meat," she muttered in her tongue, not caring if she was understood or not.

The flaring nostrils of her adversary told her that she was understood well enough.

"You can curse in that stupid, crooked, twisted tongue of yours all you like, but I spent days with him and we talked a lot, and he said nothing about you, not a word!" Some color crept into the lifeless face, the girl's cheeks beginning to burn. "He did not miss his people, and he doesn't intend to go back, ever. He told me that much."

Seketa's rage was difficult to control now, fueled by her inability to understand it all. The stupid fowl was so unreasonable, and she cared too much. Her passion was jarring in its intensity.

"Who are you?" she asked, risking another defiant refusal.

"I'm the woman whom he trusts more than anyone!" There was a challenge in the sparkling eyes, but also some deeply hidden misery. Now Seketa could see it most clearly. This girl was strong and violent, but she was unhappy too, and it had to do with that legendary messenger of theirs.

"Listen, I don't... don't know this messenger, maybe." She searched for words carefully, wishing to be understood now.

"Maybe another person. Maybe looking for another person, not your messenger. See?"

"You don't know?" Forgetting her wound, the girl straightened up, then gasped and fell back, leaning against the rock, her face drained of color again. "But you should know whom you are looking for, no?" she muttered, when able to speak. "To get into such adventure, to risk your life and your freedom this way, you need to know whom you are looking for, don't you?"

Seketa looked away, saying nothing. Yes, she had been stupid to do such a reckless deed. She knew it all by herself, with no need to elaborate on it.

"He is Crooked Tongues, right?" The girl's voice held a measure of compassion. "The man you are looking for."

"No," said Seketa, her stomach twisting all of a sudden. Since entering the accursed town, dragged there against her will, attempted to be adopted like the last of the helpless captives, she didn't think about him, too busy with her mounting troubles. "He is from this side, this side of the Great Lake. He is no Crooked Tongues."

"Oh!" The girl's relief was ridiculously obvious. "I see." She frowned. "Why are you looking for this man?"

"It long, long story." She sighed. "I hoped he is with your messenger, maybe. If not, I don't know, don't know what to do, where to look. I should not come. Should stay home." The tears were too near now, blurring her vision. "He promised, promised to come, to be back, to take me, but he did not come, and I should, should forget. Not to come here."

It was too difficult to talk now, so she stopped, her misery welling. If they survived, this girl would go back to her town, her people, her life, but she, Seketa, had nowhere to go, stuck among the enemies, with not a hint as to where to look, whom to ask, or even if she would have been welcomed if found. He had probably forgotten all about her, while she waited and waited, leaving her people in order to find him, to help him keep his promise.

"Don't cry." The clammy palm reached for her, brushing against her arm, trying to reassure. The attempt cost her companion enough pain to break with a new bout of sweat. "I'll help you to find this man. After all this is over, after we have made it out of here alive, I promise to help you. We'll find him together. I'm sure he just couldn't come. Not because he forgot. I'm sure he'll be glad to see you. Is he Onondaga?"

"Flint People," muttered Seketa, embarrassed, trying to control the trembling of her voice. What a stupid thing it was, to start crying like a baby, no better than silly Gayoah.

She blinked the tears away, then felt the stunned silence, taking in the girl's stare, her eyes wide, full of disbelief, watching Seketa as though she had suddenly sprouted horns or laid an egg, at the very least.

"What?" she asked, but the girl kept staring, her mouth gaping, her eyes ridiculously round. "What happened?"

"Oh, Mighty Spirits! It can't be you. It can't be!" The girl swallowed. "It would be just too much."

"What?" Seketa felt like shaking her companion into talking more sense. It was better to argue and hate each other than to watch the astounded, stupefied face, waiting for the silly woman to faint from all this staring.

"The scar-faced Flint youth!" breathed the girl in the end. "You can't be his girl!" The passionate gaze bore at her. "He has scars, doesn't he?"

"Scars? No. Well, yes, scars, little." She pointed to her chest. "He hunt bear, got scars, yes."

"No, his face," insisted the girl. "All over his face and his chest, yes."

"No, he no scars. Not his face."

The disappointment of her companion was again too obvious too miss. "Oh, then I got it all wrong." She grinned, but it was an artificial grin. "The wrong Flint People's man, I suppose. The youth I knew has scars all over, and he has a girl left among Crooked Tongues. He wanted to go back all the time, but the Messenger needed him, so he had to wait." She shrugged. "Maybe he went there after the Cold Moons. Maybe he brought her back already."

Seketa was afraid her head would crack from the effort to understand. Someone already went to her lands to fetch another girl? Who? And why? And most importantly, what did it have to do with her and with that mysterious messenger of theirs?

The girl laughed, at ease again. "It's all so very strange now. Since the Messenger came nothing happened that was not odd, bizarre, out of the ordinary. Of an old it was unspeakable to think of Crooked Tongues girls roaming around, seeking our men."

She clung to the only familiar thing. "That messenger, how he look?"

The girl's eyes lit. "Oh, he is impressive, outstanding. So formidable! With his eyes shining and his smile special. He is so wise, so courageous, like no other man. He speaks beautifully, even though it's difficult to understand him with that dreadful accent of your people. Still, everyone listens to him, everyone! Even Hionhwatha has listened. Even the Flint People. He is truly the Messenger of the Right-Handed Twin himself. I knew it all along, but the other people know it too now, everyone." The girl paused, her smile turning shy. "He is not making miracles, like people think. He did not sail a white canoe made out of stone, like they say. His canoe is bright but regular, made out of bark. And he doesn't do obvious wonders. But he is no ordinary person. He makes everyone listen and follow, and he will make our people live in peace. Tadodaho can struggle all he likes, but he can't change it now. The Messenger is stronger than him, and," she paused again, her cheeks coloring, "well, he will make it all happen. I know he will."

"But he come, come other side of the Great Lake?"

"Oh, yes, he speaks with that dreadful accent of yours."

Two Rivers? Seketa felt the knot in her stomach tightening again. "And the man with him, the Flint People's man?" She swallowed. "He young? Tall? Broad shoulders?"

"Oh, yes! He is a handsome youth, and very good, good

warrior, great friend." The girl's grin was almost playful, full of memories. "We used to argue all the time. I hated him in the beginning. He is violent and short-tempered, and he came from Little Falls, the filthiest town that ever existed and—"

But Seketa stopped listening, her heart thundering too loudly, interrupting with her ability to hear. It all fit, *all of it!* It was him, him and no one else. But the scars all over his face? He had not enough scars to call him 'scar-faced youth' like this girl did. There were some small cuts, that all boys had, and then there were the bear claws' marks, but nothing to make it stand out.

And then she gasped, remembering the fateful night on the shores of her home-lake, with Two Rivers inspecting the canoe, with her and Tekeni embraced, clinging to each other, exchanging promises, but unable to kiss even, with his lips cut and his face cut, and his chest and his ribs even... Oh, Mighty Spirits! She fought for breath, seeing the girl staring at her again, wide-eyed.

"What now?"

"It's him!" She heard her voice trembling, low and distorted, her breath coming in gasps, impossible to control.

"Do you think? But you said your man has no scars—"

"Yes, the scars, he must, he must scars now, yes." Her head reeled so badly, she pressed against the cliff, afraid to lose her balance and fall into the falls.

"Oh well, if it's him, then all is well." The girl smiled broadly. "He didn't forget you, I can promise you that." Her smile kept widening. "He even made me promise to take care of you when he brings you here, if he is too busy sometimes, or if something happens to him." The amusement was spilling out of the crinkling eyes, transforming the pale, haunted face, making it look breathtakingly beautiful. "Who would predict you would find me all by yourself, throwing yourself into my care before he came to remind me of my promise." She beamed. "Oh, he will be stunned, and so very excited. I can't wait to tell him! And the Messenger, he will be relieved, too. He felt bad about not letting him go and fetch you last autumn. He said he would come, too."

"He did? He was? He wanted?" It was truly difficult to breathe now, with her elation welling, filling her chest with so much joy she wanted to jump onto her feet and scream into the roaring chasm.

"Oh, yes. He could talk about nothing else. He made me promise to help." A smug, female grin twisted the generous lips. "I told him to go last autumn. He was afraid you wouldn't wait for so long, and I thought about it, too. But obviously we were wrong, weren't we?"

She remembered the dreadfully long winter moons. "I wish he come then. I wait and wait, and he not come. It was terrible."

The girl's face darkened. "I know. I had a bad winter, too."

Now it was Seketa's turn to reach out, to caress the smooth, golden arm, scratched and muddied, but still pleasant to touch. This girl was very attractive, and she was in love with Two Rivers, following the pattern set by many women.

"He is special, yes, special man. Man of the prophecy and the visions, but," she hesitated, searching for words. "But he is special, special person, too. No one, not like him. Different. My cousin Iraquas want to follow, admire so much. And Tekeni, yes. And some others, but not many. Your people open, listen new ideas, yes?"

"No, they are not." The girl shook her head. "But they will listen to him, too. Like Flint People and their neighbors. They will listen because he won't allow them not to." The hopeful gaze clung to her, full of expectation. "He will return here, won't he? It would not be like him to abandon my people, not keeping his promises, no?"

Seketa hesitated. "Yes, he keep promise, he decent, he won't lie. I think he come, come soon."

But she wasn't sure. She knew Two Rivers so little. Just the rumors and the general distrust of her townsfolk, and then discovering this man through Tekeni, but too late to see who was right and who was not. He was so good to the Wolf Clan's boy, so decent, so kind, but Tekeni was worthy of all of it and more. She would have done anything for him, as well.

"I think he come, yes. Soon." She hoped her smile did not relate her uncertainty. He would do anything for his ideas, yes, but what about this girl? Would he keep his promises to her? She shook her head, getting rid of the irrelevant thoughts. "But we can't, can't wait on the cliff, no? So first, we get up, or down, save our lives, yes? Then wait for our men. Or go find, yes?"

The smile of her companion made her feel better. Wide and free of shadows, it gave her hope. They both were in trouble, not likely to survive, but they were not alone anymore, and maybe, with a little help from the Great Spirits…

"We try to climb down as we planned," said the girl briskly, echoing Seketa's thoughts. "We can do it!"

CHAPTER 19

"So, the legendary Messenger has finally deigned to come to our humble town."

Despite his shortness, Tadodaho was undeniably imposing, his shoulders so wide they made him look square, his impressively broad chest covered with tattoos, decorated by a row of bear claws, his arms wide, encircled with leather thongs of exquisite beadwork, the feathers of his headdress soaring, adding to his height.

The man wore his shortness as a constant challenge, decided Tekeni, watching intently, his skin prickling, sending rays of alarm down his spine. They were in no particular danger, no more than when visiting the People of the Mountains not so very long ago, and yet he could not make the bad feeling go away. It set his nerves on edge. Something was wrong, but not in the way of the disappearing sun. This danger was closer, more tangible, of a more common nature. But what?

Despite Two Rivers' determination to go on all by himself, his anxiety to ensure his girl's safety overcoming his good sense and his dedication to his mission this time, they arrived at the shores of Onondaga Lake leading an impressive following. The multitude of people from all over this side of the Great Sparkling Water, those who had came to High Springs following the Messenger and the locals, were not about to stay behind; and it was good to see the excited citizens of High Springs joining the procession, making their flotilla of canoes crowd the rivers they passed.

Entering Onondaga Town was a sort of triumph, especially for Hionhwatha, reflected Tekeni, following at some distance, close enough to make sure Two Rivers was protected from anything unexpected, yet keeping in the shadows. Too many respectable leaders crowded the proximity of the Messenger, grudging each other the closest positions. The obvious advantage Hionhwatha held over the others now made many frown. It didn't seem to bother the formidable Onondaga man, but Tekeni did not crave this sort of attention. He just wanted to make sure Two Rivers was safe, protected from anything violent, a knife or an arrow. The Crooked Tongues man was an experienced warrior, but sometimes he had been too sure of himself, too careless, indifferent to his own safety. Until the agreement with the Onondagas was reached it was safer to keep a close eye on the man.

According to all accounts, Tadodaho was not to be trusted, but now, upon seeing the man, Tekeni felt the hair on his nape rising, his danger signals up, shouting loudly. Oh, no! Two Rivers could not be allowed to meet such a man all alone and on the enemy's battleground. Hionhwatha was good, but not good enough. The former War Leader seemed to genuinely like the Crooked Tongues man, but he was not a close friend, and he thought about himself and his people before anything else.

"It is a great honor to be received in a settlement as important as Onondaga Town," he heard Two Rivers voice, ringing calmly, clear and well-heard. "The prospect of sharing a pipe with the leaders of the Onondaga People fills my heart with joy."

The great man stood there, his legs wide apart, hands folded upon the satisfactory padded chest, dressed simply in a plain loincloth and undecorated leggings, wearing the basic jewelry, his hair tied behind his back, his face unpainted, such a glaring contrast to the obvious efforts of his adversary to look rich and important.

Tekeni's heart filled with pride. Oh, Two Rivers needed no decorations, no feathers or paint to convey his undeniable importance. The power his eyes, his whole being, radiated was more than enough. This is why they listened to him, all of them, those richly dressed people, powerful leaders of five nations. They followed him, and they accepted his guidance because he was above all of them put together.

"The Onondaga people are not sharing their pipes as readily as the other peoples may have. Our tobacco is of the highest quality, and our pipes are all exquisitely carved, their beauty and delicacy are renowned all over the land." Tadodaho's broad face smirked, the challenge in it lurking, not very well-hidden, spilling out of the squinted eyes. "The Messenger might have wasted his time traveling to Onondaga lands, tiring his followers on a futile journey."

"No time spent in the quest of the Great Peace is time wasted," said Two Rivers calmly, not moving a muscle. "The Right-Handed Twin desires to see his children living together, side by side, managing their affairs in peace, not ruining the world of his creation. His message is clear, and I bring it to every place I travel. I came to Onondaga lands now to deliver the message."

People were murmuring, crowding the ceremonial ground in the shadow of a huge maple tree, listening avidly. Oh, yes, they came here to listen, realized Tekeni, his hope growing. They were not as close-minded as their uncompromising War Chief. Their wide-opened eyes and attentive faces told him that they were actually full of anticipation, hopeful. They wanted the change.

Tadodaho's laughter shook the air. "Oh, but we have seen people presuming to represent our revered Great Spirits. They claimed speaking their minds, but upon closer inspection, they were nothing but pitiful creatures with malicious agendas and personal goals, wishing to achieve nothing but power and influence. You are an outsider, a man with no home, no family, no roots. You have nothing but your tongue and your way with words, to use it to the best of your ability, to try and impress people." His bracelets rang as the man raised his arms, reinforcing his words, conveying his apparent astonishment. "And it turns out that not only the people of the east, but our esteemed neighbors to the west are oh-so-easily impressed. Enough to follow a desperate stranger set on disrupting our way of life. Enough to let him lead our people into a wild scheme with no future."

Oh, but this man was good. Tekeni held his breath, feeling more than seeing the doubt creeping into the faces around him, the locals and their guests alike.

"I do no such deeds," said Two Rivers more loudly, his voice having only a slightly strained tone to it. "I came here from the other side of the Sparkling Water, because the Great Spirits wanted me to do so, sending me here to do their bidding. I have roots and I have family, but I left them in order to bring the message of peace. I sacrificed the comfort of my old life, because the Right-Handed Twin wished me to do so." A wide gesture of the man's hand indicated the crowds who watched, spellbound, afraid to miss a word. "The people who chose to listen are wise people. They are not afraid of the change. They are not afraid to see beyond the obvious. They are brave and courageous, and their ears are opened, their minds are pure. The seed of peace and concord fell in a fertile field, and it will bring beautiful fruits to sustain our people and their children, and the children of their children, for endless moons to come. We are the People of the Longhouse, brothers and cousins, who should live in peace with each other, governed by laws of our clans and their mutual dwellings."

Elated, Tekeni listened to the familiar voice, ringing in a complete silence. Even the birds seemed to stop chirping and the wind went still, listening too. Oh, Two Rivers spoke beautifully, although on their journey here he had not been in his best. Edgy and impatient, the Crooked Tongues man seemed to be thinking mainly about the Onondaga girl and the dangers she had been exposed to, giving little thought to the impending encounter with the important Onondaga leader, the last of their opponents.

He made Tekeni and Hionhwatha worried, but now, none of his impatience showed, although while heading toward the meeting place Two Rivers' eyes darted in quite a few directions, seeking the girl, of that Tekeni was sure. And finding not a hint of her presence in the town. Which was odd. She must have been here, somewhere. She could not have just disappeared from the surface of this earthly world.

Tadodaho was answering, saying more of the hate-filled words, but Tekeni stopped listening, glancing around, instead. Two Rivers could handle this last of the important encounters, he concluded now; the Great Man was in no particular danger. There was no need to guard him so closely, but if he, Tekeni, managed to find the girl, it would give his friend much reassurance, allowing him to concentrate for real, with no nagging worries.

Easing his way carefully, he moved toward the back of the crowd, listening to the murmuring people. The farther he got the freer they talked, mostly younger women, exchanging their opinions rather than listening, chattering all at once, more concerned with the foreigner's looks and handsomeness than anything else. Women! He shook his head, uncomfortable with the glances he drew.

"He is too young to be the true messenger of the Right-Handed Twin," one of the women was saying. "The War Chief is right. He is just a man who seeks power."

"Then why have the others listened, eh?" cried out another. "He brought here all the peoples we have heard of, aside from the Crooked Tongues. Think about it! Even our people from High Springs came."

"Maybe he is a sorcerer. Maybe he put some sort of spell on them all," said a short, broadly built girl.

"Oh, please!" They all glared at the girl who had spoken, united for a change.

Tekeni hesitated, thinking about his next move. Here, on the edge of the crowd, away from his peers, his foreignness was more prominent. He could not just wander this town, not yet. Maybe after Two Rivers had bested the War Chief, this way or another, but not now.

"Also, he could never best our War Leader this way. He could never—"

"With so many followers and all the other nations behind him, he can do whatever he wants!" This came from a young man, clearly a warrior, who stood leaning heavily against a tree, his leg bandaged, the cut upon his shoulder open and glaring, his face haunted, pale and thin, glittering with sweat. "No matter how, he made the others listen, so it leaves us with not much choice."

Catching Tekeni's glance, the warrior glanced at him coldly, then looked away, while the cute, round-faced girl who stood beside him, supporting him with one arm, kept staring, wide-eyed. He knew this sort of glances and it annoyed him, the open fascination of it irritating, making him wish to scream into her face that yes, he had scars and it was none of her stupid business, may the gods-cursed Yeentso rot in the realm of the Evil Left-Handed Twin for all eternity.

"The High Springs girl said he was that impressive and not truly old. I remember it most clearly." The women's chattering was annoying as well, but it provided diversion and saved him the necessity to ask questions, maybe.

"She said nothing about his looks!" called several women at once.

"But she said he was impressive, mysterious, the real messenger, and that he could do magical things."

"Oh, you all are talking nonsense. I was her friend, not the lot of you!" The girl who said that was short but pleasantly round, with her skin smooth, inviting to touch. "She didn't like this sort of questions. She said he was above any of this. She was impressed with him so! Her eyes were shining every time she talked about him."

"And where is she now that her messenger has come? I would expect her to be there in the thickest of the crowd, drinking in every word of the foreigner, eh?"

"Maybe she would start arguing with the War Chief again," said one of the women with a chuckle. "Like she did on the

Maple Ceremony."

The other girls covered their mouths, but the warrior and his pretty supporter, who was still watching Tekeni, seemed to be puzzled as he was, not a part of the joke.

"Come, Hanowa, where is your newfound friend?"

"And how should I know?" The girl called Hanowa glared at the others, oddly enraged. "She just disappeared, and it has nothing to do with me."

"What do you mean 'disappeared'? I saw you two in the fields only this morning! Or was on the day before this one?"

"Yes, it was on the day before this one. And since then, I haven't seen her." Another frown crossed the girl's round face as her eyes darted aside, clouding. "Well, since last night. We were right here, behind the maple tree. Don't you remember?"

Two other girls nodded, while the rest raised their eyebrows.

"She must have left the way she came. Suddenly and with no reason."

As they went on, discussing the possibilities, Tekeni stopped listening, peering at the girl called Hanowa, disturbed. That one knew more than she was telling, of that he was sure, and the High Springs girl, the authority on the mysterious messenger, must be no other than Two Rivers' woman. And she was missing – again.

He saw the girl hesitating, then beginning to ease away. Fascinated, he slipped after her, trying to attract as little attention as he could, which was a difficult task. The wounded warrior's girl was sneaking glances in his direction, now shy and self-conscious, dropping her gaze every time his eyes met hers. Damn silly woman!

He cursed silently, then watched his prey disappearing behind the nearby longhouse, even her back full of tension, hunched in a guilty way. Oh yes, she must know something! Paying the people around no more attention, he hurried after her, diving into a narrow alley that the walls of two longhouses created. She was rounding another corner, almost running now.

Reaching the farther end, he saw her hesitating in front of

one of the buildings' facades, as though pondering. The wind rustled in the nearby bushes, and no people seemed to be anywhere around.

Having no time to think it all through, he covered the distance with two powerful leaps, grabbing the girl from behind, locking her in his firm grip, covering her mouth with his free arm. She didn't even struggle, too stunned by the unexpected attack as it seemed.

"Tell me where the High Springs girl is!" he hissed into her ear, his heart beating fast. If caught doing this, harassing a local woman, he would be done for, ruining their mission along the way. "Tell me now or I'll kill you."

The girl seemed to stop breathing, going completely still in his grip. He wondered if she was about to faint.

"Tell me now, and I will let you go," he said, moderating his tone. "Now!"

He felt the shudder taking her, the face under his palm twisting, turning clammy with sweat. Easing his grip upon her mouth, he tightened the one around her shoulders, ready to evade a kick that would most likely come.

"Tell me!"

The twitching increased. "It's not my fault," whimpered his victim, her lips wet and unpleasant against his palm. "I didn't do anything… I didn't mean it. It's not my fault!"

"Where is she?"

"I don't know. I swear I don't! The War Chief only told me to invite her to the ceremonial ground… her and the other girls… He said to ask… ask about the Messenger again." His palm was now awash with tears, and worse. Disgusted, he fought the urge to let her go. "I swear I don't know what he did to her."

He tried to make sense out of it. "So you were on the ceremonial grounds with her? Last night?" He remembered what the women said. "And then what happened?"

Her body was heavy against his, sagging, trembling with fear. If she fainted, he would learn nothing.

"Listen! I won't hurt you if you tell me the truth, the whole of it. I'm going to let you go now, if you promise not to scream or run away." He eased his grip slightly, gauging the reactions of her body. "Promise!"

"I promise," she whispered, but when he backed away, she swayed and almost fell, waving her hands, hopeless, until he caught her again, to support more than anything.

Her eyes were so wide-open they looked ridiculously round, the enlarged pupils making them turn almost black. The glimpse of his face did nothing to reassure her, he concluded, but there was no time for any more reassuring talk.

"Tell me now what happened on the ceremonial grounds."

The girl wiped her face, smearing all sorts of fluids upon it. "We talked, she and the other girls. She told us about the Messenger, answered questions. Like she always did." With a loud hiccup interrupting her speech, she paused, sniffing loudly. "She was a good girl. Strange and mysterious, but a nice person. Even though she had no patience for normal conversations, I befriended her because she was interesting. Not to do her any harm. She talked about nothing but the Messenger. She made many people listen. But then there was the Maple Ceremony, and she was the best among our dancers—"

He had no time to listen to the Onondaga girl's adventures in this town. "Tell me what happened after you talked last night."

"She disappeared." The girl sniffled again. "She wasn't in our clan's field in the morning."

"Was she living in your longhouse?"

"No, in the neighboring one. With Gwayeah's family."

"Who is Gwayeah?"

"The woman who sheltered her." The girl's eyes lit with hope. "I can introduce you to her. Maybe she knows where she went."

He paid her words no attention. "Why was the War Chief angry with her?"

"She argued with him, on the Maple Ceremony."

"About the Messenger?"

"Yes."

Oh, Mighty Spirits! The thought of her dead, probably cut and dumped somewhere in the woods, made him feel sick. He remembered her face, her large, pleasantly tilted eyes, the way she had always spoken, so straightforward and honest, so full of passion, a bitter enemy, then the closest of friends. Why couldn't she have just waited patiently?

"I didn't mean to betray her," the girl was whimpering, her words slurred, barely comprehensive, a new bout of tears taking her. "I'm so sorry!"

"Do you think the War Chief killed her?"

The girl shrugged. "I don't know. I think yes."

He cursed loudly, seeing her shrinking under his furious gaze. He didn't care. Without that filthy, tearful rat, *the traitor*, the Onondaga girl might have still been alive. Oh, curse them all into the underworld of the Evil Twin. Why her, of all people?

"Get away from her!"

The shout echoed between the bark walls, rolling down the alley. Tearing his knife out of its sheath, Tekeni whirled around to see the wounded warrior limping toward them, clenching a bow, an arrow out and ready, attached to the bowstring, staring into his, Tekeni's, face. Stomach tight, he watched the ragged palm clutching the fathered shaft, stretching the bowstring lightly, not about to shoot, not yet.

"I do her no harm. I came to ask questions, peacefully, but if you don't drop the filthy bow, I'll kill you both before you know it. You can't best me, not in your condition."

The warrior grunted. "Get away from that girl and go back to your people. Or get out of here. You have no business to run around this town. Our leader didn't agree to listen to your Messenger yet."

He watched the hand on the bowstring trembling slightly, the man's face covered with sheen of perspiration. It was evident that it cost him an effort to stand unsupported, the wound on his shoulder oozing, the round-faced girl, the one who had stared at Tekeni earlier, again by the warrior's side, an inseparable shadow.

"I'll ask my questions, then I'll go back to the people I came with. Not only my people, but all the wise people from all over our side of the Great Lake. Those who have enough courage to listen."

"To listen to the foreigner presuming to manage our affairs?" The man's hands trembled more visibly now, from rage more than exhaustion as it seemed. "Our people are wiser than your savages from the east. They are not as easily fooled."

"Or maybe they are just cowardly and stupid." Ready to leap aside the moment the bowstring would start shifting, Tekeni felt more than saw the Hanowa girl still there, hardly breathing by his side. "It's not only the east now, but the west as well. Four powerful nations came here, following the Messenger, listening to his words. Four mighty peoples from either side of your lands saw the truth, the truth that your people refuse to see with the stubbornness of angry children." He shook his head, watching the trembling hand pulling at the string, the squinted eyes boring at him, blazing with rage. "And it's not that the Onondaga people are not wise or courageous. High Springs and the surrounding villages have listened already. They came here following the Messenger. Even the people from the villages and towns of your shores of the Great Sparkling Water came. It's only Onondaga Town is cowardly, afraid of the wrath that its ruler, blinded with rage, might send its way." The bowstring shook, pulled a little tighter. "I hope we won't stay for longer than today, because I feel that this place is contaminating me, making me wish to purify my spirit with a generous offering to the Right-Handed Twin."

"You speak just like her," muttered Hanowa.

"What?" Afraid to take his eyes of the half-stretched bow, he glanced at her, forgetting all about her presence, or that he threatened to kill her only a short time ago. Apparently, she was still there, despite the opportunity to run away.

"Onheda. The girl who disappeared. You speak just like her about the Messenger."

Onheda! Yes, that was her name. His chest tightened with pain. Only half a day late! Would he be as late when crossing the Great Sparkling Water? The thought made him sick.

The warrior stood motionless, but his round-faced girl brought her palms to her face, covering her mouth. "You are looking for that girl, too?" she mumbled, her words muffled.

"Who are you?" asked Hanowa suspiciously, suddenly very sure of herself and not especially friendly.

The round-faced girl seemed as though about to run. "We… we are not from… from Onondaga Town. We just came…" her words trailed off under the scornful glare of the warrior.

"We are as Onondaga people as anyone else," he stated firmly. "We don't have to explain anything."

"But you are not from this town," pressed Hanowa.

"No."

Suddenly, Tekeni felt a surge of hope. "It seems that we are all looking for the same girl who disappeared last night, aren't we? So why don't we try working together?" He took his eyes off the man and his bow, the string now relaxed, almost slacking, and looked at the round-faced girl with as affable an expression as he could muster. "When did you see her last?"

But the girl's face fell. "I didn't see her since we came here. I tried to tell them not to take her away, but I was too sick. And my brother, he almost died." Her pleasant looking face twisting, she peered at him as though asking for forgiveness. "I tried to tell them not to take her away, but they didn't listen."

He held his breath. "Who took her away? When?"

"She is talking about another girl, you gallant rescuer," said Hanowa, her smile challenging. "Not the High Springs girl you are looking for. Unless you are busy rescuing all women in trouble." The generous lips twitched, forming a slightly derisive grin. "The foreign girl was even prettier, come to think of it. Might be worthy of your time."

"Oh, shut up!" Enraged, Tekeni turned toward the sneering local, causing her to take a step back, her smile gone. "Think where the War Chief might have put the High Springs girl if he wished to keep her alive. Think hard!" He looked at the other pair. "Was your girl somehow connected to the Messenger, too?"

"She was very curious about him, yes," said the warrior grimly, his bow still high. "She sailed the Great Sparkling Water looking for him."

"She what?" cried out Tekeni and the Onondaga Town's girl in unison.

"Yes, it's very odd. She was no captive." The young man shrugged with his good shoulder. "I came out to tell them that this morning, the moment I came back to life, as they weren't prepared to listen to my sister." He shot the girl beside him a disapproving look. "But she disappeared since last night. The clan that wanted to adopt her was furious. They think she might have run away."

"Last night," Tekeni narrowed his eyes. "The same night the High Springs girl disappeared."

"Maybe they both ran away," said Hanowa, suddenly hopeful. "Onheda – to put as much distance between her and the War Chief, and the foreigner for only Great Spirits know what." Her grin flashed with sudden light affability. "Maybe they both went looking for the Messenger, while he was busy traveling here. I suggest we go back and listen to him, eh?"

"Yes, I suppose." Tekeni sighed, thinking about Two Rivers. He wouldn't take the death of his woman well, not this time. He would kill malicious Tadodaho, and then there would be no peace, not for real. The proud Onondaga people would never enter the union if one of their leaders was to die at the hand of the foreigner organizing it all, the divine messenger or not.

"Yes, maybe they both ran away," said the warrior, turning to go, his fingers digging into the supportive shoulder of his sister, leaving a print. He was not in the best of shapes, reflected Tekeni, pondering whether to offer his help or not. "She was the most courageous woman I ever met. Pity she didn't wait. If she had stayed, I would have helped her."

"If she had stayed, she wouldn't have the need to travel at all.

She would have gotten her Messenger, hale and ready." This Hanowa was a spicy thing. Tekeni couldn't help liking her.

"We'll send someone to High Springs right away. If she left, she would go there, with or without the other girl." He shrugged, his gloom returning. "But something is telling me it is not that simple. I doubt the Onondaga girl would just run away like that, unless he threatened her. Did he?"

"Oh, yes, he did. On the Maple Ceremony. But she didn't leave then."

"Then she wouldn't have left now, either."

"But he was after her now. He made me spread the trap." The girl quailed under his gaze, losing most of her newly gained spark. "It was more serious than just an empty threat," she finished, her voice trailing off.

"There must be a place, somewhere, anywhere, a place where he would lock her if he thought she might be of use to him alive."

"A cabin, somewhere," suggested the warrior, limping beside Tekeni, trying to keep up with the briskness of their pace. His voice dropped to a mere whisper. "This man is renowned for his powers. If he wanted her dead, she would be found dead. On her bunk in her longhouse, or anywhere else, apparently untouched. He can do that. He did it to Hionhwatha's family." A shrug. "There was no need to kidnap her in order to kill."

Tekeni suppressed a shiver. "Then she must be alive, somewhere!" He glanced at the warrior, grateful. "Maybe your girl, too."

"The girl I *came here with*," the man stressed his words pointedly, "has no quarrel with the War Chief of Onondaga Town. She is in no danger from this man, but she will face danger from every other direction now. It was silly of her to run away. She didn't even speak our tongue."

"What tongue did she speak?"

"The Crooked Tongues, obviously."

His heart missed a beat, then threw itself wildly, fluttering in his chest. But it could not be; it was not possible!

"How…" He swallowed. "What did she look like?"

"I know where he might have put her," cried out Hanowa, making them all jump. If Tekeni's heart was out of tempo already, now it leaped all the way up into his throat. Dizzy, he made an effort to concentrate, pushing the wild thought about *her* crossing the Great Lake away. It was simply not possible.

"What? Where?"

"There is this place by the falls." The girl's voice dropped to a whisper. "People were talking about those cascades. There is a magic there, and these days, no one dares to come close. The falls are vicious, and they have claimed many lives. But once we sneaked to see and, well, there was a hut there, and the smoke was coming out." The girl paused, her voice hardly audible now. "The girls wanted to go back, but I made them stay and we waited, and then the War Chief came. He was not a War Chief back then, Hionhwatha was, but well, our current War Leader came later on, with some people, and they were carrying something, or someone, maybe. It was wrapped in hides, and it moved. Oh, Mighty Spirits! It was so frightening. We ran away the moment they got in, but I heard about this place later on, many times. And well, he might have taken her there, might he not?"

Tekeni tried to make his head work, his heartbeat calming, but his mind still in a jumble. He had to talk to this warrior, ask about that other girl. A Crooked Tongues girl! He felt his chest tightening again.

"How far away are the falls?" he asked, pleased to hear his voice ringing calmly.

"Not far. You will have to follow the lake shore, then, when you see a spring and the small rapids, you turn into the woods and follow the trail until you hear—"

"I'm not going to look for this place all by myself!" Wondering if he had taken it too far, Tekeni stared back at her. "You will come with me." He measured the sun, perturbed. It was already well past its highest, and he would need to wait for Two Rivers to finish the talks. He could not just rush away on dubious missions without saying a word. Or could he? "You said it's not far. You will be back in no time." The girl was still gaping at him. "You betrayed her, so you owe her this."

"If we set off now, we won't be back before nightfall," protested the girl.

"You said it's not far!"

"Well, it's more than just a few steps out of the town." The cheeky spark was back, and he breathed with relief. She was going to take him there. But he still needed to go back and see how far Two Rivers had progressed out there on the town's square. "If you want to get there fast, you will have to run all the way. Then we'll be there before Father Sun is getting near his resting place."

He looked at the other two, assessing the warrior's condition. No, this one would not be able to keep up. The thought that must have reflected in his gaze, as the warrior's eyes flashed with anger. "I can make it, even if it'll take me longer to get there."

The round-faced girl began sobbing all at once. "No, you can't. You need to rest. You will be sick again—"

"Stop it," he hissed, glaring at his sister. "Seketa saved my life. I owe her this."

And then her name was the only sound, and the world went still, losing its color. He stared at the man, seeing his face clearly, the beads of sweat, the pale, haunted features, the pressed lips, the stony, unwavering eyes. The other voices were no more, and the wild pounding of his heart was the only sound left, thundering in his ears. They were talking to him, the man and the other girl, but their words were muffled, ringing strangely, as though spoken in an unfamiliar tongue.

"Come," he breathed, finding it difficult to utter even this single word.

Hanowa struggled, but he clasped her arm tightly, almost dragging her off her feet.

"What are you doing?" cried out the warrior, grabbing Tekeni's arm in his turn, helping the girl to break free.

Tekeni felt none of it, too stunned to think about his actions. She was there, somewhere out there, exposed to all sorts of dangers, *looking for him*!

"We have to get to the falls now!"

The girl stepped back, frightened, but he spent no more time on their puzzled glances, rushing away, desperate to find the shortest way out of the town and down the lake, oblivious of the voices coming from the gathering and the glances he drew as he rushed past the edge of the crowds. He didn't care. Just to reach the lake shore. To snatch one of their canoes would speed the matters up, but this way, he might miss the spring and the turning point.

"Wait, please!" The girl's voice reached him as she caught up with him, flushed and gasping. "Why are you running? Wait."

"Are you taking me to the falls?" he barked, not slowing his step.

"Yes, but not running all the way."

"You said there would be a clear trail by the spring."

"Yes." She panted beside him as the tobacco plots and the wide gap in the fence swept by, disappearing behind their backs.

The breeze from the lake greeted them, cooling his burning face, but his heart was thumping all the same, his thoughts rushing about, impossible to control. She was here, somewhere here, on *his* side of the Great Lake, having achieved the impossible by crossing it, somehow, against all the odds. She was looking for him, facing more dangers than one could count, while he was busy with Two Rivers and the Great Peace, postponing his journey over and over, missing her oh-so-dreadfully but thinking her safe, far away but safe, protected, sheltered among her people, not running all over the enemy's countryside, vulnerable and alone.

Oh, Mighty Spirits!

CHAPTER 20

Two Rivers stared at his rival, fighting the urge to tell the man off, to do whatever he wanted, to go and fight the united four nations, if he liked. The long, wearisome argument dragged on, with Father Sun reaching its zenith, then climbing down, but lingering, as though curious to see what would happen.

Nothing good, was Two Rivers' conclusion. They were wasting their time, with the annoying leader of Onondaga Town arguing in the way that made it clear that he was enjoying listening to himself, making a show for the benefit of his people. Nothing he, Two Rivers, said would make any difference. The man was set against joining the union, knowing that his enemies were caught in their own ideology, united and strong, and yet powerless, unable to force the reluctant neighbors because such an act would disrupt everything that was achieved with so much effort through the last span of seasons. May the malicious, dirty warmonger rot in the underworld of the Evil Twin!

He could smell the aroma of the upcoming feast spreading, tickling his nostrils, promising a rich meal. It did nothing to alleviate his mood. He was hungry, and the feast signaled approval, acceptance of the townsfolk and, most importantly, of the Clans Mothers. The dwellers of Onondaga Town, even its leading citizens, wanted in, making no secret of it. If only the loathsome Tadodaho was not as insistent, not as intentionally offensive, not as annoying in his stubbornness and this obnoxious refusal to listen to a reason.

He watched the broad, ragged, lived-in face, the scar crossing the wide chin, the dark eyes squinted, glittering with a barely

concealed satisfaction, as though the man knew something he
did not, as though there was another advantage he was not in a
hurry to use. It made Two Rivers' skin prickle. If on the
battlefield, he would suspect a fresh force of especially fierce
warriors was hidden somewhere not far away, to join the
fighting when the time was right. The man was so sure of his
victory, but why?

"My people are powerful and proud. They are not made to
be a part of the crowd. Unless leading, of course." Grinning,
Tadodaho took his time filling his pipe, inhaling the fragrant
smoke, offering none to his guest. Such an impolite brute!

"The time has changed. There is no shame in being a part of
the union consisted of five proud, powerful nations. There will
be no inequality, no leadership of any sort. Your people have
nothing to fear. By joining our League of Five Nations they will
gain power and lose none."

He waited a little before stuffing his own pipe, so as not to
appear to be emulating his adversary. However, when the
smoke began climbing up in a thin sliver of blue, he sucked on
it, then offered the beautifully carved object to the formidable
man. It was the pipe he'd received from the Swamp People as a
cherished gift, an exquisite work of dark wood and engraved
figures, with an eagle sitting on top of it, spreading its wings.

Tadodaho's eyes brushed past the beautiful object,
concealing his appreciation well. His grin flickered as he shook
his head, refusing the gesture. Two Rivers stifled a curse, feeling
the people who watched them tensing with anger. They were
sitting together beside a small fire, out of earshot now,
conversing privately, but it wouldn't be long before his old or
his newly acquired allies, all powerful leaders in themselves,
would get up in anger and leave. Or maybe begin insulting each
other. He felt like cursing at length and leaving himself.

"We are the People of the Longhouse," he repeated, instead.
"We should live in peace and equality, like the brothers we are.
Your people are dwelling in the middle of our longhouse. They
are offered to be the Keepers of the Central Fire. It's a great

honor. Why would they be reluctant to take it? Are they afraid of the responsibility such a position requires?"

He said it more loudly, hoping the crowds surrounding them would hear, repeating for the benefit of those located too far away to listen. He had mentioned it before, more than a few times, getting no appreciation from the uncompromising leader, but now he was talking for the benefit of the crowds. Would they have enough sense to go against their formidable leader? How naive he was to think that this special concession, presented in the right way, would impress the tough beast.

He made an effort to clear the furious thoughts off his face. Let the old scoundrel think he could talk for days on end, until that one gave in. Or dropped dead, which would be a better solution. *Don't let him know you are at the end of your patience and about to explode.*

"Oh no, the Onondaga People are not afraid of a challenge. They can deal with even greater responsibility of leading your union to great achievements and victories."

"There will be no leading nations in our union!" He made another effort to keep calm. The man's audaciousness knew no bounds! But then, of course, he was trying to unsettle him deliberately, to make the revered Messenger lose his temper, do something violent maybe, to prove himself human, and not an especially worthy human at that.

As though reading these thoughts, Tadodaho smiled, then sniffed the air. "It seems our women are determined to make us share our food with the revered guests. Women are the power one has to reckon with, are they not?"

"Yes, they are. The Clans Mothers are wise and farsighted. Their opinions are worthy of listening to."

The man leaned forward, as though about to share a secret. "And they are always ready to make us listen, if we forget."

"Yes, they are." He felt the urge to back away, his skin prickling as though a dangerous animal just moved into a closer proximity, an old wolf who, until now, was sitting on its back legs, licking its whiskers, its eyes attentive, not in a good way.

"Even the young women can be a nuisance sometimes, holding too much power or giving the man trouble in other ways." The man's gaze deepened. "Or working for them, promoting their interests, loyal until the very end."

He stared into the squinted eyes, seeing the wariness, the anticipation, the cold amusement flickering in the dark depths. His heart slowed its beat, sliding into the cavity of his stomach, to lay there like a dead weight.

"Some women are loyal, beautiful, heedless of their private interests. Heedless of danger. It can be a sad business sometimes, don't you agree?"

Now it was his turn to lean forward, but he didn't notice himself moving at all. It's just that the man was very close now, his face changing, the wariness increasing, and the tension.

"Where is she?" He didn't recognize his own voice, so strange, low-pitched and growling it sounded, like the rumbling of the thunder deep inside the earth.

The old leader moved back only a little, straightening up, bringing the pipe to his mouth, still calm and composed, but the fingers wrapped around the old wood were white from the force with which they clutched the carved object.

"She is alive and well." A cloud of smoke came out. "Waiting for you, maybe."

"Where?"

"In due time."

"Not in due time – now!" Again, he could not recognize his own voice, with this stony ring and the growling sound of the occurring under the earth.

"After we talk about the terms." Suddenly, the gaze boring at him wavered, slipping sideways, brushing past the fire and the people sitting not so far, watching intently. "Would you like to talk in privacy?"

He leaned closer. "No, I would not."

The wave of relief took him, the realization that the meaningless talk was over. This whole thing was over, but he had no regrets. He tried, he did his best, but it was all very trying. It's good this was going to end now. In killing this man, he would be doing the people he'd come to like and admire a great favor.

He saw the eyes staring at him widening. The mask was slipping off, and the man underneath it sat alarmed, thrown out of balance, almost nervous. It gave him no satisfaction.

"I will take a great pleasure in killing you, and I don't need privacy to do that. When my flint will be slitting your throat, the bad spirits will be released, and your people will breathe freely again."

The man swallowed. "You can't kill me now in front of everyone. It will put an end to your mission." His nostrils widened, as he evidently gathered the remnants of his rage. "That is, if you managed to kill me at all."

"Oh, yes I will manage!" He tried to control the trembling, his body crying for the action, hands itching to grab the hilt of his knife. "I will cut your filthy heart out, and I will feed it the wolves, before I leave the lands of your people. Morsel by morsel, I will make the whole forest feast on your rotten flesh, and then I will pray to Gadowaas to close the gate to the Sky World, to refuse your spirit reaching even for the smallest, most meaningless star. You will wander between the worlds until nothing is left, tormented and forgotten. It will happen. *It will!*"

He felt the silence descending like a cloak, with not a breeze and no buzzing of the midday insects, the sun dimming, turning grayish, lacking its vividness. Or maybe it was just him. The people around seemed to be the same, watching intently, probably trying to hear, but the man in front of him froze, and he knew he felt the sun dimming too.

"If she dies, you will pay the price," he growled in a voice that made him shiver himself.

"She is alive and not harmed." Tadodaho's lips were pressed tight, although his eyes flickered with uncertainty, openly perturbed. "I do not require much in exchange for her life."

"You get nothing but your worthless life in exchange for hers!"

"I get more than this." Suddenly, the man's eyes returned to calmness, although no more derisiveness glittered out of the dark depths. Firm and concentrated, they gazed at him with almost earnest sincerity. "I've seen your strength, Messenger, and I accept your Tidings of Great Peace. My people will enter your union, and they will be the Keepers of the Central Fire. They will be represented by fourteen elders, as the number of our towns and villages, and they will watch the proceedings very carefully, ready to settle the differences between the east and the west." The man paused, and Two Rivers watched the strong jaw jutting, the eyes turning into stone, as his own eyes were, he was sure of that. "As the Keepers of the Central Fire, my people will have the final say on every decision, every law, every agreement our Great Council of the Five Nations reach."

"No one will make final decisions." He struggled against his rising hope, not ready to believe it just yet. "Every representative will have his say."

"And yet, our people will be the last to express their opinions."

He thought fast, his worry for her nagging, but his hope escalating. The last or the first, what did it matter, as long as the decision had to be reached unanimously, by voting of every member of the council? Didn't the man realize that?

And then he knew that yes, indeed, the man did not know about the unanimous voting. He had mentioned it privately to Atiron before the Cold Moons, and he had repeated it on the gathering of the eastern nations, at the lands of the Standing Stone People, when struggling to make them listen. But then it all got very hectic, the spontaneous ventures into the western nations' lands, with no opportunity to discuss the details of the proposed union. And if Tadodaho didn't know about the unanimous voting, then he could grant him his wish now, very grandly at that.

He gathered his anger back before looking at the man hard, trying to convey the hatred he felt. The vile creature was too shrewd, too canny to be deceived easily.

"If she is returned to me alive and unharmed, I will agree to your terms." He let his gaze relate most of his fury. "But only if she is here before sunset. *Unharmed*."

"I'll send someone to fetch her," said Tadodaho at once, curiously relieved. "She'll be here by sunset. Unharmed."

"Take me there now. I don't trust your cronies."

"But you trust me." The smile was back, a provocative, goading grin. "With your life even."

"You will not be able to take my life in a thousand seasons to come. But I will always be there, ready to keep my promise to feed you to the wolves and make your spirit wander for all eternity should anything happen to the people close to me. I can do all of it and more. I came to bring peace, but I am skilled in the art of war and the darkest of sorcery. You had better not test my patience ever again." Disregarding the veiled gaze, deriving no pleasure at the wariness and the uncertainty it held now, he sprang to his feet. "Now, keep your side of the bargain, War Chief."

CHAPTER 21

Seketa rested against the slippery stone, leaning on it with her entire body, forcing her mind off the roaring abyss down below. If she slipped she would be done for, she knew, crushed to pieces at the bottom of the narrow canyon, her limbs broken, her head bashed, her blood washed away by the fiercely gushing water.

Sinking her teeth into her lower lip savagely, she resumed her climbing, determined. There was no point in thinking about any of it. She'd either make it all the way up, to sneak back into the cabin and get a good, long, durable rope, or she wouldn't. There was no other way out of this.

Earlier, after being certain that the man who had shot at them was gone, they tried to go down, hoping to descend the trail all the way to the bottom of the falls. Yet, less than halfway, they got stuck, with the cliff getting steeper and steeper, with less and less places to step on until it turned into a solid, glittering, polished surface. By that time, the Onondaga girl was too weak to go on anyway, her wounded arm trickling blood, her face having no color at all, leaning on Seketa so heavily, she felt like fainting herself. She had had a sleepless night full of unpleasant adventures behind her too, her life powers not at their best.

So they had rested for a while, trying to decide what to do, letting the sprays of the angry cascades wet their sweaty faces. Those soaked their clothes, refreshing and cooling, but irritating in the constant noise they created. It was difficult to hear one's own thoughts in the deafening roar.

"You go back... back up," groaned the Onondaga girl.

"Climb back. Don't return to the town. Be careful of that man with the bow." Wearily, she wiped her face with her good arm. "Don't go back to Onondaga Town. Go to High Springs. There is a trail. It begins at the lake shore, by the spring. Will you find your way back to the lake?"

"Yes." Nodding, Seketa wiped her eyes in her turn. The sprays of thousands of drops made her blink constantly, interfering with her ability to see. "Remember way, yes."

"Good. Then when you reach the lake, go as though returning to Onondaga Town, but when you see the spring, turn into the woods and follow the trail. It will bring you to High Springs in the end." The girl stifled another groan, trying to find a better position against the wet rock, a broken shaft sticking out of her upper arm, oozing liquids. "Two days of walk, but you can make it faster if you hurry. In High Springs, seek out Hionhwatha. Tell him I sent you. Tell him the Messenger will want you unharmed and in good spirits, so he is to take care of you until he comes." Her gaze turned away, glittering with wetness that had nothing to do with the flying droplets this time. "When you see the Messenger, tell him I tried. Tell him I did my best. Tell him…" Her voice shook and broke, as the exquisite face twisted, the glittering eyes closing, the colorless lips pressing tightly, quivering. She was truly beautiful, and so very courageous.

Seketa suppressed her own tears.

"You tell this. Not I. You tell when meet the Messenger," she said firmly, hearing her own voice loud and not trembling, overcoming the constant thundering. "I climb, get rope. Then we make you climb, together, yes. Not leaving, not going away. High Springs go together, you and me."

There was an unmistakable flash of hope in the eyes that opened abruptly, not blinking against the mist. A smile curved the generous lips.

"You can't drag me all the way up, rope or not. But I thank you for this thought. You have much courage. You will make a great wife to the scar-faced warrior. He deserves someone like you. So make sure to get to High Springs in one piece." The girl's grin widened. "When you see him, tell him Onheda said his Flint People are an ugly lot. Tell him I still think this way. Tell him to make a home anywhere but in his Little Falls. His rotten town is no good for a treasure like you. Tell him I said my spirit will haunt him forever with ugly curses if he makes you live in Little Falls." Her laughter trilled, overcoming the thundering of the water. "He knows I can curse well."

The laughter died abruptly as the girl shut her eyes, exhausted, but Seketa kept staring, suddenly uneasy. There was an obvious past between Tekeni and that beautiful, brave, witty woman, older than herself but not by much. Those baiting remarks that she was supposed to pass along related a sense of deep comradeship. Were those just friendly words, or was there more to it? Was Tekeni fascinated with this sparkling female once upon a time? Was that why he was in no hurry to come?

She pushed the troublesome thoughts away, concentrating. "I climb up, get the rope. Then we'll see, yes. Maybe get help, somehow."

"Don't endanger yourself," pleaded the girl, clutching Seketa's hand between her sweaty palms. "Better run for High Springs right away."

But Seketa wouldn't hear any of that, and now here she was, jumping the slippery stones, fighting off her exhaustion and fear, not knowing what awaited her up there if she managed not to fall to her death in the next few heartbeats.

It was not yet near dusk when she reached the top, falling onto the wet grass and just lying there, grateful, her muscles cramped, aching, begging to be left alone, to rest, just for a little while. With an effort, she forced herself up, listening intently. Only regular sounds disturbed the peacefulness of the afternoon, the wind rustling in the bushes and the birds chirping in the trees. The anonymity of the woods beckoned, but she turned the other way, going along the edge of the cliff, remembering the trail they had followed while escaping the hut. *Oh, Mighty Spirits, please, let it be empty.*

She would find a good rope, or she would repair the one she had cut in the attempt to break free this morning, and then, somehow, she would reach the Onondaga girl again. They would tie the rope around her, and this way, the climb would be possible, maybe. She pushed her doubts away. One thing at a time.

The trail was there, calming in its tranquility. Pleased with herself for locating it so quickly, she rushed on, careful to make no sounds.

The hut looked deserted, its entrance opened and gaping, but as she peeked in, her heart missed a beat, because it was not empty, not abandoned. Eyes adjusting to the semidarkness with difficulty, her senses reached out, feeling a foreign presence, her ears picking up a light breathing. The man seemed to be asleep, his bow, most likely the one that had shot at them this morning, within an easy reach.

She hesitated, then saw her bag, untouched, lying where she had left it this morning. Taking a deep breath, she tiptoed toward it, her steps soundless upon the earthen floor. The man didn't move, his breathing light, even. Maybe she could look around. Just to snatch a rope, a long string of any sort, and she would go back, satisfied. It had to be long and made out of leather, not of plants. Fibers, however many, may not be strong enough. Why wouldn't such a place have a rope?

There was a pile of utensils in the far corner. Holding her breath, she slunk toward it, moving the plates carefully, eyeing the jumble of clothes underneath it, hopeful. A pair of leggings cut into ribbons and tied together could work, couldn't they? A knife, she needed to get a knife!

Determined, she looked around, absorbed. Too absorbed. The sound of the man's steps did not penetrate her mind before he was upon her, moving with the speed of a pouncing predator, one moment asleep on his mat, the next across the room, grabbing her shoulder, making her sway.

She fought him desperately, slipping away from his grip. A mad dash toward the doorway had her stumbling before he was beside her again, faster than she was, not as clumsy or panicked.

Squirming wildly, pushing and kicking, she tried to break from yet another stony grip, the safety of the woods beckoning. But for a chance to run into the bushes and be gone!

"Stop fighting, you wild beast," he hissed, backhanding her, making her ears ring. "Why did you come back?"

She bit his hand as he tried to make her face him. He groaned and struck her again, so hard she slipped out of his grip and went flying against the wall. Dizzy, she kept still for a moment, wishing the world would stop spinning.

"Why did you come back?" He watched her warily, coming closer and standing above, measuring her with a certain amount of interest. "I would expect you to be back at the town by now, keeping very quiet." His eyebrows climbed high. "Not running around, stealing things."

"I no steal, I need, need rope," she said, desperate.

"What for?" His eyes flickered with growing interest.

"I..." Hesitating, she remembered overhearing the previous night's conversation, when the Onondaga girl grew so frightened. The man who kidnapped them wanted her alive, and unharmed. She remembered that most clearly. And if she was not to be harmed, then why not...

"Please, need help," she said, gambling. "Please."

"Eh?" His face was now a mask of bewilderment mixed with an open amusement.

"The other, other girl, she stuck, need help. I come, get rope. Help climb."

The amusement fled. "You are talking nonsense. The other fox died. I shot her and saw her falling into the falls."

"She no died. Wound, yes, but no dead." Narrowing her eyes, Seketa peered at him, not liking the way he looked at her now, his gaze turning measuring, greedy. "Leader want alive, he said again and again, want her alive, no harm. He said—"

"Stop talking nonsense. She is dead. I saw her." He leaned forward, grabbing her shoulders once again, pulling her onto her feet. "Yes, the War Chief needed her alive, but she was a wild cat, and she jumped to avoid being caught. You will tell him this, if asked. Is that clear to you?" His breath was upon her face, so very close she felt like gagging. "But he said nothing about you, did he? So I can harm you all I like, can't I?"

Before her dread could get the better of her, making her limp with panic and helpless, her instincts took over, forcing her knee up, acting with no coordination with her will. Crushing into his groin with a desperate force, it sent a shaft of pain up her leg.

The man doubled over as though cut, the air hissing, escaping his lungs in a ridiculous sound. He seemed as though about to fall, or maybe to curl around himself. She didn't wait to see it. Dashing toward the doorway, she burst into the clearness of the outside, racing madly, crashing through the bushes, where muffled voices seeped from between the trees. She could hear them most clearly, coming from the woods, following the trail, probably. Panicked, she turned to detour, but her foot slipped, stumbling over protruding roots, sending her flying forward, head first.

Struggling to her feet, too frantic to pay attention to the pain, she saw a glimpse of another figure, and the fright it gave her returned some of her sanity, making her roll away into the thickest of the shrubs instead of jumping up and running again.

The man from the hut was out there now too, yelling and cursing. She tried to crawl away, but her skirt caught at the branches and thorns, and then they were upon her, both of them, their voices ringing above her head, making no sense. They were screaming at each other, then the blows came. The man from the hut went flying into another maze of branches, but jumped back quickly, his knife flashing.

Then a girl she did not recognize was beside her, pulling her gently, helping to free the torn dress.

"Come, come," she murmured. "Don't be afraid. It's all good now."

"Who you?" groaned Seketa, the sounds of the fight still on, making her dizzy.

"Hanowa. From the town. Don't you remember? I remember you." The girl frowned. "Where is Onheda? She was with you, no? Please, tell me she isn't hurt."

"Onheda? Who Onheda?"

The girl's face fell. "Oh, she was not with you!" Growing quiet, she just sat beside Seketa, leaning against the same tree, her shoulders sagging.

The fight subdued, with her pursuer falling beside them, his limbs flipping, awash with blood, bubbling with his mouth, trying to scream. Terrified, they both jerked away, while the other man knelt, murmuring a prayer, delivering the final blow.

Her nausea was getting the better of her, but before she could turn away in order to vomit discreetly, she caught a glimpse of the man's face, and her heart came to a total halt. One heartbeat, then another. Nothing happened in her chest, while her mind went numb, absolutely blank.

He looked different, not the boy she remembered but a man, truly a man, wide-shouldered, imposing, dangerous. It was as though many hunting seasons had passed, many summers and many cold moons. He was a stranger, but her heart, which came to flutter wildly now, making her nausea so much worse, told her that it was him, despite the weathered, scarred face and the blood splattered across it, and the air of cold violence he radiated. This man, this warrior, was him, the Wolf Clan boy, *her chosen mate*!

Fighting for breath, she tried to overcome her dizziness, afraid to lose her senses, because if she fainted, he might go away, disappear again, and then she would have to look for him anew, wandering these dangerous lands, miserable and alone.

He was kneeling beside her now, his arms holding her, pulling her up, reeking of blood, like the last time when they had been together. But now it was not his blood, and his arms were holding her strongly, the warmth of his body forceful, not weakened by wounds.

"You," he was muttering. "You... you are here. I found you. Oh, Mighty Spirits, you are here."

His words trailed off, turned incomprehensible, but still he was whispering in her people's tongue, and it made her feel at home, helped to calm the wild pounding of her heart.

"You didn't find me," she murmured, pressing closer, enveloped in his warmth. "I was the one to find you."

It was nothing like their farewell, when he was wounded and hurt, or their kisses and their lovemaking before the filthy Yeentso ruined it all for them. Now it was this man, almost a stranger, a dangerous, formidable warrior full of scars, holding her, and yet, it was him, his arms, his strength, and her body fitted against his perfectly, like it always had. She was home at long last, after so many moons of loneliness and despair.

"I had to look for you," she repeated, snug against his chest. "I couldn't wait any longer."

His arms were trembling, pressing her so tightly that she found it difficult to breathe.

"Yes, yes, you found me," he murmured, his voice breaking, his shudders making her tremble along with him. "I don't deserve a woman like you."

And then the other girl was beside them, and she was talking to him in that foul-sounding foreign tongue of theirs, and she felt him tensing, making an effort to control himself. He released his grip, just a little, and, while able to breathe again, she was disappointed. In his arms, it felt good, safe, *home*.

"Did you happen to see another girl?" he asked, lifting her face with one hand, peering at her from above. They used to be of almost the same height, but now she was barely reaching his forehead, and again, it was difficult to recognize him, with all the scars and the wide, strong, weathered features of his. His smell and touch were welcome, familiar, but the rest of him belonged to the unknown man, a handsome warrior, a fascinating stranger. Then she saw his smile, and all was well again. The hesitant, shy smile was his and his alone.

"She disappeared at the same time, you see?" he went on, unsure of himself. "Maybe you know what happened? She was tall and pretty, and fierce, very sure of herself. Maybe—"

"Yes, yes, I know. Of course I know!" Panicked again, she broke free from his embrace. "She is down there, by the falls. We need to get to her. We need to hurry." Frantically, she looked around, meeting the wide-eyed stare of the other girl. "We need to hurry! There might be a rope in that hut, back in the woods. We need to run there first. Please." Grabbing his arm, she pulled, annoyed with their stares. "I was there earlier, before that man woke up. Please, we need to hurry!"

"Where is she?" he asked, blinking.

"Halfway down the falls! She can't get out, she is stuck there."

He came back to life all at once. "Where exactly? Show me the place!" Now it was again the warrior speaking. "You go to that hut and see if there is a rope there," he tossed toward the other girl, switching to their tongue effortlessly, already walking toward the hut. "Come, hurry." His arm wrapped around Seketa's shoulders, propelling her on, gently but forcefully. "Show me the place."

It was all happening too fast. Her mind in a haze, she let him pull her on, trying not to stumble on the entanglements of roots and the muddy, slippery ground. Her legs didn't seem to shake outright, but they felt wobbly, as though about to give way any moment.

"Is she wounded?" he asked, his hand still around her shoulders, supporting.

"Yes, yes, she is!"

He tensed visibly. "How badly?"

"Not badly, but she can't climb. I came up to get a rope. I thought I could pull her up, maybe."

"How did you two get down there?"

"We escaped." She pressed closer, although it did nothing but hinder their step. The memories of the morning made her need of his warmth and protection soar.

"Tadodaho?" he hissed between his clenched teeth, pressing her tightly yet not slowing down.

"What?"

"The man who kidnapped you, who was it?"

"I don't know. I think—"

He halted so suddenly, she lost her balance and would have fallen but for the tightness of his grip. Startled, she was about to demand an explanation, but his eyes told her to keep quiet, and his arms tightened protectively, signaling her to stay still.

The voices were nearing, a group of men hurrying up the trail, or maybe crashing through the bushes. She pressed against his chest, her heart thumping.

"How far is that cabin?" demanded the familiar voice, a voice she would recognize anywhere. She felt Tekeni relaxing all at once.

"Not far, and you don't need the cabin," he shouted as another voice was answering, calm but somehow anxious. *The voice of the man who had kidnapped them.* She pressed closer into his embrace.

"What are you doing here?" cried out Two Rivers, bursting from behind the trees.

"Looking for your girl. What do you think?" Tekeni's eyes flashed with a hint of amusement.

"Where is she?" demanded Two Rivers, not amused in the least, his face a foreboding mask.

Oh, this one had changed to the point of being unrecognizable as well, another man to grow in stature, not physically maybe but otherwise. The Messenger of the Great Spirits, oh yes. Awed, Seketa just stared, as more people surrounded them, the man who kidnapped them, dressed in all the glory of his high status, and many others.

Tekeni grew serious again. "Somewhere down there. Seketa is taking me to that place."

Two Rivers' eyes widened all of a sudden. "Oh, Mighty Spirits," he muttered, staring at her, but blinking as though trying to clear his vision.

"Let us go. She is wounded."

He whirled at the War Chief, causing the man to take an involuntary step back.

"She was supposed to be in the cabin, unharmed," muttered the man defensively.

"Well, obviously she is not." Not waiting for Seketa's guidance, Two Rivers turned around and rushed up the incline, toward the roaring of the cascading water.

"It's not in the end of the trail," she whispered into Tekeni's ear, indicating the right direction with her eyes. "I came up somewhere around there."

And then more shouting followed, and everyone was frantic or angry, so she gathered her strength to leave the safety of his arms and led the way, blessing the spirits for making her remember. It was unsettling to be away from his warmth, but she needed to make an effort. Only this once, because after all this was over, with the Onondaga girl rescued and saved and taken care of, she would not leave his arms, not even for a heartbeat, she promised herself. Not even to sleep or eat or do her needs in the bushes. She would stay in his embrace for long days and nights to come, to make it up for the dreadful waiting and the harsh journey, and all the hardships. She had found him, and it had been worth all the sacrifices. He had been worthy of even more than this.

Smiling to herself, she sought him with her gaze while they had been busy crowding the slope, talking all at once, arguing. About what? She didn't care. In the end, Two Rivers won, as always, and she came closer and caressed Tekeni's arm as he frowned, watching his friend disappearing behind the edge of the cliff.

CHAPTER 22

Fighting for a foothold on the slippery stone, Onheda clenched her teeth, the pain in her shoulder pulsating, sucking on the remnants of her strength. The damn arrow was still there, fluttering in the fleshy part of her upper arm, easy to pull out, but not when one is tottering above the roaring chasm, needing every bit of one's concentration and the sharpness of one's senses to hang on.

It had been a while since the Crooked Tongues girl left, jumping the slippery stones, quick and as nimble as a pretty squirrel. She was probably up there already, looking for that rope. Or maybe running away.

Onheda shrugged with her good shoulder. The girl didn't owe her much, meeting in the way they did, sharing an evening of unpleasant adventures. If she had listened to her, Onheda's, advice and ran away, she had been a sensible person.

Having regained her breath, she reached for another crack between the stones, digging her fingers into the cavity, bettering her grip. How did she get to such a steep cliff again? She must have lost the way.

To grind her teeth again helped. If she was to die here, she would do it while trying to find the way out; not curled around herself and dying of starvation. And she would not jump into the falls to hasten her end, the way she had contemplated doing when the girl disappeared out of sight. No! It would be no meek, helpless death, and no taking her own life, either.

A desperate push with her right foot saw her a little higher, huddled on a small shelf, panting, careful not to touch the annoying stick, lest it'd bring more of the sharp, cutting pain.

Oh, Mighty Spirits, but for a little more of her old strength. If not for the filthy arrow, she would have been in great shape, the dull ache in the back of her head or not. She would have been up there before the foreign girl even, running for High Springs as fast as she could, damn the ugly man who had shot at them into the underworld of the Evil Twin!

Had the girl found a rope? Would she come back?

Thirsty, she turned her head toward the thundering water, trying to catch the flying sprays. It didn't help, so she licked the wetness off the clean-looking spot on the stone in front of her. How strange it was that she met the scar-faced youth's girl, of all people, the girl who, instead of waiting, did the unspeakable by crossing the Great Sparkling Water, the impossible obstacle, all by herself, setting upon a journey to find her lover. A tale worthy of a storyteller, to repeat by the winter fire, with the groaning of the wind and the thumping of the snow. A story of love!

She smiled, imagining the scar-faced youth's surprise in seeing her, that brave girl of his. Too bad she was not destined to be there, to see it for herself. The girl was worthy of an outstanding man like him, so pretty and determined, so courageous, a true companion. He had planned on crossing the Great Lake for so long, worried that she wouldn't wait. Oh, how silly men were sometimes; how stupid to judge women by their own faults. A man could forget, but rarely a woman. Had the Crooked Tongues man forgotten?

She clenched her teeth, pushing the sadness away. If she was to die soon, she would not embark upon her Sky Journey disappointed or downcast. She would go proudly, with her head held high. If he had forgotten, then he was not the man worthy of her love. And if he had not, then he should have made an effort to find her before she died, struggling to make his dream come true.

He would be sorry, when he found out, of that she was sure. But how sorry? He praised his mission above anything else, not ready to put it aside for any reason. But then, she had known it all along. He had never lied to her. They should not have fallen in love, and he had said he struggled against it. And failed. Oh, how pleased she had been to hear that back then. But maybe it was not for the best. Maybe but for the wonderful lovemaking in the woods, she would have gone home as intended, forgetting all about the strange foreigner and the impossibility of his wild ideas of peace between warring nations.

Closing her eyes, she curled against the cold firmness of the stone, the pain seeping out of her wounded shoulder, slow, unhurried, taking her life forces away. Maybe she wouldn't die of starvation, she thought. Maybe it would happen faster, in a more merciful way. But for a chance to see him one more time! One more glimpse of his prominent, foreign-looking face, with those high cheekbones, as sharp as though chiseled out of stone, and his eyes, large, dark, penetrating, shining eerily sometimes, sparkling with amusement more often than not. Not a person one would expect the Great Spirits to send, but their messenger nevertheless. How else had he made them all listen, in one short span of seasons uniting two fierce enemies, the eastern nations. And her people, too. Tadodaho would give up eventually, sooner or later. This is why the man resorted to filthy means like kidnapping her. He was desperate, knowing the end of that struggle.

Sighing, she forced her eyes open. It was good that she had escaped, not leaving the filthy man with the means of blackmail. At the cost of her life, she left the Messenger free to do the right thing, not to give up on account of her.

Would he?

Fighting her exhaustion, she straightened up carefully. Oh, she had better climb on. If she had the slightest chance of survival, she'd better give it a try.

Her hand slipped, but she managed to regain her balance, groping for another cavity, clinging to the wet surface with her entire body, the pain in her arm unbearable. A stone rolled from under her foot and she cried out, desperate. *Not now, not yet!*

With the last of her strength, she clung to the slippery rock, afraid to breathe. No more stones fell, but the shelf was now narrower, not wide enough to crouch on it even, and her strength was vanishing fast, sucked by the pulsating pain and the wild pounding of her heart.

Two Rivers worked his way down the cliff, concentrating on his step, watching for signs, dominating his fear, but barely. He never liked climbing, either rocks or trees, but since the test of the falls, he'd come to detest heights in general, especially if accompanied by the deafening roar of cascading water. It made him nauseated, and his stomach remained so tight, he could not let in a deep breath. And just when he needed the ability to breathe deeply.

The stones under his feet were wet and slippery, the chasm down below alarmingly deep. It was the test of the falls all over again, curse their filthy spirits into the afterlife of the endless wandering, every one of them who had made him jump or climb.

Regaining his balance on yet another perilous edge, he paused, then hurried on. He might be too late already. Tekeni's girl said they were halfway down the cliff, stuck, so he must have been very close, yet there was no sign of Onheda anywhere around, and the thought of her lying on the bottom of these falls, her broken body carried away by the vicious stream, made his limbs go rigid with rage, pushing his fear away, giving him strength to go on.

He needed her, he realized. Needed her desperately. If she died, something of him would die with her, and nothing would be the same. The Great Peace, even if still achieved, would be pale, grayish, lacking in color, not something as wonderfully meaningful as it might have been with her by his side. He had spent a long winter and spring away from her, but the knowledge of her being out there, waiting for him, impressed with his new achievements, was the one to push him on. He knew he would return to her in the end, he knew it all along, but like always, he was blind, mistaking her for just another woman, more enticing than the rest, but still one of many.

Oh, but she had been anything but that, and he should have known better. She was not prepared to wait patiently. How could she, with all her spark, her courage, her immense inner powers? Of course she was anxious to do actual deeds, to help, to impress him, maybe. Hionhwatha had not exaggerated while claiming that she came to him, offering help. Of course she did this, ready to head into the heart of the danger, to do vital things, to make the most stubborn people listen. She was no less the messenger than he was, doing no less for the Great Peace than he did. And she paid for it with her life.

He ground his teeth until his jaw hurt, then went on, determined. Would he have to go all the way down to the bottom of the falls? Tekeni's girl said they were stuck halfway, but for the lack of strength or the lack of passable trail, he didn't know, didn't care to ask. If forced to jump the last part of his journey, he would do it, he decided, licking the blood off his lower lip, where his teeth tore at it. Dead or alive, he would find her, no matter what. Without it, there would be no Great Peace, unless they decided to proceed with his enterprise on their own. He would not be a part of it, knowing that she died because he cared for nothing but his mission.

The trail ended with a suddenness that startled him, making his heart leap in fear. Far below, the water raced, crashing against the sharp rocks. He stared at it for a heartbeat, frozen, afraid to breathe. It was worse than Little Falls, far worse. She could not survive this fall, not even if youths with a canoe were waiting down there, ready to fish her out. He was lucky not to be required to jump these cascades, with or without Tekeni's rescuing scheme.

Heart beating fast, he scanned the angrily swirling surface, seeking her broken body, but it was vacant, indifferent, racing on undisturbed, although the shelf he stood on displayed signs of life. There was a piece of a torn dress, fluttering in the crack between the rocks, and there were dark stains upon the wet stones, not washed out by the constant drizzle.

Kneeling, he studied it, his breath coming in gasps. He was late, by only a little, but late. She had evidently been there, struggling to stay alive, while he was busy lingering in Onondaga Town, talking to its filthy leader, concerned with nothing but his purpose in life, indifferent to the people who loved him.

The noise of the falls made him wish to curse aloud. It closed on him, pressing from every direction, eager to claim his life too, not satisfied with hers only. So this was the sound she had heard last, the roaring water hungry for her blood?

He could not get enough air. The trembling was getting worse, the convulsions in his chest unbearable. It was terrible, suffocating. It made him sick with desperation. He could not even see properly now, not even the blurry shape of the shelf he crouched upon.

Reaching for the piece of cloth, he tore it off, not wishing for this place to have any remnants of her, the filthy cliff that made her die.

Wipe away the tears, cleanse your throat so you may speak and hear...

The words didn't work, although he said them aloud now, screaming to overcome the accursed thundering.

She had died alone, afraid maybe.

No! Not afraid. Not her. He could imagine her radiant eyes, sparkling with fury, refusing to accept her fate. She went off as unyielding, as daring, as proud as she lived.

The knowledge didn't make him feel better. He needed her, her cheeky, challenging, spicy presence, her laughter, her smile – that surprisingly shy, unguarded smile of hers – and the way she had touched him, when finally in his arms, hesitant and tender, then passionate and so full of love.

As his fist hit the rock, again and again, he winced with pain, but it made him feel better, refreshed him a little. He deserved all the pain in the world for making her fight alone. He deserved worse than this. When threatening filthy Tadodaho with eternal wandering of his worthless spirit, he didn't know he was the one deserving that.

He rose to his feet, fearless now. The long climb up would calm him, provide a wonderful opportunity to think, or maybe to fall to his death. He didn't care. It was tempting to stay here until nightfall. He didn't want to face people, not even Tekeni, but Tekeni would be the first to climb down here should he not return in a little while.

As for Hionhwatha, the man who had sent her here, or Tadodaho, the man who had kidnapped her, oh, he wasn't sure he would be able to face either of them without doing something violent, ruining the chances of the Great Peace, achieved with so much effort and hard work. To sacrifice it all was wrong, even for her memory. He had no right to let his temper fray, and yet he wasn't sure he would manage.

A stone rolled, bouncing off the steep cliffs to his left. He peered at it, puzzled. Someone must have been coming down, following another trail? Why? *And why wouldn't they leave him alone, for the Great Spirits' sake?*

Wiping his face, he looked up, squinting against the flying droplets. The muffled figure was poising on a sort of a shelf, far enough removed to let him compose himself, before the newcomer would reach him. He hoped it was Tekeni, tired of waiting, and not some well-meaning local, trying to be of help.

Scanning the steep cliff, his gaze returned to the figure, seeing it still frozen in the same pose, clinging to the wall, not moving. He shielded his eyes, then held his breath, taking in the fluttering skirt, the only part of the frozen form that moved. A woman! But how?

The next thing he knew, he was leaping up, heedless of his step, frantic to reach the other trail.

"Hang on! Don't move!"

The yells rang in his ears, distracting, and he wasn't sure it was him who yelled, but who else was around to do that?

The falls roared below his feet as he jumped a small chasm, landing on his hands and knees. There was a way to detour it, probably – for how else had she gotten there? – yet he had no time to look for a better course.

Now directly below her, if still too far removed, he struggled against the rough stones, scratching his limbs, sometimes wavering dangerously, with only the strength of his fingers separating him from the turbulent void. He didn't pause. Any moment, she would loosen her grip, slipping to her death, to plummet past him, so close yet unreachable.

But oh, no! he thought, clinging to the wet stones, pushing with his elbows and knees, oblivious of his tearing skin. Not this time, not after he had lost her already.

"Don't move!" he shouted again, close enough now to see her clearly, pressing against the wall, standing on the tips of her moccasins, so ridiculously narrow was her shelf – how did she get there at all? – her skirt torn and fluttering along with her matted hair, the soft curve of her cheek clearly visible, scratched and dirty, pressed against the glittering rock, the dark stiffness of the material under her shoulder suggesting blood, *her blood.*

A few more wild leaps that should have seen him plummeting into the falls, and he was close below, on a relatively comfortable step, his elbow propped against another rock, in a good enough position to catch her and hold on, should she fall abruptly.

"Now slip down carefully," he gasped, struggling to catch his breath, his heart thundering in his ears. "Don't let it go right away."

Her hands shook as she strained to separate her fingers, which must have been numb from holding on for so long and with such desperation.

"Don't be afraid, I'm ready to catch you." He felt his own limbs trembling, from the effort, and from fear. The waiting was unbearable. Why did it take her so long?

"Carefully. Just slide down. Don't fall back."

His hands shook with every heartbeat, the sharp edge of the cliff jutting against his body, making the ordeal worse. She was still clinging onto the slippery wall, although her hands managed to release their grip. Now it was the pure ability of her body to keep her balance, as though after dedicating all of its inner powers to hanging onto the small perch, it refused to lose what was achieved with so much effort.

He shifted upwards as far as he could without sacrificing the security of his position. He would need all of it and more when taking on her weight. His free hand wrapped around her waist.

"Now!"

With a small cry, she slipped down and he clenched onto her, fighting for balance, feeling himself tottering for a moment, his body clinging to the wet stones, struggling for control. Her eyes were shut, and she was trembling so badly he was afraid she would tip them both over, after all. Her sobbing was quiet, uncontrollable, like that of a child. He didn't think about his next step. For once in his life, he didn't care. The feeling of holding her, warm and alive, even if wounded, hurt, and crying, was the most exquisite sensation, to melt into it and to forget all about the outside world.

The moons of misgivings, of longing, of indecision were no more. He had found her, and he would not let her go, not again, not if he could help it. If Tadodaho was to materialize in front of him now and demand to let her drop in exchange for his people joining on the humblest of terms, with only a few representatives and no final say, he would tell the old sorcerer to go and dump himself into the falls, he knew. The thought made him chuckle.

"What's funny?" she whispered into his chest, not daring to move a muscle and still sobbing, but somehow sounding more of her old, challenging self.

"I just thought that Tadodaho might feel like jumping into the falls now."

Her giggle, mixed with a hiccup, made his laughter more difficult to control. "Maybe we should help him."

"Yes, maybe we should. Then I won't have to keep my promises."

She lifted her face, peeking at him carefully, like a small

creature ready to dive back into the safety of his arms.

"Am I dead?" Her eyes peered at him, their frown obvious. "I thought I managed not to fall when this cliff began breaking, but now I'm not so sure."

"What are you talking about?" He shifted her carefully, now, with the first wave of the euphoria over, aware of the roaring chasm and the slippery stones jutting everywhere. To get her back to safety, he would have to go down first, back to the beginning of the trail. There was not much hope for him to climb up from where they stood, not while carrying her.

"The way you materialized out of the drizzle, ready to save me, it can't truly happen. I'm either dreaming or dead," she insisted.

"You still can die if we don't hurry. We need to bring you up before nightfall. I don't like that stick in your arm."

He watched her frown deepening, enjoying the spark in her eyes and the sight of her lips quivering, fighting a smile. "I thought you would like it."

His happiness swept him. Oh, but how he missed those baiting remarks of hers. "No, I don't. It doesn't look good on you. And all the mud and dirt. You need to wash up."

The smile won. "You are complaining!"

"Yes, I am. When I told you to wait for me at Jikonsahseh's I didn't plan on hopping all over Onondaga Falls, trying to fish you out of chasms. I thought Onondaga women were more patient than that."

"And I thought Crooked Tongues were not so slow in doing things, taking so many moons to complete simple tasks."

The wideness of her smile took his breath away. Muddied, bruised, and haggard she might be now, but her beauty was still there, unmarred, making his heart race, the beauty of her face and the beauty of her spirit. Oh, she was not one of many, never, never that! And he was a coward trying to convince himself of the opposite.

Her lips were cracked, dry, and bruised, and yet their taste made his head reel. It was a homecoming.

"I'm starting to believe it might be true and I'm still alive," she whispered, her mouth opening against his, not shy, not retreating, but inviting and eager to explore.

"If that's the proof that you needed…" He heard his voice ringing throatily, the reactions of his body disturbing, making it difficult to keep their balance on their slippery perch. He needed to break that kiss.

As though hearing his thoughts, she moved her face away, diving back into the safety of his chest.

"Yes, I need some proof," she muttered. "I need a lot of proving."

"You'll get all of it and more. But first, we take you up there." Briskly, he measured the slope towering above their heads. No, he could not climb up, not while carrying her. "We move back down to that cliff. From there, we'll climb up easily."

"If not for the stupid wound!"

"How did you get shot?" Taking most of her weight, he helped her down to another shelf, sliding beside her, not letting her go, not trusting her ability to keep straight under the circumstances.

"That stupid lump of rotten meat," she said painfully, steadying herself, making an obvious effort to be easy on him. "He chased us to the falls." Clinging to him, she closed her eyes as he picked her up in order to jump over a narrow crack between two rocks. "He was shooting, like the stupid, useless, fat rodent he was. The Crooked Tongues girl argued, but after I was hit, she dove down here with no additional word."

He tried to regain his breath, leaning against the craggy surface, resting for a moment. Slender and wonderfully built, she was still not an easy burden to carry while jumping cliffs.

"Who kidnapped you?" It was essential to keep her talking. It took both their minds off the danger.

"The War Chief, who else?"

She tensed as he jumped yet another crack clumsily, wavering and slamming his side against another rock, his arms shifting their grip of her, brushing against the broken shaft of the arrow. "Sorry."

"It's all good," she gasped, then narrowed her eyes, peering at him. "I overheard the War Chief saying that I'm not to be harmed. I swear, I don't know how he knew... What did he..." Her voice trailed off as her gaze dropped, avoiding his.

"They say he is a sorcerer. He must have guessed." He clenched his teeth, proceeding up the trail now, relieved to head in the right direction at long last. There would be a few difficult places to forge, he remembered, but it looked as though they might make it, after all. "Hionhwatha should never have sent you here. I wanted to kill him when I heard."

Her smile was faint, atypically shy. "I wanted to go. I was tired of waiting."

He leaned against another wall, dizzy from the effort. But for a gulp of water, and maybe some rest. The deepening dusk made him hasten his step.

"I'm sorry for not coming back earlier. I should have come, or at least sent a word."

"I think I can walk here." She slipped out of his arms when he paused again, exhausted. "It's just the climb that makes it difficult, because of the annoying arm." He watched her frowning, biting her lips. "I was angry with you, yes, but well, I knew you've been doing important things." She beamed all of a sudden. "We heard all about your exploits. Both eastern nations are now following you, united, not warring anymore. And now my people! Hionhwatha did a wonderful work in High Springs. People there are waiting for you. And even here, in Onondaga Town." She frowned again. "I talked to people, many people. They are waiting for you, too. It's only Tadodaho you need to remove."

"This man is not standing in our way anymore, either." He pulled her closer, wrapping his arm around her waist in order to support, but enjoying the touch immensely.

She stopped abruptly, gasping. "What do you mean? Did you fight him already?"

"I talked to him. He agreed to join." Happy with the effect, he pulled her on. "He had seen the reason, like all of them."

"You talked to him?"

"Yes. He saw the strength of my arguments." It felt good to tease her this way. He grinned happily. "Why are you staring at me?"

"Because it doesn't make sense. He was... he was so against you. He wanted you to come and fight him. He kidnapped me to use against you. He would use anything he can to bring you down."

His happiness fled. "He kidnapped you to get concessions for his people, that's all. The filthy rat knew he can push only up to a certain point."

For a few more heartbeats, they proceeded in silence.

"Did he? Did he get... those concessions?" Her eyes were so firmly upon the slippery rocks that he glanced there involuntarily, to see what she was seeing.

"Yes, he did, but I can deal with it." He picked her up again, feeling her wavering, losing most of her spark. "I'm not looking forward to explaining it all to the others, though. They will be furious."

"What did you concede?"

"Well." He let out his breath, the necessity to talk wasting more of his precious energy, but, at the same time, distracting in a good way, keeping his thoughts away from the rapidly deepening dusk and the long way yet ahead of them. "First of all, the meetings will be held on your people's lands, around this Onondaga Town, probably. But this is not what will bring trouble to me. People did agree, tentatively, that it's only fair that the meeting of the Five Nations will be held halfway from everyone."

"Five Nations?" Her eyes were as round as two plates, gaping at him in astonishment. "It can't be!"

"Five nations, of course, five nations. You knew what the plan was."

Ridiculously proud, like a child that hunted his first rabbit, he suppressed his grin, fighting the urge to stop and rest for another heartbeat. They needed to reach the top soon, before the darkness fell and made it impossible to pick their way among the slippery rocks. If worse came to worst, he would shout until Tekeni heard him and came down bringing a torch. But for that, they needed to be as close as possible, not drowned out by the deafening cacophony of the falls. Why didn't Tekeni have enough sense to follow, or to come down here now, like he always did? Then he remembered the girl.

"That Crooked Tongues girl, how did she end up with you?"

Her smile beamed at him. "I think all the impossible things happened to me since I argued with the War Chief on the evening of the Maple Ceremony."

"You argued with Tadodaho?"

"Well, yes, I did. I know I shouldn't have." Her smile was wide, free of guilt. "But you know how it is."

"I know how it is with you. From now on, I will keep a close eye on you, woman. You get into trouble too easily."

"I helped. I made the people of Onondaga Town aware of you and your good intentions."

He pressed her closer. "I know that, too. Without you, we would not be received in this town at all. You made it possible for us to come and talk to the War Chief when the time came."

Her smile was again a marvelous sight that made his heart quicken. "I didn't do that much, but I tried." Although pale with the loss of blood and exhaustion, her cheeks colored nevertheless. "You are the one to do wonders, not any of us, those who are helping you. I now believe that you are truly the Messenger of the Great Spirits. I talked about your divine mission so much, I came to believe you are not a mortal man at all."

"I don't know what I am," he muttered, embarrassed by her words and her gaze, so full of wonder and adoration. "But I know that I enjoyed the blessing of the Great Spirits when I found you alive and not dying; and not angry with me, either. Tomorrow, at dawn, I will make an offering, thanking the

Right-Handed Twin for his wonderful benevolence and goodwill."

Her gaze deepened. "I'll come with you and join your prayer."

And then they knew there was nothing to be added, their gazes locked, telling it all.

Which was one of the most wonderful things about her, he thought. She asked for no promises or declarations, no vows, no protestations of love. She was a law unto herself, a woman like no other, and he would make every effort to not let her go again. There was no need for words or promises. She knew. The depth of her gaze told him that.

CHAPTER 23

The first rays of sun caressed Tekeni's face, sliding down the opening in the tent, pulling him out of the pleasant dream. He had been in the middle of a river, floating rather than sailing, looking for fish. He must have been a heron, or some sort of a water bird, and the trout were splashing all over, sparkling with silver, promising a good hunting day.

He stretched lazily, not opening his eyes, not yet. Still half dreaming, snuggled in her warmth now, instead of that magical river, he pulled her closer, just in case. She felt so soft against his skin, her head nestled upon his shoulder, the tips of her hair tickling his face.

He listened to her calm, even breathing, then to the chirping of an early bird that was fussing near the roof opening, making a nest, most probably. Today was going to be important, and he should have been dressed and out already, heading toward the nearby valley in order to ensure that all was in order.

The First Gathering of the Five Nations was to be held here, near Onondaga Town, an event of an unheard-of proportion, its importance rivaling no other happening in the history of his people since the world had been created by the Right-Handed Twin and his grandmother, the Sky Woman. Just to live in time to witness such a thing was a privilege worthy of immortal souls. As for being a part of it... Oh, Mighty Spirits, his luck knew no bounds. He had witnessed the idea of the Great Peace being born, had seen it gaining power, had helped it turn into reality, step by step, little by little. Two Rivers was the creator, the man of the vision, the power behind the whole thing, but he, Tekeni, was his right hand, his most trusted friend and companion. Without him, the Great Peace might not have been born at all.

He smiled, then opened his eyes a fraction, reluctant to get up, but ready to leave the dream by now. Just a few more heartbeats of peace, and the wonderful sensation that the touch of her skin sent down his stomach, like rays of sunshine, warming every corner of his being, making it alive.

Ten dawns spent together in their small, pretty tent on the lakeshore, the dwelling they had been given to celebrate their union – two foreigners, belonging to no clan of the Onondagas – were evidently not enough. He craved her touch all the time, feeling the separation like a physical pain each time he had been required to leave her side. Quite often, as there was much to be done in order to prepare the First Gathering of the Five Nations, to make it proceed perfectly and with no hitch.

Two Rivers had been busy traveling again, bringing the leaders and the important people who hadn't come yet, inviting them personally, as persuasive as always, but now having a great authority as well. A personal invitation from the Messenger of the Great Spirits, the Great Peacemaker himself, was of a huge importance, so the people flocked readily, their camps overflowing Onondaga Lake's valley and its surroundings. Which kept the Great Man mainly away, trusting Tekeni and Hionhwatha to make it all ready, with the Onondaga Town's council helpful but lost, and Tadodaho smirking, watching affably enough, but doing nothing to help.

Oh, but those were busy days, with so many things that needed to be organized, food and entertainment, running all over, sending hunting parties far and wide, as not to exhaust the local woods, pacifying the Mothers of the Clans, who were elated by the honor of hosting such an important meeting but not overly happy with the amount of additional duties it put on the town's womenfolk; and last but not least, making sure the guests were not arguing or fighting, getting angry with each other, the enemies of yesterday now suddenly made brothers.

Toward the end of each day, his head would reel, and his legs would hardly support him, but then she was there, always there now, waiting for him to come home, soft and pliant and so wonderfully welcoming, her smile shining, her arms enveloping him, taking the tiredness away.

Not bored and not frustrated, because her days were not spent in loneliness, with the Onondaga girl usually around, spending more time in their tent than in the town, but melting away the moment he would return. Onheda was a sensible person, and he was glad Two Rivers was about to make her his woman. If anyone could handle the Crooked Tongues man, the fierce Onondaga woman was the one.

Still smiling, he stretched, then opened his eyes, suddenly hungry. She was watching him, the smile upon her lips beautiful, holding a mystery. Deep in his thoughts, he didn't notice her lifting her head, but now here she was, towering above, beaming at him.

"You are awake," he muttered, pulling her closer, hesitating. His body craved to feel her, but his eyes demanded to see her looking at him like that.

"For ages," she said. "Since before there was a light."

"Why didn't you wake me up?"

She laughed. "I didn't dare. You were so tired yesterday, you could barely see or eat."

He lifted his hand, running his fingers down the delicate curve of her cheek. "I was useless, wasn't I?"

"Yes, you were." Her laughter trilled, filling his heart with so much joy he felt like whooping, or maybe yelling something wonderfully loud, a blood-freezing war-cry. "You left your young wife wanting, and today is the big day, so you will have to be up and running again. Some husband I found myself."

"Oh, yes?"

He pulled her again, more forcefully now, shivering with the touch of her skin against his. To have a tent all for themselves was an unheard-of privilege. They could sleep naked all they liked, as no one would pass through their cozy dwelling on their way in or out, heading along the long corridor. Their frequent visitors made sure to create some noise, announcing their presence before storming in. Both dwellers of longhouses, where the decency required a sort of coverage most of the time, they weren't accustomed to such luxury, but as it was, they had found nothing to complain about, delighted in that unexpected development. It was good to make love whenever they wanted, with no consideration to the other people and their privacy. Their true married life would begin with their arrival at Little Falls.

She laughed, but when he enveloped her with his limbs, she melted against him, murmuring words of love, as she always did. Her voice was more beautiful than the trill of a flute, softer than the a murmuring of the wind, at least to his ears, so he held her, fondling, caressing, not in a hurry to kiss, wishing to hear more. And then they were one, one with the wind and the sun, and the world waking with all of its wonders, offering nothing but happiness and contentment; one with the pulses of their bodies, tuned to each other perfectly, belonging in one another.

Later, she made a breakfast for him by warming yesterday's meal of some meat and beans, munching on cornbread in the meanwhile.

"It's your fault your woman is lazy," she said, giggling, as he fished a piece of greasy meat out of the pot with an obvious lack of enthusiasm. "You keep her in bed all the time. She will bear you plenty of children this way, but you will be starved soon, all thin and underfed, unable to go out."

"I don't mind," he said, snatching one of her muffins, instead. "I will have a cause to stay home, too. Making more children."

"As though they will let you stay." She made a face, the tip of her tongue sneaking out, making him wish to push the food away and love her again, no matter how much he was needed elsewhere. "I'm lucky they don't know what you are eating in the mornings. Such an important person, the second most important man in these lands, the right hand of the Great Peacemaker himself, the man who is expected to organize it all and tell everyone what to do—oh, they would skin me alive if they knew that I jeopardize the health of such an irreplaceable dignitary."

He caught her skirt as she swept by, heading out to bring him water.

"Jeopardize me one more time before I go." She struggled to break free, but he was stronger, pulling her into his lap, laughing. "I'll drink on my way out, and there will be a great feast after the ceremony. I'll eat then. But I won't get to have a beautiful woman before this day is over. And it's not good for my health, to contain my desire for so long."

"There are plenty of annoying, filthy-tempered local beauties who would be only too happy to help you with this," she said, avoiding his kiss. "I saw them staring at you wherever you go. This whole town would be too happy to have you having them."

"What nonsense!" Having received that kiss, he kicked the half-empty plate out of his way, careful to make it slide and not overturn, then laid her on the earthen floor. "You are a jealous, headstrong woman, but I don't mind you guarding me and my honor. I touched no other woman when away from you, and I will touch none now that you are with me. We made a promise, remember?"

Her gaze deepened, filling with so much love, his heart squeezed. No, he didn't deserve this happiness. Or did he?

"Yes, I remember. We made a promise, and we were true to our hearts." Her arms enveloped him, pulling him into her warmth, into the wonderful passion that only her skin and her love could offer, of that he was sure.

"But they do look at you," she said afterward, after another bout of love left them breathless, drifting in too much happiness. Towering above him, her hair caressed his chest as he floated, too fulfilled to move a limb. "All those annoying foxes. Even Onheda agreed when I asked her. She said that yes, many girls would love to have you sharing their bunks, with their longhouses only too happy to have you in the family." Her eyes sparkled. "She said I came in time. After the First Gathering, many would have started pestering you."

"You both are talking so much nonsense," he said, grinning reluctantly, embarrassed. Surely the people who were staring at him, many girls among them, indeed, were startled by his scars, fascinated maybe, but not in this *other* sort of a way. It must be repulsive, this sight. He blessed the spirits for not making it repulsive in her eyes.

Her eyebrows were raised high, so he felt obliged to confess.

"They are staring at me because of the scars. Thanks to that filthy rat Yeentso, I stick out in the crowd, but not in the way I want to."

However, the usual wave of rage whenever bringing up the hated name, never came, dissipating in the adoration her gaze radiated.

"But you are so silly," she chortled, running her fingers alongside his face, tracking the scars, outlining the patterns they created. "Oh, how silly you are, handsome, beautiful man of mine. But I love you for that too, for being so humble, never seeing how important, how outstanding, how vital to everyone you are. And how handsome, too. Only truly great men are humble about themselves and their achievements, and I am lucky to have one such all for myself."

He stared into her eyes, drawn into their glow, knowing that nothing mattered and anything bad that had ever happened, and that was yet destined to come, would turn into nothing, to melt and disappear in the intensity of her love.

Unable to say a word, he drew her close to him and stayed still, relishing the wonderful sensation. She was his guiding spirit, and the future held only good things. He knew it for certain now, because of her.

Onheda watched the colorful mess of the valley spreading

beneath her feet, her heart squeezing with pride. People from all over their side of the Great Lake were walking about, talking and gesturing, their excitement unconcealed. The clusters of their tents stuck out everywhere, impossible to separate.

She could see the People of the Mountains strolling proudly, coming out of the encampment situated at the farther edge, encased cozily between two hills, as though still in their hilly west, a single feather in their headdresses peering into the sky, erect and as proud as those people were. By now, she'd learned that this was the way to tell them apart. Two Rivers had told her all about it, and about the mysterious disappearance of the sun in exactly the right moment, when he came to their lands, uneasy and in a hurry, in a hurry to reach her.

She had listened to him wide-eyed, as captivated by his account of this journey as with the terrifying occurrence itself. Oh, but he had mastered the tongue of her people! It was a pleasure to listen to him now, not only a great orator, but a storyteller, as well. Oh, how proud of him she was!

Her gaze slid down, brushing past the encampment of the Swamp People, with their headdresses sporting a single feather as well, but this one being tilted in a somewhat playful way. They were talking and gesturing, and although standing on the top of the hill and unable to hear their words, she knew that their agitation was peaceful, not that of disagreement.

Her people camped in the middle of the valley, and it made her proud that even here, at the First Gathering of the Five Nations, Onondaga, the People of the Hills, enjoyed such a prominent place. But of course! Her people were powerful, and they deserved a special position. It was only fair. She was secretly pleased with the fact that filthy Tadodaho did manage to squeeze out of Two Rivers quite a few favorable concessions. On the surface, she fumed, disgusted at the way the immoral man managed his affairs, kidnapping her for the purpose of blackmailing the Messenger; but very deep inside, she was pleased, pleased that the Crooked Tongues man backed down on important things in order to save her life. And also that this way, her people got a more prominent place than the others, to keep it that way for the long summers to come.

"See there, in the middle of the valley? In this cluster of tents, by the great tree?" she said, addressing the Crooked Tongues girl who was standing by her side, as immersed. "These are people from High Springs, my town."

"Yes, see," said the girl thoughtfully. "Your people, see. We go, say greeting?"

"No, not yet."

The girl's grasp on their tongue did not improve much, which was no wonder, truly. When not with Onheda, she spent her time alone, in the pretty tent given to the newlywed couple belonging to none of the Onondaga clans. Had either of them belonged to this nation, they would have been offered a place in the relevant clan's longhouse, but as it was, these two received an undeserved amount of privacy. A lucky couple.

Onheda suppressed her grin. Even if the scar-faced youth had not been able to speak like Crooked Tongues when necessary, the girl had probably entertained him in the manner that involved no idle talk. Whenever she, Onheda, came visiting, and if he was still there, they would peek out guiltily, hurrying to cover the mess of their tent with no smells of cooking involved. Oh no, these two spent their time on no silly talk. What would they do after moving into a longhouse? she wondered, amused, pleased for them, liking them both a great deal.

"We'll go and greet them in a little while," she said, grinning. "Did you talk to him?"

The girl tensed. "Yes, I talk."

"What did he say?"

"He say strange, no good, why do this. He say need think, think a lot. He not like the idea."

"Well, it's the beginning. I'll talk to him, too. I think it's the best, don't you?"

"Yes, yes, I think yes."

The girl nodded eagerly, her face alight. Prettier than ever now that more than ten dawns had passed since the end of their wild adventures, she beamed at her, and Onheda could not but marvel at her companion's beauty. Such an exquisite creature!

Good food, plenty of rest, and lovemaking with the man the courageous thing loved strongly enough to risk her life and freedom to find, clearly agreed with her, adding a special glow to her skin, making her eyes shine and her figure round up in a favorable way. Wherever she went, people were turning their heads, but no man dared to as much as smile at her, because they all knew whom she belonged to, the second most powerful man in the League of the Five Nations, the scar-faced warrior who had seen hundreds of battles and on whom the Divine Messenger relied entirely.

Suppressing her grin, Onheda remembered the last autumn, with the three of them traveling to seek the recluse of Onondaga Lake, Hionhwatha. What they had been if not a foreigner with strange ideas, an angry, frustrated youth, and her, a woman with no homeland. Oh, how much had changed, and all in a few short moons, less than a whole span of seasons.

"Yes, you talk and I talk, and we make listen," repeated the girl, flashing a smug, purely female grin. "Women good do that, no?"

"Yes, we do that," laughed Onheda, enjoying the easy comradeship. Through the last ten days, she had grown to regard this girl as a true friend, a rare occurrence, as normally, she didn't like the company of her fellow women. This was why she had suggested that, when done here in Onondaga Town, they should persuade Tekeni to take a permanent residence in High Springs, along with Two Rivers, instead of returning to his Little Falls.

Why should the two men separate now that the Great Peace was achieved? They would still surely need to work close together, as much still needed to be done in order to maintain the whole complicated structure, to strengthen it up. The Crooked Tongues man needed his most trusted friend, and what was there for Tekeni to seek in his Little Falls, anyway? He hadn't lived in that town since he had been a boy, and he had no close family there, while his woman deserved a better life than the annoying place had to offer, of that Onheda was sure. Anitas was still there, and some of her filthy friends, too. Why should the Crooked Tongues girl suffer those on a daily basis?

As the men were the ones to move into the longhouses of their prospective brides, Tekeni's girl would need to be adopted first, and if so, why should she wish to be adopted into the Flint People's clans and settlements, and not into a friendlier place like High Springs? Unless Tekeni wished to live in his town, but Onheda most sincerely hoped he was more attached to Two Rivers than to the memories of his childhood.

Smiling, she scanned the crowded valley with her gaze, seeking *his* figure among the groups of people. The Messenger had spent so much time talking, persuading, calming the most agitated spirits, pacifying, readying them for the grand event. Still, he had always found time to be with her now, to talk and cuddle and make love. In the evenings, or early mornings sometimes, they would sneak away into the woods, or to the more secluded shores, and love and talk, and then love some more. It was never enough for either of them, but they would separate peacefully, in perfect accord, to sneak out again the moment they could, craving each other's company.

He made no secret of their love, paying no attention to the people's raised eyebrows, declaring that the moment the First Gathering was over, he would return to High Springs with her, to ask the Grandmother of her longhouse for permission to live there and share Onheda's bed.

Oh, how thrilled it made her feel, how elated, how fulfilled! He would make her his woman, and the Grandmother of her longhouse would never even dream to refuse, because if she were to hesitate for one single heartbeat, Onheda would leave, to go anywhere he went and never look back. And if some discontented people didn't like his special connection with the Onondagas, accusing him of giving her people a better place because of her, well, it was their narrow-minded problem. She and the Crooked Tongues man were meant to be together, and to think that she had known it all along, but so very stupidly had lost her patience only a moon and a half ago.

"Let come, go there, listen what say." The girl's voice interrupted her thoughts, and she stifled a laugh, ready to bet that the little fox saw her scar-faced husband somewhere there in the crowds. Why else would her eyes light in such a way, with her entire body tilted forward like that of a deer ready to burst into an unrestrained run?

"Yes, let us go down there and give our poor men support," she agreed with a chuckle, putting her arm around the girl's delicate shoulders. "They will need every bit of it today, won't they?"

***

Two Rivers peeked into the wide pit, inhaling the smell of the fresh earth with enjoyment. The thick tree had stood there only a few days ago, an unconquerable forest giant, spreading its branches and roots, casting a blissful shadow, impossible to take down. Yet, now here it was, lying across the grass, defeated.

"Please, be of good spirit and don't grudge us taking you down," he muttered, addressing the *uki* that must have resided in this forest dweller. "Please, take the sacrifice you made kindly and watch over the people who will bury their weapons under your roots."

He remembered eyeing that giant tree in the middle of the valley, only a few days ago, coming back briefly, returning from Little Falls and heading toward the Swamp People's main town. So many peoples and settlements needed to be visited, invited personally, persuaded sometimes, with many others asking for no more than a few words of reassurance, little encouragement, fine promises.

Many leaders of the four neighboring nations were suspicious, displeased with the prominent place he was offering to the Onondagas. The permanent meetings were one thing, a bearable concession, and so was the ensuing position as the Fire Keepers. It made people frown, but not overly so. There was sense in such an arrangement. After all, the Onondagas, indeed, resided in the middle of the metaphorical longhouse, right between the four nations. It was logical to meet in their lands and to entrust them with the keeping of the Great Council's fire.

However, their position as the orbiters, as the watchers, the people who would have a final say in every discussion, every conflict, every deliberation, made many eyebrows fly high, many foreheads crease direfully. This privilege smelled of leadership, and although Two Rivers explained again and again that the unanimous nature of the voting rendered any such advantage null and void, many remained incensed, needing to hear more reassurances before conceding to come at all.

Sighing, he straightened his shoulders, trying to pay no attention to the permanent tiredness that made his head ache and his limbs heavy, crying for rest. It was the lack of sleep, he knew, and the general tension, making it all ready for this day – *the day* – bringing the nations together for the first time, all of them represented well, ready to commit to the future he had engineered for them.

"What a rare pleasure to catch the Great Man alone, deep in thoughts and not besieged by hundreds of people wishing to share their doubts." Tekeni's words broke into his reverie, welcomed.

"I wish today were already over," he said, making sure to keep his voice low. He might have been alone for a heartbeat or two, but many eyes followed him, suspicious or expectant, it didn't matter.

"It will be a great day, for many generations to remember," Tekeni's voice rang firmly, the amusement in it gone. "Our children, and the children of their children will live according to your laws and rules, and they will always remember you, the Messenger of the Right-Handed Twin himself, the Great Peacemaker, who made it all possible."

He felt the words slipping into his soul, warming it, making it come alive with confidence.

"Since when have you been dealing with prophecies?" he asked, trying to cover his embarrassment.

"Since this morning. I woke up, and here it was, the prophecy." The young man laughed, pleased with himself.

Since finding his girl and taking her to be his woman, he had grown to become even more imposing, a future leader without a doubt, already leading so many enterprises, listened to and respected despite his young age, in peace with himself and his world, a content man.

"And that's the best you could do with your morning? I thought your pretty woman kept you busy most of the time."

Another bout of satisfied laughter. "Oh, yes, she does. She made me forget all this silliness. But she is not here now, so I remembered." The merriment fled as suddenly as it came, but the contentment remained. "It's Strawberry Moon already. The hot moons are upon us, and I keep thinking about the previous summer. We were in such a different place back then, but look at us now."

A wide gesture of the muscled arm encircled the tents and the multitude of people, strolling around, watching the medicine men toiling above a large fire lit at the base of another imposing tree, preparing the ceremony, the dancers in their colorful attires ready to help the prayers, to make them fly high, carried by the fragrant tobacco smoke, to reach the Great Spirits and receive their benevolent blessing.

"It was a good span of seasons, yes." Two Rivers smiled, suddenly calm, full of confidence, too. "There is still much work to be done, but yes, we did it. Together." He turned his head, holding his companion's gaze. "You are one of the most important parts of the Great Peace. I wouldn't have succeeded without you. Never mistake that."

He watched the high cheekbones taking a darker shade.

"I just helped where I could. I'm not the important part. You are the heart of the Great Peace. You would have managed without me."

"No, I would not. I think about things, I talk to people, but many times, you are the one to implement my ideas without even the need to ask. You are always there, making it all work." He pointed at the fallen tree. "See this? I wanted to pull this tree out, to bury our weapons underneath its roots. It is an important part of today's ceremony, so I told you that and I went away. And when I came back the tree was down, an impossible feat, if you ask me. But you did it all the same. Like you always do."

"Oh, that one." The young man laughed, embarrassed. "It was not an easy thing. It took me long to understand how to do it, days of digging around and pulling with ropes." He shook his head, grinning. "Hionhwatha helped. He was amused in the beginning, said it was impossible, but still he agreed to give me the requested amount of men to make it all work. Which was a blessing, because otherwise, I would have had to ask Tadodaho, risking another sneer and disdainful glance of his. The damn old skunk." Scornfully, Tekeni snorted. "Are you sure you have to make this man your first representative, with such pomp and in front of everyone?"

Two Rivers sighed. "Yes, I have to, and please don't argue with me about that. I have had enough heated protests from all the rest of your people and all their neighbors and their former enemies."

"Why not?" Tekeni's face cleared of shadows. "When was I questioning your decisions, anyway?"

"If you are so obedient, agree to wear the headdress with the deer antlers on behalf of Little Falls." They had had a long argument about it last night, and for some days before, with the young man refusing adamantly, not wishing even to hear about the idea of becoming a member of the Great Council.

"I can't. Atiron is better fitting."

"I know he is, but I want you to take this position. I know you are too young for that, but you learn fast, and you will make a wonderful representative with the passing of summers. It's a lifelong position. If you don't take it now, you might not be able to reach it in the future."

"I don't want it now, and I don't want it in the future," said Tekeni, his voice firm, inviting no argument. When the young buck got into this mood, even Two Rivers knew better than to argue.

"You are making a mistake."

"Maybe, but this is my decision."

"Oh well, have it your way."

For a few heartbeats, they stood in silence, watching the tongues of smoke twirling upwards, reaching for the sky, carrying the softly murmured prayers.

"If you don't want to be in my council, representing your Little Falls, you may just as well follow your woman's idea of living elsewhere."

The young man turned his head abruptly, peering at Two Rivers, wide-eyed. "How do you know about that?"

He let his grin show. "It was my woman's idea, not yours. She thinks Seketa won't do well in Little Falls. She thinks she will be happier in High Springs."

Tekeni's eyes clouded. "She may be right about that," he muttered, his face closing.

"Well, then, why not? If we are about to settle, both of us, then why not in the same place? Like the good old times, eh?"

He wanted to ask why Tekeni thought his woman would not be happy in Little Falls, then decided against it. Whatever happened during the Cold Moons they had spent there, it was none of his business to inquire. Maybe the young man had fooled around with another girl, just like he himself was not ready to face Kahontsi, not with Onheda by his side, or without her for that matter.

"Maybe. Maybe we'll do that." Tekeni's smile was happy, free of guilt or heavy memories. "There is still much work to be done here, isn't there?"

"Oh, yes, there is. We'll have to watch the proceedings very closely, making sure all is working and there are no breeches, no cracks in our Great Law of Peace. It will take us long summers to make it work for real."

Tekeni's smile widened. "Would you believe if I confessed that I was looking forward to it? It would be boring to go back to the life of a hunter. I like the challenges you provide better. My father was a great warrior, a great leader, but I don't want to be like him. Not anymore. I want to stay and make sure our people live in peace."

"Then we shall do just that, Old Friend. And now, let us step onto our new path."

Patting the young man's back, relating in this single touch all the appreciation, the love, and the gratitude he felt, Two Rivers strolled toward the fire and the wide-branched tree in the way that signaled them all that the ceremony was about to begin.

They were crowding around, watching intently, some hopeful, expectant, some wary, some suspicious. He paid it no attention, his confidence restored, the exhaustion and misgivings gone, not to return.

"*I am the Messenger of the Great Spirits,*" he began, his voice clear, ringing strongly, carried by the strengthening breeze. "*And with the power of Five Nations, I open our First Gathering in the shadow of the Great Long Leaves Tree.*" He looked at them gravely, strangely calm now, knowing the right words, not afraid of the power given to him. "*The Tree of Great Peace will always belong in the Onondaga Nation, in the territory of you who are the Fire Keepers.*"

The silence prevailed, and even the birds stopped chirping, listening too, aware of the solemnity of the occasion.

"*Under the shade of the Tree of the Great Peace we spread the soft, white, feathery down of the earth thistle as seats for you, Revered Leaders. There shall you sit and watch the Council Fire of the Confederacy of the Five Nations; and all the affairs of the Five Nations shall be transacted at this place before you, Tadodaho, and the thirteen other Onondaga representatives, by the Confederate Leaders of the Five Nations.*"

He pitched his voice higher, knowing that when speaking to the large crowd, his words would carry further, reaching more people. But the breeze was there, helpful, spreading his words.

Oh, yes, the Great Spirits *were* listening!

"*Roots have spread out from the Tree of the Great Peace, one to the north, one to the east, one to the south, and one to the west; and their nature is Peace and Strength. Our Peace will be this of strength and not weakness, and our union will be invincible. Yet, if any man or a nation outside the Five Nations shall obey the laws of the Great Peace and make known their disposition to the Leaders of the Five Nations, they may trace the roots to the Tree, and if their minds are clean and they are obedient and promise to obey the wishes of our Great Council, they shall be welcomed to take shelter beneath the Tree of the Long Leaves.*"

That came down surprisingly well. They peered at him, mesmerized, not incensed by the possibility of more people joining the union. His heart quickened. Oh, yes, he would send messengers to *his* side of the Great Lake, and not in the too far away future.

"*To you, Onondaga brothers and the other Confederate Leaders, I have entrusted the caretaking and the watching of the Five Nations Council Fire. When there is a matter to be discussed and the Great Council is not in gathering, a messenger shall be dispatched either to you, or to the other Onondaga leaders, the Fire Keepers, or to their War Chiefs with a full statement of the case desired to be considered. Then you shall gather together and consider whether or not the case is of sufficient importance to demand the convention of the Great Council, and if that is the case, you shall dispatch messengers to summon all the Confederate Leaders to assemble beneath the Tree of the Long Leaves.*"

His gaze held that of Tadodaho, stern and unwavering, relaying to the man that the prominence of his place would come with a price. Then he went on, addressing the Onondagas, instructing them to the correct way of keeping the Council's meeting place clean and pure. *Oh, yes, you will work for the prominence you gained while blackmailing me*, he thought. *You will work hard for it.*

He turned toward the other representatives.

"*The leaders of each nation shall be divided in three groups, and while the first two would discuss and deliberate, the third group will listen only, and if an error is made or the proceeding is irregular, they are to call attention to it. But when the case is right and properly decided, they shall confirm the decision of the two parties and refer the case to their brothers of the other nations."*

He named them one by one, starting with the People of the Flint, all nine representatives, pleased to offer to Atiron the honor of working on behalf of Little Falls, now the most influential town of the eastern lands. Tekeni's prophecy had come true.

"The People of the Flint and the People of the Mountains shall be the Elder Brothers, first to discuss any matter between themselves. Then they shall refer to the Younger Brothers, the Swamp and the Standing Stone People on the opposite side of the fire."

He was afraid that so many technicalities would send them all snoring, but they were listening, wide-eyed, so he went on, encouraged, describing their future responsibilities more at length than he intended to, enjoying their attention.

The women's duties came next, as he elaborated on the way the representative's Clan Mothers were to nominate the members of the Great Council. With an appropriate solemnity, he named Jikonsahseh to be the Mother of the Nation, pleased to offer her such a high status. He had traveled to meet her in the beginning of this moon, inviting her personally, giving the old woman the honor she deserved.

The use of the purple-white *wampum* strings that Hionhwatha wove with such expertise came next. The strings were to play an important part, made in a special fashion each, to commemorate a law, an event, and occasionally, yes, a position. Each representative was to be granted a *wampum*, to swear his integrity and the pureness of his intentions and to keep it as long as he was to remain the member of the Great Council, a lifetime position but one that could have been taken away should the man show less than enough respect for the people he represented. As always, the Clans Mothers would be the ones to decide.

The belt Hionhwatha had given him back in High Springs, the beautiful, long, white-and-purple design representing Five

Nations, was shown, and every leader had sworn his loyalty to it and the Great Council of the union.

By the time the ceremony of burying their weapons under Tekeni's uprooted tree arrived, Two Rivers' voice was rasping and his throat hurt. The sun was very high in the sky, but the people's attention didn't waver, and no one sneaked away to allay his thirst or hunger. The important ritual went on uninterrupted, and then the deer antlers were placed on the heads of the leaders, symbolizing their newly acquired status, now that they were aware of their responsibilities.

It was only when Father Sun was halfway through its journey toward its resting place, the smells of the upcoming feast began to tickle everyone's nostrils, and then it was that. The new world was born, the world of his dream, the world of his vision.

He watched them strolling about, talking to one another, hurrying toward the food, all the people who warred on each other so relentlessly, with so much venom and fury, ready to sacrifice it all, their lives and the well-being of their families in order to achieve another victory, another conquest, more captives, more destruction. Now they worked together, talking, sharing responsibility, affable and at peace with their world. How fast it had happened! How ready they were to change their minds.

His excitement welled, along with his anticipation. Much work was yet to be done. He was to make sure all the laws were memorized and followed, recorded by various *wampum* belts, revered until no one would dare to break them, or twist for the sake of their private advantage. Much work, much satisfaction.

He saw Onheda's slender figure slipping out of the crowd, a steaming bowl in her hand, hurrying toward him, nimble and graceful, oh-so-very beautiful in her festive dress and with her hair flowing freely, not constricted by strings or combs. She had danced earlier through the ceremony, a skilled dancer, and the vision still filled his mind, making his stomach flutter with a special kind of reverence and a deep gratitude.

His heart quickened, beating faster and faster. Not only the people of this side of the Great Lake were made to live in peace and prosperity, but his own private canoe seemed to be reaching a calmer harbor, after all. This woman was the gift of the Great Spirits, a personal prize for all his efforts and the hard work.

"You look mighty pleased, oh Great Peacemaker of the Longhouse People," she whispered, offering a cup of fresh water before the plate, knowing what he needed the most. "A shell-string and a pair of good moccasins for your thoughts."

"I was thinking how blessed I am," he said, watching her, fighting the urge to pull her closer, to hug her in front of everyone, scandalizing them all. "The moment the First Gathering is over, woman, we are heading for High Springs, full speed, running all the way. I want to put in my request before some other pushy hunter gets in, charming the old Grandmother of your longhouse into agreeing on your behalf."

Her laughter trilled, making the urge to pull her into his embrace overwhelming.

"The Grandmother of my longhouse would know better than to refuse the Revered Peacemaker, the greatest hero of all times, for all generations to remember." Her gaze softened, turned serious, losing its mischievous spark. "And you will be remembered this way, I know you will. In many hundreds of summers from now, people will still remember your name, speak it with reverence and respect, the name of the most amazing person that had ever walked on our Turtle Island, the creation of the Sky Woman's world."

His breath caught, he stared at her, seeing the glow of her eyes, radiating her love and admiration, but more than this. It was a prophecy, oh yes, uttered in the same words Tekeni used earlier, before the ceremony. *Would it truly happen this way?*

He took a deep breath, not truly caring. As long as the union he had created survived, and the Great Peace held, and this woman and his friend were still with him, he was content, happy; happy at long last, he who had never known real happiness before.

AUTHOR'S AFTERWORD

The third book of the "Peacemaker Series" keeps tracing the events outlined in the Peacemaker legend, following various versions of it.

Indeed, according to the story, having proven the divine nature of his mission to the People of the Flint (Mohawks), the Peacemaker began working for real. Backed by this powerful nation and their goodwill, he had approached their immediate neighbors, the People of the Standing Stone (Oneida), who had proved relatively easy to convince. The message of the Good Tidings of Peace fell on attentive ears, although it must have taken a few gatherings and more than a few arguments to make two enemy nations sit beside the same fire.

The People of the Great Swamp (Cayuga) joined the proposed union as eagerly, but their neighbors to the west, the fierce, warlike People of the Mountains (Seneca) remained suspicious. Divided already, they followed two different leaders, spreading along the lands up to Genesee River, a natural boundary. What seemed to be uniting both disagreeing leaders was their mutual dislike of foreigners trying to pry into their people's affairs. However, the Great Peacemaker was not about to go away. Or to take a 'no' for an answer. Accompanied by the leaders of the three other nations, he had sailed into the lands of the stubborn westerners, to talk and to persuade, by another miracle if necessary.

The meeting might have not been very well going, as at some point the Peacemaker was reported to make "the sun disappear from the sky." Indeed, in August 1142, around the relevant site of upstate New York (Ganondagan, near modern-day Victor, NY) a full sun eclipse has occurred according to the list displayed on NASA Eclipse Website. There were more eclipses above this area, a century earlier, and a few centuries later, too, but those were either not full or occurring at the wrong time of the year or a day to fit the event described in legend.

This or that way, after witnessing such a glaring prove of the divine displeasure, the Mountain People (Seneca) joined promptly, with no more arguments or debates.

With the backing of four powerful nations, the Great Peacemaker could turn to the last of the reluctant, the Onondagas. In the lands of the People of the Hills (Onondaga) all was not well. Tadodaho, the man responsible for Hiawatha's family's death, was still strong, still influential, still adamant in his refusal to listen to the message of the Great Peace. He was reported to be a powerful sorcerer, with twisted limbs and snakes for a hair. The Peacemaker and Hiawatha went to see him alone.

According to many versions of the legend it was a long tedious meeting. The old sorcerer refused to listen. Snakes twisted in his hair, and his ears were closed to reason. The sun climbed its usual path and was about to descend to its resting place, and still the Peacemaker talked, refusing to give up. In the end, the old sorcerer was convinced. He allowed the Peacemaker to comb the snakes out of his hair, his twisted limbs straightened and he joined the Great Peace.

Judging by the Peacemaker's wonderfully detailed, well-recorded constitution, it might not have been that simple. Onondaga People had definitely received a special place in the Great League of Five Nations. The meetings of the confederacy were to be always held in Onondaga lands, making its inhabitants into the Keepers of the Central Fire.

In the Great Council these people were represented considerably more heavily than any other nation – fourteen Onondaga representatives as opposed to nine Mohawks, nine Oneida, ten Cayuga and eight Seneca. Tadodaho was to preside over the meetings, having a position of an arbiter, and a power of veto. Not that the power of veto gave the Head of the Great Council any clear advantage, as the voting was required to be unanimous, thus in fact granting every member of the council power to veto any decision.

Still, these positions of honor and additional power may have been the ones to tip the scales on that famous snakes-combing meeting. The Peacemaker was a great man with a grand vision and a brilliant thinking. He might have thought of those concessions to lure the man he needed to join on his free will. In the end there was no inequality in the Great League's procedures, honorific titles or not.

So the Great League of the Five Nations (the Iroquois) was born, to blossom and prosper for centuries to come. But what about the Great Peacemaker himself? Did he stay to sit in the government of his creation? Did the position of a representative or an arbiter/observer suit the person of his drive and passion?

Those questions and more are attempted to be addressed in the fourth book of The Peacemaker Series, "**The Peacekeeper**".

ABOUT THE AUTHOR

Zoe Saadia is the author of several novels on pre-Columbian Americas. From the glorious pyramids of Tenochtitlan to the fierce democrats of the Great Lakes, her novels bring long-forgotten history, cultures and people to life, tracing pivotal events that brought about the greatness of North and Mesoamerica.

To learn more about Zoe Saadia and her work, please visit
www.zoesaadia.com

Made in the USA
Columbia, SC
22 January 2019